The Leek Club

By Paul Mann

The Long Game

Other books by Paul Mann

Season Of The Monsoon
The Ganja Coast
The Burning Ghats
The Witch's Code
The Britannia Contract
The Traitor's Contract
The Beirut Contract
The Libyan Contract

Acknowledgements

Human memory is far too fallible to be relied upon and I owe a sincere debt of thanks to all those who helped with the research for 'The Leek Club.' Foremost, Ian and Elizabeth Prentice, who provided me with the most comfortable accommodations at their home near Hadrian's Wall while I took the train into Newcastle every day to do research at the city library. Elizabeth and I grew up together at West Lea and she was invaluable in helping with recollections of places and events from the 1950's. She and Ian gave generously of their time, driving me to various locations around Bedlington and Northumberland to refresh my memory. In addition to the assistance rendered by the staff of the Newcastle City Library I must thank the staff of the Bedlington Town Library, especially in relation to the Northumberland Miner's Picnic, which was held at Bedlington throughout the 1950's. I also referred often to local histories of Bedlington compiled by Evan Martin and Stephen B. Martin. I want to thank Alan Henderson, also of Bedlington, who gave generously of his time and knowledge about the growing of competition leeks and the extraordinary history of leek shows in the northeast. I am especially grateful to my wife, Nancy, for her endless encouragement and patience, and to our amazing daughters, without whom this book would not have been written.

- Paul Mann.

For Nancy.

Furthest, fairest things, stars, free of our
humbug,
each his own, the longer known the more
alone,
wrapt in emphatic fire roaring out to a black
flue.

Briggflatts *by Basil Bunting*

1953

Queen Elizabeth the Second ascends the throne while Edmund Hillary and Norgay Tenzing ascend Mount Everest. Top wireless programmes are The Goon Show starring Peter Sellers, Spike Milligan, Harry Secombe and Michael Bentine; Life With The Lyons starring Ben Lyon and Bebe Daniels. Top movies: Shane starring Alan Ladd; From Here To Eternity starring Burt Lancaster and Deborah Kerr. Hit songs: Don't Let The Stars Get In Your Eyes by Perry Como; You Belong To Me by Jo Stafford and How Much Is That Doggie In The Window by Lita Roza.

Home and Garden

Ever since he was a lad he'd spied on his neighbours. Sneaking around after dark, shinning up drainpipes, peering through the curtains to catch them at their worst. Sandra Metcalfe in curlers, painting her toenails in bed, pallid flesh boiling out of her half slip like porridge. Albert Watson drunk and giggling as he pissed on the living room fire and filled the room with pungent clouds of steam. Bobby Burns riding 15 year old Eileen Purvis in an arse slapping frenzy on the cold kitchen lino while trying not to wake her parents upstairs. This past spring Eileen had married George Abbott, the draper's son, thinking nobody but her knew the likely father of the bairn she carried. The man in the dark knew all their flaws, all their secrets. He liked the feeling of power it gave him, the feeling of seeing without being seen. Like looking through the eyes of god.

He strolled across the playing fields with loose limbed swagger, a shadow in the darkness. He passed gardens where late season carrots, turnip and cabbage still grew, gardens with pigeon lofts, rabbit hutches and chicken crees, gardens where dogs left out for the night knew his scent and raised no alarm. The only sound of his passing was the squeak of rubber soles on wet grass, the dew so heavy it seeped through his plimsolls and chilled his feet.

He came to the McBride house and paused. Robbie McBride, his wife, Nellie, and their two young sons were in bed. The house next door was empty and in the next house along was Mrs. Oliver, a widow who lived alone. She was listening to Henry Hall and the BBC Dance Orchestra on the wireless. Old folks' music but loud enough to drown out any noise from outside. The man in the dark unhooked the wire on the back gate and slipped through the sagging stake fence. A path of packed earth between twin rows of angled bricks cut the garden in half and led to the washhouse. The houses were all the same; semi-detached red brick shells arranged in the shape of a 'Q' with a grassy oval in the middle. In front of each house was an apron of lawn bordered by flower beds. Out the back were a washhouse, a coalhouse and a vegetable garden. There were houses like them on council estates the length and breadth of Britain. Homes for heroes in a country still knackered by the War. Cement columned lampposts lit the fronts of the houses with a harsh white glare but did not penetrate the darkness out back. Smoke from thousands of coal fires thickened the low lying cloud and blotted out the moon and the stars.

He trod warily, the straight razor in his pocket bumping lightly against his thigh. Halfway down the path he stopped, crouched into invisibility and opened the razor. It was too dark to see his intended victims but he knew they were there.

He eased forward, feeling his way past carrot fronds and waxen leaved cabbages till he found what he was looking for. Resting on one knee he gripped the smooth bone handle of the razor and cut into mute white flesh. He cut quickly in a rhythmic, slashing motion as the BBC Dance Orchestra played 'Anything Goes,' and he didn't stop till he'd savaged every one of them. When he was finished he backed out carefully, folded the razor back into his pocket and strolled home humming happily to himself.

It was Robbie McBride's habit to get up early so he could have a tab and a cup of tea in peace. He lit up a Woodbine, put the kettle on and went to get the daily bottle of milk from the front step. He pressed his thumb gently into the middle of the silver foil cap so it came off without tearing and decanted the milk into a white tea mug careful to get all the cream in the neck of the bottle. He put the foil cap back on the bottle, poured his tea and stirred in four heaped spoonfuls of sugar. Then, mug in one hand, tab in the other, he stepped out the back door for a breath of what passed for fresh air in the coalfields of East Northumberland. Short set with a sinewy build and untidy black hair he wore work pants and vest, galluses dangling at his sides. The cement path was cold and damp under his bare feet but after six years in the dungeons of the Doctor Pit he barely noticed. He took a sip of tea and pulled on his tab till he'd filled his lungs and, with a sigh of pleasure, exhaled a plume of smoke into the grey air. There was nothing like the first tab of the day and it always tasted best before breakfast.

His gaze wandered over his scrupulously tended garden till he came to his leeks. He tensed at the signs of disturbance. He hurried down the path spilling hot tea on his hand but not noticing. When he saw the extent of the damage he groaned. He threw his tea and his tab aside, dropped to his knees and shuffled along the first trench, taking the wilted green and white ribbons tenderly in his hands. He'd planted two trenches, each with 10 leeks, and they were the best he'd ever grown. Fat barreled beauties with creamy flesh and broad bladed leaves. He was going to pull them for the show at Netherton Club two days from now but there was nothing left. Nothing at all to show for a year of toil. There'd be no new furniture for the house this year, no trophies to join the gleaming display on the sideboard. And worse - no new seeds to carry his prizewinning strain forward. An upsurge of anger carried him to his feet and to the back fence.

"Ye bloody bastards," he shouted. "Ye cannit beat is fair, can ye, ye dorty bloody bastards…"

His words caromed along the houses and scattered like starlings across the fields. He shouted for a minute or more till exhausted by his rage. Some of the neighbours came out to see what was wrong and he turned away, back to his ruined garden and the questioning faces of his wife and kids at the back window. Somebody else watched him too, from next door. A tall, sparely built man in his early 30's, thinning blonde hair combed back from a high forehead. He stood on the path between the house and the washhouse and wore a civilian jacket with a blue police shirt, black police tie, black police trousers and black police boots. Robbie had no idea how long he'd been there.

"Aye, an' wee de ye think you're lookin' at?" Robbie said.

The man inclined his head to one side. "Get on wi' the neighbours ahlreet, de ye?"

The next day Northumberland Police Constable Jimmy Bright moved his wife, Pat, and their son, Nick, into the house next door to the McBrides.

*   *   *

Coronation day was to be unforgettable. Nick came in from the playing fields to find his mother at the mirror over the fireplace smearing soot on her face. She wore a sleeveless red dress with white polka dots and around her shoulders a red and white checkered tea towel tied at the throat to make a shawl. Her auburn hair was tied up in a cloth printed with bluebells and knotted at the forehead into a turban. She'd already blackened her arms and legs and painted her toenails the same neon red as her fingernails. Nick watched her smooth the soot into her neck and face, taking extra care around the eyes, dipping her fingers into the chimney when she needed more. When she was finished she plucked a lipstick from the mantelpiece and used it to exaggerate the size of her lips.

"Mrs. Leese is havin' a fancy dress party fo' the coronation," she said without looking away from the mirror. "Ah'm goin' as a black mammy."

Nick had forgotten it was coronation day. There were posters of the young Queen Elizabeth and Prince Phillip in some front windows around town and souvenir plates and mugs for sale in the shops but otherwise not much excitement at all. Nick's dad said it was because Bedlington was a Labour town and only Tories supported the royal family. Nick's dad was a polis. A working class Tory. Something else to set him apart from the neighbours. The Northumberland Constabulary had moved him and his wife and son onto the council estate at West Lea with the idea that putting police families among the general population would set a civilized example to the natives. But they'd barely unpacked when Bright warned his wife not to get too friendly with the neighbours: "Because ye nivah knah when ah might hae to lock one o' the buggas up." Which was why Nick was surprised him and his mam were going to a fancy dress party at Mrs.

Leese's house even if it was for the coronation. His mam leaned into the mirror, tilted her head this way and that till she was satisfied and snapped the lipstick shut. She reminded Nick not so much of a black mammy as Kali, the Hindu goddess of death and destruction.

"Ye can wear ya dad's uniform an' go as a polis," she said.

His dad's police tunic reached down to his feet and his mam had to roll the sleeves up so he could use his hands. She tucked the emergency whistle into a breast pocket and gave him his dad's truncheon to carry, which was so heavy he had to hold it with both hands. The helmet slid down over his eyes and she had to shorten the chinstrap to almost nothing and tip the helmet back on his head so he could see where he was going. Then she went into the kitchen and returned with a plate of cheese and beetroot sandwiches and the frying pan.

"The fryin' pan's ganna be me banjo," she said.

Nick shuffled across the street behind his mother to Mr. and Mrs. Leese's house. Alf and Kitty Leese were an older couple with no children of their own so they had plenty of time for the local kids. A retired engine driver from the Doctor Pit Mr. Leese would wash his black Ford Anglia every Saturday morning and entertain the kids with stories about his adventures as an explorer up the Amazon directing their attention to his vaccination scars, which he said were the bites of giant mosquitoes. The front door was open and inside a mob of cowboys, pirates and princesses ravaged the coronation day spread. Several tables had been pushed together to form one long table that reached from the front window to the back. The tables were of varying heights and sizes, covered with mismatched tablecloths and set with platefuls of sandwiches cut into triangles, a daintiness wasted on kids who crammed food into their mouths as if it might be taken from them at any second. After years of rationing they'd got used to going without and had never seen such plenty: Spam sandwiches, meat paste sandwiches, cheese and tomato sandwiches, egg and tomato sandwiches, cucumber and watercress sandwiches, tinned salmon sandwiches, sausage rolls, cheese scones, thick slabs of sly cake, buttered tea cakes and an assortment of jam tarts.

Several other mams were there to help. John Gordon's mam in a Union Jack sash and a fireman's brass helmet had come as Britannia. Dave Foster's mam in a floor length frock, knitted shawl and a tiny hat with a broach was Old Mother Riley and Mary Beecroft's mam had come as Dick Whittington's cat in a pantomime costume with limp ears and a moth eaten tail. A crescent of little Union Jacks hung across the front window, there were paper flags on the tables and crepe paper ribbons in red, white and blue garlanded the light shades. Tacked to one wall was a Union Jack poster with a portrait of the new queen at its centre and on top of an upright piano were two coronation plates of the Queen and Prince Phillip. At least Kitty and Albert Leese were loyal subjects.

Mrs. Leese, wearing a Union Jack pinny and matching paper hat, came out of the kitchen to make Nick and his mother welcome. She found a place for Nick at the table and he happily discarded his dad's helmet and truncheon and joined in the general assault on the food. His mam did a quick party turn, strumming the frying pan and singing a few bars of 'Oh Susannah,' which brought squawks of delight from the other mams. Mr. Leese offered her a drink and she asked for a rum and orange. When the kids had eaten till they could eat no more they went outside and played tiggy-in-the-bay, chasing each other and screaming the way only kids could with bellies full of food. The grown-ups sat at the plundered tables and enjoyed a smoke break while Mrs. Leese turned on the wireless so they could listen to the BBC broadcast of Max Robertson describing the royal procession from Westminster Abbey to Buckingham Palace. In the background could be heard the cheers of a crowd estimated at more than a million.

"Mind it's warth sayin,' tha's nae other country in the world has tradition like wors," Jean Gordon said and expelled a cloud of cigarette smoke toward the ceiling.

"An' wa forst on top o' Moont Everest an' ahll, divvent forget," Eadie Foster added. "That's somethin' the yanks cannit say fo' once."

"No, wa not finished yet," Nick's mam said.

"Not the day at any rate," Mr. Leese said. "We're on top o' the world the day."

"Whey aye man," Mrs. Leese said and lifted her glass in a toast. "Top o' the world, iverybody, top o' the world."

They listened till the newly crowned queen and her consort appeared on the balcony at Buckingham Palace then Mrs. Leese turned the wireless off and they set about clearing the tables and washing the dishes. After a while a few kids straggled in looking for more to eat and their mams decided it was time to take them home. It was then that Nick's mam discovered she'd forgotten the house keys. She and Nick were locked out and would have to wait till his dad came home from work some time after six. Mr. and Mrs. Leese didn't seem to mind and brought out what scotch, rum and gin they had left along with a few of bottles of cordial. Seeing this Jean Gordon decided to stay and keep them company. Nick passed the time with John Gordon, the two of them crawling around under the tables pretending they were tunneling out of a prisoner of war camp. John was the same age as Nick and the kids had nicknamed him Spelk because he was as skinny as a sliver of wood. Around half past six, the Bright's next door neighbour, Nellie McBride, looked in to say she'd just seen Nick's dad come home.

"Stop bein' sae helpful will ye, hinny," Mrs. Leese said.

"To hell wi'm noo," Nick's mam said. "Wa ganna stay here till wa blotto."

"Ah think it's owa late fo' that divvent ye?" Jean Gordon added. "Ah think wa' ahlready blotto."

They cackled like hens and Nick's mam took her time finishing her drink before she collected her frying pan and went home, Nick trailing after her. But when she tried the front door it was still locked. She rattled the knocker and waited for a response but there was none. She tried again, longer this time, but still there was no answer. She bent down to shout through the letterbox, lost her balance, staggered backwards and fell down on the lawn with a flustered "whoops-a-daisy." She struggled back to her feet and decided to try the back door. Nick followed and around the back they found his dad's police bike propped against the coalhouse wall. Upstairs the bathroom light was on. She tried the back door but it too was locked. She stared up at the bathroom window, a muted yellow light shining through the dimpled glass.

"God knahs hoo lang he'll be up there if he's havin' a shite," she said. She banged on the back door and shouted up at the bathroom window: "Jimmy…wa locked oot…come an' open the door."

She and Nick waited but there was no answer.

"This is ridiculous," she said, growing agitated. "He's been yem haff an ooah, he has to be finished bi noo." She banged on the door and shouted up at the window again and this time there was a muffled reply. She couldn't make out what he said but at least he'd heard her. A few more minutes passed and when it became apparent that he still wasn't on his way down to open the door she lost her temper.

"Ye oppin this door reyt noo," she screamed at the bathroom window and kicked the back door so hard it rattled in its frame.

Next door, Nellie McBride looked out to see what the commotion was about.

The bathroom window opened a fraction and Bright called down: "Can ye not wait a minute, woman, ah'll be doon as soon as ah can." And the window closed again.

"A minute," she shrieked. "Ye spend haff ya bloody life in theyah."

She looked around then went into the washhouse. Nick heard the banging of something heavy and she emerged dragging the ladder. It took her a few tries but eventually she got it propped against the house and managed to extend it till it rested against the bathroom windowsill. She climbed up and banged on the window with her fist.

"Ye come doon an' oppin the door this minute," she shouted. And she kept banging till the window swung open again. From below Nick saw his father's astonished face.

"Are ye wrang o' the bloody heed, woman?"
"What are ye deein' in there?"
"What de ye think ah'm deein'?"
"Ye cannit still be havin' a shite."
"Whey, ah am still havin' a shite if ye must knah."
"No ya not. Naebody normal teks this lang to have a shite."

"Hae ye seen the state o' yasel'?" Bright said. "What are ye deein' dressed up like a bloody golliwog?"

"Ah took the bairn to a fancy dress party across the road an' ah locked wi' oot," she said. "Could ye not hear is bangin' on the door?"

"Aye ah could hear ye," he said. "De ye expect is to stop in the middle of a shite to come doonstairs an' oppin the door fo' ye?"

"Ah don't believe ya still havin' a shite."

"Well ah am still havin' a shite an' ah cannit hurry it up just for ye. Noo haad ya whisht an' ah'll be doon in a minute."

He went to close the window but she grabbed it and yanked it from his grasp and saw that in his other hand he had a copy of the Daily Mirror.

"Ya not still havin' a shite at ahll," she screeched. "Ya readin' the paper. Ah cannit get back in me ahn hoose an' you're in there readin' the bloody newspaper."

"Can a man not hae a shite in peace?" he shouted back.

Nick saw Nellie McBride put a hand over her mouth. Other doors

8

opened along the houses as the neighbours came out to see what was happening.

"Naebody teks the time ye tek to hae a shite."

"Well ah'm sorry if me arse doesn't work fast enough to suit ye."

"Ye've had ya shite an' noo ya just sittin' there readin' the paper."

"Ah'll be finished when ah say ah'm finished."
"Ye should be finished bi noo."
"Ah'll finish in me ahn good time."
"If ye divvent hurry up ah'll kick the bloody door doon, Jimmy, an' ah mean it."
"Is it ahlreet if ah wipe me arse forst?"

"If ya not doonstairs to open that door in the next minute, ah swear to god, ah'll kick it off its bloody hinges."

Nick's father disappeared back inside and closed the window after him. Nick's mam started down the ladder but in her temper she went too fast and missed her footing. She screamed and fell, her legs slipped between the rungs and caught by the knees so that she swung downward like a hinge and slammed into the ladder with a loud grunt. The ladder shuddered but stayed upright and she hung there upside down, afraid to move. Slowly, her polka dot dress slid down her body till it covered her head and shoulders leaving her black calves and doughy white thighs for all the world to see. Nick watched as she flapped her arms like a trapped moth and called for help and all along the houses the neighbours laughed.

*   *   *

When Bright had a day off he usually worked in the garden. He wouldn't call himself a serious gardener, certainly not as serious as Robbie McBride, but he grew enough to save on the groceries. The front garden and the back garden were badly overgrown when he moved in and he had to use a spade to edge the lawn out front and a pair of garden shears to trim the grass enough to get the push mower into it. Nick's mam weeded the borders and planted snapdragons, pansies and violets. Other gardens around the estate were flush with roses, chrysanthemums, daffodils, tulips and lupins, flourishes of colour that softened the brick and cement landscape. The back garden was clogged with thickly tufted grass anchored in clayey yellow soil and it had been hard work to dig it out. When he'd turned the garden over Bright went to work breaking down the heavy clay, airing it and digging in a couple of bags of lime. He'd started a compost heap to which was added potato peelings, vegetable scraps, tea leaves and eggshells but it would be another year before it yielded any usable compost. In the meantime Bright did what the neighbors did and scrounged up manure wherever he could find it. Fresh manure was a valuable commodity and whenever a horse drawn milk float or a grocery van came on the estate it was followed by eyes at every window. The moment the horse deposited a fresh mound of manure on the road the nearest housewives scrambled to be first outside with a bucket and shovel.

Bright planted staples like potatoes, carrots, turnips, parsnips, peas and runner beans as well as salad vegetables like lettuce, radishes and scallions. But not tomatoes. Without a greenhouse the growing season was too short for tomatoes. He had planted a dozen leeks for cooking, not for show, which was why he hadn't bothered to set up a proper leek trench. When his leeks were fully grown they would look like pencils compared to the cannon sized monsters Robbie McBride grew. Since they'd moved in the Brights had learned little about the McBrides except that Robbie was a miner at the Doctor Pit and everybody in the family was short. Short enough for Nick's mam to say they lived next door to a family of garden gnomes. The McBrides had named their first son, Robbie, after his father so they were known as Big Mac and Little Mac, even though Big Mac was no more than five foot six in his pit boots. Little Mac was every bit as talkative as his father but his three year old brother, Keith, hardly spoke at all, which led some to think he was a bit slow. Big Mac's wife, Nellie, was little more than five feet and had frizzy brown hair and a harried manner. Whenever Bright was in the garden and Big Mac was home it wasn't long before he would come outside and try to engage Bright in conversation. Bright had tried ignoring him but Big Mac was immune to hints of any kind. As Bright liked to say: "it went streyt owa his heed." That Saturday morning Bright was hoeing weeds when Big Mac wandered out with a mug of tea in his fist and a half smoked tab stuck to his bottom lip. As usual his hair was uncombed, he was unshaven, he wore a vest and work pants and his braces at his sides. Like many short men he walked with his chest thrust out, as if to assert a manliness that might otherwise be in question. He came up to the back fence and greeted Bright cheerily.

"Good fettle the day then, Jimmy?"

"Good enough," Bright said without looking up.

"Garden's comin' alang canny."

"Aye, canny."

"Ya not bothered aboot leeks fo' show, but?" Big Mac's cigarette bobbed on his bottom lip and sprinkled ash on his vest.

"No, not for show," Bright acknowledged. "Leek an' potato soup, leek puddin', that sort o' thing."

Encouraged, Big Mac gestured to a wooden barrel by the washhouse and said: "If'n ye want ye can help yasel to me liquid manure. Ah've got plenty and it meks a big difference in mah opinion."

The barrel had a removable lid and was filled with water in which Big Mac had suspended one of Nellie's old nylon stockings filled with sheep manure. The manure leeched into the water to create a potent liquid fertiliser that attracted a summer long cloud of bluebottles.

"Ah'll manage," Bright said.

"It's not just good fo' leeks, ye knah," Mac persevered. "It's good fo' iverythin'."

Bright looked up from his hoeing and said: "Ah'm sure it is, Mac, but ah don't want it."

Mac looked hurt. "Ahlreet, Jimmy. Ah'm just offerin'. Just tryin' to be friendly, like."

Bright felt guilty. He stopped and rested a hand on the hoe.

"Ah knah, Mac, an' ah divvent want to seem ungrateful but ye hae to understand, ah cannit be tekin' favours. A polis cannit be beholden to naebody. It has nowt to do wi' ye, it applies the same to iverybody."

It wasn't true but Bright hoped it would be enough to keep Mac from pestering him.

Big Mac took the cigarette from his mouth, hawked and spat a gelatinous grey pellet far into the garden. Compared to Bright, Big Mac's garden was a model of organisation, dissected by wooden boards and parceled with pieces of string threaded with gold, red and silver foil milk bottle tops and twisted strips of newspaper to deter the birds. In the middle were his leek trenches, fenced off from the rest of the garden with a mesh of chicken wire interlaced with strands of barbed wire to discourage a return visit from the leek slasher. It wasn't just the loss of a year's crop that hurt, it was the loss of fresh seeds from a prizewinning strain. Leek seeds had a short shelf life and the germination rate declined dramatically after one year so that the loss of a season's leeks could set a grower back several years.

"Ah was hopin' wi ye livin' next door t'is folk'd leave me leeks alone," he said.

"Ye divvent need me wi' Stalag 17 there," Bright said.

"Aye, mebbe," Mac said. "But ah think it meks mair of a difference when ye've got the polis livin' next door."

"Ah wouldn't coont on it."

"Surely naebody would hae the narve to come in here an' hae a go at me

11

leeks wi ye livin' reyt next door," Mac said.

"From what ah've seen tha's buggas 'roond here would steal the bed oot from under ye, nae matter wee ye hae livin' next door," Bright said.

Mac looked frustrated.

"Ye knah what it teks to grah competition leeks noowadays, Jimmy. Ah've put years o' me life into breedin' champions…years. Ah brought me leek trench w'is from me last hoose an' ah've built it up ivery year since."

Bright knew. To serious leek growers the right soil was critical and all of them had their own formula. After years of building a leek trench to the point of perfection it was common for growers to dig up the soil, bag it and take it with them when they moved.

"An' ah'm tellin' ye ya not the only one, Mac," Bright said. "It's a problem iverywhere. From what ah hord tha must hae been 20 blokes from ahll owa Bedlin'ton had leeks slashed last year an' wi niva caught one o' the buggas that did it. If ye don't catch them in the act ya not goin' to catch them. An' it's not goin' to stop as long as tha's buggas willin' to spoil another man's hard work to get what they want. Wi haven't got the manpower to guard iverybody's leek trenches, Mac. Dee what other folk dee when it gets close to show time, park yasel ootside wi the poker of a night and when ye cannit dee it hae Nellie tek a torn."

Mac looked dismayed.

"Ah cannit dee that, Jimmy. Ah cannit expect Nellie to sit ootside ivery night when ah'm on the fore shift. Not when she has the bairns to look after durin' the day. An' ye've seen the size o' wor lass. Hoo's she ganna stop somebody comin' in the garden an' deein' whatever they want?"

Bright shrugged and went back to his hoeing. "Weel, ah'm sorry then, Mac, because ah cannit dee it fo' ye."

Big Mac dawdled a moment longer then slung his tea dregs into the garden.

"If'n ye change ya mind, Jimmy, ye can help yasel from the barrel any time ye want. An' ah divvent want nowt in retorn."

Bright grunted and continued chopping at the weeds.

*   *   *

In the winter the house got so cold Nick often woke up with frost in his hair. The main source of heat was the living room fire, which his mam would bank up with coal before going to bed to keep it burning long into the night. But, when the last embers died out, heat leached rapidly from the house leaving only pockets of warmth where each body lay curled underneath layers of blankets.

The blue puppy dog hot water bottle with the red bow tie that Nick took to bed turned cold as a brick overnight and had long since been kicked onto the floor. When the alarm clock woke him at seven thirty for school it was impossible to see outside because the bedroom windows were whorled with frost inside and out. He lingered as long as he could in the cosy stife of his cocoon, bracing for the frigid scamper to the bathroom where he would fill the sink with hot water so the steam would take the chill off the air. Then he would wash and dry himself in a hurry and get dressed before the air cooled.

His mam got up with him on school mornings to light the fire and put a pot of Scotts Porridge Oats on the oven. He didn't like porridge but it was hot and he could get it down once he'd stirred in a couple of spoonfuls of sugar. He and his mother spoke very little in the mornings. She did her duty then left him to eat at the kitchen table while she perched on a thatch topped stool by the fire in her dressing gown and smoked her first tab of the day. With the porridge weighing inside him like a cannonball Nick would finish dressing in the hall, zipping his navy blue corduroy jerkin right up to the chin to anchor his balaclava under the collar and keep out the cold. Last he would pull on a pair of mitts his mother had knitted, sling his satchel over his shoulder and join the other kids making their way to the bus stop like a procession of midget bank robbers, the fronts of their balaclavas rimed with frozen snot.

From the time Nick stepped out his front door to the time he stepped into the classroom he wondered if this would be the day he'd be beaten to death for being the polis's son. But not today. Today brought only the usual gauntlet of insults. It started as he crossed a strip of open ground to the bus stop with Spelk, Dave and Mary, the frozen grass crunching under their feet like broken glass. Sean Mullen was waiting for the bus with his younger brother, Stephen, and with them were Brendan and Owen Leary. The Mullens and the Learys were Irish immigrant families at the bottom of the estate who lived lives of noisy chaos amid packs of dogs, chickens and kids allowed to run wild. The head of the Mullen clan was Patrick, a bushy haired coal sorter at Netherton Colliery who supplemented his income with a bit of poaching and anything else that brought in an extra quid. His neighbour and best pal was Michael Leary, who was rumoured to be a former IRA man and was now a shot firer at the same pit. Patrick and Michael shared the belief that anything in England that could be carried on the back of a lorry was theirs for the taking. Nick's dad had said if the police could get rid of the Mullens and the Learys they would rid themselves of half the petty crime in Bedlington. Waiting with the Mullens and the Learys was Brian Boyle, who came from an Irish family at the top of the estate. While the Mullens and the Learys were Ulster Catholics and the Boyles Ulster Protestants they'd set their differences aside in the face of the universal hostility of the English. Just last August Nick and Spelk had found Brian on his front step wanking his dog, Prince. When Spelk asked what he was doing Brian had answered: "He likes it."

"Hey look," Sean Mullen called as he saw Nick approaching, "it's Bright, Bright, soft as shite."

The others turned to see and Brendan Leary added: "Whey if it isn't P.C. Stupid's son," and they sniggered to each other.

"Hey, Bright, ya name should be stupid, not Bright," Sean said.

"Are ye any relation to P.C. Stupid?" Brendan added.

"Just ignore them," Mary told Nick. "Ignore them and they'll stop."

Nick wished it was that easy. Girls had no idea. Boys had no choice. The aggression directed at them by other boys was unrelenting. Girls were non-combatants, they were left alone to play their happy little schoolyard games like skipping rope and hopscotch. Nick could only imagine how wonderful it must be to go through a day where all there was to worry about was who wasn't talking to who anymore.

There were also two women at the bus stop, plump and anonymous in headscarves and heavy coats, their presence no deterrent to the Mullens and the Learys.

"Bright, Bright, soft as shite," Stephen Mullen took up the chant from his older brother as Nick reached the bus stop.

"Hey, Bright," Sean said. "Are ye fuckin' stupid like ya mutha an' fatha."

With that one of the women turned on him.

"That's quite enough oot o' ye, Sean Mullen," she said. "Ye just try keepin' that dorty mooth o' yourn shut fo' once."

Nick recognised her from the Top End paper shop where she worked behind the counter and sometimes sold him sherbet and liqorice. He didn't know her name but whoever she was he was grateful to her. Sean gave her an insolent look and was about to say something but she stepped up to him and wagged a finger in his face.

"An' divvent ye gi' me any o' ya impittence neither or ah'll smack that look right off ya face fo' ye, ye just see if ah don't."

Sean hesitated but said nothing and turned away smirking.

"He's a right little sod that one," the woman said as she rejoined her friend. "He's nivah happy unless he's tormentin' somebody."

A glum silence settled punctuated by furtive muttering and an occasional laugh from the Mullens and the Learys. It seemed an age before Raisbeck's single decker bus came wheezing and rattling down Netherton Lane. The two women got on first, followed by the Mullens, the Learys and Brian Boyle then Mary, Nick, Spelk and Dave. The bus was standing room only, the air rank with cigarette smoke and the fog of steaming, wool-clad bodies. Condensation drizzled down the windows and puddles of filthy water collected on the floor. Nick kept near the front of the bus away from the Mullens and the Learys. The bus was filled past capacity but the driver stopped on Ridge Terrace anyway to take on more passengers who somehow managed to cram themselves in except for a couple of young pit lads who rode in the stairwell beside the concertina door. It was only a couple of minutes to the Top End where the Catholic kids got off to go to St. Bede's. For those standing in the aisle it was a tight squeeze as passengers pushed their way to the front of the bus. Sean Mullen went to jab an elbow into Nick's stomach but Nick was ready and used his satchel to block the blow. Brendan Leary was next and he stepped on Nick's foot and ground down with all his weight. It wasn't enough to hurt but Leary was so close Nick caught a waft of unwashed flesh and grimaced. Satisfied, Leary sauntered off with a grin.

That left Brian Boyle on his own at the back of the bus. As a Protestant Boyle went to Whitley Memorial Junior School, the same school as Nick and the others, but he had no friends there. He was big for his age, sexually precocious and without warning would spew out strings of obscenities at whoever happened to be around. He'd achieved a certain notoriety early on by calling Miss Chivers 'a smelly owld cunt.' Miss Chivers was a flinty spinster in her sixties with a deeply ingrained hatred of children. She grabbed Boyle by the hair and banged his head repeatedly against a radiator admonishing him with each clanging blow to "mind-your-tongue-when-speaking-to-your-elders."

She only stopped when Brian started to bleed and Isabel Clarke ran to get the headmaster. Brian's parents never complained because they believed however severely he was punished he'd probably asked for it. Violence was a well established form of child control at school and at home. One parental favourite was to march their bairn down to the front gate, take down his or her underwear and administer a sound smacking to the bare arse while other kids watched. And at Whitley Memorial the arithmetic teacher, Mr. Hall, liked to bend kids over between the desks and use a blackboard ruler to see how far he could drive them up the aisle. The headmaster, Mr. Nicholson, kept an arsenal of canes in a glass display case in his office. Of varying thicknesses each one was identified by different coloured bands and feathers. He'd also given each cane a nickname and would use them according to the severity of the offence. A minor offence might bring a couple of stinging strokes across the hands from the whippy 'Cecil,' while something more serious would merit a dozen paralyzing strokes across the backside from the much sturdier 'Toby.'

The bus stopped at the school gates and Nick and the others dispersed into the mayhem of the schoolyard. Whitley Memorial was a monument to late Victorian provincialism steeped in soot. The roofs were grey slate and the corridors two shades of bile. The classrooms were starkly white, the desks stained with age and carved with dates and initials that went back before the First World War. The girls and boys toilets were outside, stinking brick cubicles enclosed by U-shaped walls the boys competed to piss over. There was a high brick wall along the back boundary of the cement paved yard and a couple of prefab classrooms to accommodate the first wave of baby boomers. The yard sloped gently down to a playing field, which made it ideal for ice slides and there were already half a dozen underway. Leather soled shoes made for faster slides and there was keen competition to see who could go fastest and furthest. Most kids slid standing sideways, arms out for balance, but some liked to hunker down and wrap their arms around their knees to reduce wind resistance.

Nick rolled his balaclava up into a cap and took his turn on one of the longer slides. The only problem was the bad lads liked the longer slides too. The bad lads excelled at all things physical. They threw themselves into any challenge, heedless of danger, and were forever breaking their arms and legs or cracking their heads open and they wore the scars as badges of honour. Not that sliding was inherently dangerous, it was just the bad lads enjoyed making it dangerous.

Bumper Barrett was standing near the bottom of the slide talking to his mates when he turned and casually stuck a leg out as Nick came down. Nick jumped it but lost his balance and sprawled onto the ice to a chorus of jeers. He got to his feet, his mitts shredded, droplets of blood seeping under skin peeled back like wood shavings. His mam would be mad but he couldn't tell her because she might complain to the school and all that would happen was that Barrett would give Nick a proper hiding. All school had taught Nick was that childhood was anarchy beset by random cruelties and grown-ups were, for the most part, useless.

*   *   *

1954

Roger Bannister breaks the four minute mile; food rationing ends. Wireless listeners tune in to Hello Playmates with Arthur Askey. Top films are On The Waterfront starring Marlon Brando; Seven Brides For Seven Brothers starring Howard Keel and Jane Powell; The Dam Busters starring Richard Todd and Michael Redgrave. Top song hits are Such A Night by Johnnie Ray and Shake, Rattle and Roll by Bill Haley And His Comets.

Child's Play

There were few words Nick wanted to hear less than: "Ye'll be stayin' wi ya Aunty Dot the day."

Nick hated his Aunty Dot. She was much older than his mother and a hard life had left her shriveled, bitter and quick to see the worst in everybody. Her husband, Ray, no more than a couple of shoestrings knotted together, was as affable as she was miserable and deferred to her on everything. They had two children: Irene, 20, a replica of her mother, and Eric, who was a few years older than Nick and for some reason jealous of what he perceived to be Nick's cushy life. But Nick had no choice. His mam and dad were going to Newcastle for the day and Dot was the only person who would take him. Not that she did anything to look after him. She shoved him outside with the other kids for the day and when he came back his parents would be there to take him home.

Dot's house was on Cumberland Avenue, which faced Westmoreland Avenue to form a pair of pincers that held between them a grassy elipse ringed with trees and bushes. The kids had made hideaways in the bushes so they were hidden from the prying eyes of grown-ups. Nick knew Eric and his pals had a refuge under a hawthorn bush near the top of the avenue. As he approached he smelled cigarette smoke and heard furtive voices then silence. He found Eric with two of his mates, Trevor and Clag, a ginger haired lad with a crust of pimples on the back of his neck. Clag got his nickname for complaining during a PE class one hot day that his knackers were 'claggy.' When the three lads saw Nick they groaned. They sat cross-legged on the ground with playing cards and a few coins scattered on a scruffy blanket. Next to the gnarled trunk of the hawthorn bush was a pile of empty beer bottles.

"Ah put me tab oot cos o' ye, ye thick cunt," Eric said. From behind their backs the other lads produced the cigarettes they'd been smoking. Eric lit his dump off Trevor's tab and they resumed their card game. With nothing else to do Nick hunkered down to watch. They were playing brag for hapennies, pennies, thruppeny bits and the odd sixpence with Clag doing most of the winning. At one point Eric asked Nick if he had any money and when he said no Eric said: "Ya not much use fo' owt are ye?" Nick's mam had given him two bob but he had no intention of telling Eric.

After a while Eric and Trevor got tired of losing to Clag, picked up what was left of their money and considered what else they might do to amuse themselves. Eric leaned into the other two and there was a whispered exchange, which Nick assumed was about him. Then his cousin turned to him and said: "If ye want to stay ye hae to dee a dare."

Nick was wary but he wanted to show he could do any dare they could come up with. There was a half mad old man called Dippy Dawes who lived alone at the bottom of the avenue. Eric said Nick had to knock on Dippy's door and goad the old man into chasing him. Nick had seen Dippy from a distance, a gnomish man with bow legs and knew he could outrun him.

"Ye hae to gan up the path an' knock on the door wi'oot 'im seein' ye," Eric said. "Cos if he sees ye comin' he'll be waitin' ahint the door an' he'll oppin it an' pull ye in and naebody'll ivah see ye again."

It took a while for Nick to memorise what they wanted him to say because they kept laughing. Most of the words were swearwords and he had to admit it would be fun to shout them out around the houses. When they were ready they left their little hideaway, walked down the elipse and crouched behind a holly bush across from Dippy's front gate. With the moment at hand, Nick hesitated.

"Gan on then ye soft shite," Eric said. "What are ye waitin' for?"

Nick shut out the voices of caution that clamoured inside his head and crossed the road. He paused at the gate, looked round to make sure there was no-one to see, and crept up the path. His heart raced. What if Dippy wasn't a man at all but an ogre whose house was littered with the bones of missing children? Nick put a foot on the front step and lifted the knocker. His hand shook. Now was when it would happen. He banged the knocker three times then turned and ran down the path so fast his feet barely touched the pavement. When he reached the middle of the road he stopped and waited. The door opened and Dippy peered out. He was bald except for a few wisps of white hair and he had a big and misshapen nose and a drooping lower lip shiny with slaver. He wore a dirty collarless shirt, baggy pants fastened under his belly and his feet were bare. He looked around and saw Nick in the road.

"Did ye knock on mah door?" he demanded, his voice unexpectedly powerful.

"Yar a fuckin' bugga," Nick shouted.

"What?"

"He's haff deef, ye hae te shoot looder," Eric said from behind the holly bush.

"Yar a fuckin' bloody bugga," Nick shouted louder, the words echoing up the avenue.

"I knah ye," Dippy said. "Was it Norma sent ye?"

"Fuck off ye fuckin' cunt."

"Hadaway an' shite," Dippy retorted. "An' tell Norma she can fuck off an' ahll."

Nick was shocked. He hadn't expected Dippy to swear back at him. He returned to the script.

"Yar a shitty arsed bastard."

Dippy muttered and stepped outside and Nick spun around and ran for the bushes. He heard a shout behind him and a half brick whooshed past his head and crashed through the holly bush prompting shouts of alarm from the other side. Nick skidded under the bushes, regained his footing and ran up the grassy oval like a hare from the hounds. He was almost at the top before he paused to look back and see if Dippy was coming after him. All he saw was Eric, Billy and Clagg running behind him, laughing.

"That was fuckin' great," Clag said.

"He threw a haff brick at him," Trevor said. "A fuckin' haff brick."

"If it hit him it would hae fuckin' killed him," Clag added.

"He just missed is," Nick said.

"He come that close to hittin' ye," Eric said holding his thumb and forefinger inches apart. "Ye jammy bugga."

They scuttled under the hawthorn bush and watched to see if Dippy would come looking for them, but he didn't. The three older boys lit cigarettes and went over Dippy's reaction again and again, comparing it to past encounters. until it began to grow stale. They returned to whispering between each other and when they stopped Clag got up and left.

"Where's he goin'?" Nick asked.

"He's just gannin' yem fo' a minute," Eric said.

Nick realised he was hungry and thought he might go up the street and get something to eat but then Clag came back with his young sister, Brenda. She was the same age as Nick with curly fair hair tied in white ribbons. She wore National Health glasses and a shapeless summer frock. Her legs were scratched and brown and on her feet she wore scuffed green sandals. Clag told her to sit down and the whispering began anew. Nick and Brenda eyed each other curiously. The whispering stopped and Clag said: "Brenda, come owa here an' lie doon." The older boys shuffled aside to make room for her on the blanket.

Brenda looked uncertainly at her brother. "What for?"

"Ah telt ye, it's a game wa playin', that's ahll," Clag said.

"What are ye goin' to do to is?" she asked.

"Nowt," Clag said. "Honest, wa not ganna dee owt to ye."

"Ya not goin' to hurt is are ye?"

"Divvent be sae daft," her brother scoffed. "Naebody's ganna hort ye."

"Cross ya heart, hope to die?"

"Aye, cross me heart," Clag said and crossed his chest.

Brenda went over to the blanket and lay down, arms by her sides, feet together. Her eyes flitted suspiciously around the gallery of faces watching her. Clag said to Nick: "Noo ye lie on top of ah so ya lookin' at ah, like."

It was Nick's turn to be suspicious. "What for?"

"Ah'm tellin' ye, it's just a game," Clag said.

"She's just a lass," Eric sneered. "She's not ganna hort ye."

Stung, Nick crawled over to Brenda on his hands and knees and lay down on top of her. Like him she was skinny and their bones dug into each other. Their faces inches apart Nick saw only bafflement in her eyes. Her breath smelled of milk.

"De ye feel owt?" Clag asked.

"Ow," Brenda said.

"What?" Clag said.

"He's hortin' is," Brenda said.

"Where's he hortin' ye?"

"He's pullin' me skin."

Nick eased himself up to ease the discomfort for both of them but it didn't help.

"Where's he pullin' ya skin?" Clag asked.

"Me stomach," she said.

"De ye not feel owt else?"

"No," she said, annoyed. "What am ah supposed to feel?"

Eric asked Nick: "Do ye not feel nowt?"

"No," Nick said, every bit as baffled as Brenda.

"De ye not feel owt…good like?" Clag persisted.

"No," Nick said.

Trevor said: "Tha not deein' it reyt, they hae to move. He has to gan up an' doon on ah."

"Gan on then," Eric urged Nick. "Gan up an' doon on ah." Nick wanted to leave but Eric grabbed him by the seat of the pants and bounced him up and down on top of Brenda.

"Ow," Nick protested as his trousers pinched his crotch. "That horts."

"Ow," Brenda said. "Get him off is."

"De ye still not feel owt?" Clag asked.

"No ah don't," she said. "Ah want to go home."

Exasperated, Eric released his grip and Nick climbed off Brenda. As she sat up Trevor said: "They've got tha claes on, that's why it's not workin'. Tha supposed to tek their claes off to dee it reyt."

Brenda scrambled to her feet. "Ah'm not tekin' me clothes off," she said.

Nick felt the same stab of alarm. "Ah'm not tekin' mine off neither." He was horrified at the thought of a girl seeing his willy.

"Ah'm goin' to tell," Brenda told Clag, her voice rising. "Ah'm goin' to tell me mam ye tried to get is to tek me clothes off."

Clag looked panicked. "Divvent ye dare…we were only playin'."

Brenda seemed to enjoy the effect her threat had on him. "Ah'm goin' to tell me mam," she said and started out from under the hawthorn bush.

"Brenda, divvent…" There was a pleading note in her brother's voice. He dug into his pocket and pulled out some of the money he'd won at cards. "Ah'll gi' ye a tanner if ye don't tell. Ye can get a Mars bar fo' a tanner."

Brenda stopped as her brother held out a sixpenny piece.

"Mind, ye divvent say nowt…ivah," he said.

She snatched the sixpence and darted away and they heard her skipping down the avenue singing: "Ah've got a sixpence…ah've got a sixpence…"

"Fuckin' hell." Clag shook his head. "She better not say nowt or me dad'll fuckin' kill is."

Eric turned to Nick and said: "Mind, ye divvent gan tellin' naebody neither."

Nick stood up and said: "Ah'm goin' an' all."

Eric grabbed hold of his arm. "Ah'm warnin' ye, ye say owt to anybody an' ah'll fuckin' kill ye. Ah mean it, ah'll fuckin' kill ye."

Nick pulled his arm free. "Ah'm not tellin' anybody," he said and ducked out from under the hawthorn bush. He walked quickly up to the top of the avenue and along Ridge Terrace to the Top End chip shop to buy some fish and chips for lunch and, try as he may, he couldn't make any sense out of what had happened.

*   *   *

Nick was jolted into wakefulness by the sound of his mother's raised voice. It was late, his dad had come home from work and she was going off at him. Her tone was scalding, as if something malignant had erupted out of her, an evil spirit that once released into the air spiraled up the stairs and into Nick's room where it lodged in his chest, something ugly and barbed that made it painful to breathe. He lay there in the dark and listened.

"Ya nivah here an' ye cannit be workin' ahll the time 'cos ye come yem smellin' o' beer so ah knah ye've been oot drinkin' wi' ya police pals," she railed. "But ah nivah get across the doors from one day to the next, div ah? Ah'm stuck between these four walls wi' the bairn ivery day and naebody to tahk tee. As far as you're concerned all ah'm good for is cookin' and cleanin' and deein' ya laundry. Ye divvent want a wife, de ye, Jimmy? Ye want ya mam back to look after ye. Somebody to be ya skivvy. Ah might as weel be a bloody prisoner here for ahll the life ah hae wi' ye."

Nick cringed beneath the covers. Bright had worshipped his mother and her early death from cancer had left him devastated. Yet, somehow he kept his temper. Nick heard the formless drone of his father's voice as he tried to calm her down but his calmness served only to incense her further.

"Divvent ye patronise me, Jimmy, divvent ye dare bloody patronise me," she shouted. "Ah knew it was a mistake te marry ye. Ah didn't want to marry ye in the forst place. Ah didn't love ye then an' ah don't love ye now. If ah'd knahn this was the life ah was goin' to hae wi' ye ah'd nivah hae bloody married ye."

The barb in Nick's chest flexed and dug its talons deeper. Was it true what she said? That she didn't love his father? That she'd never wanted to marry him? That she felt trapped at home with only Nick for company. Nick's universe was a small one, confined to a small house on a small housing estate in a small town. His mother and father were the pillars of that universe and if those pillars were to crumble his universe would come crashing down and then what would become of him?

Somehow his father must have found the right words because at last he managed to soothe her and their voices faded to a murmur. Nick burrowed under the blankets but it was a long time before the barb in his chest relaxed its grip enough to let him sleep. When he woke up the next morning it was as though he'd been asleep for just minutes. He was drained and his eyes felt raw as if he'd been crying. But he wouldn't say anything to his mam and dad about what he'd heard. He would pretend he'd heard nothing so life could go on as if nothing had happened. A pretend life until he was old enough to strike out on his own.

*   *   *

Detective Inspector Jack Shepherd knew what he wanted. He wanted Jimmy Bright to be his new detective. Shep was in charge of the detective branch that covered Bedlingtonshire, which sounded grander than it was because its total manpower consisted of himself and one plain clothes constable. For the last 18 months that had been Alec Newell, an earnest young man whose greatest flaw was that he took his job seriously. Newell thought he should solve every crime that came across his desk and that was the last thing Shep wanted. Crime had been good to him. Crime was job security. Shep intended to guard its mysteries well enough to make himself indispensable but not so much that it looked like he wasn't doing his job. And Newell had never grasped how fine a balance that was. Newell didn't drink either and that annoyed Shep. To Shep abstinence was a sign of weakness - or worse. If Newell hadn't been married Shep would have thought he was queer.

It was a raw Sunday night in November and Shep stood out of the rain in the doorway of the police station at the Top End and waited for Bright to finish his shift. The high peaked Victorian Gothic police station sat on a hill that overlooked the town's major crossroads, which carried traffic between Bedlington, Ashington, Morpeth and Newcastle. It was a little after six and the town was quiet with few cars and fewer people on the rainswept streets. From where he stood Shep could follow the downhill arc of the streetlamps on Front Street to the Market Place. In the blurred sepia light the stolid mercantile architecture was picturesque. But, for 200 years, the business of Bedlington had been coal and behind the quaint facade miles of rowhouses pressed up against the pit-head like piglets at a sow's belly.

Without hint of irony the top end of town was called the Top End and the bottom end of town the Bottom End. As well as the pubs that clustered around both ends there were two working men's clubs, one known as the Top Club, the other the Bottom Club. Shep favoured the back room at the Top Club for discussions of the type he intended to have with Bright.

He heard the door open behind him and looked around to see Bright, still in uniform, leaving for home.

"It's a grand night when tha's nowt for the polis to dee," Shep said.

"Ah'm not complainin'," Bright responded.

"Ye in a hurry to get yem?" Shep asked.

"Whey, ye knah…the wife's expectin' is."

Shep knew. He'd heard how Bright had been late for Sunday dinner once and his wife had thrown it out on the front lawn; plate, cutlery and all.

"Ah only need haff an' hoor o' ya time," Shep said. "Tha's somethin' ah want to tahk to ye aboot in private." He sensed Bright's hesitation. "It's ahlreet, ah'll gi' ye a lift yem after," Shep said. "Ye can leave ya coat an' helmet in the car. Ah've got a spare coat ye can wear owa ya uniform."

Shep's aqua blue Austin A40 was parked around the corner from the police station in Catholic Row. In the back he kept a spare raincoat, a pair of wellies and a bottle of Cutty Sark. Bright left his police coat and helmet in the car and put on the spare coat for the short walk to the Top Club. With no traffic around the two of them bypassed the zebra crossings and cut across the intersection, past Dr. Trotter's pink spired memorial water fountain to the Top Club. The bar was almost empty but even a few drinkers were too many for Shep. He caught the attention of Alf, the head barman, and signaled that he and Bright were going to the back room. The room was cold and dark. Shep switched on the light, tossed his hat onto a padded bench by a corner table, unbuttoned his raincoat and sat down heavily. He rubbed his hands to warm them, leaned to one side and expelled a loud fart.

"Tornip," he said and reached into a jacket pocket for his cigarettes. Across from him Bright rummaged for a Senior Service while Shep lit one of his unfiltered full strength Capstans. Shep was a coarse man with coarse appetites and a once powerful physique that had turned to flab. His thinning hair was combed back from a complexion of scorched pumice and the thumb, forefinger and middle finger of his right hand were stained with nicotine. Summer or winter he dressed the same, a loose cut suit in dark olive, white shirt, tie knotted just off center, light brown Gabardine and matching trilby. The joke at the station was that he had identical versions at home for every day of the week.

The door opened and Alf wheezed in, his laboured breathing a legacy of 30 years down the pit.

"Weather's not fit for a dog to be oot the night, Mr. Shepherd," he said.

"Depends hoo thorsty the dog is," Shep answered. As a Detective Inspector he hovered somewhere between two dialects; the pitmatic he'd grown up with and a posher version for his superiors. He and Bright each ordered a pint of Fed. When Alf returned and Shep showed no sign of paying Bright reached into his pocket. Shep motioned to him to put his money away.

"It's tekkin' care of," he said.

He picked up his pint, drank half of it in a series of practiced swallows and put the glass down with an appreciative grunt.

"Ah wondered if ye might hae given some thought te the idea of detective work, Jimmy," he said. "De ye think that would be somethin' that would interest ye?"

Bright was surprised. He'd given no thought at all to the idea of becoming a detective. As a Detective Inspector Shep could second men to the detective branch as needed as long as he had the approval of John Robson, the inspector in charge of uniform branch at Bedlington. Most of the uniformed men welcomed it because it meant overtime pay. Bright had worked a few shifts for Shep, mostly surveillance, watching the movements of villains in and out of one place or another. Just this summer he'd taken part in a raid that nabbed a welder from Sunderland who was wanted for attempted murder and had been hiding out at his sister's house at Sleekburn. But Bright didn't think that was enough to single him out for Shep's attention.

"Ye mean transferrin' ovah, full time like?"

"Full time," Shep said.

Bright was interested. It would mean more money, a clothing allowance, expenses, and if he did well, a shortcut to a sergeant's stripes. A man usually worked plainclothes three to four years before he could expect promotion and Bright wondered why Alec Newell was leaving after just 18 months.

"Does Alec want to go back into uniform or does he not know aboot this?"

"Alec's not cut oot for detective work," Shep said.

"Ah thowt he was supposed to be deein' ahlreyt."

"He only thinks he is," Shep said. "He doesn't hae the right porsonality. He's not patient enough. He wants iverythin' to happen streyt away and it doesn't work like that."

Bright sipped his pint. From what he'd seen Alec put in long hours.

"So ah tek it he doesn't know?"

"No, he does not." Shep plucked a strand of tobacco from the tip of his tongue and flicked it away. "An' he won't know till ah'm sure of his replacement."

"Hoo de ye think he's likely to take it?"

"Ah'll give him a good recommendation. Ah've got nowt against the lad porsonally, ah'm sure he'll dee var' weel back in uniform."

Bright nodded but he foresaw complications, not least of which was that Alec might think it was Bright's idea to replace him, which was the kind of thing that could poison the atmosphere at a small police station like Bedlington.

"Aye, but why me?" Bright asked.

Shep finished his pint and pressed a service button on the wall. "Ah've been keepin' an eye on ye. Ah've seen the way ye handle people. Ye hae a natural manner so folk feel comfortable wi' ye, but ye get the job done ahll the same. That's a knack. Ye cannit be taught that and Alec doesn't have it. He doesn't mean to but he rubs folk the wrong way so they won't open up to him, an' when people won't open up to ye you're not goin' to get the information you need te dee the job right. Ninety percent of what we dee in plainclothes is information, the rest is hoo we use that information."

"Ah thowt his numbers were good," Bright said.

"His numbers *are* good," Shep said. "Ah'm the one wee does them an' ah've been makin' him look good, but ah cannit keep deein' it forever. The truth o' the matter is ah've given him the easy jobs because ah cannit trust him wi' the hard jobs an' that can only go on for sae lang. He's antagonised some o' me best informants, blokes it's tekkin' is years te cultivate. Ah hae to get him oot soon afore he does serious damage."

The door opened and the two of them stopped talking while Alf delivered two fresh pints. Bright was tempted by Shep's offer but he wondered if there was anything else the D.I. wasn't letting on about.

Shep read his eyes.

"Tha's a lot mair to detective work than folk realise, Jimmy. It's not just aboot numbers. It's not just aboot lockin' blokes up. If ye look at it wi' a clear an' analytical mind it's what police work is supposed to be aboot; prevention, not apprehension." Alf had gone but Shep leaned towards Bright and lowered his voice a level. "Ah've been deein' this fo' a while noo. Goin' on 26 year barrin' me time in the army, an' there's not much that goes on in Bedlington wi'oot me knah'n aboot it forst. If ah hear some silly bugga is goin' to knock owa the Market Place Post Office ah'm not goin' to wait till he does it an' gives some poor owld biddy a heart attack. It sarves the police, it sarves the community, it sarves iverybody better if ah put a word in the right ear an' the Post Office doesn't get knocked owa at ahll. That way naebody gets hort an' ah divvent hae te gan chargin' aroond like a bull in a china shop. That's what keeps the numbers doon - but tha's nae paperwork that can show ye that." He leaned back. "Crime is nowt mair than porsonnel management, Jimmy. That's ahll it is, porsonnel management. Alec doesn't understand that an' he nivah will."

Bright could see the sense in managing villains to keep the crime rate down but he could also see the danger in getting too cosy with them. He could think of a few clever buggas who'd try to use the polis as much as the polis used them. Shep might think himself wiser than most but it was murky terrain that existed only in his mind and Bright wasn't sure he could navigate his way through it any better than Alec Newell.

"Ye see, Jimmy, most villains are naewhere near as clivvor as they think they are," Shep continued. "That's why they keep gettin' caught. An' most of their crimes are penny ante stuff. It's only when they get carried away wi' themselves they start causin' trouble. For instance, it doesn't bother me one iota that Tommy Locke has haff a dozen runners workin' the pit rahs. Ah knah wee they are, ah knah what tha deein' an' ah knah where te find them."

Tommy Locke was the transport depot foreman at the Doctor Pit who'd run an illegal bookmaking business for years.

"Folk work hard an' tha entitled te a few pleasures otherwise life wouldn't be worth livin' would it?" Shep added. "They want to have a flutter on the horses, that's ahlreet bi me. It's their money. They win a couple o' quid every noo an' then, it keeps them happy and Tommy meks enough to tek the wife an' kids to Butlin's ivery year. Good fo' him. But it's not riches beyond ya wildest dreams is it? An' as lang as that's ahll Tommy does he's not ganna get any grief from me. But if he gets owa ambitious an' tries to mek a fool oot o' is he knahs ah'm ganna come doon on him like a ton o' bricks."

Bright knew a dozen villains in Bedlington who fell into the same category and he was inclined to agree; if tolerating their smaller transgressions kept a lid on more serious crime it might be a worthwhile exchange. There had never been a bank robbery in Bedlington, nobody had ever held up the Co-op or the Post Office. There were a few too many break-ins but most crime in Bedlington was alcohol related; pub brawls, street battles and domestic assaults. And there was no guarding against the occasional crime of passion; the husband who throttled his nagging wife, the wife who took a poker to her abusive husband. For the most part it was as Shep said, a balancing act. But what was it that Shep saw in Bright that made him seem so much more suited to the job than Alec Newell? Was he more accommodating than Alec? Less scrupulous perhaps? And how much did it help that he was known to enjoy a drink? Still, they weren't reasons to turn it down. Pat might be a bit more understanding about his hours if she saw more money coming in. And why worry about Alec? If Shep was right Alec was better off in uniform branch anyway.

"Ah'll hae te think aboot it," he said. "Ye warn't lookin' for an answer streyt away were ye?"

Shep looked discomfited. "What's tha te think aboot?"

"Ah'd like to discuss it wi' the wife."

"Aye ahlreyt then," Shep conceded grudgingly. "But ah'd like to knah afore the end o' the week."

Bright looked at his watch and saw that half an hour had passed. At least he had some good news to deflect Pat's ire when he got home. But Shep wasn't done yet.

"Seein' as ye brought it up tha's somethin' else that needs to be said an' it concorns ya wife."

Bright's guard went up.

"Ah don't want ye takin' this offer unless ye've got iverythin' sorted oot at home," Shep said. "Ah knah ye've had some problems wi' your lass but if you're goin' te come over to plainclothes she has to understand ya ganna be workin' ahll oowahs. She won't know when ya comin' yem 'cos ye won't know when ya gannin' yem. Ye hae to be crystal clear wi' ah on that, Jimmy. She married a polis, she has to know that workin' ahll hours comes with the job. Other wives get used te it, she'll hae te get used to it an' ahll."

Bright knew word of his wife's behaviour must have got back to the police station before now but, nonetheless, he felt a prickle of resentment.

"Some wives adapt better than others," Shep went on. "But tha's one thing ye can be cartain of, Jimmy. Ye won't get ahead in the police force unless ye hae a wife wee's willin' te make some sacrifices on your behalf. An' on ah ahn behalf an' ahll. An' ah've yet to meet the wife wee objected to mair money comin' in."

It was easy for Shep to talk. He and his wife lived separate lives. Audrey Shepherd had long since resigned herself to the fact that Shep was the kind of man who would keep his own hours no matter what. She'd built a life for herself that focused on her two married daughters, her grandchildren and flower shows. More often than not she was away visiting and when she was home she and Shep slept in separate bedrooms.

"A wife has to know ah place," Shep continued. "What ah'm offerin' ye here is a chance te take a big step forward an' it's not hor place te haad ye back. Ye hae to mek ah see that, Jimmy, because the wrang wife can ruin a man's career. Ah've seen it happen teym an' teym again."

Bright nodded but he had no idea how Pat would take the news.

"Ah'll tahk tiv ah," he said.

"Ah can ask for nae mair than that," Shep said. He finished his second pint and added: "We'll hae one for the road eh, an' then ah'll get ye yem."

*   *   *

When Shep pulled up outside Bright's house it was getting on for ten and the windows were dark.

"She must hae gone to bed early," Bright said. He got out of the car, took his helmet and overcoat off the back seat and thanked Shep for the lift.

"If she's mad at ye tell ah she can blame me," Shep said before he drove off.

Bright closed the front door quietly so as not to wake Pat and Nick upstairs. He hung up his things in the hall and went into the living room where the fire was almost out. Usually Pat banked it up before going to bed but the coal bucket was full and the house felt cold. She must have forgotten. At least she hadn't thrown his dinner out. He found it under a plate on the countertop next to the cooker; a couple of slices of pork in a puddle of congealed gravy with a soggy slice of Yorkshire pudding, boiled potatoes, tinned peas and carrots. He turned the oven on low, put his dinner in to warm and went upstairs. The door to the bedroom was open but he didn't want to disturb Pat by turning on the light so he stood in the doorway and listened for the sound of her breathing. He heard nothing and when his eyes adjusted to the dark he saw the bed had been made but there was nobody in it.

He looked in on Nick to see if she'd fallen asleep in there but there was only their son, asleep and apparently unaware he'd been left on his own. Bright went back downstairs and saw her mac and her fleece lined boots were missing from the front hall. He looked on the mantelpiece, the sideboard and in the kitchen but there was no note to say where she'd gone. He wondered if she was at a neighbour's house but that was unlikely given how late it was. Bright felt a growing unease.

He went back upstairs, turned on the bedroom light and looked through her dresser drawers to see if any of her clothes were missing but everything seemed to be there. He opened the cupboard and their one suitcase was still there along with his Navy kit bag. He went back downstairs and switched off the oven, his appetite gone. There was a half bottle of Lamb's Navy Rum in the sideboard and he poured himself a good sized nip, lit a tab and settled on the couch to wait. He loved his wife but when she lost her temper she lost all perspective and didn't seem to care how much harm she did. He was fairly certain she'd gone somewhere to punish him. To show him how it felt for her to be out and for him to wait at home not knowing where she was or when she'd be back. She might have gone to Dot's. It wasn't far so she could have walked but it would have been a while ago or he and Shep would have seen her on the road. She could have gone to Ashington but that was unlikely. Her mother might take her in but her father wouldn't. Her father had no time for her nonsense and gave the impression he was glad to have her out of the house.

Bright threw more coal on the fire, stoked it back to life and poured another nip of rum. He must have nodded off because the next he knew the clock on the mantelpiece was striking twelve, the fire had gone out and he felt cold. But still there was no sign of Pat. Resigned, he went upstairs and got into bed. The next time he awoke it was to see Nick standing at the foot of the bed dressed for school.

"Where's me mam?"

Bright had to think for a moment. "Ah think she went over to your Aunty

Dot's. She must hae decided to spend the night."

"Is she comin' back?"

Bright thought it an odd question. "Of course she's comin' back," he said. "Do ye need is to mek ye some breakfast?"

"No," Nick said and went downstairs. Bright heard him collect the milk off the front step then go the kitchen and get himself some cornflakes. Something about the matter-of-fact way Nick had asked if his mam would be coming home bothered Bright, as if his son wouldn't mind that much if she didn't. Soon afterwards Nick called upstairs to say he was leaving for school.

"Be a good lad," Bright called back. "Work hard." The front door closed and the house fell silent. Outside he heard Nick greet his friends, their liveliness a stark contrast to the cheerless silence in the house. Was that the extent of his fathering to his son, Bright wondered? 'Be a good lad? Work hard?' He spent hardly any time with Nick. His son was growing up a stranger to him much as he had grown up a stranger to his own father and he had no idea what to do about it. Unable to go back to sleep he got up and relit the fire. With just him in it the house felt lifeless so he switched the wireless on for company and made himself a cup of Nescafe. He lit his first tab of the day and stood at the front window looking through the net curtains at a world steeped in grey light.

She came home around nine thirty. He watched her walk up the path, eyes down, a half smile on her lips, knowing he'd be watching her. He opened the front door before she could put in her key.

"Oh hello," she said with affected lightness. "Ya back then."

"Ah meyt weel say the same thing aboot ye," he said.

She hung up her coat, kicked off her boots and put on her slippers.

"Are ye ahlreet?" he asked.

"Whey a'course ah'm ahlreet," she said. "Why wouldn't ah be?"

"Where were ye - at your sister's?"

"Oh, ya interested are ye?" she said and went through to the kitchen to make herself a cup of instant coffee. He followed and waited while the kettle boiled.

"Ah hae a right to know, Pat. Ah am ya husband. Ah just want to know ye were ahlreet."

"Ah just telt ye, ah'm perfectly ahlreet," she said. She pronounced it 'perfect' instead of 'porfect' or 'parfect,' to maintain a certain coolness.

"Were ye…at your sister's?"

"An' what if ah wasn't?"

"Just answer the question will ye, Pat. Were ye at ya sister's last night or not?"

"Ye don't like it when the shoe's on the other foot, de ye?"

"Ye mean ye want to knah if ah'd worry aboot ye if ye were oot ahll night? Of course ah bloody worried aboot ye, what de ye think?"

"Oh well, that's nice to know then, isn't it?" she said and tossed her hair the way she'd seen Bette Davis do in a film once. She took her coffee into the living room, sat on the stool by the fire and used a spill to light a tab.

He went after her. "Ye could hae at least left a note sayin' where ye were goin'."

"An' what if ah didn't feel like leavin' a note?" she said, staring into the fire. "What if ah didn't want ye to know where ah was goin'?"

"Why wouldn't ye want is to know where ye were goin'? Wi are married, ye knah."

"Oh, ye noticed did ye?"

Her disdain was unbearable. Bright wanted her on any terms, whether she loved him or not.

"Ah divvent dee it on purpose, Pat," he pleaded. "If ah don't come straight home from work tha's generally a good reason."

"Tha ahlways is," she said.

Bright remembered what Shep had said the night before.

"Ah'm a policeman, Pat. Ah don't ahlways hae the luxury o' comin' straight home the minute ah get off work. Sometimes tha's things te dee. Important things. An' when a superior officer says he wants to tahk t'is aboot somethin' ah hae to pay attention."

"Aye, but it's funny hoo these tahks always hae to happen in a pub isn't it?" she said.

"It was Shep wee wanted to tahk, not me," he said. "De ye not want te knah what it was aboot?"

"No, Jimmy, ah don't," she said. "Because whatever it was it was obviously more important than me."

Bright sighed. "Pat, tha's nowt in me life more important than ye, man. But if ah've telt ye once ah've telt ye a thoosand times, this isn't a nine to five job. Ah'm a polis. It's not a lot different to bein' in the navy. Ah hae to dee what ah'm telt when ah'm telt."

"An' in the meantime ah'm supposed to stop livin' am ah?" she said. "Well, what if ah just felt like havin' a bit o company last night? What if ah just felt like a drink an' somebody to tahk to? Somebody wee'd listen to me for a change?"

The thought of her with another man was like a shard of glass in his heart.

"Were ye at your sister's or not?"

She let the silence draw out then said mockingly: "Of course ah was at me sister's. Where de ye think ah was, galavantin' aboot wi' me fancy man?"

Bright was so relieved he didn't know what to say, so he asked: "Did ye enjoy yasel'?"

She looked at him to see if he was being sarcastic.

"It was better than sittin' here starin' at these four walls by mesel' ahll neet, if that's what ye mean."

"Ye left Nick on his own."

She shrugged. "He wouldn't have been on his own if ye'd come yem at the time ye said ye were comin' yem, would he? He's your son as weel as mine." She'd slid back into the vernacular, she was softening.

"Ye didn't hae to stay oot ahll night, Pat."

"Oh, ah was supposed to wahk back on me own, was ah? Wahk past the cemetery late at night ahll by mesel'? Is that what ye wanted is te dee?"

Apparently she wasn't afraid to walk past the cemetery in the dark on her way to Dot's. But there was nothing to be gained by pressing her further. Bright had to be at work for noon and he hadn't had anything to eat since the day before. His dinner from last night sat in the oven untouched. All he had to do was warm it up. She might like that. She'd see he appreciated what she did for him.

"Ah hae to eat somethin' afore ah go into work," he said. "Ah'll hae last night's dinner ye made, ahlreet? It won't go to waste."

She shrugged indifferently, stared into the fire and smoked her tab.

He ate alone at the kitchen table and when he was finished told her how good a dinner it was. She didn't answer. He went into the living room and put his hands affectionately on her shoulders.

"Ah divvent dee it to vex ye, pet, really ah don't. Ye knah hoo much ah love ye."

She made no response. He sighed, went upstairs and got ready for work. When he came back he was in uniform. He stood over her, feeling awkward, his helmet cradled in his arm.

"Ahll bein' weel ah should be yem by haff past six the night," he said. He bent down to kiss her and she allowed him to kiss her cheek.

That night he was home on time, as promised. And the next night and the night after that. And he said nothing about Shep's offer. That Saturday he had the night off and he got in some Newcastle Brown Ale for himself and some Guinness for Pat so they could relax together at home. Later, when they went to bed, she allowed him to make love to her.

33

Whith the end of the week come and gone and Shep had still heard nothing he beckoned Bright into his office, an untidy wood framed glass cubicle next to John Robson's office. Both offices were open to the high ceiling, which made for hushed conversations when anything confidential had to be discussed. Shep's office was cluttered with cardboard boxes to hold the overflow from a couple of filing cabinets and a desk barely visible under a heap of folders, memos, notebooks, bulletins, graphs, maps, letters, newspapers and other random scraps of paper. Bright closed the door behind him but remained standing. He didn't want to be in Shep's office for long.

"Hae ye made your mind up aboot that matter we discussed?" Shep asked.

"Ah have, boss," Bright said. "An' ah don't want ye to think ah'm not grateful, because ah am. But ah don't think this would be the right move for is at this time. Ah think ye know things haven't been the best at home lately and, honestly, it'd be temptin' fate..." He let his words trail away.

Shep looked up at Bright's bland oval face, his guileless blue-grey eyes.

"Then you're a fool te yasel', Jimmy," he said. "You're a fool te yasel'."

The next month Alec Newell went back to uniform branch and Dickie Prichard, an ambitious young polis who'd come to Bedlington the year after Bright, was appointed Shep's new detective constable. And Bright never said a word about any of it to Pat.

1955

Newcastle United wins the FA Cup for the third time in five years; Samuel Beckett's 'Waiting for Godot' opens in London leaving audiences baffled. On the wireless Grace Archer dies in a fire. Top draws at the box office are The Colditz Story starring John Mills and Eric Portman; Love Is A Many Splendored Thing starring William Holden and Jennifer Jones; Doctor At Sea, starring Dirk Bogarde and Brigitte Bardot. Top of the Hit Parade are Softly Softly by Ruby Murray and Never Do A Tango With An Eskimo by Alma Cogan.

Lovely Things

In the spring of 1955 the lives of the Brights changed from black and white to colour. Nick's mam got a job managing a dry cleaner's on Vulcan Place at the Bottom End and the effect of more money coming in was transformative. The improvements began with the quality of food. Nick's mam bought apples, oranges, pears and bananas and put them in a fruit bowl on the sideboard like posh people did. She bought better cuts of meat. She bought cakes and pastries. And she took Nick to Newcastle to buy clothes. Usually she bought his clothes at the Co-op in Bedlington or Ashington where the only choices were blue or grey. Going to Newcastle was an adventure because it was filled with motion and spectacle. Picture houses with the latest films, theatres with big name stars, swanky hotels and restaurants and department stores like palaces with rumbling escalators that led to floor after floor of lovely things. The streets bustled with life; shoppers, tradesmen, office workers, medical students from King's College in flowing scarves, crafty eyed businessmen in smart suits and smashing office girls in high heels who trotted along the pavement like ponies.

Nick's mam took him for lunch in the cafeteria at Fenwick's where he had pie and chips and a strawberry milkshake. At British Home Stores she bought him a pair of khaki shorts, some T-shirts and a pair of sandshoes. She bought his dad a couple of summer shirts and herself a pair of lightweight slacks, walking shoes and a camel hair jacket. When Bright cautioned her about how much she was spending she laughed it off and said now she had her own job she could tick it on. To Nick it was proof that money could buy happiness. What he didn't know was that the trip to Newcastle was a prelude to even broader horizons. That summer his mam and dad bought a motorbike and sidecar combination. A 600cc Panther with a single seat sidecar like a little maroon boat with its own windshield and a black canvas hood with Perspex windows. It was second hand but it didn't matter because it was going to take them on holiday all the way to Nottingham.

Nick's Aunty Vi and Uncle Don lived in Nottingham. All he knew about them was what he'd heard from his mam and dad. Vi was a couple of years older than Pat and the two of them had been close when they were young. Unlike Nick's mam, who served in the Women's Land Army during the War, Vi spent the war years in service to a rich family in London. She'd dropped her accent and copied the manners of her employers in the hope of marrying up in the world. But, when the offers never came, she married Don, a sergeant in the Royal Artillery who she met at the NAAFI off Picadilly Circus. After the war he took her home to Nottingham where he got a job as a surveyor with the city council and bought a house with an orchard in the village of Arnold on the outskirts of the city.

The day of departure the Brights were up an hour before dawn. It was nearly 200 miles from Bedlington to Nottingham and it would take all day to get there. They squeezed their one suitcase behind the red vinyl seat in the sidecar and put everything else in pillion bags. Nick's dad wore a black oilskin motorcycle jacket that zipped from throat to thigh. It had roomy chest pockets and side pockets that fastened with brass studs and a broad collar that flapped like bat's wings in the wind. With it he wore black leather gauntlets, a flat cap and goggles that covered the top half of his face. Nick's mam wore her new slacks and camel hair jacket and a scarf to keep her hair in place while she rode pillion. She made Spam sandwiches with HP sauce to eat along the way and filled a flask with hot coffee. Nick was locked in the sidecar with a bottle of pop, a packet of crisps and a handful of comics to last him on a journey his dad estimated would take up to ten hours.

The most direct route to Nottingham was by the Great North Road, the A1, which ran from London to Edinburgh. They would go through Newcastle to get onto the A1 then head south through Scotch Corner, York and Doncaster. All being well Bright said they should get to Nottingham by tea time. Nick liked riding in the sidecar because the roar of the motorbike engine and the rush of wind across the canopy made him feel like he was a Spitfire pilot: World War Two fighter ace, Rockfist Rogan, zooming up on enemy convoys, strafing lorries and tour buses, strewing the road with burning wreckage and the tumbling bodies of old age pensioners.

They made good time till they reached York whose streets hadn't changed since the days of Oliver Cromwell and they had no choice but to crawl along for a couple of hours. On the other side of York they stopped at a lay-by for lunch and Nick went with his dad for a slash behind a hedgerow. His dad had removed his goggles so the top half of his face was white and the bottom half grey with road grime. It was another five hours before they trundled into Arnold tired, dirty and steeped in exhaust fumes.

His aunt and uncle's house was easy to find; a square Victorian tower three stories high that looked as if it had been set down at random in a quaint English village. Flanking the road was a brick wall with an open farm gate and a gravel track that led up the side of the house. The house overlooked a front lawn and across the road was a pasture where a dozen or so Jersey milk cows grazed. Behind the house was a small courtyard with a washhouse and coal house. The orchard, which covered about three acres, reached from the road up past the house for about 200 feet where it ended in an impressive hedgerow atop a steep earthen bank. Beneath the fruit trees was a grassy meadow splashed with buttercups and daisies.

When Nick met his Aunty Vi he saw the same unsettling gleam in her eye that he saw in his mam and his Aunty Dot. Yet, her crinkly haired husband, who had the weathered look of a man who spent his life outdoors, was the essence of affability. It was then Nick realised his mother, his Aunty Dot and his Aunty Vi had all married the same man. A man whose temperament was the opposite of their own. A man who would not stand up to them.

Nick got his bag out of the sidecar and followed his parents inside. Despite the warm summer air the house felt cool. His aunt and uncle had no children and their home was geared to the comforts of grown-ups. The living room had high windows but heavy curtains kept out the sunlight. Glum pastorals hung on the walls and the furniture was old and dark. A pair of armchairs with worn cushions bracketed an iron fireplace shielded by a screen embelished with wrought iron ivy leaves. The most modern piece of furniture in the room was a radiogram with a collection of neatly stacked 78's and LP's by the likes of Louis Armstrong, Frank Sinatra and Peggy Lee. The most lived-in room was the kitchen, which had an enormous square table in the middle of the floor and a cast iron cooking range that took up most of one wall. A walk-in pantry was stocked with jars of stewed apples, pears and plum jam made from the fruit that came out of the orchard. A wide staircase serviced the upper stories. On the first floor was his aunt and uncle's bedroom with an adjoining sitting room and a separate bathroom and toilet. On the second floor was a guestroom where Nick's mam and dad would sleep, another toilet and a room that was used for storage. Nick's bedroom was on the top floor, an attic room with faded floral wallpaper, two single beds, a wardrobe and a washstand. Gabled windows overlooked the orchard and the courtyard. To spare guests the trouble of finding their way downstairs to the toilet in the middle of the night a jummy had been placed under his bed.

Nick's mam and dad recovered quickly from the rigours of the road. All it took was a drink or two and they revived like a couple of inflatable dolls. Don and Vi kept a well stocked cocktail cabinet, there were two crates of beer in the pantry and they'd got in a crate of Guinness just for Pat. They started their holiday that night as they meant to continue - by drinking till they couldn't drink anymore. Vi put out some cold ham, cheese, bread and home made pickles and Nick drank lemonade while the grown-ups turned themselves into drunken gargoyles. When they could drink no more beer and Guinness they broke out the whisky, gin and rum. It was around this time Nick's mam and dad sent him to bed so they could relax properly. He lay in bed unable to sleep as shrieks of laughter echoed up the stairs late into the night.

The next day Nick's mam and dad took him into Nottingham on the bus and they went to Nottingham Castle where he had his picture taken beside the statue of Robin Hood. Afterwards they visited the captive remains of Sherwood Forest to see the Major Oak. The next day his Aunty Vi took them to a small Saxon church in the village where deep grooves worn into the vestibule stones were purportedly made by the outlaws sharpening their arrowheads. But the evenings were devoted to drinking.

One night the grown-ups went out to a local pub and parked Nick on a bench by a window with a glass of lemonade and a packet of crisps. In a corner of the lounge the open lid on a stand up piano beckoned and, after a view drinks, Pat and Vi could ignore its invitation no longer.

"Come on, Pat, give us a song, like you used to do in the NAAFI," Vi said.

"Are ye sure nobody minds?" her younger sister answered.

"Of course nobody minds," Vi said.

Pat went to the piano, teased out a few rills then eased her way into Vera Lynn's 'White Cliffs Of Dover.' Next she did 'Sally' by Gracie Fields, for which she earned a round of applause from the other drinkers. She followed it with another Gracie Fields hit, 'Wish Me Luck As You Wave Me Goodbye,' which got everybody's feet tapping.

"Pat, play 'Who's Your Lady Friend," Vi called out and she picked up her drink and went to stand by the piano. Nick's mam played a boisterous 'Hello, Hello, Who's Your Lady Friend' with Vi joining in and encouraging everybody to sing along. From there it was like a party amongst old friends. In quick succession she thumped out 'Down At The Old Bull And Bush, Roll Out The Barrel, My Old Man Said Follow The Van' and 'All The Nice Girls Love A Sailor.' She made jokes, bantered with the other drinkers and took requests. She played old time crowd pleasers like 'Lily Of Laguna, Maybe It's Because I'm a Londoner' and 'Roamin' In The Gloamin'.'

Watching through the window it felt to Nick as if he was watching a film where his mother and his aunt were the stars. The two of them thrived on the attention, his mam working the room instinctively while Vi, drink in hand, conducted the singalong. They were having the time of their lives and everybody there was their audience. Nick saw that this was his mam at her happiest. These were the times she was most alive and the rest of her life was inbetween.

At last it was closing time and the landlord's call of 'time, ladies and gentlemen please,' was met with groans. They all spilled into the summer night laughing and singing, reluctant to let the moment go. New friendships had been forged and there were reluctant partings to be made. When Nick's mam saw him waiting by the bench she remembered suddenly that they'd brought him with them.

"Ahh, me bairn, me bairn," she cried and enveloped him in her arms, pressing him to her body with its commingled aromas of sweat, gin and Evening In Paris. "Ya mutha loves ye son, ya mutha loves ye." She held him so tightly he had to pull away so he could breathe. "Ahh, don't ye like to see your mutha enjoyin' herself, hinny?" she chided him. She turned to the others and said: "Look, he's jealous, he's jealous of his mutha havin' some fun." They laughed and Vi said: "He bloody well better get used to it then," and they laughed all the more.

At last they disengaged themselves from their new found friends and went their separate ways to the scattered refrain of 'We'll Meet Again.' The night was starless with only a thumbnail moon to light the way home across the fields. A swing gate led into the first field and they giggled and pushed each other into single file so they could get through. Nick's mam let out a scream as his dad pushed after her and grabbed a fistful of her arse. Don said: "Hey you two, wait till you get home before you start that." There was some muttering not intended for Nick's ears followed by loud cackling from his mam and his Aunty Vi. The drink made them happy. Turned them into big, happy kids without a care in the world. They linked arms on the path and sang 'Show Me The Way To Go Home.' The way to the next field was over a stile and Bright and Don made a show of taking each of their wives by the waist and swinging them over as they let out girlish squeals. The next field was the cow pasture that led down to the road past Don and Vi's house. In the dark they could hear the cows coughing.

"They winnit bite us will they?" Nick's mam asked.

Don and Vi laughed. "Cows don't bite," Don said. "If the bull was in here he might have a go at you but they don't keep the bull in this field."

"Aye but there's plenty o' somethin' else an' ah just stepped in it," Nick's dad said.

"Shit for luck," Nick's mam said and they all cackled again. When they got home they were barely in the door before Vi suggested a nightcap.

"Whey aye, man," Nick's mam said. "Ah divvent knah aboot the rest o' ye but ah'm just gettin' started."

Nick didn't have to be told to go to bed but before he could leave his mother grabbed him by the shoulders, spun him around and kissed him sloppily on the cheek.

"Ooh, look at his face," she said, laughing. "He hates that don't ye, Nick, ye hate your mam doin' that."

As he climbed the stairs he used his sleeve to wipe away his mother's kiss.

*   *   *

The next day was the day before the Brights were to begin their marathon journey home and they decided to spend it quietly. Nick played in the orchard most of the morning and in the afternoon his mam and dad and his Aunty Vi came up to get some sun. Vi wore a wide brimmed straw hat with a gauzy pink scarf trailing from the brim and carried a bag that held her knitting, cigarettes, a flask and some plastic cups. They spread blankets under a pear tree and made themselves comfortable. Nick's mam wore a green and white woolen bikini she'd knitted herself so that each of her breasts looked like it had its own tea cosy. Great gingery tufts of pubic hair jutted out from her bikini bottom and varicose veins clustered like blackberries on her calves and ankles. It was why she never bared her legs at the beach, but here she felt safe. Vi wore a pale blue one piece swimsuit with a white skirt that complemented her glassine skin. Nick's dad wore baggy blue swimming trunks and his bony white body and beet red head reminded Nick of a matchstick man.

Vi poured each of them a cup of lemon and barley water and they smoked and chatted in the drowsy air, their conversation punctuated by the click of knitting needles. Bright finished his tab, lay on his back, spread a handkerchief over his face and was soon asleep.

"It annoys me the way he can do that," Nick's mam said.

Hot and thirsty from playing in the sun Nick went over to see if he could have some lemon and barley water too. Vi poured him half a cupful and he drank it quickly.

"That's all you're going to get, mind," his aunt said.

Nick shrugged and put the cup down.

"An' what do you say?" his aunt added.

"Mind your manners, Nicholas," his mam said. "Say thank you."

Nick offered a grudging 'thank you' and returned to his perch in an apple tree where he amused himself tossing apples at the squirrels that came to raid the fruit. After a while he heard the tinny beep of a car horn as his Uncle Don announced his early arrival home from work. Don parked the council van next to the house and walked up to the orchard.

"Finished early today," he said. "I wasn't getting much done. Can't imagine why after last night."

Nick's dad stirred at the sound of Don's voice.

"How are we today then Jim?" Don asked.

Bright sat up and mashed his lips together dryly.

"Ah divvent knah aboot anybody else," he said, "but ah could morder a pint."

"Hair of the dog eh, Jim?" Don said.

"Ah've hord tell it can work wonders," Bright responded.

"Well, the sun's past the yardarm," Don said. "Reckon I could bring a couple of bottles up."

"If you're going to bring a couple of bottles for yourselves, would you mind bringing a couple for us too, ducks" Vi said. "What do you think, Pat, you good for a Guinness?"

"Ah'm always good for a Guinness," Pat said with a stagey grin.

Don went back down to the house and when he returned he'd changed into a pair of ex-army shorts and a shirt he wore open to reveal a chest that was little more than a vest stretched over a wire coathanger. He carried with him a clinking haversack and he sat down and opened a bottle for each of them. From his eyrie Nick watched them revive from a fresh infusion of alcohol. They drank and talked and as it so often did their conversation turned to the war years that were still so fresh in their minds. Nick heard endless such conversations among family and friends and didn't understand how they could recall so fondly something they were supposed to hate so much. In one breath the war was nothing but dread and suffering and in the next it was the best years of their lives.

"You get to see The Dam Busters yet?" Don asked.

"Ah'm waitin' for it to come to Bedlin'ton," Bright said. "When it came to Newcastle the queues were aroond the block."

"Very good picture," Don added. "Heavily dramatised of course but true to life. The Colditz Story was good too."

Bright said: "The most true to life picture about the war ah've seen - from the point of view of the Navy anyway - was The Cruel Sea. Not as good as the book mind you, but it gave ye a good idea what convoy duty in the North Atlantic was like."

"Ah took Nicholas to see 'The Red Beret' when it came to Bedlin'ton," Pat said. "It had Alan Ladd in it, ah thought it was really good."

"You've always been soft on Alan Ladd," Vi said.

"Alan-short-arse-bloody-Ladd," Nick's dad said.

"That's the kind of thing that sends me right up the wall," Don added.

"They have to put a yank in a picture where there shouldn't be one. They have no respect for the truth."

"If ye listen to the yanks the forst two years o' the war nivah happened 'cos they waren't in it," Bright said.

"I don't forget that we stood alone for those two years," Don said. "We were fighting every bugger by ourselves - the Germans, the Eyeties, the Japs - and the yanks kept givin' us gyp because we weren't winning enough battles. They sat back and made a fortune off us and if they hadn't been bombed into the war at Pearl Harbour they would have let us go under. And it's a bloody good job for them we didn't."

Nick's mam and his Aunty Vi had fallen unusually quiet.

Don continued: "The thing is the first time the yanks went up against the Germans was a disaster, a complete bloody disaster. After we kicked the Germans out of Egypt we were pushing the buggers back across the desert and the yanks were supposed to stop them at the Kasserine Pass in Tunisia and the Germans made mincemeat out of them. And if it wasn't for our armour it would have been a hell of a lot worse. But I don't think we'll be seeing too many films from the yanks about the Battle of Kasserine Pass any time soon, do you?"

"Aye but that's the yanks fo' ye," Bright said. "Last in, forst to claim ahll the glory."

"We had a saying in the desert," Don said. "When the Germans flew over the British ducked, when the British flew over the Germans ducked, when the Italians flew over nobody ducked and when the yanks flew over everybody ducked."

The four of them laughed and, with their bottles empty, Vi suggested they go in for dinner. But dinner was incidental to their thirst and they continued drinking late into the night. The next morning Nick's mam and dad got off to another slow start. By the time they'd taken their first sip of tea Nick was washed, dressed and packed. But he had a dilemma. He'd never used a jummy before and he knew nothing about jummy etiquette. Nobody had emptied it for him and now it was full, a potful of stale piss under his bed. It didn't seem right to leave it behind and it hadn't occurred to him that he should empty it daily into the netty the next floor down and now it was too late. And it was so full he didn't fancy his chances of getting it down a flight of stairs without spilling it. He'd have to do the next best thing. He opened a window, picked up the jummy with both hands and edged his way across the room. It was a big chamber pot with raised pink rosebuds on the side and felt to Nick as if it held a couple of gallons. He rested it on the window sill and, holding the handles tightly, tipped it outwards. The contents cascaded down the side of the house, a twirling amber ribbon in the morning sun. And then he heard a scream. Even distorted by horror it sounded like his Aunty Vi. It was followed by angry shouts from his mam and dad. A door slammed and there were thudding footsteps on the stairs. Nick dropped to his knees, put his hands together in prayer and looked up to the ceiling.

"God, if you're there…"

*   *   *

"Howay buggalugs, get ya coat on," Nick's dad said. "Ah hae to gan owa to Netherton, ye can come wi's for the ride."

Nick was sprawled on the living room carpet with his cavalry fort, arranging his blue coated troopers, a few of Robin Hood's outlaws and some British Army soldiers with Sten guns to fight off an imminent Indian attack across the carpeted prairie. His dad had just come in from work and Nick jumped up, glad of the chance to get out of the house.

"Where ye goin'?" his mam asked. She sat on the settee smoking, listening to Jack Demanio on the wireless, a sheaf of discarded football pools on the coffee table.

"To see a man aboot a dog," Bright answered playfully. "Ah hae to tahk to Ken Bossey the club secretary. Ah'll not be lang but ah thowt the bairn might like to see the show."

"Ya not stoppin' for a drink?" she said.

"No, ah'll not be stoppin' for a drink."

"Ye promise?"

"Aye, ah promise."

"Ye meyt as weel bring somethin' back then," she said. "Ye can bring is a couple o' Guinness."

"If it'll mek ye happy, pet, ah'll bring ye a barrel o' bloody Guinness," he said and kissed the top of her head.

It was only a few minutes from West Lea to Netherton on the combination but Nick didn't mind. It was fun to ride pillion instead of in the sidecar. He squinted happily into the wind as they rumbled past stubbled wheat fields under a chalky September sky. The farmland ended abruptly at the turn off just before Netherton Village and Bright had to slow down to navigate the rutted and cratered colliery road made from compacted coal dust.

Netherton Working Men's Club was an annex to the old Miners And Mechanics Institute and stood on a rubble strewn expanse of open ground where stunted weeds struggled to survive. The Institute, built in the 1880's, was a brick building two storeys high. The annex had been built as a single storey extension between the wars and both were stained by coal dust to a deep claret color. Just after the club the road divided, the right fork curving around to the pit head 200 yards away, its cage tower stark as a gallows. There were offices, workshops, baths and a canteen on the south side of the pit head and beyond them rail sheds and a siding where an overhead bucket conveyor dumped coal into waiting rail wagons. Past the siding was a no man's land of slag heaps and pools of scummy black water. When the wind blew from the coast six miles away it snatched dust from the slag heaps and drove a fine black spray inland, staining laundry on the line, sifting under doors and windows. When it rained streams around the colliery ran black as tar. The left fork led about a hundred yards to the northern side of the pithead and rows of cottages where miners and their families had lived since the first shaft was sunk in the 1860's. Grim, grey and slouched with age the tiny cottages were kept determinedly neat and tidy by the miner's wives.

There was a car park on the sheltered side of the club with a couple of motorbikes and a single car, a cream and brown Vauxhall Cresta. Ken Bossey's car. Most miners walked to the club from the pit rows in their Saturday night best and tried not to soil their shoes on the way. Bright parked the combination against the club wall and turned off the engine and the noise from inside the club swelled to fill the silence. The original entrance to the Miners And Mechanics Institute was a rarely used pair of double doors with a lintel of stone scrollwork but everybody used the entrance the Institute shared with the club. Nick's dad pulled open a swing door with a frosted window on which an arch of blocky gold letters proclaimed: 'Netherton Working Men's Club and Institute Union.' Underneath the arch was the CIU crest that signified the biggest working men's social, fraternal and political organisation in the British Isles.

Inside, a clammy heat washed over Nick and his dad like a gust of steam from the pit baths. Nick found himself in a crowded lobby where an older man with a severe haircut and the scorched complexion of the heavy drinker sat at a folding table checking membership cards and tickets to the show. On the table were an almost empty pint glass and an overflowing ash tray. Behind him a placard on an easel announced: 'Netherton Working Men's Club and Institute Union Annual Leek Show, 1955.'

"Hoo's ya fettle the night then, Maurice?" Bright addressed the older man.

"Canny man, canny," Maurice replied. He looked Bright up and down noting that he wore his motorcycle oilskins over his uniform but had unbuttoned the tunic and removed his tie.

"Ye heyah fo' the show, Jimmy?"

"Actually ah'm heyah to see Ken Bossey," Bright said. "Ah browt the lad alang to see the show if that's ahlreet."

"Whey aye man, just mek sure he keeps to the main hall, that's ahll," Maurice said. "The judgin' was this afternoon so the names o' the winners are ahll oot. Ah'll send word to Ken that ya here." He waved them in without asking to see a membership card or a ticket.

Nick followed his father through a jostling crowd of men that spilled out of the bar into the hallway. It was one of the biggest nights of the year and they had bathed and Brylcreemed themselves to a high gloss. Most wore dark suits with white shirts, plain ties and starched white handkerchiefs folded into their breast pockets. Some of the older, retired miners wore the livery of an earlier era, black woolen suit with flat cap, waistcoat, watch chain, collarless shirt and white scarf knotted at the throat. Many wore a red or white carnation in their lapels. Almost all wore lodge badges. And the noise was such that they had to lean into each other to make themselves heard. Cigarette smoke formed an oily stratus at the ceiling and the floor was sticky with spilled beer. Dodging elbows and pint glasses Nick was glad to reach the main hall where the crowd thinned out appreciably. He was quite unprepared for what he found; a room grander than any he thought could exist in Bedlington's blighted landscape. The walls were paneled with oak as dark as tea and reached two stories to an arched ceiling supported by solid oak beams. Affixed to the walls were wooden tablets with columns of names in gold lettering memorialising miners who had fought and died in wars from the Sudan to the Boer War, the Great War, the Second World War and the Korean War. Hanging from the walls were gold fringed tapestries which Nick's dad pointed out were not tapestries at all but lodge banners fastened to poles so they could be carried in parades. The banners were emblazoned with crossed pickaxes, cage towers, rising suns and hands clasped in friendship with slogans that proclaimed: 'Prosperity Through Industry,' and 'Strength In Unity.'

The hall had a churchy reverence to it and in a way it was a church, a shrine to all that miners held sacred. He'd grown up thinking of coal mining as dirty, dangerous and dehumanising with little about it that was worthy of celebration. Yet here there was only celebration; the coal miner's world was built on traditions that went back generations. Traditions of brotherhood and charity, of pride and patriotism. Thriving as it did in such bleak surrounds there was something inherently noble about it. However often their country had failed the miners they had never failed their country. And along the way they had cultivated customs of their own, the breeding of racing pigeons, whippets and that curious creature the Bedlington Terrier - and the growing of the finest leeks in all the world.

Nick had never seen so many leeks gathered in one place. Rows of tables draped with green felt cloth had been set up on the polished hardwood floor bearing artfully arranged displays; leeks as long as a man's arm, leeks with barrels as thick as a man's thigh, leeks with pearlescent flesh whose carefully rinsed roots were spread like silken tresses on a pillow. Their savory aroma filled the hall with a lush and fecund tang.

"Ye might want to shut ya gob afore ye start catchin' flies," his dad said.

"It's...fantastic," Nick said. He would never have guessed there could be so many different kinds of leeks, long leeks, intermediate leeks, pot leeks, leeks that stood alone or were entered in pairs or threes. And when it came to the prizewinners, with their ribbons and rosettes, he could see little difference between the big and beautiful leek that came in first and the big and beautiful leek that came in last.

"Hoo do they tell which one's are the best?" he asked.

"Aye, weel, that's a good question, isn't it?" his dad answered. "That's why leek show judges get called names warse than a referee at a footbahl match."

"Ah cannit see any difference between them," Nick said.

"Ye hae to have the right eye an' even then it's hard to tell just by lookin' at them," his dad said. "The judges measure them lengthways an' then the corcumference, an' then they work oot the cubic capacity o' the barrel."

"The barrel?" Nick repeated.

"If ya ganna tahk aboot show leeks ye hae to knah what ya tahkin' aboot," his dad continued. "They call the white bit, what ye might think of as the stalk, the barrel. The leaves are called flags, the roots are called the beard." He spaced the thumb and forefinger of his right hand lengthways against the barrel of a leek. "For a pot leek ya lookin' fo' the whiteness o' the barrel, what they call the blanch, to be a good five to six inches from the bottom o' the leek to the button but nae mair than that." He indicated the point on the leek where the barrel divided into leaves. "That right there, that's the button," he said. "If the blanch is owa long or owa short ya not ganna dee as weel. Then they measure the leek aroond. Usually three times; at the top o' the barrel, at the middle an' at the bottom to come up with the average corcumference. An' when they've done that they can work oot hoo many cubic inches are in the barrel. The more cubic inches ya leek has the better ya ganna dee in the show."

"Ah didn't knah there was sae much arithmetic in leek growin'," Nick said. He hated arithmetic.

"Aye there is that, bonny lad," his father answered. "It's why ye hae to dee good in ya sums at school, 'cos when ye grah up ya ganna come across it in ahll manner o' things."

"So ye hae to measure ya leeks afore ye put them in the show?" Nick said.

"Ye dee if ye want to enter ya best leeks an' ye divvent want any nasty surprises when the judgin' starts," his dad said. "Then, if the dimensions are right, the judges look at the appearance o' the leek. It has to be fresh, that's why most o' these leeks would hae been pulled an' weshed just yisterday or the day. But ye cannit pull it if it's owa close to seedin' 'cos that'll get ye disqualified. Then tha lookin' fo' blemishes on the barrel, any marks or bruises that'll tek points off ye. If the barrel feels soft to the touch they'll take points off ye for that. If any o' the flags are torn or frayed they'll take points off ye for that. If the leek is owa light they'll take points off ye for that an' ahll." He gestured around the room. "Ahll these leeks that didn't get the top prizes hae somethin' wrang wi' them that ye or me might not be able to tell. The winner has to be as close to porfect as ye can get."

"What happens to them when tha finished heeyah?" Nick asked. "Do they get eaten."

"Some dee but not ahll," his dad said. "Some o' the top prizewinners will tek them yem an' replant them an' if tha lucky they'll get a canny batch o' seeds off them in a couple o' weeks. They'll use them seeds te grah a new crop of champions next year an' what they divvent use they'll sell."

"They sell the seeds?"

"Oh aye, there's ahlways folk wee want to buy seeds from a top prizewinner. That's when the grower can mek some canny money - an' ye can be sure the tax man doesn't knah owt aboot it either."

Nick was impressed. "Hoo much money?"

"A bob or two a seed," his father answered. "Mebbe more if the seeds come from a long line o' winners - an' a good leek will produce a couple o' hundred seeds. Mind, ye hae nae way o' knowin' if a grower's sellin' ye the right seeds unless ya there when he collects them. Some growers hae nae intention o' sellin' tha best seeds 'cos they divvent want some other bugga tekkin' the top prizes away from them. They'll sell ye seeds from tha less successful leeks an' if ye divvent win any prizes at next year's show ye divvent knah if there's somethin' wrang wi' the seeds or somethin' wrang wi' the way ye grew them." He seemed amused by Nick's amazement. "Son, iverythin' that's wrang in human nature, ahll the greed an' spite ye can imagine, it ahll goes on aroond leeks just like it does wi' owt else o' value. Wherivah tha's money to be made ye'll find folks up to nae good - like slashin' Robbie McBride's leeks. It's not 'cos some bloke doesn't like him, it has nowt to dee wi' that, it's te tek him oot the competition."

As they moved along the line of prizewinners his father mouthed each grower's name.

"Freddy Knox, ah knah him. Complete bloody waster. He's been oot on compensation wi' a bad back the last fowah year. Doesn't keep him from bendin' owa in the garden though. He collects the dole so he can spend ahll his time growin' leeks an' racin' pigeons. Ray Gaskell, he's from West Lea. Doesn't knah his arse from his elbow. God knows hoo he got this far this year. Dave Dwyer, he's from Netherton, he come in forst last year. Kevin Healey, ah locked him up for knockin' the daylights oot o' his best mate last year." He paused in front of Paddy Mullen's entry, which had come in 149th out of the show's 350 entries. "That's the highest he's ivah come. Sarves him right if it's him wee slashed Robbie McBrides leeks. It's only won him a pair of blankets." A little further along they came on Robbie McBride's pot leek at number 93. "Just made it into the top hundred this year," Bright said. "It's ganna tek him a while to come back, poor bugga."

Finally they came to the table where the winning entries in the pot leek class sat next to a three foot high silver cup where the grower's name would be engraved with the other winners going back to the 1880's.

"Eddie Gill, another bloody villain," Bright chuckled. "Ah knah ahll these buggas. Ah've locked most o' them up for one thing or 'tother."

"Jimmy, ah just hord ye were heeyah…" Nick turned to see a man approach his father with his hand outstretched. Ken Bossey had the dark good looks of a film star and the manner to go with them. He shook Bright's hand and clapped him on the shoulder. "Has naebody got ye a pint yet?"

"No, an' ah've been here at least five minutes," Bright said.

"We'll soon fix that," Bossey said. "A pint o' Fed is it?"

"That'd be champion," Bright said, breaking the promise he'd made before leaving home.

Bossey disappeared briefly and returned to tell Bright a pint of Fed was on its way.

"So, this'd be your lad is it?" he said, giving Nick an appraising look.

"Aye, this is Nicholas," Bright said. "Ah thought he meyt like to see what a leek show's ahll aboot."

"An' so he should," Bossey said and offered his hand. Nick hesitated. It was the first time he'd met a grown-up who wanted to shake his hand.

"Gan on, ye can shake hands wi'm, he's not ganna bite ye," his dad said.

Tentatively, Nick shook Bossey's hand.

"Whey, he's a bonny lookin' lad," Bossey said. "Are ye sure he's yours?" They laughed and Bossey added: "So what do ye think of the show this year then Jimmy?"

"Var' impressive from what ah've seen," Bright answered. "The lad here says it's fantastic."

"Fantastic eh? Whey he's obviously as clivvah as he is good lookin'," Bossey said. "We've had a record settin' year this year, Jimmy. An' the highest quality ah've seen in the time ah've been club secretary. An' that's despite the bother some o' the top growers have had." He gestured to a pair of pot leeks on a nearby table, their flags arranged as carefully as fine cloth. "Look at these two…" He rolled the two leeks together so that each barrel pressed tightly against the other. "See that, Jimmy," he gave Bright a nudge. "Nearly as bonny as wor lass's big white arse."

Bright smiled and turned to Nick. "Gan on doon the bottom an' look at the prizes while ah tahk to Mr. Bossey," he said. "Ah'll come an' get ye when wa ready te leave."

Nick did as he was told and wandered down to a low stage at the end of the hall. There was a crowd between Nick and the stage and when he'd threaded his way through to the front he saw why. Rearing up in front of him in tier after gleaming tier was a pyramid of household treasure. Furniture polished to a high shine, pots and pans that sparkled, crystal glassware that glittered like diamonds. Numbered cards matched each prize to its winner. That year's top prizewinner in the pot leek class had won a set of living room furniture that included a settee with walnut armrests, two armchairs, a coffee table and a solid walnut sideboard. Second prize was a bedroom suite with double bed, wardrobe, dresser and vanity, third prize a Formica topped kitchen table and chairs. Other prizes included a radiogram, a grandfather clock, bicycles, a Royal Doulton dinner service, a pressure cooker, an Irish lace tablecloth, bed linens, a quilt, a lamp standard, a ladies' leather handbag, a hip flask, bottles of rum, whiskey and gin all the way down to last place, a crate of Newcastle Brown Ale.

Nick felt as if he'd strayed ito Ali Baba's cave. Anybody would have been happy to take home any of the prizes on display. Miners made around 15 pounds a week and a bottle of whisky cost nearly three pounds. Eddie Gill might be a villain, as Nick's father said, but as long as he kept winning at the leek show he could refurnish his entire house for free.

Somewhere behind him Nick's dad was coming to the same conclusion.

Ken Bossey told Bright: "If'n ye want, Jimmy, ah'll put ya name forward at the next meeting o' the Membership Committee. Ah can pretty weel gar'ntee ye'll get in."

Bright finished his pint before answering. "Aye, gan on, then," he said. "It's aboot time."

"Consider it done," Bossey said. "Ye ready for another pint?"

Bright hesitated. "Ah suppose ah might as weel hae one for the road," he said.

*　　*　　*

Appearances mattered to Ken Bossey. Every day he went into the club he wore a jacket with a clean white shirt, a club tie fastened with a gold and maroon tie pin and matching cuff links. His thick black hair was always neatly brushed, his slacks pressed and his shoes polished. He also kept a spare jacket, shirt, razor and shoe shine kit in a cupboard in the club secretary's office. He was always cheerful, always ready to pull pints behind the bar or help the cellarman tap a new barrel of beer and he made sure the beer was kept to the exacting standards of a membership of expert beer drinkers. He chaired the Operating Committee, the Finance Committee and the Membership Committee and exercised more control than the Club President, who represented the club at official ceremonies and charitable events. While the president made speeches, presented prizes and posed for photographs Bossey was happy to stay in the background. The club's employees knew him as a man who never lost his temper, was slow to criticise and quick to compliment. He never took a sick day but when any of his staff was in the hospital he made sure they got a card and a fruit basket. In return they gave him their unwavering loyalty. And those who knew him well knew that behind the easygoing manner was a shrewd mind. He left nothing to chance and he knew everything that went on at the club, however trifling.

There were only five applications to be considered at tonight's Membership Committee meeting; three from colliery apprentices who had reached legal drinking age; one from a former steelworker from Consett who had recently started at the pit and the last from Jimmy Bright. Bossey had told nobody about Bright's application. There were seven members of the committee, including himself, and only three others were present: John Jacks, who lived at West Lea, Bob Gillespie from Netherton and Claude Turnbull from Bedlington.

As usual the business of the meeting fit on a single typed sheet of paper and the wording for each item was kept deliberately vague so committee members wouldn't have too much time to worry about the details of what Bossey wanted expedited. The committee was the easiest on which members could serve and meetings were usually over before they'd finished their second pint.

A few minutes after seven-o-clock Bossey asked his secretary, Doreen, to close the committee room door. The room fell quiet except for the tap of Doreen's heels as she returned to her seat. She sat next to Bossey, shorthand notebook open on her knee, pencil in hand, a glass of Muter's Lemonade in front of her. The five of them were gathered at one end of a magnificent oak table flanked by 20 chairs upholstered in green leather and brass studs. Ken and Doreen sat on one side and John, Bob and Claude sat across from them. All but Doreen smoked, including Claude who was 68 and retired and couldn't stop despite his blackened lungs. Each man had a fresh pint in front of him except for Ken, who made do with a gill, and barely touched it, but always had a drink on hand to show he was one of the lads.

He started the meeting with a roll call then had Doreen read the minutes of the last meeting, which were accepted unanimously because nobody but Ken and Doreen remembered what happened at the last meeting. The only correspondence was a letter from the wife of a recently deceased member challenging the exclusion of widows from the club on the death of their husbands, to whom Bossey would send the standard reply that there was no support among the membership for changing the rule that barred unaccompanied women. He wouldn't tell her the reason why, which was because for 60 years other member's wives hadn't wanted widows coming to the club to steal their men.

Under new business there were no expulsions or disciplinary matters to be decided and the committee instructed Bossey to send out the usual reminder to members who'd fallen behind in their dues. As expected, when he came to new applications there was little discussion about the mine apprentices or the former steelworker and all were approved unanimously. When he came to the last application he read it slowly and with emphasis: "James William Bright...Police Constable, Bedlington."

He let the words hang in the air and John Jacks, a mine electrician in his forties, was first to seize on them.

"Jimmy Bright...would that be the polis wee lives just doon the road from me?"

"That would be correct," Ken answered.

"It's a bit unusual isn't it," Bob Gillespie said. A colliery engineer in his early thirties he was the youngest man in the room and, after Bossey, had the quickest mind. "Would this be the forst time the club's had an application from a polis?"

"Tha's nivah been a polis in the club that ah can remember," Claude Turnbull said.

"It's the forst time this club has had an application from a polis," Bossey confirmed. "But it wouldn't be the forst time a polis has been a member of a Bedlin'ton club. Jack Shepherd has been a member at the Top Club goin' on 15 year noo an' there are other clubs in the northeast an' other parts of the country that hae polises as members."

"That's thon big bastard..." Jacks began then looked at Doreen and said: "Cross oot the word 'bastard,' if ye divvent mind hinny...that's thon big bugga... ah mean detective at the Top End?"

53

"That'd be him," Bossey said.

"But he'd hae to be a special case would he not?" Jacks added. "Bein' a polis an' ahll?"

"He's not a special case," Bossy said. "Ah tahked to Col Beatty, the secretary at the Top Club, an' he said Shep was admitted when he was a sergeant an' he qualified because the polis is a workin' man just like the rest o' the membership. The only problem that came up was when he was promoted to Inspector and there was some discussion aboot whether he was still a member o' the rank an' file or a boss. The decision was that if he got promoted any higher than Inspector he'd likely hae to go but till that happens he's ahlreet."

Jacks shifted in his chair. "Ye knah what I'm gettin' at Ken. Havin' a polis in the club meyt mek some folk uncomfortable. They meyt feel they hae to watch what they're sayin' ahll the time. The members come here to relax an' enjoy themselves, they divvent want to worry aboot the polis watchin' iverythin' they dee an' say."

Gillespie said: "What ah'm wonderin' is, if it's ahlreet fo' the polis to join, why mair o' them haven't bothered? Why is Jimmy Bright only the second one in Bedlin'ton to apply?"

Bossey shrugged. "In some places they hae tha ahn clubs. Ah knah the police in Newcastle hae tha ahn club an' ah believe there's one at Wallsend an' ahll. Some are telt streyt oot not to fraternise wi' the locals. Some meyt just think tha not goin' to get enough oot o' it te mek it worth their while."

"So why does Jimmy Bright want to join noo?" Gillespie asked.

Bossey smiled. "Same as the rest o' wi, ah expect, the polis likes his beer an' doesn't want to pay pub prices ahll the time." He added: "His fatha is a retired miner in Ashin'ton where he's been a member o' the Ashin'ton Club gannin' on 50 year. An' he has a brother wee's a member there so there's a history o' family membership. Jimmy Bright might be a polis but he comes from a minin' family."

"Ah don't hae anythin' against the polis," Claude Turnbull said. His voice had turned phlegmy and he paused to spit into his handkerchief. "Ah've knahn some good an' ah've knahn some bad in me time an' ah understand the polis has a right to drink in peace as much as the next man, but ah agree wi' John. Ah cannit help but wonder hoo him joinin' might affect the rest o' the membership. Not iverybody is comfortable aroond the polis, ye knah." He paused. "Ah suppose what ah'm sayin' is ye never knah when the polis is off duty, when he might hear somethin' he can haad against ye later on."

"That's exactly what ah'm sayin'," Jacks added. "Wor responsibility is to the existin' membership. They hae a right to drink in peace an' are they goin' to be able to dee that wi' the polis stannin' at the same bar they are? An' mind, ah hae nowt against Jimmy Bright either, he seems a canny enough bloke from what ah've seen of him." He hesitated. "Ah'll tell ye one thing though, that wife o' his doesn't haff gi'm some gyp."Bossey Ken said. The others, including Doreen, smiled. Bossey added: "Ah can only tell ye what Col Beatty telt is aboot Shep. He said tha was a few at the Top Club had misgivin's when they let him in but they've nivah had any bother from him or because of him. None at ahll. In fact, Col says havin' him in the club has helped them oot a teym o' two."

"An' hoo's that then?" Jacks asked.

It was the question Bossey had been waiting for.

"Ah'll put it like this…" He paused. "Doreen, pet, put ya pencil doon fo' a minute would ye please, there's a good lass." Doreen put her pencil and notebook on the table, sat back and folded her arms. Bossey went on: "Col says it's probably worked oot in tha favour havin' Shep aroond because him bein' a member o' the Top Club means he's got a cartain loyalty to that club, if ye get me drift. Col says he's been a big help on licensin' matters an' he's saved them a ton o' money on solicitor fees. An' far from him listenin' in on what others are sayin', Col says he's telt them things that's helped club members from time to time."

"Aye, like what?" Gillespie asked.

"Ah'll gi' ye an example," Bossey said. "Ye ahll knah Phyllis Ritchie?" Phyllis Ritchie was the wife of Doctor Bernard Ritchie, a well known Bedlington GP. Together they owned Spring Bank Farm which raised prize winning Herefords. Phyllis Ritchie was a staunch Protestant, a teetotaller and an animal lover who'd dedicated her life to public service and raising money for charity, especially animal welfare. She'd been appointed a Justice Of The Peace some 10 years before and risen to the position of Chief Magistrate for Bedlingtonshire. She had famously punished Ted Pollock a former milk man, when he managed to pull off a trifecta. After a night of drinking on money he'd stolen from an RSPCA donations box Pollock had set out on his milk round only to lose control of his float going down to the Furnace Bank bridge. He had jumped clear as the horse, pushed by the float, ran off the road, down the bank and into the River Blyth where, trapped in its traces, it drowned. Pollock escaped without a scratch only to have Phyllis Ritchie remand him to Newcastle Assizes with the recommendation that he be sentenced to the maximum and resulted in him going to jail for three years.

"It nivah horts to knah somebody wee can put in a good word fo' ye at the reyt time." Bossey continued. "Ye nivah knah when ye might hae a bit o' business ye need some help wi', or when ye need the reyt porson to help ye oot of a spot o' bothah. An' ah think it goes wi'oot sayin' that if ye knah somebody wee's comin' up in front of ah it could mek ahll the difference in the world if ye had ah ear ahead o' time." He leaned back in his chair. "Ah cannit put it any plainer than that."

Turnbull was first to speak. "So, you're sayin' wi should let the polis in because he knahs the right folk?"

Bossey chose his words carefully. "Ah'm sayin' Jack Shepherd has been a good member and a valuable asset to the Top Club and ah don't see why Jimmy Bright couldn't be a good member and a valuable asset to this club, an' that's ahll ah'm sayin."

"It's not what ye knah it's wee ye knah," Gillespie sniffed.

"Aye, an' when has it ivah been any different?" Jacks added.

Bossey shrugged. "It's what makes the world gan 'roond, Bob. We didn't mek the rules, wa just followin' in the footsteps o' them wee went afore wi."

The table fell silent and Bossey was happy to let it drag out. Then Turnbull said: "Ah cannit deny a man admission to the club fo' bein' a polis. He's a workin' man like the rest o' wi, nae better, nae worse. Ah hae nae objection to him joinin' if he wants."

"No, me neither," Jacks said. "If he can dee wi the odd good torn while he's heyah so much the better. It's not much different to when ah dee a bit o' electrical work to help the club oot from time to time. Wi' ahll dee that."

Bossey looked to Gillespie who slowly shook his head. "No, ah've got nae objection to the man neither."

"An' if some folks hae to watch tha gob when he's aroond that's not ahltogether a bad thing either is it?" Bossey added. The mood at the table eased and he gestured to Doreen to pick up her notebook and pencil.

"Ahlreet," he said. "Ah move wi approve the application of James William Bright. Ahll those in favor?"

One after the other Jacks, Turnbull and Gillespie said: "Aye."

"It's unanimous then," Bossey said. "Jimmy Bright is approved."

*   *   *

Nick's mam decided this would be the best Christmas they'd ever had. She bought a tree so big it filled the bay window and its fragrance perfumed the whole house. She bought tree lights whose tulip shaped covers were painted with figures from fairy tales. She had Nick help her decorate the tree with silver garlands, plastic icicles and baubles that refracted the light into sparkling rainbows. They draped the tree with tinsel and on top his mam placed a spectacular gold and silver foil star. Around the walls she hung multicoloured paper bells and paper chains that criss crossed the ceiling. On the coffee table she put out boxes of chocolate brazils, sugared almonds, licorice allsorts, dates and mixed nuts. And she baked like Nick had never seen her bake before; Christmas cake, Christmas pudding and mince pies. She bought a turkey, a pork roast and bacon to wrap around the chipolatas, more food than the three of them could possibly eat at one meal. She was a joy to be with, tireless and good natured. She had her moods, it was true, but when she was happy she made everybody around her happy. When she was done the house looked, felt and smelled like everything Christmas was meant to be.

Nick woke up early Christmas morning too excited to sleep any more. In the pre-dawn gloom he saw a stack of presents at the foot of the bed and ran to tell his mam and dad Santa had been. Despite the earliness of the hour they put on their dressing gowns and came to his room to watch him open his presents. He was overwhelmed by how many presents there were; a Hornby Flying Scotsman electric train set, roller skates, a cowboy outfit, a game of Cluedo, the Beano and Oor Wullie Christmas albums and a Cadbury's selection box. Afterwards Nick carried them downstairs and put them under the tree while his mam and dad smoked, drank coffee and tried to wake up. They had mince pies for breakfast and Nick's mam and dad had a nip of whisky with their coffee. Nick's dad was delighted with his presents, which included a shaving set, a calfskin wallet, a box of his favourite Turkish Delight, a carton of 200 Senior Service and a bottle of Lamb's Navy Rum. He apologised for having only got Pat a pair of sheepskin lined slippers but she shrugged off his concerns and put them on in place of her old and worn slippers. And she seemed equally happy with the Pink Camay soap and bath salts Nick had got her.

The rest of the day had a dreamlike quality about it. There was so much of everything, so much to eat, so much to play with. And when they sat down to Christmas dinner it was so lavish Nick felt like they were in a picture in a posh magazine. His mam and dad had tippled all day and they drank beer and wine with dinner. When they came to the Christmas pudding his mam doused it in brandy and lit it so it was wreathed in blue flames. Nick was allowed to have a piece of pudding but not the sauce, which his mam had laced with rum. Afterwards he lay in front of the fire and read his Oor Wullie album while his mam and dad sat on the settee and smoked and drank. It had been a perfect day and the Christmas his mam had always wanted. Until her mood turned.

"Hoo much did ye spend on me slippers?" she asked Nick's dad.

"Ah cannit tell ye that," he said in mock surprise. "It's a present."

Nick pretended to keep reading but his hair prickled like hackles on a dog.

"It couldn't hae been more than ten bob," his mam said.

"Aye, but it's the thought that coonts, isn't it?" Bright responded.

"Ye couldn't hae thought aboot it that much," she said.

"Pat, ah didn't hae time to dee ahll the Christmas shoppin' ah wanted," Bright said. "Ah would hae got ye more if ah'd had the time."

"It's funny hoo ye ahlways hae time to go to the pub wi ya pals but ye divvent hae time to go Christmas shoppin' fo' ya wife."

"Let's not tahk aboot it just noo, eh," Bright said. "We've had a lovely day..."

"Aye, because ah worked me fingahs te the bone te mek it special fo' the two o' ye," she interrupted. "An' ye didn't gi' it a second thought did ye?"

Bright lowered his voice. "Pat, ah'm sorry if ya disappointed. Tell is what ye want an' ahll get it fo' ye."

"It's owa late noo." Her voice went up an octave. "Ah dee iverythin' ah can te mek Christmas special an' ah get nowt back in retorn. Iverythin' ah dee is tekkin fo' granted by the both o' ye."

"Wi nivah take ye fo' granted," Nick's dad said.

"Ye've got a funny bloody way o' showin' it then don't ye, Jimmy?"

"Do ye not like the slippers?"

"It has nowt to dee wi' the slippers," she shouted.

Nick wanted to get up and leave but was afraid it would only draw her ire.

"Look, Pat, ah'm sorry," Nick's dad said. "Tell is what ye want an'..."

"What ah want is fo' ye to show a bit of appreciation fo' once in ya life," she yelled into his face. "Christmas is supposed to be aboot love. Ah did ahll this fo' the two o' ye because ah love ye. But neither one o' ye feels the same way aboot me de ye? Apparently neither one o' ye loves me."

"Pat, ye knah that's not true," Nick's dad said.

"Ya selfish, Jimmy, selfish through an' through - an' he's just the same." She gestured dismissively at Nick. "He teks afta his fatha ahlreet just like ye tek afta your fatha. You're ahll the same, ye just take, take, take, the lot o' ye."

"Come on, hinny…" Bright put a hand on her arm but she pulled away.

"Don't ye bloody touch me," she said. "Ye see this…" She snatched up the wallet she'd given him for Christmas and flung it at him. "Ah got ye this oot o' love. That's what Christmas is supposed to be aboot…love. Iverythin ah got ye ah got because ah love ye…" She threw the word 'love' at him like an insult.

And then something happened that Nick never could have imagined. His dad sobbed. An anguished, crippled sound that spilled out of him like vomit. And he jumped up from the settee and ran upstairs, sobbing.

Nick felt sick and stunned. She'd made his dad cry. A man wasn't supposed to cry. Not his dad. His dad was a polis. Folk on the street wouldn't believe it. Jimmy Bright, the big hard polis reduced to tears by his wife. He'd never live it down. The lights on the Christmas tree still glowed, the ornaments still sparkled, the gold and silver star on the top of the tree still shone but everything had changed. She'd given them Christmas, she could take it away.

1956

Thousands of civilians are killed as Soviet forces crush an uprising in Communist occupied Hungary; Egypt's President Nasser closes the Suez Canal cutting off oil supplies to Britain and France. Tops at the Box Office are Davy Crockett, King Of The Wild Frontier, starring Fess Parker; The King and I starring Yul Brynner and Deborah Kerr. Most popular TV show is Hancock's Half Hour with Tony Hancock and Sid James. Biggest song hits are The Ballad Of Davy Crockett by Bill Hayes; Green Door by Frankie Vaughan and Heartbreak Hotel by Elvis Presley.

Where There's Muck

The new year wasn't 48 hours old when Bright began his preparations to grow prize winning leeks. His first stop was Cec Tyler's greenhouse at the Doctor Pit allotments. Nick clung to the back of the Panther as they rode through deserted streets the day after New Year's Day, the wind so cold it made his teeth ache. At the Top End they turned down Glebe Road and halfway down the hill turned into the allotments. Many pitmen had worked the same allotments for years and put up sheds and greenhouses that had the look of permanency. Most miners grew vegetables for the kitchen and almost all grew leeks for food and show. But the allotments weren't just a source of sustenance, they were a green oasis in an industrial desert, a refuge where a man could escape the domestic clamour of home. Sheds sheltered wheelbarrows, gardening tools, watering cans, seed trays and plant pots of all sizes, but there was also an upturned beer crate or two that served as a seat where the miner could sit and enjoy a tab, a bottle of beer and a bit crack with his neighbour. Tacked to the wall were pictures of Jackie Milburn snipped from the Chronicle or some bikini clad beauty from the Reveille. And in winter a paraffin heater generated enough warmth to make a shed or greenhouse cosy on the coldest day.

Nick's dad steered the combination along the back lane that serviced the allotments, bouncing over puddles frozen hard as concrete. He stopped about a third the way down beside a slab of plywood that served as a gate. The gate was fastened with a bolt and Nick followed his dad inside fumbling with benumbed fingers to slide the bolt behind him. His dad led the way along a narrow footpath, the muddy boot prints of autumn frozen underfoot. The allotments were a labyrinth of footpaths and chicken wire fences that separated one garden from another. On some sections of path duck boards had been laid down but were sleeved in ice and it was safer to skirt them. In every direction Nick saw the skeletons of last year's gardens; frames and trellises white as bones under a thick coating of frost. Many of the gardens were littered with the frozen scraps of last year's crop, which would be worked into the soil in the spring. Despite the barrenness of winter every garden had its own compost heap, a silent Vesuvius from which stray wisps of heat escaped in defiance of the punishing cold. Downhill from the allotments were the slate roofs of the pit rows, sulphurous columns of smoke rising from every chimney to taint the underbellies of the clouds.

Nick's dad made a couple of turns and the two of them came up on a large greenhouse behind whose streaming glass panes the bulky figure of a man could be seen. Bright tapped on the wood framed doorway and the figure inside stopped what he was doing to open the door. Nick stepped into dreamy tropical warmth. The greenhouse was about 12 feet long, eight feet wide and seven feet high at its peak. The floor was packed earth with wooden boards laid down the middle. Girdling the inside of the greenhouse at waist height was a broad wooden shelf on which sat numerous seed trays, each about four inches deep and filled with soil. Under the shelf were stacks of dirt rimed clay pots of varying sizes. At the back of the greenhouse was a paraffin heater set on bricks with a tin flue to vent the fumes.

"Hoo's ya fettle the day then, Cec?" Bright inquired.

"Fine fettle, Jimmy, fine fettle," Cec answered. "Yasel?"

"Nivah better, man," Bright said.

"An' wee's this young lad?" Cec said, nodding at Nick.

"This is me son, Nicholas," Bright said. "Nicholas, say hello to Mr. Tyler."

Nick shook Cec Tyler's hand, which was as big as a shovel.

Bright added: "Ah thowt it was time he larned somethin' aboot grahin' leeks."

"Aye weel, ah'm not so sure he's come to the right place for that," Tyler said amiably.

Cec Tyler was a broad chested man in his 50's. His sandy hair was salted with grey and curled untidily around a bald scalp, his complexion ruddied by foul weather and fine ale. He wore a sleeveless leather tunic lined with sheepskin over a woolen army shirt, baggy brown corduroy pants and hobnail boots that scraped on the wooden boards. Cec ran The White Hart, a short walk down Glebe Road, but spent much of his time growing leeks, a world in which he had been immersed for most of his adult life.

"Mr. Tyler has forgotten mair aboot grahin' leeks than most blokes aroond here will ivah knah," Nick's dad said.

"Aye that's the trouble," Tyler said. "Ah think ah've forgotten most o' what ah used to knah. Last year ah didn't start a night watch on me leeks soon enough an' ah got caught oot."

In the years before the war and just after, Cec had been among the top winners but the shows had got bigger and the competition fiercer. It had been a few years since he'd taken first prize in any show, though he usually managed to place in the top 10. He was still perceived as enough of a threat for slashers to cut the best of last year's leeks.

"Ah divvent knah why they bothered wi' me," he said. "It's been a while since ah took the top prize yem."

"Ya still the man wi' the best seeds in Bedlin'ton, but," Bright said.

"That's as maybe," Cec said. "But it's not a guarantee o' grahin' the best leeks any mair is it?"

What he said was true. Seeds with a sound pedigree were just a beginning as growers experimented with ever more innovative ways of nourishing their leeks.

"So, ye want to get some show leeks started, Jimmy?" Cec said. "Ah feel it's only fair to warn ye it can tek owa ya life."

Bright knew. He'd watched his own father put countless hours into building up his trenches and fussing over his leeks the closer it got to show time. It would be a while before he could put up his own greenhouse at West Lea and in the meantime he'd do what other growers without greenhouses did. He'd pay somebody like Cec to get his leeks started then transplant them into his own garden come May.

"Hae ye thowt aboot what kind o' leeks ye'll be grahin'?" Cec continued. "Ah grah mainly Musselburghs but ah hae a few blokes gannin owa to Lions an' they're not a bad strain, they've had some success wi' them. Ah hear some blokes are tryin' News O' The World leeks an' ahll but ah divvent knah owt aboot them an' ah stay away from what ah divvent knah."

"Ah'll be fine wi' Musselburghs," Bright said. "They're what me dad grew an' they've done ahlreet fo' ye owa the years."

"They're the most dependable strain, in my view," Cec said. "Ah'll be happy to get them started for ye but after that ya on ya ahn." He paused. "An' ah don't want ye blamin' me if ye divvent win nowt ya forst year, mind."

Bright smiled: "Ah'll be owa the moon if ah even place this year. Ah just want to get a good strain started an' we'll see hoo ah go from there."

"Aye, good enough then," Tyler said. "Hoo many do ye think ye'll ye be wantin', Jimmy?"

"Ah think two dozen to start," Bright said.

"De ye want to start them from seeds or pods?"

"Ah knah some blokes swear by pods," Bright said. Pods were leeks grown from bulbs but required more attention in the early stages. "Does it matter as lang as they come from a good home?"

Tyler looked doubtful. "Some blokes want nowt but pods because they think they can get better quality an' accelerate the growth as they come on but it's an ahful lot o' bother in the forst few weeks. The seeds come from the same strain as the pods an' ah use only me top prize winners."

Bright got the impression Cec was less bothered about starting from pods than he was by growers coming to his greenhouse too often in the first few weeks of growth.

"Ah'll be fine wi' seeds," Bright said. "It hasn't done ye any harm."

Cec nodded. "Ye can weed oot the runts orly enough when ya startin' from seed, an' it gis ya best ones time to settle. Ah'm not one for choppin' and changin' them aroond ahll the time when tha that smahll."

"That's good enough for me," Bright said.

"Tell ye what ah'll dee, Jimmy, ah'll put aside a tray o' 50 fo' ye an' ye can thin them oot to suit yasel. An' ah'll not charge ye any extra. Hoo does two pund soond?"

"Soonds champion to me, Cec," Bright answered. Two pounds for 50 leek seedlings was a bargain considering they came from top quality stock and the price included greenhouse space and heat for four months.

"Ye win any prizes this year divvent forget to say where ye got them," Cec added. "Ye want me to dee the pottin' or will ye be deein' ya ahn?"

"Ah think ah might dee me ahn pottin', Cec," Bright knew Cec was giving him a bargain and didn't want to take advantage. "That way ah cannit blame ye if owt gans wrang."

"Just as ye like, Jimmy. Do ye hae ya ahn pots or will ye want to use mine?" Bright wasn't sure and Tyler added: "It depends if ye want to keep the pots. If'n ye want to keep them ye should bring your ahn to tek yem. Otherwise ye can use mah pots an' bring them back when ya done. Ah've got a ton o' pots an' it'll not cost ye nae mair."

"Ah'll use your pots this year then, Cec," Bright said. "Ah divvent want to bugga me leeks aroond any more than necessary."

"That's hoo ah feel aboot it," Tyler said. He gestured to a dozen nearby seed trays that awaited their first planting. "Ah'll set ye up wi' one o' these an' put ya name on it so ye can come back any time an' see hoo tha deein'. An' it'll not dee any harm fo' the polis to be seen comin' aroond regular like."

After the warmth of Cec Tyler's greenhouse the walk back to the combination was brutal and Nick was shivering when he climbed on the back of the motorbike. By the time they'd gone up to the Top End, down Front Street, past the empty market place to Jessop's the butchers Nick was chilled to the bone. He'd never been to Jessop's because his mam bought most of their meat from the Co-op at the Top End but he was learning just how many people in Bedlington his father knew.

Jessop's was on Front Street East, its facade painted dark green and above the window in black letters on a yellow background were the words 'Jessop and Son, Fine Butchers.' After the name, in smaller letters, were the words 'Established 1924.' Because it was still a holiday the white enamel display trays in the window were mostly empty except for a few links of sausages, some slabs of darkly glistening calf's liver and a couple of curled ox tongues. Hanging stiffly from steel hooks in the unheated store window were the unskinned carcasses of half a dozen hares.

Bright pulled the combination into an archway beside the butcher shop and parked. The archway was about 30 feet deep and led to the back yard though the way was blocked by a solid wooden gate topped with iron spikes. Nick got off the bike and swatted his arms against his body to get his blood circulating.

"Ah thought it was a hol'day the day," he said.

"Not fo' iverybody," his dad said. "The polis still has to work an' the butcher still has to dee his slaughterin' fo' the week."

Nick had never given much thought to how his Sunday roast got to the butcher's shop. From time to time he'd seen a refrigerated delivery van parked in front of the Co-op with blood streaked carcasses hanging inside, which the driver and the butcher's assistants would heave over their shoulders and carry into the store. But, it had never occurred to him that there was a place in Bedlington where live animals were killed.

His dad opened the latch on a small door set in the larger gate and the two of them stepped into the back yard. The yard was enclosed on three sides by high brick walls and on the fourth was the back of the butcher shop and the flats that overlooked Front Street East. The tops of the walls were encrusted with cement studded with broken glass. Set against two of the walls were a couple of small livestock pens, each accessed by a stable door that could be closed at the top to keep the animals inside from seeing what awaited them. There was also a small open pen where a good sized pig trotted fretfully back and forth. Against another wall was the slaughterhouse where the animals were funneled one at a time into a narrow wooden slot to be dispatched by the slaughterer. Huge worn flagstones were spattered with blood and animal excrement. The floor of the slaughterhouse was caked with blood soaked sawdust to keep the butchers from slipping. Steam trailed upward from carcasses that swung from meat hooks at the back of the slaughterhouse. The air was rank with the stench of animal guts.

The voices of the three men doing the slaughtering reverberated between the walls as they went about their bloody business. All three wore wellies and rubber aprons streaked with blood and animal fat. Despite the cold none of them wore gloves. One of them was an older man, who Nick guessed was Ken

Jessop, the butcher. His son, Derek, in his early 20's, had the same dark brows as his father. The third was Ronnie 'Thorpie' Thorpe, a teddy boy from Millbank whom Nick knew by reputation. Last year Thorpie and one of his mates had gone out on a rainy Saturday afternoon with a handful of sheep's eyeballs in their pockets. As they made their way down Front Street they took it in turns to bump into old biddies with umbrellas while the other stuck a sheep's eyeball on an umbrella prong and staggered around the footpath with a hand over one eye screaming that she'd put his eye out.

Bright and Nick waited inside the main gate till the older Jessop noticed them.

"Ah'll be wi' ye in just a jiffy," the butcher called over. "Wi hae one mair an' wa done for the day."

"Tek ya time, man," Bright answered. "Wa in nae hurry."

Nick put a hand over his mouth and nose to keep out the stink and watched Jessop lead a black heifer across the yard with a rope attached to a ring in its nose while his son applied a stick to its rump. The heifer tried to dig its hooves into the flagstones and rolled its head violently from side to side to escape the butcher's grip. Blood poured from its snout and when Nick saw its eyes he realized it knew.

Jessop and his son manouevered the heifer into the pen and pushed it down the narrowing chute till it reached a dead end where Thorpie slid a metal gate in behind so it could go neither forward nor backward. Excrement and urine poured to the floor as the heifer raised its head above the rails and let out a series of plaitive bellows. Jessop retrieved a large pistol from a nearby bench, leaned over the topmost rail, pressed the muzzle against the calf's skull and pulled the trigger. There was a loud bang and Jessop yanked his hand back revealing a long bolt that extended from the muzzle. The calf went down with a crash, legs splayed, tongue lolling from its mouth. With the animal down Thorpie opened the slot and he and Derek took a pair of steel hooks attached to chains that hung from a rail in the ceiling and jammed them through the calf's hind legs, below the hocks. Together they hauled on a pulley till the calf was fully suspended, its head swinging loosely a couple of feet foot above the floor, blood drizzling from the wound in its skull. They manoeuvered the beast over a sunken grate where the elder Jessop steadied it, thrust a wide bladed knife into its throat, drew the knife sideways and released a cascade of blood. Next he took a cleaver and hacked at the calf's neck two or three times till the severed head came away in his hand. He lobbed the head onto a nearby bench where the tongue would be removed later to be turned into cold cuts and the brain to be sold for sweetbreads. With the head gone he made a shallow incision the length of the calf's belly to the bloody stump of the neck, worked the blade under the hide to loosen it and made fresh incisions the length of each leg. Then he and his son each grabbed two fistfuls of hide around the rump and, pulling downward with all their weight, peeled away the hide as smoothly as taking off a glove. Once the hide was removed it was thrown into a bloody pile against the wall to be sold for a few shillings each to a tannery in Gateshead.

With its head and hide removed the calf had been turned into an amorphous lump of meat. Jessop then plunged his knife into the calf's belly near the rump and sliced all the way down to the truncated neck so that the belly opened like a trapdoor spilling a pile of organs and entrails onto the grate in a gust of foul smelling steam. Nick took out a handkerchief and held it to his face. There was something medieval about it, something indecent, as if it was the kind of thing a civilised society should no longer be doing. Still he watched as Derek Jessop played a hose of warm water around the inside of the carcass, cleaning it, using his free hand to remove stray pieces of intestine. Next he hosed off the pile of innards on the grate as Thorpie sorted through them retrieving the heart, liver, kidneys and stomach linings, tossing them into enamel pails nearby. Lastly he sorted through the calf's intestines, unraveling them from their tight coils, holding them up for Alan to flush with the hose so they could be used for sausage casings.

Wiping the grease and gristle of slaughter on a filthy towel Jessop sauntered over to where Bright and Nick waited.

"Under the corcumstances ah'll not shake hands wi ye, Jimmy," he said.

"Ah imagine ye could dee wi' one o' these," Bright said and offered a packet of Senior Service.

"Ah could that," the butcher said and leaned forward to take the proffered cigarette in his mouth. Bright took one for himself, lit Jessop's cigarette then his own.

The butcher sucked hard and the tip of the cigarette glowed red. "Ahlways tastes best at the end o' a good day's wark," he said.

"Forst thing ah dee at a crime scene where there's a body is light up a tab," Bright said. "It doesn't smell a whole lot different te this."

"Ah divvent notice it anymair," Jessop said. "Ye get used te it."

Nick watched Derek and Thorpie in the background up to their knees and elbows in animal parts and wondered how anybody could get used to that.

"Hoo aboot ye, young lad," Jessop said, winking at Bright but directing his words to Nick. "Ye wouldn't mind workin' here would ye? Wi could use a good lad to clean up afterwards."

Nick's eyes widened in alarm.

"Be a bit pocket money fo' ye," his father said.

Nick shook his head, unwilling to open his mouth and let the smell inside.

"Got a weak stomach hae ye, son?" Jessop said.

Bright said: "Ah can mind when me an' me brother and sisters would skin an' clean rabbits at yem fo' me fatha. Wi couldn't be owa picky durin' the Depression."

"Whey aye, man," Jessop added. "If wi couldn't afford to gan to the pictures we'd put a dog in wi' the chickens fo' entertainment." The two men seemed to enjoy their little joke at Nick's expense. "So, ya lookin' fo' a bit o' blood an' offal for the garden, are ye, Jimmy?" Jessop added.

"An' some hoof an' horn if ah can get it," Bright said. "Dee ye hae owt for grindin' bone?"

Jessop used a bloody thumb and forefinger to take the cigarette from his mouth and blew twin cones of smoke down his nose. "Wi divvent hae any need fo' it, Jimmy. Ah can keep some hoof an' horn back fo' ye, an' a few bones, but ye'll hae te find a way te grind it yasel. If'n ye knah somebody at one o' the pit workshops they might grind it fo' ye."

Bright nodded but he was already asking enough favours. He had a sledgehammer at home that would do.

"Ye startin' from scratch?" Jessop asked.

"Fo' ahll intents and porposes," Bright answered. "The soil at West Lea is ahll clay. Ye cannit grah owt unless ye condition it forst, an' its ganna tek a fair bit o' conditionin'."

Jessop nodded. Most of the surface soil around Bedlington was yellow clay and it took years to build it up to the point where it was rich enough to grow show leeks.

"Hoo many trenches ye lookin' at?"

"Two to start wi'," Bright answered. "Twelve leeks in each trench."

Jessop thought for a moment. Nick, half listening to their conversation, watched Thorpie go over to the pig pen on the other side of the yard.

"An' when will ye be needin' it?" the butcher asked.

"Late March, orly April," Bright answered. "Soon as the frost is oot the grund an' ah can work the soil."

"Ye'll need aroond 10 gallon for each trench," Jessop said.

Nick watched Thorpie enter the pig pen and try to back the pig into a corner.

"Ten gallon fo' each trench?" Bright repeated. "Ye reckon ah'll need that much?"

"To brek doon the clay an' torn it into somethin' manageable, aye," Jessop replied.

"Twenty gallon o' blood an' offal?" Bright said.

"Aye, blood an' guts, mostly large intestines," Jessop said. "We'll mince the guts fo' ye, we'll even thrah in some coo shite if ye like an' not charge ye any extra."

On the other side of the yard Thorpie had the pig cornered but when he made a lunge it darted away leaving Thorpie grasping at empty air. He changed tactics, instead of trying to grab hold of the pig he threw himself at it, trapping it against a rail. As the pig thrashed and squealed Thorpie took hold of its hind legs, dragged it out of the pen and over to the slaughterhouse.

"Ah can always find plenty o' that," Bright responded to Jessop's joking offer of free cow manure.

"The good thing aboot blood an' offal is it breks doon var' quick." Jessop said. "It's the best thing ye can use te condition a garden in a hurry. But ye mind tha's other things ye hae te add te the soil te get the balance reyt. It's ganna tek a few year afore ye can expect to grah show winners."

"Ah'm just tryin' te get off te a good start," Bright said.

Nick watched Thorpie struggle to hold the squirming pig still so Derek could put the bolt gun to its head.

"Right ye are then," Jessop was saying. "Gi's a call a week or so afore ye need it an' ah'll put 20 gallon to one side fo' ye."

"An' what are ye lookin' at fo' cost?" Bright asked.

But Jessop's mind had moved on and he asked: "Ye might want to think aboot gettin' some shoddy an' ahll." he said. Shoddy was sheep's wool that added nitrogen to soil when it rotted. "Ah've hord some say it's better than coo manure 'cos it keeps addin' nitrogen owa time."

"Ah haven't hord much aboot it one way or t'other," Bright said. "But ah doobt it could tek the place o' good coo manure."

"Depends wee ye listen te," Jessop said. "Some say it adds more on top o' the coo manure. The reason ah mention it is we'll be killin' lambs fo' Easter an' wi could keep a bit o' wool aside for ye, if ya interested."

While Bright pondered Jessop's offer Nick stayed stayed fixed on the life and death struggle across the yard.

"Fuckin' be still, ye twat," Thorpie swore at the pig while Derek dodged around them, the primed bolt gun in his hand. "Fuckin' be still or ah'll fuckin' strangle ye." Thorpie lay full length on the pig's back and used his weight to hold

it down, clenching its ears tightly in his fists to steady its head so Derek could get
a clean shot. The younger Jessop grinned at the spectacle of Thorpie mounted on
the pig.

"Get on wi' it, man," Thorpie yelled. "Ah cannit haad it ahll fuckin' day."

Derek saw his moment, pressed the gun muzzle to the pig's skull and
pulled the trigger. There was a loud crack and the butcher's son stepped away,
the extended bolt of the gun dripping by his side. Thorpie rolled off the pig but
not fast enough to avoid a geyser of excrement that gushed out of the pig's rump
splashing his face, arms and hands.

"Ye fuckin' cunt!"

Thorpie aimed a kick at the pig that would have connected had the pig
not taken off across the yard squealing, blood pulsing from the hole in its head.
The dead pig circled the yard coming close enough to Bright, Jessop and Nick
that the three of them had to step out of its way. They watched the pig run,
waiting for it to drop in its tracks, except that it didn't, it started another lap of
the yard, still squealing.

"It's the narves," Jessop said. "Sometimes they'll dee that."

Thorpie chased after the runaway pig, grabbed it by the tail and pulled
back hard so the pig's hooves flailed uselessly against the slick flagstones.

"Ah divvent think ah'll bother wi' the shoddy," Bright decided. "Me fatha
swore by coo manure an' he did ahlreet."

"Good enough, Jimmy," Jessop said. "De ye hae a van to transport it in?
The buckets'll tek up a bit o' space an' ye'll need to secure them so they divvent
tip owa on the way yem."

"Ah think ah knaa where ah can find one," Bright said. "So what are wi
lookin' at in torms o' price? What's 20 gallon of blood an' guts ganna cost is?"

Jessop sucked on his bloodied cigarette and shook his head. "It'll not cost
ye anythin', Jimmy. We'd be givin' it to somebody else or hoyin' it away. If ye
want te come an' get it you're as welcome te it as the next man."

Bright hesitated only a moment. A favour accepted was a favour owed.

"Right ye are then, Ken," he said. "Ah'll see ye a couple o' month from
noo."

Bright and Jessop turned their attention to the spectacle playing out
behind them as Thorpie, red faced and panting, hung onto the pig's tail until its
scrabbling feet finally gave out and it lay still.

Jessop said: "Ye can stop buggarisin' that pig noo afore the polis teks ye
away fo' havin' owa much fun."

*   *   *

All the kids liked to watch Spelk's dad eat. Joe Gordon had been known to eat slugs plucked glistening from cabbages in the back garden, to drop freshly dug worms down his throat, to pop a live mole in his mouth and chew it like a pastie. When his wife, Joyce, served him fish he ate everything, head, skin and bones. When he ate crab he ate it like a sandwich, claws, shell everything. Sometimes Joyce complained about living with a man who didn't care what she put it front of him, but unlike other wives she never had to worry about what to make for dinner.

The Gordons lived two doors up from the Brights and Spelk had become Nick's best mate. The two of them played everywhere together, in the open fields, among the giant boulders of the open cast mine that passed for the old west, and in the old cemetery that made the perfect haunted forest. The cemetery was across the fields from West Lea and divided into three parts, an open, grassy area for newer burials, an older section that had filled up a few years earlier and the abandoned section whose graves went back 300 years. The abandoned section covered 40 to 50 acres and thickly overgrown with trees and brambles. With no living descendants to care for them the graves of the deceased had long since fallen into disrepair. Headstones were crooked and broken and tree roots pushed into the graves to draw nourishment from the richer soil underneath. None of that bothered the kids. They played among the long decayed remains with gleeful indifference, building tree houses, tunneling through the brambles and using the graves as toilets.

The first time Nick had gone over to Spelk's house was in mid-summer and Mr. Gordon was tending to his garden. He'd picked a caterpillar off a lettuce and offered it to Nick who shook his head. Mr. Gordon bit the caterpillar in half, let the remainder wriggle in his fingers for a moment then popped it too into his mouth and returned to his gardening.

Spelk said his dad learned to eat anything when he was a prisoner of the Germans. It was an explanation that raised as many questions as it answered and one hot summer day Nick got the answers to those too. It was late morning and Mr. Gordon was on the back step cleaning his boots and shoes. Leanly built with tautly muscled arms his close cropped dark hair was greying at the sides and the lines in his face were etched deeply even though he was only in his thirties. He sat with his long legs stretched out over the path, his bare toes splayed like chicken feet. He spoke without exaggeration, without the need for effect and all the time he worked on his shoes.

He left school at 14, he said, and worked down the pit till he was 17 when he joined the Royal Northumberland Fusiliers hoping to see something of the world. War broke out in the autumn of 1939 and his regiment was sent to France with the British Expeditionary Force. For the six months known as 'the phony war' he said the only danger he faced was dying of boredom.

"Wi were stationed just ootside o' Abbeville," he said. "Ah thowt wi might get to see somethin' o' France, at least meet some of the local lasses but wi might as weel hae been a thoosand miles away 'cos the officers wouldn't let wi gan into the toon itsel'. They didn't want wi fraternisin' wi' the locals an' givin' the British Army a bad name. So it was drill, clean ya gear, polish ya byuts an' more bloody drill."

But in May of 1940 the German army struck at France and the Low Countries with an army of almost a million men. A quarter of a million British soldiers were pushed back toward the sea and a hastily assembled rearguard, including elements of the Royal Northumberland Fusiliers, was ordered to hold off the Germans so the British Expeditionary Force could be evacuated from Dunkirk.

"It was chaos, total bloody chaos," Mr. Gordon said. "Wi were thrown back into a smahl pocket aroond Dunkork, ahll different units mixed up wi' each other. Tha were stragglers mixed in wi' refugees tryin' te reach the coast an' Stukas comin' owa an' bombin' wi whenivah they felt like it. There was nae bugga in charge until some o' the officers started roondin' up blokes to try an' moont some kind o' delayin' action. Wi'd been fightin' fo' the better part of a week bi then an' wi were knackered an' sick o' fahllin' back, an' from what wi could tell it wasn't any better at the coast. At least where ah was ye could get into the woods an' hae some protection from the Stukas. So, me an' a few other lads fell in wi' a bunch o' Jocks an' set up machine gun positions to dee what wi could to slow the Jarmans doon. Wi knew we'd end up deed or prisoners o' war but wi worn't ganna let the Jarmans waalk ahll owa wi like wi were nowt' neither. Wi thowt wi meyt as weel mek the buggas work fo' it."

The British rearguard action inflicted such heavy casualties on the Germans their advance on Dunkirk was delayed long enough for 338,000 British and Allied soldiers to escape to Britain through the miracle of the small ships. But the price paid by the men left behind was terrible.

"The officers were goin' by tha experience o' the Forst World War, thinkin' this would be a gentlemanly sort o' war, like, so naturally the lads went along wi' them," Mr. Gordon said. "They fought till tha ammunition ran oot an' when they couldn't fight nae more they surrendered - an' they were massacred by the Waffen

SS. The whole bloody lot o' them. Lads from the Norfolks, the Cheshires, the Warwickshires, hundreds o' them were shot by the Jarmans after they surrendered.

"Ah knew none o' this at the teym o' course, ah just didn't want to be tekin prisoner. So, when wi ran oot o' ammunition it was ivery man fo' hissel an' ah went to grund. Ah knew hoo to look after mesel in the woods like, an' ah was in there nearly two weeks, livin' off pond wettah an' bords eggs and owt else ah could find. Ah torned 19 when ah was in them woods. Ah mind ah had a couple of handfuls o' frogspawn fo' me birthday dinnah. Ah was thinkin' if ah hid oot lang enough ah could mek me way to the coast an' find a way across the Channel somehoo even if ah had te swim yem. Ah was plannin' on travellin' at night and layin' up durin' the day but ah got caught the forst day sleepin' under a hedge 'cos some Jarman soldiers hord is snorin'."

Mr. Gordon was taken to a collection point for Allied POW's back in Abbeville then he and several hundred others were marched eastward.

"Folk alang the way come oota tha hooses an' tried to gi' wi food an' drink but the Jarmans wouldn't let them," he said. "Wi didn't stop till it was gettin' dark an' ahll they gi' wi' was a bowl o' soup an' a piece of breed an' then they locked us in barns an' pig sties fo' the neyt."

After two more days of marching the prisoners reached a railhead where they were loaded into cattle cars and transported deep into Germany, a journey that took another two days.

"They nivah fed wi an' they packed wis in like sardines," Mr. Gordon said. "Ye couldn't move so ye had to piss an' shite where ye stood an' aftah a couple o' days it was a bonny smell, ah can tell ye that. When wi got to the POW camp they shaved wa heeds, hosed wi doon, hoyed de-lousin' pooder owa wi an' give each o' wi a bowl o' tettie soup an' a piece o' greasy sausage, an' that was wa lot."

For the next year Mr. Gordon was shuffled from one POW camp to another and eventually ended up in a camp near Dresden where he remained till February 1945 when the war in Europe was coming to an end.

"It was a big camp an' tha were ahll sorts there; British, French, Polish, Russians. They kept the Russians separate from the rest o' wi 'cos the Jarmans didn't think o' them as human bein's. They were scared o' them, but. The guards wouldn't gan into the Russian part o' the camp unless they had te. Ah remember in the winter o' 1944, the Russians rioted 'cos they warn't gettin' enough to eat an' the guards fired on them but that didn't work so the guards torned the dogs loose on them an' that quietened things doon fo' a bit. The next day the Russians hoyed the bones oot an' that was ahll that was left o' the dogs."

Despite the warm sun on him Nick shivered nonetheless.

"Ye were ahlways hungry," Mr. Gordon said. "Ye went to bed hungry, ye woke up hungry an' believe me there's nae pain in the world like it. Ye feel like ya stomach is tyin' itsel' in knots. Ye stop pissin', ye stop shittin' 'cos tha's nowt inside ye to come oot. An' the closer it got to the end of the war the warse it was 'cos the Jarmans had hardly enough to feed themsels bi then so wi were gettin' soup that had next to nowt in it an' breed that was nowt but sawdust. The only reason ah got through it was because ah hardened mesel' to eat owt ah could get me hands on. Ah dug for worms an' ah ate them. Ah ate forky tails an' maggots an' blackclocks. Ah caught mice an' rats an' ah ate them. An' ah wasn't the only one wee did it. The blokes wee couldn't bring themsels to dee it, they were the ones wee didn't last."

The final collapse of Germany came swiftly. The fire bombing of Dresden by the Allies and the rumble of guns from the advancing Red Army to the east started a panic among the local population. Stories of atrocities committed by Russian troops drove columns of German refugees westward to the safety of the British and and American lines. But as one ordeal came to an end for Joe Gordon another was about to begin.

"Wi noticed the number o' guards thinnin' oot fo' a couple o' weeks," he said. "They didn't want to be aroond when the Red Army got there because they knew what the Russians would dee te them. Then one day wi woke up an' ahll the guards had nicked off. The gates were locked but there was naebody in charge an' the gun toowahs were all empty. The forst thing wi did was break into the kitchens an' eat owt they left behind. But tha wasn't much, a few tetties an' snaggies, that's ahll. So wi just waited for the Russians to get there. But the trouble wi' the Russians was they didn't knah what to dee wi' wi so they were ganna keep wi locked up in the camp till some bugga somewhere made a decision. Ah thowt to hell wi' that. Ah didn't trust the Russians anymair than ah trusted the Jarmans. An' ah hadn't gone nigh on five year as a prisoner o' the Jarmans just to be a prisoner o' the bloody Russians. As soon as ah saw me chance ah was off. Ah foond some claes an' shoes in an abandoned hoose an' ah started wahkin'. It was easy 'cos tha were sae many refugees on the roads ahll gannin' the same way. Ah wahked fo' six weeks, livin' off the land, sleepin' rough, brekkin' into hooses an' tekkin what ah needed. Ah stayed weel clear o' any toons 'cos the RAF an' the yanks were gi'n them a reyt pastin'. Ah kept to the back roads as much as ah could an' ah managed to stay oot o' bother septin' fo' one time ah nearly got mesel shot by some owld Jarman gadgie wee caught is robbin' his hens."

Days later he realised he was getting close to the advancing Allied lines.

"Ah could hear bombin' in the distance an' durin' the day tha were these geet big bloody columns o' smoke on the horizon so ah knahed somebody was catchin' it. Ah decided ah better lay up 'cos ah didn't want to get killed by me ahn side while ah was tryin' to cross the lines. So ah stayed put for the best part of a week an' the whole time the bombin' an' the shellin' nivah let up."

Until one day the bombardment ended and a massive pall of smoke on the western horizon told of the destruction that had taken place. Mr. Gordon resumed his trek and came to a railway track that led him toward the smoke. Gradually the landscape changed from farmland to what had once been the outskirts of a major city but was now nothing but devastation.

"We'd done a good job on them, ah'll say that," Mr. Gordon continued. "Tha was nowt left stannin', just ruins and bomb craters as far as ye could see. Ah seen folks sittin' ootside what was left of tha hooses weepin' an' wailin' an' carryin' on an' the like, an' ah didn't feel the least bit sorry fo' them. Not afta what they did te us. As far as ah was concorned they desarved iverythin' they got."

Eventually he came to what had once been a major railway terminus but was now a wasteland of shattered rail cars and twisted rails and he saw a squad of American soldiers guarding German POW's who'd been put to work clearing the rubble.

"Mind that was a sight fo' sore eyes," he said. "It was worth wahkin' fo' six weeks just to see that."

But when he tried to identify himself to the Americans he couldn't make himself understood.

"They didn't knah what to mek of is," he said. "They couldn't understand a word ah said. An' they'd been telt to be on the lookoot fo' SS men an' the like tryin' to get through the lines so they put is under guard and marched is off to tha company headquarters fo' questionin'."

At company HQ he learned he was a prisoner of the 82nd Airborne and he was in Essen, which the Americans had entered a few days earlier. It was only when he was questioned by an American captain that he was finally able to make himself understood.

"But he didn't believe ah'd wahked ahll the way from Dresden," Mr. Gordon said. "Neither did ah when he telt is hoo far it was. Ah'd wahked nearly ahll the way to the bloody Rhine, nigh on three hunnerd mile. An' ah hadn't wahked in a streyt line neither. So ah'm stannin' there thinkin' ah've been a prisoner o' the Jarmans, ah've been a prisoner o' the Russians an' noo ah'm a prisoner o' the bloody Americans, what else is tha? But he was a clivah bugga this captain an' he radioed a British armoured unit a few miles up the road an' he telt them me story an' then he torns t'is an' he says: "What's the nickname fo' Newcastle United?" An' streyt away ah says: 'The Magpies' an' he passed it on to the English bloke on the otha end an' then he give 'is the thumbs up and said they were sendin' somebody te pick 'is up. Thank Christ for footbahll eh?"

It was only then he felt he could relax, though he was to learn quickly that five years of privation had changed him forever.

"This yank captain g'is a tab, the first real smoke ah'd had in nearly five year, an' ah couldn't believe hoo good real baccy tasted. Then he had one o' his lads tek is te tha field mess to get is somethin' to eat an' ah'll nivah forget it as lang as ah live; a corn beef sandwich an' a cup o' coffee. That's ahll it was but it tasted like nowt ah'd ivah had in me life before, that's how good it was. An' ye knah what else? Ah couldn't finish it 'cos ah thowt ah was ganna spew it reyt back up. Me stomach had shrunk to the size of a bloody farthin'. Not only that, it giv is a shockin' pain in the gut an' ah was fartin' an' belchin' somethin' ahful. After five year o'eatin' owt ah could get me hands on ah couldn't eat owt normal any mair. Ah had te train mesel to eat normal again. An' if normal isn't normal any mair ye nivah really get back to bein' normal de ye? But te this day ah'm grateful for owt wor lass puts in front of is, an' ah divvent care what it is because whatever it is ah'll eat it."

*   *   *

Bright wheeled to a stop outside Harry Armstrong's house on Poplar Grove and used a pedal to prop the bike against the kerb. Armstrong hadn't renewed his dog license and it was a slow enough afternoon that Bright had decided to get some air and ride down and tell him he had a week to renew his license or pay a fine.

Bright went up to the front door and knocked but there was no answer. He waited a minute then knocked again but nobody came. Harry was a fitter at the Doctor Pit and was on the late shift so he should have been home. Reluctant to go back to the station without anything to show for his time Bright went to the house next door and knocked there. A woman in a pinny came to the door, a worried look on her face.

"Y'ahlreet, hinny, it's not ye ah'm heyah for," Bright reassured her. "Ah'm lookin' fo' ya neighbour, Harry Armstrong. Ah've knocked on his door but ah cannit get an answer. De ye knah where he meyt be?"

"Eeh, he should be in," the woman said. "Ah saw him come yem orlier an' ah haven't seen him gan back oot."

Bright thanked her and went back to Harry's house and this time hammered on the door with a clenched fist.

"Oppin the door, Harry, ah knah ya in there," he shouted.

There was no immediate response and Bright was about to bang on the door again, harder this time, when it opened. Harry appeared in bare feet, work pants and collarless shirt. He rubbed his face as if he'd just woken up.

"Ah was just haein' a bit kip," he said. "What's ahll the racket aboot?"

"Ye in the habit o' ignorin' the polis when he comes to the door?" Bright said.

"Ah didn't knah it was ye, Jimmy," Armstrong answered. Bedlington was small enough for most of its residents to know the police by name.

"Aye, weel noo ye dee, what are ye ganna dee aboot it?"

"Dee aboot what?"

"Divven't come it wi' me, Harry. Ye knah bloody weel what ah'm heyah for."

Harry looked mystified. "No, ah don't, honest."

"Ye divvent think ye can keep somethin' like this from the polis fo'ivah de ye?" Bright added. "What'd ye think naebody would notice?"

"Ah divvent knah what ya tahkin' aboot."

"Noo ya just insultin' me intelligence," Bright said. "What div ah hae te dee, come in and get ah mesel?"

Armstrong hesitated, looked down at his feet. "Ah didn't think anybody would notice," he said glumly.

"Be serious, Harry, hoo could wi not notice? It's not like it's the kind o' thing ye can keep a secret, ye knah. Wa paid te tek notice o'these things."

"She's in the back garden," Armstrong said.

"Ah don't give a bugga where she is," Bright said. "Are ye ganna tek responsibility for ah or not?"

"Ah buried the both o' them in back garden," Harry said. "Ah thowt they should be together. De ye want is te show ye where?"

"What would ye...?" Bright began and stopped when he realised he and Harry Armstrong were talking about two quite different things. He took his handcuffs out of his back pocket. "Ye betta gis ya hands," he said.

Harry obligingly put his hands out and Bright snapped the handcuffs shut on them.

"Noo ye just stay heyah an' behave yasel'," Bright added. "Ah'll be back in a minute."

He got back on his bike, pedaled to the corner shop and used their phone to call the Top End. The duty sergeant, Bert Fry, picked up.

"Ah'm ganna need some assistance doon heeyah," Bright said.

"What's the matter, Jimmy, can ye not handle an expired dog license on ya own?" Bert asked.

"Ah think Harry Armstrong just confessed te killin' his wife," Bright added. "Weeivah ye send, tell them they better bring a couple o' shuls wi' them."

*   *   *

The Saturday after the last frost seeped out of West Lea's gluey soil Bright reversed the Black Mariah into the back yard of Jessop's the butchers. Waiting for him were 10 pails filled with blood and offal. Ken Jessop had also filled a couple of sacks with horns, hooves and shank bones. It took Bright and his police mate, Evan Thompson, only a few minutes to load the pails and sacks into the back of the van and secure them between the benches where prisoners were usually confined. Bright thanked Jessop and drove his gory cargo home taking extra care on the corners. At West Lea the two of them unloaded the pails and sacks then Thompson took the Black Mariah back to the police station.

Bright had busied himself in the preceding two weeks gathering materials he considered essential to the establishment of his leek trenches. He'd filled half a dozen coal sacks with cow manure from Spring Bank Farm, he'd filled another half dozen sacks with slag from Netherton Colliery and a couple of sacks with seaweed he'd collected from the rocks at Cambois. He'd dug two trenches laid out east to west where they would get the most sun. Each trench was about ten feet long, two feet wide and two and a half feet deep. They were formidable trenches. They showed he'd become a serious leek grower. Nick watched his dad walk along the trenches emptying one pail after another, staining the yellow clay a dark rust colour. Then, using a garden fork, he worked the blood and offal into the clay.

Nick was fascinated. Ever since he'd seen the prizes at the Netherton Club show he'd understood the allure of leeks and wanted to know more about the alchemy of growing prizewinners.

"Can ah help?" he asked.

"Ah think the clay's owa heavy for ye, son," his dad answered. "Ye'll just be in the way."

Despite the rebuff Nick stayed to watch. When Bright finished digging in the blood and offal he dumped the slag into a crumbly black pile and began spreading it along the bottom of his trenches. Then Big Mac came out from next door, tea in one hand, cigarette in the other.

"When ah saw the Black Mariah ootside ah thowt ye were comin' te lock is up."

"Not the day," Bright said.

"Ye've decided te grah show leeks after ahll then, eh Jimmy?"

"Aye."

"Ah hord ye joined the club, like."

"Aye."

"Ah thowt it must hae been 'cos ye were thinkin' o' showin'."

"Aye."

"Ah see ya beddin' it doon wi slag?"

"Aye."

"Ah bed mine in each year wi' straw. Ah think it drains betta than slag an' it breks doon quicker, like."

Resigned, Bright stopped shoveling and said: "Tha's plenty o' lime in the slag to brek doon the clay, Mac. Ah hae blood an' bone fo' extra conditionin' an' coo manure an' seaweed fo' fortiliser. Ah think ah'll be ahlreet."

Mac nodded. "Ye ganna be wantin' any liquid fortiliser?"

"Ah'll get them bedded in forst," Bright said. "Mek sure ah get the pH level right then see hoo ah go from there."

"Weel, like ah said before, ya welcome to help yasel' any teym ye like."

"That's very generous o' ye, Mac but ah should be ahlreet this year," Bright said.

"Noo ya goin' into the shows mebbe weeivah's been slashin' me leeks will leave the both o' wi alone," Mac said.

"Ah wouldn't be so sure," Bright responded. "You're still a threat, ah'm not. But ah tell ye what, Mac, ah'll keep an eye on your leeks an' ye keep an eye on mine this year. The two o' wi can look oot fo' each other, hoo's that?"

Mac brightened. "Aye, that'd be great." He tossed the dregs of his tea into the garden and turned to go inside. "Between the two o' wi, wi should be able te keep the bastards at bay, eh?"

Bright grunted and went back to spreading the slag. When he was finished he dragged the sacks of cow manure and seaweed into the garden.

"Ah could help wi that," Nick said.

Bright wiped his brow with the back of his hand. Sweat misted his scalp and there were damp patches on his shirt.

"If ye really want to help…" he began but just then Nick's mam came out with a cup of coffee and a couple of tabs. She handed the coffee and a lit tab to Nick's dad and the two of them stood in front of the washhouse, smoking and batting away bluebottles.

"What'd he want?" Nick's mam asked, nodding at the McBride's house.

"Ahh, he's just bein' a bloody pest again," Bright said. "He wants is to be his porsonal security guard fo' his leeks."

"What did ye say?"

"Ah telt him ah could keep an eye oot fo' his an' he could keep an eye oot fo' mine. Mebbe that'll keep him quiet fo' a bit."

"Just as long as neither o' ye think ah'm ganna sit up nights wi' a poker when it gets te show time," she said.

"Ah wouldn't expect ye tee, hinny," he said.

"Hoo much more de hae te dee?"

"A fair bit," Bright replied. "Ah want me trenches set up good an' proper afore ah stop fo' the day so they'll be nicely bedded in when ah transplant me seedlin's next month. The slag an' the manure an' the rest of it has to be properly settled so it'll not shock the seedlin's or ah could lose the lot o' them."

"Ahh, poor little buggas," she said.

"Ye wouldn't credit the things some blokes'll dee to look after tha leeks," Bright added. "Ah've seen some put blankets on them at night to keep them warm, ah've seen some feed them broon ale streyt from the bottle. Ah've even hord tell o' some blokes wee sing to them."

Amazed, she said: "What de they sing to them?"

Bright shrugged. "Cushy Butterfield."

"No they don't ye skitty bugga," she said and slapped his arm.

Nick watched them so playful together. At times like this they could be mistaken for the happiest couple on earth.

When Bright finished his coffee and his tab he turned to Nick. "So, ye want to mek yasel' useful do ye?"

Nick perked up at the prospect of being included. His father shook a sackful of cattle horns, hooves and bones out onto the cement path. Some of the hooves still had tendons and fur attached and scraps of gristle clung to the shank bones. Bright got the sledgehammer and the laundry basin from the washhouse and rested his hand atop the sledgehammer.

"Ye use the mell to crush the bones," he said. "Like this." He put a cow horn into the basin, lifted the sledgehammer a couple of feet, let it drop and the cow horn cracked. He did it a few more times, reducing the horn to splinters and producing a tablespoonful of powder. He passed the hammer to Nick who needed both hands to hold it.

"Ye divvent hae te worry aboot swingin' it or owt," his dad said. "It's heavy enough if ye just keep liftin' it up an' droppin' it like ah showed ye, ye should be ahlreet. Just be careful what ya deein', ah divvent want to stop what ah'm deein' just because ye've missed the basin an' flattened ya toes."

Bright went back to chopping and mixing the cow manure and the seaweed. Nick lifted the hammer and let it drop onto the horn splinters as he'd been shown, each time producing perhaps a thimbleful of powder. It took him nearly an hour to produce a cupful. His arms and shoulders ached and it occurred to him that his father had given him the job so he would tire quickly and go back inside. He dropped the hammer onto a shank bone to no effect. He did it a few more times producing only a few chips and realised he'd never reduce a whole shank bone to powder. Discouraged, he put the sledgehammer down.

"Ah cannit dee it any more," he said.

He half expected a dismissive response but instead his dad said: "Ye lasted langer than ah thowt ye would."

He stopped what he was doing and came over and patted Nick on the shoulder. "Tha's a lot o' hard work gans into mekkin' leek trenches isn't tha? Especially if ye want to grah champions."

"De ye need a lot o' groond up bone?" Nick asked.

"Iverythin' ah hae heeyah is heeyah fo' a reason," his dad answered.

"Ah divvent knaa hoo owt could grah in that," Nick said. "It ahll looks like poison."

"Aye, weel, it's a funny thing aboot gardenin' in Northumberland," his dad said. "Folk look at the slag heaps an' iverythin' an' they think nowt worthwhile could ivah grow here an' that's where tha deed wrang. In point of fact, iverythin' ye see here that looks like it should be bad fo' gardens is good fo' them. Slag might look like it's nae good for owt but it's the best stuff in the world for leeks. It has lime in it te brek doon hard soils an' ye need that to hae good drainage because leeks like plenty o' wettah but they divvent like to sit in it. The other thing lime does is it neutralises acid in the soil. Ahll soil has a certain amount of natural acid in it and by puttin' in coo manure ya addin' te it. Coo manure is nearly ahll nitrogen, an' that's good for leeks, but as it breks doon it can get a bit acidic an' that's where the slag comes in because it's the lime in the slag that keeps the soil from gettin' owa acidic for the leeks to thrive."

Nick noticed how enthusiastic his dad had become talking about leeks.

"Slag actually meks the trench quite a hospitable place fo' leeks," Bright continued. "But on top o' that, slag has phosphorous and phosphate an' potash an' they're ahll things that leeks need te grah big an' healthy. Especially phosphorous. Anybody wee knahs owt aboot leeks will tell ye leeks use a lot o' phosphorous. But another thing aboot slag is the phosphate an' the potash in it are natural fortilisers an' what they dee as the coo manure an' the other fortilisers brek doon is they work as bindin' agents fo' the nitrogen that's bein' generated an' that ahll feeds the leeks a lot more efficiently than if ye were to put nae slag in the trench at ahll.

"The other thing is, because leeks tek a lot o' nitrogen, ye need ahll these different things workin' together. Blood and guts, coo manure, seaweed ahll breaks doon owa different time periods an' keeps feedin' ya leeks a steady dose o' nitrogen. Animal blood breaks the soil doon an' conditions it quick, like. The coo manure not so quick an' the seaweed is slow. So, ye've got this fast release, medium release and slow release o' fortiliser gannin on in ya trenches ahll through the year. The trick is to get it just right so ya leeks are comin' into tha prime just when the leek shows come 'roond in September. So," he looked down at Nick, "ah need the poodered bone to condition the soil owa a lang time. Poodered bone is aboot the slowest actin' substance ye can get but it's top stuff for keepin' ya soil conditioned. Ye cannit really dee wi'oot it."

He gestured vaguely toward the horizon. "Tha's an ahwful lot o' folk see the pits an' the pit rahs an' they think nowt worthwhile could ivah come oot of a place like this, but they're wrang. What they divvent understand is that iverythin' that looks wrang wi' the place is what meks it reyt fo' growin' leeks. Even the soot that comes oot the chimney is good fo' the garden. Ye spread some soot aroond an' it keeps the snails and slugs off ya vegetables and owa the winter the soot'll wesh into the grund an' add more potash te the soil. Ye could just aboot bury a leek in slag an' soot an' it'll thrive. Ahll it needs is a good wesh an' it'll come up shinin' like a new pin."

"Ah'm sorry ah couldn't smash more bones," Nick said.

"Ah divvent ye worry yasel' aboot that, bonny lad," his father said. "Ah'll get aroond to it soon enough. We'll let it settle fo' a few weeks an' it'll be nicely bedded in fo' when ah dee me transplants."

It was the first time Nick had seen his dad so excited about anything. He felt an unexpected surge of affection for him. It was the closest they'd ever been and it was all because of leeks.

"Ye mark mah words, son, we'll mek folk sit up an' tek notice," Bright said. "Wa ganna grow champion leeks here…champion leeks."

*   *   *

That May Nick's parents went on holiday without Nick. They took the

Panther to the Isle Of Man for a week to see the TT races with Evan Thompson and his wife, Betty, who had their own motorbike.

Nick couldn't have been happier. He had the house to himself. He could do what he liked, eat what he liked, go to bed when he liked. His mam and dad left him ten bob and if he felt like it he could have lollies and lemonade for breakfast. The next day he nearly burned the house down.

He'd come home from school hungry and decided to make chips. He sliced more potatoes than he could possibly eat, put them in the chip pan and went off to read the newly delivered copy of Tiger. He lay on the living room floor absorbed in the trials of Roy Of The Rovers when he heard a crackling noise and looked around to see a banner of blue smoke unfurling out of the kitchen. He ran into the kitchen and found the chip pan on the cooker in the corner spewing flame. Without thinking he wrapped a tea towel around his hand and grabbed the handle of the chip pan. He held it as steadily as he could and carried it to the back door while burning fat spattered the kitchen like beads of molten lava. He opened the door, flinched as the flames fanned back at him and heaved the pan into the garden where it erupted with a loud whoomph and a spectacular fireball that flared up over the rooftops. Horrified, he watched the chip pan burn itself out in an oily scrawl and wondered what would happen when the neighbours told his mam and dad. But when he peeped outside for any sign of reaction there was none. It was as if an artillery shell had exploded among the houses and nobody had noticed.

When the pan had cooled he took it inside and soaked it in a sinkful of hot soapy water. It took him the best part of an hour using several Brillo pads and a knife to clean off the blackened crust. The yellow plug of lard his mam used to fry chips had vanished in the explosion and he would just have to tell her he threw it out accidentally, which was close to the truth. Fortunately for him the smoke stains around the cooker easily washed off the oilcloth wallpaper. There was some minor scorching of the ceiling but a good rub with the dishcloth smeared the distemper around enough so all that was left was a faint smudge. When he'd finished with the kitchen he got the shovel out of the washhouse and turned over the scorched topsoil where his dad had planted his potatoes. It could have been worse, another few feet and the pan would have landed among his leeks.

The next day was a Saturday and Nick spent the morning as he often did, playing around the houses with Spelk and Dave till it was time to go to the matinee at the Prince of Wales. It cost sevenpence each to get in and tuppence for a bag of lemon sherbert with a liqorice straw. They saw a Three Stooges short, a Woody

Woodpecker cartoon, a Mighty Mouse cartoon, an episode of Captain Video and a Roy Rogers and Gabby Hayes picture. Afterwards they fought each other with imaginary six guns all the way home. That night Spelk's mam said Nick could have tea at their house. They had beans on toast then played with Spelk's train set, robbing the train in a series of increasingly violent ambushes until it was time to go home. As Nick hopped over the back fence he wished his mam and dad would go away more often.

But Sunday was different. Sunday was the day the world stood still, when church bells summoned the righteous and everybody else pulled the bedclothes up over their ears so they could sleep in. Stranded at home Nick stayed in bed till hunger drove him downstairs to get something to eat. He had a slice of bread with golden syrup and a glass of Andrews Liver Salts. Afterwards he wandered around the house poking through cupboards and drawers looking for anything of interest and finding nothing. The middle cupboard of the sideboard was a drinks cabinet stocked with rum, whisky, gin, sherry and a bottle of sweet Italian Vermouth. There were also a few small bottles of tonic water, a jar of silver skin onions and a jar of maraschino cherries. Since his mam had gone out to work she made sure they were never without something to drink in the house. Nick sat cross legged on the carpet, took out all the bottles and sniffed their contents. The rum, whisky, sherry and Vermouth smelled alright but the gin reminded him of Domestos. He put the whisky bottle to his lips, took a sip and gagged as it turned to liquid fire in his mouth. He ran to the kitchen and drank straight from the tap but the water only spread the pain and it was several minutes before the burning eased. With his scalded tongue thrumming he put the bottles back in the drinks cabinet and decided whisky would have to wait for another day.

He resumed his wandering and eventually came to the one room in the house where he never went; his parents' bedroom. He hesitated at the door and the instant he stepped inside he was filled with the apprehension that he shouldn't be there. But he went anyway. It was different to every other room in the house, the air heavier somehow, infused with the stale perfume of parental secrets. His mother had left the room tidy, the bed made, clothes put away, everything in its proper place. He browsed her dressing table, picking through bottles of hair spray, cologne, night cream and make-up powder. There was a glass ashtray, its bottom scuffed with ash, and a copy of Nevil Shute's 'A Town Like Alice' from the library. He glimpsed his guilty reflection in the mirror and looked away. He opened the drawers and poked through the brushes, combs, curlers, clips, powder puffs, lipsticks, compacts, nail polish and a black lacquered box that held an assortment of ear rings, necklaces and broaches. His mother liked flashy dangly ear rings and necklaces of brightly colored beads. The lower drawers held her underwear, all the belted, buckled, strapped, hooked, elasticised, rubberised and vulcanised apparatus needed to upholster the imperfect female form. There was also an open packet of what looked like surgical dressings with the name 'Doctor White's Menstrual Towels' on the side. He picked one up and examined it wondering what kind of wound would require such a dressing. He closed the drawers and a mélange of smells wafted upward, flowery and chemical. His mother's smell.

He went around to his father's side of the bed where there was a dresser of sturdy dark wood with no mirror. On top of the dresser were a silver backed brush and comb set, a round leather cuff link box and another glass ashtray, this one bearing the coat of arms of the Northumberland Constabulary. His father liked to read books about the war and there was another library book, 'HMS Ulysses' by Alistair MacLean. There was also a black and white photograph of Nick's parents before they were married. His father wore a dark pinstriped jacket with wide lapels. There was a youthful lustre to his skin and his hair was fuller though he'd always had a high forehead. Nick's mother wore a floral patterned dress with a demure white collar and padded shoulders. Her face, plumpish but with the prettiness of youth, was framed by a bell shaped cascade of auburn hair that brushed her shoulders. People said Nick had his mother's eyes and his father's mouth and for some reason it annoyed him.

There was a built-in wardrobe with two sliding doors on his father's side of the bed and when he looked inside he found her dresses occupied most of the space with his father's clothes squashed down at one end. On the floor were several pairs of shoes, again mostly his mother's. He looked through his father's dresser but found little of interest; shirts, ties, detachable collars, several sets of braces, socks, underwear, an unused Rolls Razor and an empty silver cigarette case. He was about to close the drawer when, tucked in a corner, he saw a couple of small square packets with the word 'Durex' printed on them. He knew what they were; they were blobs and they were what a man put on his willy to have sex with a woman. Nick wasn't sure exactly what purpose they served but he'd heard them mentioned in the direst terms. It was said that when a man 'lost his blob' he lost all self-control. Which Nick took to mean that a man better have one close at hand for every possible emergency. More unsettling, the presence of blobs in his father's bedside drawer suggested his parents were having sex. Sex was such a secret thing there had to be something wrong with it. If it happened at all it should be rarely and only under clearly proscribed circumstances. It certainly wasn't something respectable people should be doing on a regular basis.

He knelt down to look under the bed to see if his mam and dad had hidden some early Christmas presents for him but instead found what looked like a pile of old magazines. He pulled a few out and was horrified to see they were picture magazines of people with no clothes on. Old people, some old enough to be grandparents. On beaches, in the country, beside swimming pools, men and women together, pot bellied and slack skinned, basking in their withered brown nakedness. What was wrong with them that they would do this, that they would behave in such a way? Was it something grown-ups did when they went away together? Was this what his mam and dad were doing with Evan and Betty Thompson at the Isle Of Man instead of watching the TT races? Was this the reason they didn't take him?

His face burning Nick pushed the magazines back under the bed and hurried to the bathroom. He felt feverish and cold water splashed on his face didn't help. His hands trembled as he dried them. He sat on the edge of the bath, his head a swirl of disturbing images, unable to make sense of what he'd seen. There was nobody he could tell, nobody he could confide in. These were secrets too shameful to reveal to anyone. Then it occurred to him that he'd brought it on himself. If the things he found were so upsetting he should stop looking. But he couldn't. Not now. He wanted to know everything, no matter how strange.

There was still one place he hadn't looked; a double wardrobe his parents kept locked all the time. The small iron key was kept in the cuff link box on his father's dresser. It turned easily in the lock and the door swung open under its own weight to reveal a dusty full length mirror on the inside. The smell of mothballs and an underlying mustiness swept out. Hanging on a single rail were dresses with thick shoulder pads he'd seen in films made long, long ago. There was also a woman's three quarter length fur coat, out of style but still soft and luxurious. In the bottom of the wardrobe were several hat boxes with women's hats adorned with pins, beads, feathers and veils that also belonged to another time. That left a top shelf too high for him to see into. He pulled over the cushioned stool from his mam's dresser and stepped up. His head came within inches of the ceiling but he could see into the darkened shelf space. In front was what looked like a fur pillow that matched the fur coat. When he pulled it out he found it was hollow with a satiny lining. A muff, something women once wore instead of gloves to keep their hands warm. Nick wondered who the fur coat and muff belonged to because he doubted anybody in his family would ever have worn anything quite so posh. There were also pairs of women's shriveled leather gloves and pairs of white kid gloves his father wore on ceremonial occasions. He found a large and crackly cellophane envelope and when he pulled it out a dozen starched police shirt collars fluttered to the floor like bluebirds. He picked them up and put them back and resumed his search. This time he found an old fashioned chocolate box that had come from a store in New York. He removed the lid, saw it was full of postcards and letters and sat down to take a closer look. The letters were on pale blue, tissue thin airmail paper and postmarked New York, Boston, Halifax and St. John's, with dates between 1943 and 1945 when his father was on North Atlantic convoy duty. The sentiments expressed in his father's small, neat handwriting were always the same; declarations of undying love to his 'darling Pat.' Promises of the married bliss that awaited them when the war was over. The postcards were colour tints of the Statue of Liberty, the Manhattan skyline, Canadian Mounties and brilliant autumn foliage. The messages on the back were always the same; how much his father missed her and how he was counting the days till he saw her again. There were a couple of dozen letters and cards in the box, all from his father to his mother but none from her to him. He remembered her saying once that she never wrote to him because she didn't like to write and Nick thought at the time how sad that was. But his father never seemed to mind, he would joke about it as if it was just another of her endearing little eccentricities.

Nick closed the chocolate box, returned it to its place on the shelf and felt around to see if there was anything else. His fingertips brushed against some kind of coarse fabric that held something solid and heavy. He fumbled around till he got a grip on it and when he pulled it out into the light saw why it was so cumbersome, it was a Royal Navy gun holster made of blue webbing and it seemed there was a gun inside. He sat back down on the stool, set the holster on the floor and looked at it for a long time. The holster flap was held shut by a single metal stud and when he gave the flap a hard tug the stud popped open and the gun slid out onto the carpet, sinister and beguiling. It was a revolver, dark blue with a cross hatched wooden handle. He had to use both hands to pick it up and hold it steady. He turned it over and counted six empty chambers in the cylinder. It was a six shooter just like Roy Rogers used. On one side of the frame was a patch of raised print that identified it as a 45 calibre pistol made by the Samuel Colt Company of the USA. A Colt 45. The most famous gun in the world. The gun the cowboys used. His dad kept an actual Colt 45 in the house.

There was a small, ridged button on the frame but when Nick pressed it nothing happened. He tried exerting more pressure and it slid forward, the gun broke open and the cylinder folded out so the chambers could be loaded. He spun the cylinder and it turned smoothly. He snapped it shut and pulled the trigger but the trigger came back barely a fraction before it locked. Disappointed,

Nick thought it might not be a real gun after all but some kind of model. He continued looking and found another small catch on the frame, close to where the thumb would be when the gun was held in the right hand. He depressed the catch with his right thumb and heard a soft click. Then he pulled the trigger again and this time the cylinder turned, the hammer reared slowly back, released and jumped forward, striking the empty cartridge chamber with a clean metallic click. He had found the safety catch. The gun worked.

He pulled the trigger again and again, watching the cylinder rotate as the hammer rose and fell till his wrists ached from the strain. He put it down on the floor, turned his attention to the holster and found a cleaning rod and a rag with something wrapped inside. When he picked up the rag he heard the chink of metal and folded inside he found several bullets. He took one between his thumb and forefinger and held it up so he could study the brass cartridge case with its percussion cap and the lead bullet at the tip. There were six bullets. Six real bullets for a real six gun.

He wrapped the bullets in the rag, put them back in the holster with the cleaning rod, returned the gun to the holster and snapped the stud shut. He pushed the gun back into the far corner of the wardrobe shelf where he'd found it so his mam and dad wouldn't know anything had been disturbed. He put the dresser stool back where it was supposed to be, locked the wardrobe door and returned the key to the cuff link box. Before he left he looked around to make sure everything was the way his mother and father left it so they'd never know he was there.

*   *   *

Nick wanted a Davy Crockett hat more than anything he'd wanted in his life before. They weren't easy to come by because there were no raccoons in England. The only genuine coonskin caps came from America and only rich kids could afford those. So Nick resigned himself to going without a Davy Crockett hat. Until one day his dad came home with a look of triumph on his face and told Nick to close his eyes and hold out his hands. Nick did as he was told and felt the unmistakeable caress of fur on his upturned hands. Hardly daring to believe it he opened his eyes and looked at a black fur hat with white flecks and a skinny black tail with a white tip.

"Go on, put it on then," Nick's mam said.

His dad watched, smiling.

Nick looked at the hat then back at the two of them then at the hat again. Did they think he wouldn't know? Or did they think he wouldn't care that it wasn't a Davy Crockett hat at all but the skin of a dead cat? Did they really expect him to put a dead cat on his head and go outside to play? When Nick looked at the rumpled black and white fur in his hands all he could picture was a little old lady calling for her little Timmy who'd run away, never to return. Though one day she might see him bobbing past her window on the head of some kid who didn't know any better.

An awful silence yawned between Nick and his parents until his mother folded her arms and said: "He doesn't like it."

"It's not a real Davy Crockett hat," Nick said.

"There, ah telt ye, didn't ah," his mam said. "Ah telt ye he wouldn't like it. He doesn't appreciate owt wi dee for him. Ahll the trouble wi go to an' he doesn't appreciate any of it."

"De ye not like it, son?" his dad asked.

Nick had no idea how his father would react, especially if he'd gone out of his way to get what he thought was the next best thing to a Davy Crockett hat. But there was no power on earth that could make Nick put a cat skin on his head and go outside.

"Ah can tell by lookin' at him he's not goin' to wear it," his mam said. "It's been a complete waste o' time and money."

"Are ye not goin' to wear it then?" his dad asked.

Nick shook his head. "Ah cannit."

"Yes ye can," his mam snapped at him. "Ye just don't want to because it's not good enough fo' ye. Nothin' we dee is ivah good enough fo' ye, is it Nicholas?"

"Ahlreet," his father sighed and took the hat back. "Ah'm sure ah can find somebody else wi' a bairn who'll appreciate it."

Nick was relieved. But for the rest of that summer he kept an eye out for any kid wearing a cat skin hat and he didn't see a single one.

*　　　*　　　*

There was a right way and a wrong way to remove a leek from the ground. Pull it the wrong way and there was a risk of tearing the flags and the beard, which would mar its appearance and render it unsuitable for competition. It was critical not to exert too much stress on the leek by pulling it too hard or by twisting or wrenching it from the ground. A wrong turn of the wrist, an involuntary twitch could destroy in a moment a year's worth of meticulous preparation.

Bright already knew what leeks he would enter in his first show but when the day came he picked his way slowly along each trench, examining each leek minutely for any flaw he might have missed, for any stain or blemish caused by an errant snail, slug or caterpillar. When he was satisfied he used the watering can to pour water around the barrel to loosen the soil. He used a trowel to work the soil away from the leek then his fingers to clear the barrel and the beard. Finally, with the leek fully exposed, he worked his fingers gently underneath and eased it slowly upward, separating it ever so carefully from the soil's clinging embrace. When he had it clear he straightened up and held the leek, thick as a man's bicep, as proudly as if he were already holding the winner's trophy. Smeared with mud, crumbs of damp soil clinging to its beard, the leek was a thing of beauty. Bright felt its heft, admired its creamy flesh, the subtle green hues of its flags.

"That's a bonny one, Jimmy."

Nick and his mam had been watching from the footpath.

"It's not bad at ahll is it?" Bright said.

Nick was impressed. All the time and trouble his father had taken to set up his trenches had produced a promising first crop. Bright laid the leek on a clean sack and moved on to the next. He intended to enter his best pot leek on its own and his next best five leeks as a pair and a trio. He would wash and dry them as tenderly as newborn babes sprung from the womb of mother earth and take them to the club in the afternoon. The judging would be tomorrow, Saturday, and the prizewinners would be known by five-o-clock. This year the top prize was a 21 inch television set worth more than a hundred pounds.

Bright was pulling his last leek when Big Mac came out next door followed by Nellie, Little Mac and Keith.

"Looks like ye did ahlreet fo' yasel' ya forst year, Jimmy," Mac said.

Bright grunted his acknowledgement. There was no question whose leeks were bigger. Mac's leeks had broader barrels and fuller leaves and Bright had no doubt that his neighbour would place well above him this year.

"At least ah'll hae somethin' to show fo' me efforts this year," Mac responded. He unfastened a section of fence, peeled it back and stepped inside to survey his crop. He too applied a generous amount of water to loosen the soil then went to work, gently prising his first leek free. With one hand cradling the barrel, the roots dangling between his fingers, he used the other hand to grip the leek close to the button and lift it gently out of the trench. He smiled as the leek came free of the soil until the outer sheath separated from the inside and a mass of brown pulp slid through his fingers to form a stagnant puddle, leaving him holding a limp green and white sock.

Nellie and the kids couldn't see what had happened but they saw the look on Mac's face. He sat back on his heels, dumbfounded.

"It's rotten…it's rotten ahll through," he muttered. He tossed the outer skin of the leek aside and moved on to the next one. It wasn't a leek he'd chosen for competition but he had to see if whatever was wrong was confined to one leek or had spread to others. He used his hands to dig quickly around the leek, desperate for reassurance, but as soon as he picked it up the same thing happened. It was perfect on the outside but the moment he pulled it clear of the soil it expelled a putrid mass of vegetable matter back into the trench. He scrabbled along his trenches, pulling one leek after another and they all came up the same, a useless puppet and a rotten stump left in the ground.

Mac let out a wail. "Somethin's been at them, somethin's eaten them from the inside…they're ahll rotten, ivery one o' them."

Nellie looked stunned and Little Mac and Keith seemed about to cry.

Bright got up from his newly pulled leeks and went over to the fence that separated his garden from Mac's.

"What is it?" he asked. "Rust? Blight?"

"Ah divvent knah, Jimmy, ah divvent knah," Mac said dazedly. "It's not rust, it's not like owt ah've ivah seen afore."

Bright looked from Big Mac's ravaged leeks to his own. "Tha's nowt wrang wi' mine," he said. "If it was rot or somethin' ye'd think it would hae spread to mine."

"Ah knah, ah knah," Mac said. "It doesn't mek any sense, man, it doesn't mek any sense."

Mac stepped out of his leek trenches wiping his soiled hands. "Ah cannit believe it," he said. "Ah'll be wiped oot. Ah've got hardly any seeds left. Ah was hopin' to re-stock from this year."

"Is it ahlreet if ah come owa and tek a look?" Bright asked.

"What…?" Mac responded distractedly. "Oh, aye, ye can look if ye want."

Bright stepped over the fence, made his way into Mac's little compound and knelt down among the ruined leeks. He picked up a discarded sleeve and turned it over, examining it closely. He probed the viscid puddle in the ground and sniffed tentatively at his fingers. He worked his way along the trench doing the same with each one while Mac and the others watched. When he was finished he stood up, wiped his hands and looked at Mac. "Ye knah what it smells like?"

Mac shook his head.

"It smells like urine."

Big Mac looked baffled. "It smells like your what?"

"Piss," Bright said, "it smells like piss." He paused. "Just hoo much hae ye been pissin' in heeyah, Mac?"

*   *   *

He was a good Guy. Spelk had come up with a holey old jumper and a worn out pair of gloves, Dave contributed a discarded pair of his dad's work pants, Nick a frayed pair of his dad's galluses and a pair of sandshoes with worn soles. Mary Beecroft painted Guy Fawkes' face on a paper bag and her mam donated a shapeless grey hat from her days in panto. Once assembled the Guy was stuffed with old newspapers and tied together with string. Still the four of them thought something was missing. Spelk went home and returned with a red feather from his Indian headdress and stuck it in the Guy's hat. Now he was ready to meet his public.

They lifted him into Spelk's bogie, propped him up with a stick and put an empty jam jar between his legs with a piece of cardboard on which Mary had written in red crayon: 'Penny For The Guy.' Then the four of them hauled him up to the Top End to see how much money they could raise to buy fireworks. It didn't matter that their parents would buy fireworks for Guy Fawkes Night, it wasn't the same as having their own money. Their parents would buy Roman Candles, Silver Fountains, Snow Storms and Catherine Wheels but the kids wanted their own money to buy bangers, squibs and jumpy jacks. Noisy little explosives that added excitement to the season as kids roamed the town throwing them down drains, blowing up cow pats and anything else that looked like fun. The closer it got to Bonfire Night the more bold the kids became, pushing bangers through letter boxes or tying them to the tails of cats and dogs. As always the Mullens and the Learys outdid everyone in their recklessness. They and Brian Boyle used Roman Candles like pistols to fire at each other and brayed like donkeys whenever they set somebody alight.

It was also the time of year when kids reverted to pure tribalism. Every housing estate had its own tribe that competed to build the best bonfire. The kids at West Lea had an advantage because there was plenty of dead wood in the cemetery and by the time the neighbours had added pieces of scrap wood and broken furniture the bonfire was one of the biggest in Bedlington. That meant the kids who built it had to defend it against raids by kids from other estates. One year the kids from Hartlands mounted a raid but when they crept up in the dark and began stripping away the wood West Lea kids who'd hidden inside leaped out and pummeled them all the way back home.

But this year's Guy Fawkes would be memorable for reasons nobody could have foreseen. It began at nightfall with fireworks at every home where there were kids. Multi-coloured fountains of sparks lit up the houses, rockets fizzed across the sky and kids with sparklers drew frenzied patterns in the dark. When the last spark had faded the kids made their way to the back fields for the lighting of the bonfire, some of them carrying candle lanterns made from hollowed out snaggies. The bonfire was always built on the fields between the houses and the cemetery. Usually 20 or so kids turned up along with a few grown-ups to keep an eye on things but this year there were as many grown-ups as there were kids. When Nick and Spelk went to put the Guy atop the bonfire Nellie McBride hurried forward with a sheet of cardboard and hung it around his neck. Big Mac shone his torch on it illuminating the word 'Nasser' in big black letters and a cheer went up from the crowd.

That summer Gamal Abdel Nasser, the president of Egypt, had nationalised the Anglo-French owned Suez Canal cutting off Britain and France from their oil supply in the Persian Gulf. With only 30 days of oil left Britain and France had joined in a secret pact with Israel to invade Egypt and take the canal back. The invasion began at the end of October and seemed likely to achieve its goal within days but, prodded by the United States and the Soviet Union, the United Nations called for a ceasefire. Soviet leader Nikita Kruschev inflamed tensions further by threatening Britain and France with nuclear annihilation if they did not immediately withdraw their forces from Egypt. The British and the French knew the Soviet Union hadn't the ability to follow through on its threat and were all for defying Kruschev but the American president, Eisenhower, panicked and told Britain to pull out. If Britain balked the Americans threatened to wreck the British economy by pressuring the International Monetary Fund to withhold emergency loans to the British government and by dumping holdings of British securities to force a collapse of the pound. Humiliated, the British had no choice but to withdraw, which led to the collapse of the alliance with France and Israel and the abandonment of the mission to retake the canal. There was a national outcry against the United States for betraying its staunchest ally but the damage was done and Nasser's name on a piece of cardboard was enough to incite the crowd.

"Aye, bloody Nasser," Jean Gordon shouted. "Gan on an' born the bugga."

"An' put thon dozened bugga Eisenhooah up there while ya at it," Joe Gordon added.

Nick and Spelk lit the bonfire from opposite sides. Piles of newspaper mixed with scraps of greasy kitchen linoleum caught fire with a woosh and flames quickly engulfed the Guy. In minutes the bonfire was ablaze, a great column of sparks spiraling up into the night sky, the heat fierce enough to make everyone step back. The smaller kids ran around with sparklers, their giant shadows capering on the firelit houses behind. In a very short time the bonfire collapsed and the Guy vanished in a flourish of flame.

"Born you bugga, born," Big Mac shouted.

"To hell wi' the lot o' them," Spelk's mam added. "Nasser an' Kruschev an' Eisenhooah, to hell wi' the whole bloody lot o' them."

Nick was standing near Mr. Leese and heard him tell Mary Beecroft's mam: "Ah would nivah hae thought it possible the Americans would torn on wi' the way they did. Ah thowt they were supposed to be wa friends."

"Aye, an' wee needs enemies when ye've got friends like that?" Brian Boyle's mam said.

"Oh, wa finished noo," Joe Gordon added. "We hae to ask the yanks permission afore we can tek a shite noo."

"What else would ye expect o' the yanks?" Big Mac said. "They knah iverythin'."

"They showed us up in front o' the whole world," Mrs. Leese said.

"Ye cannit trust the Americans," Spelk's mam said. "They stab iverybody in the back weeivah helped them."

"They'll promise ye the world an' just when ye need them the most they torn on ye," Nick's mam added.

"Aye, ye see Anthony Eden had it ahll wrang," Joe Gordon added. "What wi should hae done was declare war on the yanks and then surrender streyt away so they woulda had to gi' wi money just like they gi' the Jarmans."

They laughed but there was little joy in their laughter.

Gradually the bonfire settled into a crater, the coals in the middle white hot. Nick sat cross-legged on the grass with Spelk and Dave and watched the faces on the other side of the bonfire shimmer in the heat. Bedtime for the younger kids came soon and the crowd dwindled to a dozen or so. A few of the grown-ups and the older kids had brought potatoes, which they poked into the embers with sticks. The potatoes baked quickly, the skins turning to char if they weren't watched. When they were flicked out onto the grass it was several minutes before they could be handled. Except for Joe Gordon who plucked a potato from the coals with unprotected fingers, juggled it briefly and bit into it like an apple. He swallowed the char and the steaming white flesh and grinned at his audience through blackened teeth.

By eleven only Nick, Dave, Spelk and his dad were left and with the next day a school day it was time to call it a night. The four of them used shovels to turn over the ashes and shake out the embers. When they were finished they stood around the smouldering grey pile and watched it for a while and thought about the impermanence of things. Then they all pissed on it and went to bed.

*   *   *

Bright was the night duty officer the Friday before Christmas when Alec Newell brought in a driver arrested for drunk driving. Alec Newell had gone out with Evan Thompson to patrol the pubs on Front Street at chucking out time when a green Riley Pathfinder knocked over Mickey Dodd on the zebra crossing at the Top End. Alec said Dodd, a mining apprentice at the Doctor Pit, had head and leg injuries but it was hard to tell how serious they were because he was lying in the road singing: 'Que Sera Sera.'

It seemed Dodd and his equally happy mates had been dawdling on the crossing making the driver of the Riley wait. The driver had tooted his horn and they'd responded with the two fingered salute and a barrage of colourful insults. The driver had eased his car forward to try and push his way through them when Dodd fell and struck his head on the road. His mates tried to drag the driver out of the car and Newell and Thompson had gone to his aid. Because he smelled of drink and was uncooperative they decided to run him in. Alec said Evan was in the process of parking the Riley behind the police station on Catholic Row.

The driver was in his late 30's, a pleasant looking man with longish fair hair he kept pushing out of his eyes. He wore a white cableknit sweater, bottle green corduroys and a three quarter length suede coat that cost more than a policeman made in a month.

"His name is Peter McMahon," Alec said. "He's from Gosforth. An architect. Has his ahn firm in Newcastle and that's ahll he'll say."

"Has he got motor vehicle registration and insurance?" Bright asked.

"Ahll seems te be in order," Alec said. "He smells like he's had a fair bit to drink, but, an' he's refusin' to take a sobriety test."

Just then Evan Thompson bustled in through the back door and dropped McMahon's papers and car keys on the counter for Bright.

"Ye'll be needin' these," he said. "Ah'll fill oot the accident report when ah get back but wi better get back oot there afore owt else gans wrang."

As Thompson and Newell left to continue their rounds Bright looked over McMahon's driving license, registration and insurance and found a business card tucked in with the license. On expensive cream colored stock with embossed

95

gold lettering it said: 'McMahon and Associates, Architects and Surveyors, Eldon Square, Newcastle-Upon-Tyne.' Eldon Square was an enclave of elegant Georgian houses in the heart of the city, most of them used as offices by upscale accountants, law firms and architectural firms like McMahon and Associates. Bright retrieved a blank arrest report and an envelope from the duty desk for McMahon's personal effects.

"Mr. McMahon, would ye empty out the contents o' ya pockets an' put them on the counter please?"

McMahon looked annoyed. "Why? You're not going to lock me up are you?"

"That depends entirely on you, Mr. McMahon," Bright responded.

McMahon had a middle class accent and Bright modified his accent as he usually did when speaking to anybody posh.

"I mean, really, do I have to get everything out my pockets?"

"Mr. McMahon, ye do realise ye've been placed under arrest fo' drivin' while under the influence of alcohol?"

"Yes, well, that remains to be determined, doesn't it?" McMahon responded.

"Not the fact that you're under arrest, Mr. McMahon," Bright said.

McMahon sighed, shook his head resignedly and went through his pockets. One after the other he put his wallet, comb, cigarette case, lighter, coins, a rumpled handkerchief and a couple of wrapped mint humbugs on the counter.

"Is that everythin'?" Bright asked.

"Yes."

Bright returned the handkerchief then listed the rest of McMahon's personal possessions noting that the cigarette case held eight Benson and Hedges special filter. In his wallet were 37 pounds and 10 shillings in notes, the loose coins in his pockets came to six shillings and fourpence. When he was finished Bright wrote McMahon's name on the envelope and tied it shut with a piece of twine. Then he turned to the arrest report.

"An' where have ye been tonight, Mr. McMahon?"

"I want to speak to my solicitor," McMahon said. "I don't have to say anything without my solicitor present."

The smell of alcohol on his breath gusted across the counter.

"How much have ye had to drink tonight, sir?"

"I'm not going to say anything until I've spoken to my solicitor."

Bright considered McMahon for a long moment then said. "Mr. McMahon, I'm not tryin' to make things any harder for ye here but ye must understand the seriousness of a drunk driving charge, especially where there's been an injury to another party."

"I'm not going to make any kind of a statement until my solicitor is present," McMahon repeated.

"Are ye willin' to submit to a sobriety test?"

"Not unless my solicitor is here to tell me it's alright for me to do so."

"Well, just so ye know, it's a separate offence to refuse to take a sobriety test," Bright said. "An' we can lock ye up for the night based on our assessment of your condition and your fitness to drive."

"I want my solicitor here before this goes any further," McMahon said.

"Alright then, just so we both understand the situation, I'm asking you formally; are you refusin' to take a sobriety test?"

"I will not say or do anything more until my solicitor is present," McMahon repeated.

Bright made a note on the report and checked the time on the wall clock. It was a little before eleven.

"And where does your solicitor live?"

"Jesmond. I can give you his phone number."

Jesmond was a middle class suburb just east of Newcastle city center.

"An' ye think your solicitor is goin' to want to come out this time of night an' drive all the way to Bedlington just because ye've got yourself in a bit o' bother?"

"He'll come," McMahon said.

McMahon was beginning to grate on Bright.

"Ahlright then, if that's the way ye want it, we'll do it your way," Bright said. "Give is ya solicitor's name an' telephone number and ah'll call him. But ah'll caution ye here an' now, if there's no answer and ye still refuse to take a sobriety test ye'll be spendin' the night downstairs in a cell."

"His name is Walter Makepiece," McMahon said. "His card's in my wallet."

Bright re-opened the personal effects envelope and retrieved the card. It read: 'Jervis, Johnson and Makepiece, Barristers and Solicitors.' The address was Gray Street in Newcastle, another prestigious location just down from Eldon Square. At the bottom of the card were the office number and a home number for Walter P. Makepiece. Bright frowned. Everything about McMahon spelled trouble.

"You just wait right there, Mr. McMahon," Bright said and went back to the duty desk to use the phone. If McMahon would consent to a sobriety test and was found to be over the limit Bright would charge him, hold him for an hour or two till he sobered up then let him go, to be summonsed at a later date. What McMahon didn't seem to appreciate was that if he insisted on bringing his solicitor in, it would take most of the night to accomplish much the same thing.

Bright tapped the business card absently on the desk deciding how best to handle the call when Shep swept in through the front door trailing beer fumes and cigarette smoke. He eyed McMahon briefly, gave Bright a curt acknowledgement and continued to his office where he rummaged in his filing cabinet and emerged a moment later stuffing a bottle of Cutty Sark into his coat pocket. On his way back out he stopped by the duty desk and, with a nod in McMahon's direction, asked Bright. "Who's this Charlie then?"

"He's a right Charlie an' ahll," Bright said, phone in hand, finger poised to dial. "Name's Peter McMahon. Bumped his car into some young lads on the crossin' near the Top Club. Evan Thompson arrested him for drivin' under the influence."

"Ah," Shep said. "He'd be the bloke who sent Sid Dodd's lad to the General in Ashin'ton then."

"That'd be him," Bright added. "Ah've tried tahkin' to him but he's not cooperatin'. Refuses to take a sobriety test, refuses to say owt wi'oot his solicitor present."

"Bit stroppy is he?" Shep said. "An' where does his solicitor live when he's at home?"

"Jesmond," Bright said.

"An' he thinks we've got nowt better to do than get his solicitor out of bed to come owa here an' hold his hand for him?"

"That seems to be the picture," Bright said. "Ah'm just callin' the solicitor now."

Shep nodded but said nothing more and walked around the counter to where McMahon stood. Bright dialed Walter Makepiece's number and listened to it ring.

"So, what have you got to say for yourself, Mr. McMahon?" Shep asked.

Bright stood at the duty desk half turned away from Shep and McMahon so he could hear the phone but keep both men in view.

"Look," McMahon raised his hands in protest. "I told the rest of them and I'm telling you, whoever you are, I've got nothing to say to anybody until my solicitor is…"

Shep punched him square in the face and sent him staggering back against the notice board above the public bench. McMahon bounced off the board and sat down hard on the bench. Blood spooled from his nose and splashed onto his suede coat.

"Hello?" a voice sounded in Bright's ear. "Hello, who is this?" An authoritative, well spoken voice.

"Is this Mr. Makepiece?" Bright asked turning away from the scene on the other side of the counter.

"Yes, who is this?"

"Sorry to bother ye at this hour, sir, this is Constable Bright calling from Bedlington Police Station. We have a gentleman in custody here who says you're his solicitor, a Mr. Peter McMahon. He's been arrested for driving under the influence and he refuses to make a statement unless you're present."

"Alright, put him on please."

Bright hesitated. "I'm afraid that's not possible."

"What do you mean, not possible?" Makepiece said.

"He can't come to the phone just now."

"Why can't he come to the 'phone? Are you refusing to let me speak to my client?"

"He's just ah…a bit indisposed at the moment," Bright said. "Ye can speak to him when ye get here."

"Bedlington Police?" Makepiece said.

"Yes sir, you come straight up the A1 from Newcastle and turn onto…"

"I know where you are," Makepiece cut him off. "Very well, tell Mr. McMahon I'll be there as soon as I can."

"Yes sir," Bright said and hung up. He turned to where Shep stood looking down at the dazed and bloodied McMahon and said: "Mr. McMahon's solicitor is on his way."

For a moment Shep showed no reaction then he walked back around the counter and said softly: "Don't call anybody else." Then he went to the toilet at the back of the police station.

Bright went over to McMahon who sat slackly on the wooden bench dabbing his nose with his blood soaked handkerchief. He looked up at Bright and said thickly: "That bastard broke my nose."

"Would ye like some water?" Bright asked.

McMahon breathed shakily then said: "No."

"A cup of tea?"

"No, I don't want anything from you."

"Can I get you an aspirin?"

"An aspirin?" McMahon said derisively.

Bright sighed. "Fair enough then, but don't say ye weren't offered. Your solicitor said to tell ye he'll be here as soon as he can."

McMahon said nothing more and Bright went back to the duty desk, leaned on it with both hands and stared at the report book. He should call John Robson, the senior officer at Bedlington, regardless of what Shep said. By doing nothing he was making himself an accessory. He should call Robson and tell him what had happened before Robson found out for himself. Besides it was possible Robson would drop in anyway as he often did on a Saturday night to see how things were going. Bright decided to get a towel and clean McMahon up a bit before anybody came. In the toilet he found Shep bent over a wash basin washing his hands, his coat and hat on a cubicle door. Bright took a clean hand towel out of a cupboard, ran some cold water into a basin, soaked the towel then wrung it out.

"Jesus, Shep," he said, "do ye hae any idea what ye just did in there? He's not some yob from doon the pit rahs ye knah."

"It'll be alright," Shep said. "It'll be alright."

"Ah wouldn't be so sure," Bright said. He went back out to McMahon and offered him the dampened towel.

"Here, you might want to clean yoursel' up a bit," he said.

McMahon waved him away. "I don't want to clean myself up," he said.

"I'm tryin' to help you here," Bright persisted.

McMahon got to his feet, wobbly, agitated. "You're trying to hide what's happened, that's what you're trying to do."

Apprehension tightened in Bright's gut. Shep had picked on the wrong bloke this time. Just then Shep came out of the toilet with his coat and hat on. He turned his back to McMahon while he spoke to Bright.

"You've spoken to his solicitor then?"

"Aye, he's on his way, he'll be here shortly," Bright said. "But ah hae to call Robson before then, Shep, ah hae nae choice."

Shep frowned.

"Just give is a minute."

He walked around the counter to where McMahon stood and in a conciliatory tone said: "Look, I'm sorry about what happened. Your solicitor should be here shortly. You'll be alright, you can use the toilet in the back there and get yourself cleaned up."

McMahon looked contemptuously at Shep. "I want my solicitor to see me the way I am," he said.

"Oh ye do, do ye?" Shep said. And he hit McMahon again, his massive fist knocking him back onto the bench, his bloodied handkerchief fluttering to the floor like a wounded bird. McMahon slumped sideways on the bench with a muffled sob while blood splashed onto the floor. Shep leaned over him and shouted into his ear.

"You can show him that an' ahll while you're at it. An' just so ye know, my name is Shepherd. Detective Inspector Jack Shepherd." Then he strode to the front door and went out into the night.

Bright leaned against the duty desk. "Christ ahll-bloody-mighty," he said to himself. "Christ ahll-bloody-mighty."

1957

Prime Minister Harold Macmillan tells Britons 'You've never had it so good'; the Soviet Union launches the first space satellites, Sputnik 1 and 2. Tops on TV are Six Five Special and The Benny Hill Show. Biggest hits at the Box Office are: The Bridge On The River Kwai starring Alec Guinness and William Holden and 12 Angry Men starring Henry Fonda and Lee J. Cobb. Top of the music charts are: Singin' The Blues by Tommy Steele; These Dangerous Years by Frankie Vaughan; All Shook Up by Elvis Presley; That'll Be The Day by Buddy Holly and The Crickets; Tutti Frutti by Little Richard; Wake Up Little Susie by The Everly Brothers; Great Balls Of Fire by Jerry Lee Lewis and Reet Petite by Jackie Wilson.

Black And White

Big Mac hunched over a set of trays in the greenhouse carefully pressing his last leek seeds into cubes of moist warm soil. It was a ritual he usually enjoyed but even as his toe tapped to Alma Cogan singing 'Dreamboat' on the tranny he was worried. He was down to 20 seeds and nagged by the fear that another total loss would mean the extinction of the champion strain he'd bred over the years. He still wasn't convinced he was to blame for the loss of the previous year's crop. He'd been pissing in his trenches ever since he'd started growing leeks, but only after a night on the beer, and it had never done them any harm before. He thought there must be another explanation but, as Jimmy Bright said, it was hard to deny the evidence of your own eyes and nose. So Mac decided that not only would there be no more slashing of his leeks there would be no more slashing *on* his leeks. And he would show Bright what real prizewinners looked like: Bright, who'd come in 293rd out of 347 entries in last year's competition and won a set of darts.

Bright's prospects for this year's leek show were the last thing on his mind as he went in to the police station and the news he'd been dreading. Bert Fry, the daytime duty sergeant, caught Bright's eye as he hung up his coat and helmet.

"The boss wanted to see ye soon as ye got back," Fry said with a nod in the direction of John Robson's office. "That bit o' business wi' Shep? Looks like tha goin' after him."

Bright nodded. It was three months since Shep had thumped Peter McMahon and Bright had expected something like this. He'd called Robson the minute after Shep left that night and Robson had come up to the station in time for a heated exchange with McMahon's solicitor, Mr. Makepiece. Makepiece had insisted that McMahon was in no condition to submit to a sobriety test and needed immediate medical attention. The amount of blood McMahon had decanted from his nose onto his suede coat left little room for argument and Robson released McMahon into Makepiece's custody. When they'd gone Bright gave Robson an account of what happened and Robson had decided to bring the maximum number of charges against McMahon so that in the event of a complaint the police would have some leverage. Bright had thought all along that McMahon would go after Shep and this was one time he didn't like being right. It presented him with the worst possible dilemma; there would be an internal inquiry and every day that passed without him telling the whole story would bind his fate inextricably to Shep's - for good or ill. And, while he believed coppers should watch out for each other, he wasn't sure Shep was worth it if things went against him. Shep was coming to the end of his career. Bright was at the start of his. Quite apart from the right and wrong of it Bright had more to lose. If the police lost the case and Shep and Bright were convicted of conspiring to pervert the course of justice the two of them could easily go to jail. At the very least they'd be kicked off the force, Shep would lose his pension and the stain on Bright's career would make it impossible for him to get a decent job anywhere. And Shep had been no help in the intervening months. When Bright had attempted to speak to him about it Shep had shrugged it off. He admitted he'd had a bit to drink that night and he remembered hitting McMahon - but only once. He dismissed the possibility of a formal complaint and, when pressed, fell back on the argument that thumping some people was the only thing that did them any good. The last thing Bright wanted was to be put in the position of protecting a man whose defence was that he'd been knocking people around for 40 years and this was the first time anybody had complained.

Bright rapped on the rattly glass pane in the inspector's office door and Robson beckoned him inside.

"Have a seat," Robson said without looking up from the papers in front of him. Bright took one of two hard wooden chairs that faced Robson's desk. The inspector's office was at the back of the room, adjacent to Shep's office, which was presently unoccupied. Both offices were identical; wooden cubicles with windows on three sides that reached almost to the ceiling and afforded little privacy even when the door was closed. The furniture was civil service drab, steel grey filing cabinets, battered desk and chairs, a chipped green metal wastepaper basket and a canted coat stand. Robson was meticulously neat with a neatly trimmed moustache and an office that was much neater than Shep's. Supposedly Robson and Shep were equal in rank but Robson was the senior officer and commanded a dozen and a half uniformed men while Shep commanded a two-man detective squad that consisted of himself and young Dickie Prichard.

Robson initialed whatever it was he'd been reading, put it in his out tray and retrieved a packet of Dunhills from his top drawer. In an unspoken acknowledgement of rank he didn't offer one to Bright. "Smoke if you want," he said and Bright took a packet of 10 Senior Service from a tunic pocket. Each man lit his own cigarette though Robson did push the ashtray a little closer to Bright.

"I had a call from the Chief Constable this morning about this affair concerning Shep," Robson said. "He's asked Detective Chief Superintendent Carroll to handle the internal investigation, reporting directly to him. The Crown Prosecutor's Office will conduct its own investigation to determine whether or not to prosecute."

Bright drew deeply on his cigarette. "Does Shep know?"

"He does now," Robson said. "I think it's finally begun to dawn on him he could be in a spot of bother."

Robson plucked a buff coloured folder from a wire tray and passed it to Bright. "This came down from the Chief Constable's office a couple of days ago."

Bright opened the folder. On top was a memo from Chief Constable Cyril Browning advising Robson of the complaint and asking him to review the contents with the officers involved. Next was a cover letter from Geoffrey Jervis Q.C., and a copy of the complaint from Jervis, Johnson and Makepiece, filed with the Crown Prosecutor's Office. The complaint detailed point by point McMahon's account of what happened in Bedlington the Friday before Christmas; how he'd feared for his safety at the hands of a crowd of drunken youths on the pedestrian crossing at the Top End; how the police had rescued him only to arrest him for driving under the influence; how he'd gone willingly to the police station where he asserted his right to speak to his solicitor and how he was assaulted by Detective Inspector Shepherd without provocation. Not once but twice. Next were copies of sworn statements by McMahon and his solicitor, Makepiece. In his statement Makepiece said despite the severity of McMahon's injuries neither Bright nor any other officer attempted to provide first aid or call a doctor. There were also photographs of McMahon's facial injuries taken from the front and sides. The stark contrasts of the glossy black and white prints served only to emphasise the damage; McMahon's eyes swollen to slits, a bloody cut across the bridge of his flattened nose, extensive swelling and discolouration, his white cableknit sweater spattered with black splotches of blood. Finally there was a copy of a medical report signed by the examining doctor at the Royal Victoria Infirmary in Newcastle, which stated that McMahon was treated for a fractured nose and cheekbone, swelling to the back of the head, facial cuts including a cut to the nose that required five stitches, and a concussion. The examining doctor's report concluded: "The injuries are consistent with a ferocious and sustained assault." And for good measure: "Mr. McMahon's hands and knuckles were unmarked with no evidence that would suggest his participation in any kind of physical altercation."

Bright closed the folder and handed it back to Robson without comment.

"That's a nice present to take home to the kids at Christmas, isn't it?" Robson said. "Mr. McMahon is a married man with two young kids. A professional man, highly regarded, a member of several professional associations. Sits on the boards of a couple of high profile charities. Seems he'd been delivering Christmas presents to his sister's family in Ashington. His sister is married to a Mr. Terence Heaton, chief accountant at the regional office of the NCB, and they have three kids. Mr. Heaton grew up in Ashington." Robson raised his eyebrows for added effect. "Went to school with Jackie Milburn, apparently. Played football with him."

Robson's words dropped like stones into a well. Everybody in Ashington claimed to know Jackie Milburn when what they meant was they'd seen him play. But then there were those like Peter McMahon's brother-in-law who, apparently, really did know him. And in the northeast Jackie Milburn was god in football boots.

"McMahon's ganna have Jackie testify on his behalf is he?" Bright said.

"It's enough that there's a family connection," Robson said. "Public sympathy will be with Mr. McMahon not the police."

Bright shifted on the hard wooden chair. Robson had a cushion for his chair but not for visitors.

"Mr. McMahon's not the innocent he's mekkin' hissel' oot to be," Bright said. "Evan an' Alec ran him in for a reason. He drove his car into a crowd on a pedestrian crossing while under the influence an' knocked over Mickey Dodd. Dodd was hurt an' ahll. There's nae mention o' that in there but there's a dozen witnesses to it. McMahon was uncooperative wi' Evan and Alec, he was uncooperative wi' me here at the station an' he was uncooperative when Shep tried to talk to him. He stank o' whisky an' he refused to take a sobriety test. He still has to answer to those charges."

"And he will," Robson acknowledged. "And it won't make a blind bit of difference because he'll dispose of those charges before this case goes to trial. Jervis, Johnson and Makepiece know what they're doing. By the time this goes in front of a judge Mr. McMahon will be able to present himself as a reasonable man willing to take his medicine. The only matter for the judge to determine will be whether Shep assaulted Mr. McMahon without provocation while he was in police custody." He tapped the ash from his cigarette. "The issue is not whether Mr. McMahon was assaulted - Shep admits he hit him - the issue is provocation. And if provocation can be established, what was the degree of provocation? Was it sufficient to justify a level of force consistent with Mr. McMahon's injuries? That's the key to winning this case or stopping it before it gets to court. Did Mr. McMahon become physically threatening after he was brought in here? We know he's never been in trouble with the law before. He's never had so much as a parking fine. We know he didn't resist arrest. And him getting a bit bolshie after a minor traffic accident is not an excuse for Shep to knock seven different colours of shite out of him. So how much provocation was there? You're the only one who can answer that."

Bright met Robson's gaze unsure of how much he should say. If he turned Queen's evidence - which could compel Shep to plead guilty - it was also possible that Shep would be treated leniently by the court and subjected to only minor discipline. Bright would have made an enemy for life and he'd be branded as somebody who wouldn't stand by a fellow officer. However he weighed his options none of them looked good.

"Ye know as much as ah do now, boss," he said.

"McMahon says in his statement that Shep hit him twice."

"He did."

"Both at the same time or on two separate occasions?" Robson asked.

"There was nae time between them at ahll," Bright said. "Shep hit him twice to put an end to his nonsense."

"And what nonsense was that?" Robson asked. "Was McMahon just running his mouth off or did he have a go at Shep?"

"He looked like he was goin' to have a go."

"*Looked* like he was going to have a go?"

"It was him who was shoutin' the odds an' carryin' on an' it was him who raised his hands forst, like he meant business…an' obviously Shep thought he meant business."

"Were his hands open or clenched?"

Bright paused then lifted his hands up, palms outward, fingers half clenched. "Like that."

"So he could have been raising his hands to defend himself against what he saw as a threat from Shep?"

"That's one way o' lookin' at it."

"That's how his lawyers are looking at it," Robson said. "And that's how they'll want a judge to look at it."

"The bloke raised his hands first, Shep just went over to talk to him."

"You know, Shep hasn't said anything to me about McMahon raising his hands?"

Bright sucked in a curl of smoke. "Ah'm not sure Shep remembers ahll that happened. He'd had his share to drink that night an' ahll."

"Aye and that'll make for a sound defence, won't it?" Robson said. "Detective Inspector Shepherd was more pissed than the bloke we arrested for drunk driving. Did McMahon raise his hands to defend himself against Shep or did he raise his hands to hit Shep?"

"Boss, ah don't know what was goin' on in McMahon's mind. Ah don't know what he was goin' to do. Ahll ah can say wi' any degree o' certainty is that while he was goin' off at Shep he raised his hands. An' you know as well as anybody, when things start to go bad ye don't wait for a bloke to plant ye one, ye plant him first. Otherwise none of us would last five minutes oot on the street."

Robson pursed his lips. "You say Mr. McMahon was belligerent?"

"He was."

"Belligerent or…just awkward?"

"Belligerent."

"To you or just to Shep?"

"To the both o' wi," Bright said. "Ah tried tahkin' to McMahon first, afore Shep had come back to the station, but he didn't want to know. He's one of these blokes who thinks rules are fo' other folk, not him."

"But he wasn't so belligerent you had to put him in handcuffs?"

Bright hesitated. "No. Ah didn't think it was necessary to put him in handcuffs."

"So he couldn't have been that belligerent? Not enough to worry you, anyway. And you didn't think he was going to do a runner?"

"No, but ah had to remind him why he was under arrest. He was definitely workin' his ticket, but he didn't raise his hands to me."

"Because you were on the other side of the counter from him?" Robson said. "You weren't standing over him?"

"That might have had somethin' to do with it."

Robson pondered Bright's response. "I suppose we should be grateful you didn't put him in cuffs because if he had been handcuffed when Shep hit him all there would be left for Morpeth to do would be to agree to whatever amount of compensation Mr. McMahon's solicitors demanded."

The two men lapsed into silence then Bright said: "Makepiece says in his statement we didn't offer McMahon any first aid and that's a streyt oot lie. Ah got him a wet towel to use fo' a cold compress an' he just brushed is off. He wanted his solicitor to see him with blood ahll over him an' he said that. He actually said that."

"Blokes have been hurt worse playing football," Robson conceded. "But Shep's always been a bit free with his hands. The only surprise is that it took so long for something like this to happen. The trouble is it reflects poorly on all of us for letting somebody like him continue on in the force. I certainly don't feel like sticking my neck out for a man who doesn't deserve it and doesn't give a toss how it affects the rest of us."

Bright took some solace in the fact that Robson shared his misgivings about Shep but he wasn't willing to take the first step that could initiate Shep's downfall.

"You see Mr. Jervis is a silk?" Robson asked.

"Ah did," Bright said.

"He's going to be working closely with the Crown Prosecutor on this," Robson added. "These are the kind of questions you're going to be asked on the stand. You're the key witness and they're not going to treat you with kid gloves."

"You think this is definitely going to trial then, boss?"

Robson nodded. "I see nothing here that would lead me to believe that Mr. McMahon and his lawyers are open to compromise. They want their pound of flesh. But it's not just Shep who's at risk, it's you, me and Evan and Alec. Let me tell you, the Chief Constable is very concerned about this case. The fact that he's assigned DCS Carroll to the investigation should tell you that. By the time this is over every one of us is going to be very well known up at Morpeth, one way or another."

"Ah can see that," Bright said.

Robson smiled faintly. "Yes, but what you don't know is the Chief Constable is planning on retiring next year and he's been recommended for an MBE to top off his career. How much do you think it's going to help his chances if a senior officer under his command is convicted of using excessive force against a respected member of the Newcastle business community? The chief made it very clear to me this morning that if Shep is innocent and his innocence is supported by DCS Carroll's findings he'll have all the resources of the police force behind him to get an acquittal. But he made it equally clear there will be no half measures here, it's all or nothing. If Shep pleads not guilty and it turns out he's not telling the truth, the whole lot of us will be out on our ear. And if Shep is guilty, unpleasant as that may be, it would be better for all concerned if we dealt with it now and got it out the way before next year. So you had better be very sure about what you saw that night and very precise in the testimony you give, Jimmy. Because if you're not, the crown prosecutor, with Mr. Jervis's help, will make mincemeat out of you on the stand."

Bright played with his cigarette for a moment then took one last drag and stubbed it out in the ashtray. "Thanks boss," he said. "For a minute there ah thought ye were goin' to put some pressure on is."

*   *   *

That spring the Bright family fortunes blossomed like the buds of May. Nick's mam left the dry cleaner's for a better paid job as the manageress of the Doctor Pit canteen and with the extra money his parents bought a car and a television set.

The car was a four year old rust red Standard Eight with a four cylinder side valve engine under a long nosed bonnet with side vents. The roof was black canvas with Perspex side and rear windows and could be folded down. It was rattly, draughty and unheated but after the combination it afforded the Brights a new level of luxury. For the first time Nick and his parents were together when they went anywhere and on Sunday drives his mother would lead them in singalongs and for a while they would persuade themselves they were happy.

The TV set was a Bush with a 17 inch screen and was connected to an H shaped aerial bolted to the chimney to capture the signal from distant Pontop Pike. The ritual of closing the curtains and settling down in front of the TV transformed the lives of the Brights as it transformed the country. With only the BBC to watch the nation was united by a television monoculture presented by men and women in evening dress who spoke the Queen's English. The novelty of having moving and talking pictures in the living room, if only for a few hours each day, meant everybody watched everything. Overnight, children's programmes like 'Bill And Ben The Flowerpot Men' and "plobalop" became part of the national conversation. 'Gardening Club' with Percy Thrower introduced viewers to a world where men wore jackets and ties to do the gardening. 'Tonight,' a current affairs programme hosted by Cliff Michelmore, carried snappy interviews with politicians and celebrities and featured a band of reporters who roamed the British Isles profiling an inexhaustible supply of eccentrics. The balding, bespectacled and baggy suited Michelmore always signed off the same way: "That's all for tonight, the next Tonight will be tomorrow night, until then, goodnight," which Nick thought the pinnacle of wit. Millions of viewers became emotionally involved in the lives of The Grove Family, The Appleyards and Dixon Of Dock Green. Live variety shows brought acrobats, jugglers and magicians into every living room along with comedians like Max Miller, George Formby, Ken Dodd, Frankie Howerd, Tommy Cooper and Max Bygraves. Comic performers like Tony Hancock, Eric Sykes, Jimmy Edwards, Dave King, Benny Hill and Bob Monkhouse were given their own TV shows with supporting casts that included the likes of Sid James, Bill Kerr, Cyril Fletcher, Dick Bentley, Hattie Jacques, Kenneth Williams and June Whitfield, who became as familiar to viewers as the corner grocer. And it was all held together by the same glue, a deftly pedestrian Britishness that satirised the banality of everyday life in post-war Britain.

The other big change in Nick's life was that he could now eat free at the pit canteen. The walk from Whitley Memorial to the Doctor Pit took 10 minutes and his first meal was his last. The canteen was a dungeon of blackened ovens, cauldrons of boiling vegetables, vats of hissing lard and walls that sweated grease. The canteen women wore stained white coats and turbans and toiled in a fog of steam and cigarette smoke. Occasionally a bloodied Elastoplast would turn up in the mashed potato and whenever some new mine apprentice asked what was for dinner the answer was: "Shit wi' sugar on."

Nick had pie, chips and peas; the pie crust tasted like wet cardboard and the filling was beef flavoured elastic. What impressed him most was the canteen ceiling, thatched as it was with thousands of glimmering stalactites, which turned out to be the silver foil from cigarette packets molded into the shape of golf tees, dabbed with spit and flicked up at the ceiling by the miners.

It was also the spring that Nick's cousin, Eric, injured himself in a motorbike accident. Eric had left school at 15 and got a job as a coal sorter at the Doctor Pit. He used his money to buy a motorbike and crashed it soon afterwards. He lost control of the bike while taking a corner on Ridge Terrace, the bike skidded one way and Eric skidded another, crossing the road in a semi-reclining position, one hand raised to protect himself till he slid underneath a parked car. He broke an arm and a leg and left most of his arse smeared across the road like tettie peelings. Nick's mam said they should visit him while he was laid up. Nick cringed at the thought. He couldn't have given a toss if Eric left whatever it was he had for brains smeared across the road. But, the next Saturday afternoon, Nick went with his mam and dad to his Aunty Dot's house in a show of sympathy.

Eric, in pajamas and dressing gown, sat in an armchair near the fireplace, his left arm in a cast, his body angled away from his left buttock, his left leg, also in a cast, resting on a stool. His sister, Irene, was there, her head bristling under a thicket of metal curlers so she would look beautiful when she went to the club that night with her husband of one year, Lennie. Nick couldn't imagine what kind of man would be attracted to a woman like Irene. With a doughy face and prominent jaw she reminded Nick of the boxer, Freddie Mills. It turned out Lennie was the same kind of amiable nonentity as her father and she had merely continued the tradition of the women in the family. Lennie had one more essential quality, he didn't want kids. Like Irene he believed kids interfered with the enjoyment of life.

Nick's mam, dad, his Aunty Dot, his Uncle Ray, Irene and Lennie gathered around the table in the living room while Nick sat on a stool on the opposite side of the steel fronted fireplace from Eric. Dot made a pot of tea, put out some scones with butter and jam and Nick resigned himself to an afternoon in hell. He emerged briefly from his misery when Irene said Eric had bought a new record that was "the worst thing ye've ivah hord in ahll ya born days." In her customary bellow she added: "Ye'll nivah believe what it's called either, it's called 'Me Balls Are On Fire.'"

"No it's not," Eric said. "It's Great Balls Of Fire."

"Same thing," Irene shouted. "Same thing."

"It doesn't matter what it is, ye cannit mek the words oot anyway," Dot said.

"Put it on, mam," Irene said. To Nick's parents she added: "Ye think ye've heard it ahll but ah'm tellin' ye, ye've nivah hord nowt like this in ahll ya born days."

"Just because ye lot divvent like it doesn't mean it's nae good," Eric said. It was one of those occasions when Nick found himself in the unusual position of siding with his cousin.

"Ahlreet, ah'll put it on for ye," Dot said and got up. "Irene's right but, ye'll not believe ya ears."

The record player was on a side table beside Eric's chair along with a stack of 78's. Dot picked a record from the top and put it on the turntable. For a few seconds there was only the hiss and spit of the record turning and then it exploded with a furious crash of piano chords and Jerry Lee Lewis yelling like a madman:

'You shake my nerves and you rattle my brain
Too much love drives a man insane
You broke my will, oh what a thrill
Goodness gracious great balls of fire.'

A tidal wave of sound swept through the room. Nick's mam sat up as if she'd been slapped. His dad looked pained. It wasn't like anything Nick had heard before either. Wilder than Elvis or Little Richard. A reckless, dangerous song to stir the blood and stun the senses.

Nick's dad shouted to make himself heard. "That's enough, torn it off for god's sake, it's bloody ahwful."

Eric grinned and for one fleeting moment he and Nick made eye contact, the only two in the room who understood. Dot lifted the playing arm off the record and the racket stopped, leaving an appalled silence.

"Did ah not tell ye?" Irene said. "Did ah not tell ye? Eh? Eh?"

"Ye cannit cahll that music," Nick's dad said.

"It's rock 'n' roll music," Eric said. "It's Jerry Lee Lewis."

"It's nivah Jerry Lewis," Nick's mam said.

"Jerry *Lee* Lewis," Eric said. "He's a rock an' roll singer from America.

That's him playin' the piano an' ahll."

"Ye cahll that playin'?" Nick's dad said. "Ye mean beatin' it te death divvent ye?"

"He's as big as Elvis in America," Eric added.

"Aye, another bugga that wants shootin'," Nick's dad said. "Ah might hae guessed it was more o' the same kind o' rubbish ye would expect from owa there."

"It's a big hit record," Eric said.

"Aye, an' it just goes to show hoo many folk hae nae bloody brains in tha heeds," Bright added.

"Was he singin' aboot what ah think he was?" Nick's mam said.

"It doesn't leave owt to the imagination, does it?" Irene added.

"Whey that's disgraceful," Nick's mam said. "To think ye could make a record like that for iverybody to hear, it's not right."

Nick sat in silence, enjoying their indignation.

"It's the young folk that are buyin' it," his Uncle Ray said.

"It's disgustin' to think what they can get away wi' noowadays," Nick's mam added.

"Ah telt ye ye wouldn't believe ya ears," Dot said sitting down.

"An' ah hope ah nivah hear nowt like it ivah again," Nick's dad said. To Eric he added: "Ye want ya heed examined, wastin' good money on rubbish like that."

Eric shrugged. "He's deein' a tour owa here soon. Ah'm ganna see him when he comes to the toon."

"Eric ah'm surprised at ye," Nick's mam said. "Ah thowt ye knew better than that."

They had no idea, Nick thought. The more they complained about it the more kids liked it. For the first time in history teenagers didn't want to be like grown-ups. They didn't want to act or dress older than they were. They wanted to be young and to have their own style, their own music, their own hairstyles, their own language. He looked up at the half grandfather clock on the wall and willed the hands to move faster. Out of nowhere, Irene announced: "Me an' Lennie are goin' to Gozo fo' wa holidays."

"Gozo?" Nick's mam said.

"Aye, Gozo," Irene repeated.

"Where's Gozo?"

"It's one o' the Greek islands."

"Hoo do ye get to Gozo?"

"Wa goin' on an aeroplane."

"Ye hae to go on an aeroplane?"

"Aye."

"So ye hae to fly?"

"Aye, we'll be flyin'."

Nick's mam turned to his father. "De ye knah?"

"Div ah knah what?"

"De ye knah Gozo?"

"So-so."

She nudged him impatiently. "Are ye ganna tell wi or not clivalugs?"

"Oh, is that what ye want to knah," Nick's dad said, laughing.

"So…where's Gozo?"

"It's next door to Malta."

"See," Irene added. "Ah said it was one o' the Greek islands."

"Hoo did ye come to choose Gozo?" Nick's mam asked.

"Wi wanted to go somewhere there was plenty o' sunshine," Irene said.

"When are ye goin'?"

"In August, fo' wa summah holidays."

"Tha's plenty of sunshine here in August," her dad said.

"Aye but it's not the same," Irene said.

"Why's it not the same?" Ray asked.

"Because it's in Gozo," Irene answered.

Ray squinted but said nothing more.

"Ye've been to Malta haven't ye, Jimmy?" Nick's mam said. "Durin' the war ye were in Malta?"

"Must hae been there at least a dozen times," he answered. "Nowt much to look at. Mind, it was bombed ahll to hell when ah was there. They couldn't dee much damage though, it's nowt but sand an' stones."

"But ye haven't been to Gozo," Irene said.

"No, ah haven't been to Gozo," he conceded. "But from what ah could tell it wasn't any different to Malta, except smahller."

"Hoo much smahller?"

"A lot smahller."

They lapsed into silence.

"It has te be big enough te have an airport," Irene said.

"Ye'd think so," Nick's dad answered.

"It must have an airport," Irene added. "Wa goin' on an aeroplane."

"It probably does noo."

"Ye mean it didn't back then?"

"No, not as far as ah knah."

Irene looked worried. "What if it doesn't have an airport? Hoo would wi get there?"

"Tha's an airport on Malta."

"But that's not Gozo," Irene said. "Hoo would wi get to Gozo?"

He shrugged. "On a boat."

"On a boat?"

"Aye, on a boat."

"What kinda boat?"

Nick's dad grinned. "The slow boat to Gozo."

*   *   *

The first Saturday in June Nick was awakened early by the sound of bagpipes. He opened the bedroom window and across the back fields saw a highland pipe band turning off Netherton Lane onto the graveled area behind the public toilets. Excited, he hurried downstairs to find his mother in the kitchen on her knees in front of the oven.

"Tha's a load o' kilties doon at the netties," he said.

"They'll be goin' to the miner's picnic," she said off-handedly. She had the oven racks on a sheet of newspaper on the floor beside a bucket of scummy grey water and was scrubbing the inside of the oven with a Brillo pad.

"What miner's picnic?"

"The Northumberland Miners Picnic," she said. "Tha's bands an' shows an' they'll be havin' speeches at the picnic grunds doon Bedlin'ton Bank. That's where ya fatha's ganna be ahll day, directin' traffic."

"The shows are here?" Nick said. Shows meant the Waltzer, shuggy boats, the ghost train, crowds and loud music.

"Aye, tha doon Millfield this year, ah think. Did ye not know?"

How was he supposed to know? His parents rarely told him anything.

"Are wi not goin'?"

"Ah'm not goin', not wi' ya dad workin' ahll day," she said without looking up. "It's more for the miners an' the unions anyway, ahll them that support the Labour Party."

The shows weren't just for the miners, Nick thought, the shows were for everybody.

"Can ah go?"

"Ah haven't any money te gi' ye," she said.

Nick didn't care, he'd saved a few bob of his own. He washed and dressed and flew across the fields to where a crowd of kids had gathered around the pipers. There were 20 or so in dark green jackets with silver buttons, their kilts and sashes in the tartan of the Black Watch. They even had dirks tucked inside their tasseled stockings. They'd set their pipes and drums on the grass so they could have a smoke and pass whisky flasks around while they waited for the parade to start. However ordinary their everyday jobs might be their highland uniforms made them extraordinary. To Nick they might have just stepped off a picture screen.

The sound of a brass band playing 'Do Ye Ken John Peel' drew everyone's attention and Nick went out to the road with the other kids to see the Netherton Colliery Brass Band approaching, their lodge banner shimmering in the sunshine. When they came abreast of the toilet block they marked time till they finished then they too stopped for a smoke and a lavvy break. Looking up Ridge Terrace towards the Top End Nick saw other bands waiting for the parade to begin, each in their own maroon, blue or green jackets and matching caps. Over the next hour the parade was extended further by the arrival of private coaches with pit bands from Cowpen, Cramlington, Barrington and Bomarsund. The crowd of spectators grew and the excitement heightened as start time approached and parade stewards came down to make sure everybody was in their proper place. The pipers put out their tabs, rejoined the parade and pumped their bagpipes back to life. Soon afterwards the signal passed down the line and one band after another started up allowing enough space between them so as not to merge into a cacophonous blare.

Nick kept time with the kilties as they marched up Ridge Terrace past the cemetery and the new secondary modern school until he got to the Top End and the crowds were so dense he couldn't see them anymore. So he joined the kids who'd climbed onto the bus railings in front of The Red Lion for a better view. From there he could see all the way down to the Market Place; the road an undulating ribbon of flashing brass instruments and swaying lodge banners with thousands of spectators on either side. It was a spectacle unlike any he'd ever seen and all the more thrilling because it was happening in Bedlington where nothing exciting ever happened. There was a feeling that normal rules of behaviour had been suspended, banished with cars and buses for the day. Everybody seemed caught up in the same delirium, some of which was due to the pubs and clubs being open all day spilling beer fumes and merriment out onto the street. Everywhere he looked Nick saw faces he knew, all of them smiling, and for the first time in his life he felt a kind of kinship with the people of the town where he lived.

The parade stopped at the Market Place around lunchtime so everybody could have a break and the bands and beauty queens could be judged. The bandsmen dispersed into pubs on both sides of the street to quench the thirst that came from blowing into trumpets and tubas while marching under a broiling sun. Those who couldn't stand the crush indoors claimed a patch of grass in front of the war memorial or sat on walls and steps where they could loosen their tunics and enjoy a pint and a sandwich made by the ladies of the Women's Institute who'd turned the Village Infants School into a canteen for the day. The parade resumed in the early afternoon and the bands marched down Bedlington Bank to the picnic grounds by the River Blyth where union bosses and Labour Party leaders from London would address the crowd. Nick followed the parade to the top of Bedlington Bank where he saw his father keeping order at the crossroads but he went no further. Speeches weren't for him and he turned instead onto Millfield East and took the back way to the showgrounds.

He heard the shows before he could see them, rock 'n' roll music booming like cannon fire across the sky, fairground organs churning and girls screaming. When he turned into the long straight stretch of Millfield South Nick saw the gaudy ramparts of the showgrounds in the distance; swirls of colour, the golden turret of the Helter Skelter and the spinning crown of the chairoplanes. With every step it increased in size and volume until at last he crossed the threshhold from the urban drab into the raucously surreal. This time of day the crowd was nearly all kids. A paradise where they could run and yell and there was nobody to tell them to stop. Batteries of coloured lights rippled and flashed, the noise battered Nick's ears and resonated in his chest. He surrendered to the maelstrom and was carried along in the current: sideshows passed in a blur; coconut shies, slot machines, roll-a-penny games, air rifles that shot out clay pipes, goldfish in little plastic bags, bobbing clouds of candy floss,

All he'd spent was sixpence on a bag of chips at the Market Place chip shop, which left him with nearly three bob to spend at the shows. He went to the Helter Skelter first, paid his tuppence, picked up a stiff bristled doormat and climbed the wooden staircase inside the tower that smelled of wood and grass. When he reached the top he looked out over the panorama that radiated out from the showgrounds. In one direction hay fields and the tree tops of Humford Woods, in the other slate roof tiles shining like fish scales. In another direction he could see past Hartlands all the way to West Lea and pick out his house where his mother toiled, storing up resentment for another day. He lowered his gaze to the swarming showgrounds below and saw Spelk and Dave at the Ghost Train. He shouted to them but his words were lost in the din. He got onto his mat, launched himself down the slide and watched the scenery spin past in a dizzying spiral, faster and faster till he hurtled out the bottom in an exhilarating rush. Grinning, he threw the mat back onto the pile and ran over to where he'd seen his mates.

"Hey ye two, where've ye been?'

"Where've ye been is more like it," Dave said. "Wi went lookin' fo' ye this mornin' but ya mam said ye'd gone."

"Ah didn't knah it was picnic day till ah got up," Nick said. "Ah went to see the kilties an' ah wahked up to the Top End wi' them."

"Ye didn't knah it was picnic day?" Dave said disbelievingly.

"Honest, ah didn't," Nick said. "Ah musta forgot ahll aboot it."

"Hoo could ye forget somethin'…" Dave began but he was interrupted by Spelk.

"What rides hae ye been on?" he asked. "Hae ye been on the shuggy boats yet?"

"Ah haven't been on any," Nick said. Then, slightly embarrassed: "Ah was just on the Helter Skelter."

"The Helter Skelter?" Dave said scornfully. "That's fo' bairns."

"Ye hae to come on the shuggy boats," Spelk insisted.

"We've been on three times," Dave said. "He doesn't want to gan on owt else."

"Ye've got to come, it's amazin'," Spelk said and he took Nick's arm and pulled him along. Nick didn't mind, he liked the shuggy boats. They were one of the most popular rides at the shows; two barges that swung backwards and forwards in increasingly steep arcs until they stood on end. There were benches inside and rope nets on the sides but no restraints to keep riders from falling. The three boys joined the queue but when the waiting riders rushed forward Spelk hung back.

"Just hang on a mo'," he said. "Ah want to see which end is best."

Others brushed past them and Nick was afraid they would miss out on the best seats when Spelk yelled "this side" and elbowed his way onto the nearest barge. Most kids preferred to sit around the sides so they could hang onto the nets. The more daring kids stood on the bench at the back and looped their arms through the netting for even more of a thrill. Spelk, Dave and Nick pushed their way into a corner and threaded their arms through the netting so they could face the opposite end.

The barge started slowly but gathered momentum, climbing higher and higher until, at the top of each swing for just a moment, the three boys hung from the nets and looked directly down on the riders at the other end. Just when it seemed they would fall the barge swung back and they were at the bottom and the riders at the other end on top, until the barge again resumed its downward trajectory. That was when Nick realised what Spelk was looking for. At the opposite end of the barge was a clutch of screaming girls whose flared skirts and flouncy petticoats flew up over their heads with each downward rush. The girls had to use their hands to hang on, which meant they couldn't hold their skirts down. For a few seconds the view for Nick, Spelk and Dave was a kaleidoscope of legs, knickers, suspender belts and stocking tops.

"Looka that," Spelk shouted in triumph. "An avalanche o' tash!"

Nick was enthralled by the sight of so much unguarded female flesh and the response of his body startled him, a surge of heat that swelled his prick and filled it with an urgent need. It strained against the confinement of his underpants, searching for a way out, demanding to be set free. Embarrassed, he squirmed to find a position that would somehow ease and conceal its expansion. There was no mistaking what it was though he'd never felt anything like it before. It was sex. For the first time in his life he was in the grip of a sexual urge. He heard Spelk laugh beside him, saw his lewd grin and knew they were all in this together, stimulated by the same reflexive lust that came from seeing the girls with their skirts over their heads. And with it came the realization…*the girls knew.*

*   *   *

While Nick struggled with the implications of his first erection, a mile away at the Top End his father returned to the police station tired, footsore and thirsty. Waiting for him out front was Shep.

"It's time ye an' me had a little tahk," Shep said. "Ah'll see ye across the road." And he left without waiting for an answer.

Bright was annoyed. Shep wasn't his boss. He didn't have to do what Shep said, especially when he was off duty. But he wasn't surprised. He'd been interviewed by Detective Chief Superintendent Carroll the previous week and come away with the impression that things weren't going at all well for Shep.

Inside, the police station seethed with discontent. Extra officers had been brought in from surrounding towns to manage the crowds and protect the Labour Party luminaries but it was never enough and tempers were running short. Bert Fry and a couple of uniformed officers from Ashington manned the front counter as if it was a barricade, taking statements from those who'd been robbed, thumped or affronted. The cells were filled with drunks and every time the downstairs door swung open a chorus of profanity could be heard from below.

Bright signed out for the day, swapped his police tunic for a jacket and went over to the Top Club. It meant he'd get home later than he promised but he was already in the shit house with Pat so another hour wouldn't make much difference. He searched fruitlessly for Shep among the crowds until he caught the eye of the club secretary, Col Beatty, who sent him to the family quarters out the back. There he found Shep at the kitchen table chatting with Col's wife, Nora, on a smoke break. When Bright came in she put out her tab and got up to go.

"Ah hope ya not leavin' on mah accoont," Bright said.

"No, it's time ah got back to work, Jimmy," she said cheerfully. "Ah'll let ye two hae ya privacy." She paused at the door. "Ah'll send in a couple of pints - ye both drinkin' Fed?"

Bright thanked her and wondered how much Shep had told her and Col about why he wanted their kitchen for a private meeting. He sat down and lit up a Senior Service.

"Ye done fo' the night?" Shep asked.

"Soon as ah can get away," Bright said.

"It'll be the wrang side o' midnight afore ah get home," Shep said. If it was a plea for sympathy it was wasted on Bright. The only reason Shep would be up late was because he'd be drinking all night. The D.I. drained his glass and said: "Looks like we'll be goin' to trial in the final quarter sessions o' this year."

Bright was struck by the use of "we," as if Bright was as guilty as Shep for the assault on Peter McMahon.

"Is there nae chance of a negotiated settlement then?"

Shep grunted. "Mr. McMahon's idea of a negotiated settlement is to see me on the dole."

Bright grimaced. "Did Morpeth not make a coonter offer?"

"Ye want to knah what tha coonter offer was goin' to be?" Shep said. "If ah pleaded guilty ah could keep me job but they'd demote is back to constable. Uniform. Ah'd serve oot me time wahkin' a beat an' retire on a reduced pension. An' still nae guarantee that'd be enough for Mr. McMahon. He wants to tek me pension away, that's what he's after. Ah told them ah'm not havin' any of that. Ah'll pay fo' me own defence forst."

Bright drew heavily on his cigarette. It seemed nobody up at Morpeth thought Shep had much of a case. More than that, anybody who knew Shep had to be wary of how he'd perform on the stand under a determined cross-examination by the Crown Prosecutor. There had to be some concern that, pushed hard enough, Shep would lose his temper and the whole thing would blow up. It sounded like Morpeth was ready to throw Shep to the wolves - and Bright had no intention of going with him.

"Ye know you're in the wrong on this one, Shep," he said. "Ye clocked the bloke good an' proper, not once but twice, an' nae provocation either time."

Shep's eyes shaded. "Is that what ye told Carroll?"

Bright was about to respond when the kitchen door opened and Alf shuffled in with a couple of pints. They waited till he'd set the glasses down on the kitchen table and closed the door behind him.

Shep leaned forward and repeated his question. "Did ye tell Carroll ah hit McMahon wi'oot any provocation?"

"No, actually, it's not what ah telt Carroll at ahll - or Robson," Bright answered. "Ah telt both o' them ye acted in self defence. But the problem is ye an' ah know that's not true. An' the closer folk look at it the less plausible it seems to them an' ahll."

"He was workin' his ticket," Shep said disdainfully. "He was moothin' off to ye an' Evan and Alec. Bog Irish prick. Comes owa here an' meks a bit o' money an' thinks that entitles him to treat the rest o' wi like shite. Ah gave him what somebody should have given him a lang time ago - a smack in the gob. Teach him to mind his manners when he's talkin' to the polis."

"Aye an' look where it's got wi," Bright said.

Shep looked hard at Bright but then something in him wavered. He leaned back, turned defensive.

"Ah knah ah was oot o' order," he said. "Ah knah ah shouldn't hae clocked him the way ah did, but there was just somethin' aboot him that got right up mah nose. But Jesus Christ, Jimmy, the bastard wants to take me pension away. It's me whole life we're tahkin' about here an' that's not right neither."

Bright picked up his pint and took a sip.

"Hae they said wee'll be defendin' ye?"

"Morrie Pickering," Shep said. "He's the one wee's been tahkin' te Makepiece direct. He said right after the first phone call that negotiatin' this was goin' to get wi nowhere. They wanted me balls right from the get-go."

Bright knew of Morrie Pickering by reputation as a shrewd old barrister who handled the trickier cases for the Northumberland Police.

"So it's ahll or nothin' then," Bright said.

Shep nodded. "That's where we're at, ahll or nothin'."

Bright stayed silent for a long time then said: "Ye knah, ah've gone oot on a limb fo' ye aboot as far as ah can go wi' this, Shep."

Shep's demeanour changed again. "Ye what?" He seemed unable to believe what he'd heard. "Ye've gone oot on a limb as far as ye can go? We're talkin' about me whole life gannin' doon the drain here…me whole life."

In his mind Bright had gone through this conversation many times, he'd considered every angle and saw no way out without it getting nasty.

"Jesus Christ, Shep, ya askin' is to lie under oath."

"Ah'm askin' ye te dee nae mair than ye've done ahlready wi Carroll and Robson," Shep said. "Assumin' what ye just telt me is the truth - that ye telt them it was self-defence?"

"Ah did," Bright said. He felt the beer in his belly turn sour. "But it's different when ya on the stand in open court. It depends on the questions ah'm asked…the way tha asked."

"Ya not goin' to do yasel' any favours if ye tell a different bloody story on the stand to what ye telt Carroll and Robson," Shep said.

"Ah telt them McMahon was uncooperative," Bright said. "Ah telt them he put his hands up when ye approached him, which he did. Ah said he looked like he might be goin' to hit ye, or at least that's how it coulda been interpreted."

"Interpreted?" Shep repeated, his face reddening. "Fuckin' interpreted?"

"Ye didn't even knah he'd raised his hands till ah telt ye," Bright said, feeling his own temper rising. "It made nae difference, ye just hauled off an' planted him one anyway. An' tha was a good five minutes atween the forst teym ye hit him an' the second teym. Ah telt Carroll an' Robson tha was nae time at ahll. What do ye think the croon prosecutor's ganna dee wi' that after what McMahon's told him?"

"It's your word against McMahon's," Shep said. "It doesn't matter what anybody else thinks; Robson, Carroll, Browning, Makepiece, any o' them. All that matters is what the judge thinks. An' ye an' me will be tellin' the same story on the stand. That's two to one, Jimmy. Two to one. And both o' wi police officers."

Bright looked away. If it was bad now, how much worse would it be in open court with everybody scrutinising his every twitch and tic?

"Ah'm just not confident hoo it'll hold up in court, Shep," he said. "Ah don't feel reyt about it. Ye knah, ye got yasel' into this an' ah've done me best to get ye oot of it, mair than anybody else has been willin' to dee fo' ye, ah might say. Ah was hopin' it would nivah get to court, that it would be worked oot in negotiation. But it hasn't an' noo ye want is to put mah career at risk alang wi' yours."

Shep lunged across the table to grab hold of Bright, knocking over their pint glasses. Bright batted Shep's hand away, the glasses shattered on the kitchen floor spilling beer and broken glass in a widening puddle as the two men got to their feet. Bright took a step back from the kitchen table.

"Ye ungrateful bastard…" Shep said, hoarse with rage. A livid white spot appeared on each reddened cheek. "Ahll ah've done fo' ye an' the one teym ah need ye ya ready te hoy is owa the side like ah'm nowt."

Shocked, Bright said: "Look at what ya deein' man. Do ye not see what ya deein'?"

Shep hesitated but only for a moment.

"Ah got ye into the club," he said. "Ah vouched fo' ye. Ye think ye would hae just waltzed into Netherton Club if it wasn't for me? If ah hadn't put in a word with Ken Bossey? Ye think folk are bein' nice to ye because you're a canny bloke? Wee de ye think ya real friends are? Robson? Carroll? The Chief Constable? Ye think any o' them gives a shite aboot ye? Look hoo willin' they are to give me up an' ah've been wi' the force nigh on 40 year. That's longer than Browning fo' Christ's sake an' he thinks he deserves a fuckin' medal. Ah knah mair aboot police work than Cyril fuckin' Brownin' will ivah knah. It's polises like ye an' me wee dee the real work. We're the ones wee clean up other folks' shite. We're the ones wee put wa balls on the line ivery teym wi set foot ootside the front door. But make just one mistake, gi' some fuckin' ponce a smack in the gob an' it's ahll owa. No pension, no thank you, no nothin', just get oot the door an' don't come back. An' these are the people ye'd choose owa me? Is that right, Jimmy? These are the people ye'd choose owa me?"

Shep was breathing heavily. His eyes darted agitatedly around the kitchen. He seemed at a loss to know what to do next. He snatched up his trilby and started for the door then stopped and brandished the hat at Bright.

"Ye better decide wee ya real friends are, lad. That's ahll ah'm sayin'. An' ye better mek ya mind up soon."

He slammed the door after him and Bright looked at the broken glass and beer on the kitchen floor. Another mess Shep had left for somebody else to clean up.

*   *   *

That summer Nick learned he'd failed the 11-plus and would be going to the newly opened Westridge Secondary Modern School on Ridge Terrace. It was by no means the worst thing that could happen and much better than going to Guidepost, which was little more than a knocking shop for teddy boys and fifteen year old tarts. Westridge had playing fields, shiny new classrooms, a fully equipped gym, science labs, woodwork and metalwork shops, an assembly hall big enough for 600 pupils and a stage with a state-of-the-art sound and lighting system. It was also modeled on the grammar school system, which meant school uniforms and a second chance for the brighter kids who, instead of being thrown on the scrap heap at 15, would get an extra year and a crack at the GCE 'O' levels, just like the kids at grammar school. The school uniform was navy blue blazer with grey flannels for the boys, grey skirt for the girls, grey or white shirt and blue and grey striped tie. There was also a school badge with the motto, 'De Profundis,' which translated as 'Out of the Depths.'

As Mr. Hemming, the headmaster of the new school, explained, it had two meanings; one to reflect the process of bringing coal out of the depths of the earth, the other the process of bringing kids out of the depths of ignorance. It all came down to the same thing, some kids weren't good enough to go to grammar school but they were good enough to be given a second chance. All they had to do was survive the resentment of their schoolmates who weren't.

It was also the summer of the royal visit. The Queen was to spend a day in Northumberland and Nick's dad was one of several hundred police officers assigned to protect her. Except Bright would be doing more than crowd control. Among the places on the royal tour was Holy Island and Bright was to be one of two police officers assigned to the launch that would carry the Queen the three miles from the mainland to the island. The duty sounded grander than it was because all they had to do was stand in the back of the boat and make themselves useful if called upon. The Queen would be accompanied by an equerry and a lady-in-waiting as well as a Special Branch officer from Scotland Yard. The launch would be provided by the Royal National Lifeboat Institution and skippered by an RNLI coxswain and crewman from the RNLI Station at Seahouses. Bright was to report to police HQ at Morpeth by 6 a.m. the day of the royal visit and join a busload of officers due at Seahouses no later than 8 a.m. Her Royal Highness was not expected there until 11 a.m. and the two constables would remain on the launch until she had been delivered safely to Holy Island and back again. While Her Majesty was on the island she would tour Lindisfarne Monastery and have lunch at the castle. Most of Bright's day would be spent waiting for HRH to arrive and depart. He would be in the royal presence for all of 40 minutes, 20 minutes on the way to the island and 20 minutes on the way back. But when word of his royal escort duty got out the neighbours, royalists or not, couldn't contain their excitement.

The afternoon of the royal visit Nick's mam was called to the front door a dozen times by those who wanted to know if Bright was back yet. When he got home a little after six he barely had time to remove his collar and tie and pour himself a glass of brown ale before a crowd of neighbours were at the front door eager to know what it was like to be so close to the Queen. They packed themselves into the living room taking every seat and leaving half a dozen others standing.

Nick's mam had opened the doors and windows to let in some air but with no breeze and so many bodies packed into one room it was stifling. Bright's normally fresh complexion had turned scarlet, sweat beaded his brow and there was a damp crescent under each armpit. He sat on a straight backed dining chair, beer in one hand, tab in the other, and basked in the afterglow of Her Majesty's radiance. The neighbours peppered him with questions: What was she like? What did she wear? How did she act? Was she nice? Did she say anything to him? No morsel was too small to be snatched like crumbs from the royal table.

He told them she was smaller and prettier than she looked on television. She'd worn a peach coloured dress with matching, broad brimmed hat, white elbow length gloves and a pearl necklace with matching pearl ear rings and she was nice to everybody.

"She said thank ye to ahll o' wi on the way there an' when wi got back she shook hands wi' ahll o' wi afore she got off the boat."

"Ye shook hands with ah?" marvelled Mrs. Oliver. "Ye touched the Queen?"

"Aye, in a manner o' speakin'," he said. "She wore gloves the whole time an' so did we. Wi were telt not to speak to ah unless she spoke to us forst an' we waren't te touch ah under any corcumstances unless she offered ah hand forst. Even then it wasn't a real handshake, nae more than a touch really."

"It makes sense," Jean Gordon said. "Ahll the people she meets, acourse she has to keep ah gloves on."

"Aye, she wouldn't want to get any jorms from touchin' the great unwashed," Joe Gordon said, grinning.

"Just imagine ahll the folk she shakes hands wi' on an average day," Brian Boyle's mam said. "If she didn't wear gloves ah hand would be droppin' off."

"Is she really bonny then, when ye see ah close up, like?" Mrs. Leese asked.

"Oh, she's a bonny lass ahlreet," Bright said, taking a drink from his glass. "She has the most beautiful skin ye've ever seen. Flawless, porfect skin. An English rose she is, a real English rose."

"An English rose," Mrs. Oliver repeated reverentially.

"Did she speak to ye directly, Jimmy?" Jean Gordon asked.

"No, not really, except to say thank you when she got off at the end."

"Did she look at ye when she spoke to ye?" Mary Beecroft's mam asked. "Did she look ye in the eye?"

"She did," he said. "When she shook me hand she looked right at is. She said 'thank you, constable' te me an' te the lad from Haltwistle. She said 'thank you' to the skipper an' his mate an' ahll. She didn't forget anybody."

"Hoo did it mek ye feel when she looked at ye?" Mrs. Leese asked.

He paused. "It's a hard thing te describe, really. She's a real porson an' ahll that but it's like ya in the presence o' livin' history an' fo' just that time when ya wi' ah it's like ya part o' history yasel."

"Were ye nervous at ahll?" Mrs. Beecroft asked.

"Not really," he said. "Ah was there deein' me job, an' in a situation like that, any special occasion really, ya just tryin' not to bugga up your end o' things."

"Aye, if it was a bit choppy he'd be tryin' not to spew ahll owa her," Joe Gordon said.

"Divvent ye be so stupid," Jean said with a slap at his shoulder. "He was in the Royal Navy."

"What's ah voice like?" Mrs. Leese asked. "Hoo does she tahk really?"

"Weel, she's var' posh o' course," Bright answered. "But she doesn't have a strong voice so ah didn't hear iverythin' she said because o' the wind."

"Ah so the Queen has wind an' ahll," Joe Gordon said.

"She was very natural is what ah'm sayin'," Bright continued. "Ah think she genuinely wanted to put everybody at tha ease. An' she looked like she was enjoyin' horsel' just bein' oot on the wettah fo' a few minutes."

"The common touch," Mrs. Oliver said. "Her uncle, King Edward, had the common touch. Some have it, some don't."

"Aye but ye nivah forgot fo' a minute wee she was," Bright added. "Ye never forgot wee ye were wi'."

"Well of course, how could ye?" Mrs. Leese added. "She's the Queen."

"Ahll telt ah'd hae to say ah was var' impressed. If she wasn't wee she is ye'd still hae to say she's a var' nice lass."

They seemed pleased by Bright's account, as if relieved that some of their most cherished beliefs had been preserved.

"Mind there was one thing ah didn't expect," he added.

They waited.

"Ye knah hoo ah said she's var' smahll an' delicate like?"

"Aye, is she really that smahll, Jimmy?" Mrs. Leese asked.

"Oh she's tiny, not much owa five feet," he said. "But what ah wasn't expectin' was that she'd be sae top heavy."

"Top heavy?" Mrs. Leese repeated. "What do ye mean, top heavy?"

"Ye knah…" Bright said with a smirk.

"Ye mean, like…" Mrs. Beecroft started.

"Aye, fo' ah size she's got a really smashin' pair o' tits on ah," he said.

And he tipped his big red head back and laughed.

*   *   *

It was Tommy Locke's habit on a Friday night, after he closed down the Doctor Pit transport depot for the weekend, to have a drink with his drivers in the depot office. A dozen or so NCB lorries delivered coal to customers around the shire and when the last lorry was parked inside the compound he padlocked the gates, collected the keys and locked them in a box on the office wall. Most of the drivers were keen to collect their pay and get off home or to the pub but there were always a few who stayed to have a drink with the boss. Locke, a swarthy man with a bit of the gypsy about him, had a club foot, which kept him on the home front during the war. He was promoted from driver to foreman when his predecessor was called up and sent to Singapore from where he never returned. Since then Locke had built up a profitable sideline as a local agent for Sammy Truscott, the bookie in Newcastle. It was easy for Locke's drivers to collect bets and drop off winnings while making deliveries, though not all of them wanted to run bets and he didn't hold it against them. But a runner like Danny Mullen was worth half a dozen other runners. Danny had the larcenous pedigree of the Mullens in him. He'd been a driver for three years and in that time he'd added more than a hundred new punters to Tommy's book. The eldest of the Mullen lads Danny had the gift of the gab and was known to have charmed more than one housewife out of her knickers while picking up bets. Shep had warned Locke not to get close to the Mullens because it would end badly, as it did for most who had any doings with them. But Danny had given Tommy no trouble and his take had gone up 20 percent while Danny had been working for him.

Locke kept a crate of brown ale in the bottom of a clothes cupboard behind his desk along with a couple of bottles of Black And White whisky. In a corner next to the lavatory was a sink with a single cold water tap and a counter with a gas burner that Locke used to boil the kettle for his tea. Above the counter was a shelf with an assortment of cups and glasses. A few battered chairs, a time clock and a few pin-ups on the wall completed the décor. Locke pulled out the crate of brown ale, set the glasses and a whisky bottle on his desk and let his drivers help themselves. Four of them stayed behind this Friday night and one of them was Danny. As usual he did much of the talking, drawing on an unlimited store of dirty jokes to keep everybody laughing. Leaning his chair back on two legs, shirt sleeves rolled high on his muscular arms, the curls of his reddish blonde hair bobbing with every laugh it was easy to see why women liked him.

Most of the drivers stayed for only one drink but this Friday night Danny lingered till the others had gone. When there were just the two of them left he told Locke he needed a favour.

"Ah want to borrow a lorry for the weekend," he said.

Locke tapped his cigarette into an old tobacco tin he used for an ashtray. Letting a driver take a lorry for the weekend was something he did occasionally but only when he could justify it to himself and management.

"Fo' this weekend?"

"Aye, fo' the morrow neyt."

"The morrow neyt?" Locke repeated. "That's a bit short notice de ye not think? What are ye deein' that ye need a lorry for on a Saturday night…or should ah not ask?"

"It meyt be better if'n ye didn't ask," Danny grinned.

Locke grunted. "Ye've got mair narve than a canal horse, Danny, ah'll gi' ye that."

"Ah can pay ye," Danny added.

"Hoo much?"

"Ten pund."

"Ten pund…fo' one night?" Locke snorted. It was more than half his weekly pay. "It's nowt legal then?"

Mullen's grin broadened. "It's not really illegal though."

"Not really," Locke echoed. "Just remember wee ya tahkin' tee here an' divvent try an' sell is a load o' shite."

"If ye want te knah the truth, that's exactly what ah'm sellin'."

"Are ye tryin' te be funny?"

"No, ah'm not," Mullen protested good naturedly. "Ah need a lorry te deliver a load o' sheep shite to blokes wee'll pay good money for it."

"Sheep shite?"

"Aye, tha's tons o' sheep shite up aroond the Cheviots. If ah can get a lorry load tha's blokes doon here ah can sell it tee fo' tha gardens. By mah calculation if ah can sell it at ten bob a hundredweight ah can mek fifty pund a lorry load."

"Fifty pund?" It was enough to give Locke pause. "Not bad if ye divvent mind shullin' shite ahll night, ah suppose."

"Ah'll tek me younger brutha, Stephen, wi's. He wants te mek some money fo' hissel' an' he's a good worker. Ah've got blokes wee'll buy it ahlreet. They cannit get it themsel's 'cos they divvent hae the transport so they'll pay to hae it delivered to tha front door. Ye knah the demand aroond here among leek growers for good manure when ye can get it."

Locke knew, though he wasn't a leek grower himself.

"Ye'll be tresspassin' on farmers' land then?"

"The moors are oppin to iverybody, Tommy. Ye can wander ahll owa an' naebody'll bother ye. Blokes gan up there ahll the time to collect sheep dottles fo' thasels. Ahll ah'm deein' is collectin' a bit mair than most. It's not like anybody else wants it."

"Ye think ye can shul two or three ton in one night?"

"It's not as bad as shullin' coal an' ah can shul a ton o' coal in less than an ooah. Wi' Stephen te help is ah'm thinkin' wi can be done in two or three ooahs. Nae bugga'll even knah wi were there, man. Ah'll be back in Bedlin'ton an' have it delivered afore the sun comes up."

"Aye an' ye can tek half an ooah to hose oot the lorry afore ye bring it back here an' ahll," Locke said.

"Does that mean ah can hae one?" Mullen brightened.

"Ye can *borrow* one," Locke said. "Ah'll tek a fiver fo' the use o' the lorry. If'n ye an' ya brutha are willin' to spend ya Saturday night shullin' sheep shite an' deliverin' it ahll owa Bedlin'ton ye desorve ivery penny ye can get. Just ye mind ye hae it back heeyah nice an' orly Sunday mornin'. An' if'n ye get stopped by the polis ah'll say ye took it wi'oot permission. Ye'll be on ya own, ye knah that?"

"Tommy," Mullen beamed. "Naebody'll knah a thing."

*   *   *

Summer that year ended with Brian Boyle crossing the Mullens as only he could. Like many lads who left school to work down the pit, as soon as he turned 16 he bought a motorbike on the never never. Despite his past behaviour it seemed not to occur to his mam and dad that Brian getting a motorbike might be a bad idea. The first house he stopped at on the way home to show off the new bike was the Mullens and it was the last friendly moment he would have with them.

Among the Mullens' many dogs was a silver grey Alsatian by the name of Rolf who liked to chase cars and motorbikes. It was a nuisance most drivers were prepared to put up with rather than anger the Mullens. The remedy was to slow down till Rolf tired of the chase and trotted back home. This course of action seemed not to have entered Brian's mind. The first few times Rolf came after him Brian tried to kick him which only provoked Rolf into biting him. This duel might have continued indefinitely had not Boyle decided it was his responsibility to cure Rolf once and for all.

The next time Rolf came after him Brian stopped the bike, took a clothesline out of a saddlebag, tied one end to Rolf's collar and the other end to the back of the bike. He remounted the bike and started off around the grassy oval in the middle of the estate pulling Rolf after him. Because it was a Saturday morning there were plenty of witnesses to what happened. For a few seconds Rolf had no idea what trouble he was in and kept up with the bike easily, barking and snapping as usual. At 10 miles an hour the rope even slackened a bit as he gained on Brian but when Brian accelerated to 20 miles an hour the rope tightened and Rolf suddenly looked about as worried as a dog could look. Brian rounded the next corner and started up the straight to the top of the oval with Rolf no longer barking and snapping but trying to keep up with the bike. When Brian looked over his shoulder and saw Rolf running flat out just to keep up he laughed. When he hit 30 miles an hour and Rolf went down in a flurry of yelps he laughed all the more. He stopped to let Rolf get back on his feet then started again. Some of the neighbours yelled at Brian as he went past but through the roar of the bike and his own laughter he seemed not to hear. By the time he rounded the top corner of the oval there was a shared foreboding among those who'd stopped to watch, a sense that something awful was imminent. Danny Mullen was the first to reach Brian and those who saw it said it was like something you only saw at the pictures. Dashing across the oval in bare feet Danny closed the distance between himself and Brian like a heat seeking missile. When Brian saw Danny he stood up on the bike's footrests, a broad grin on his face, as if inviting Danny to join in the fun. Danny leaped at him from several feet away and hit him in the chest with both feet. Brian somersaulted backwards off the bike and landed on the road with a loud "Ooof" as all the wind was knocked out of him. His bike swerved and crashed onto its side and Rolf stopped a few feet away, panting. Before Brian could move Danny was on him, punching and kicking him. Then the rest of the Mullens joined in, including Paddy and his wife, Brigid. And they would have continued punching and kicking Brian till there was nothing left but a stain on the road had it not been for the intervention of Mr. Leese and some of the other neighbours who were afraid for Brian's life. The Mullens stopped grudgingly, collected Rolf and went home.

While Brian lay in bed at Ashington General recovering from his injuries he was charged with reckless operation of a motorcycle, disturbing the peace and cruelty to an animal. And folk had to admit it all worked out well, because Brian never tormented a dog again and Rolf never chased another car or motorbike.

*　　　*　　　*

The moment Nick set foot in Westridge he was caught up in the excitement of the new. The school was new, the furniture was new, the uniforms were new and, for the most part, the faces were new. On the first day pupils were required to take an aptitude test and on the second day they were assigned to their new classes based on the results of the test. In the gleaming new assembly hall there were three rows of tables. One row was labeled Junior Remove, Second Remove, Third Remove, Fourth Remove and Fifth Remove, one row was labeled 1B, 2B, 3B and 4B and another row was labeled 1C, 2C, 3C and 4C. There was no 5B or 5C. Junior Remove meant Nick had qualified for the school's A-stream, which would get much the same level of tuition as the kids who'd gone to grammar school. He would be part of the school's five year programme that would take him to the GCE 'O' levels. Without 'O' levels in at least three or four subjects there was no hope of getting a decent job or moving on to higher education. And without being in the Remove stream there wasn't much hope of anything. Nick was glad Spelk made it into Junior Remove but Dave, who knew the words to any rock 'n' roll song after hearing it twice, was sent to 1C because he couldn't read those same words or write them down on paper. The difference between the three streams was apparent to everyone; the A-stream kids would get a second chance to make something of themselves while the rest could resign themselves to jobs as miners, factory workers and shop assistants. And the term 'Remove' was applied literally: the A-stream kids were removed from the rest of the school population. Except in the school yard where they were thrown into the general melee with kids who now had reason to dislike them. At the school's first general assembly Mr. Hemming gave an address in which he promised every pupil a new start, which prompted sniggers among those who knew it didn't apply to them.

At Junior Remove's first class Nick was relieved to see a dozen kids he knew from Whitley Memorial though the rest were strangers. In all there were 42 pupils in Junior Remove and their form teacher was Miss Wilkinson, a beefy but skilfully upholstered redhead who clopped around the room like a Clydesdale in high heels. Text books and exercise books were crisp and clean and desks smelled of fresh milled wood. But not for long. By the end of the week initials had been carved into most desks and wads of gum stuck to the undersides where they hardened into cement nipples that had to be removed with a chisel. In the schoolyard the pecking order was what it had always been; the bad lads ruled and the rest tried to keep out of their way. Whatever grand ideals may have been instilled in the classroom were trampled underfoot in the schoolyard. It was familiar terrain; academic success was a sign of weakness, hardness was a virtue. Behind the sparkling façade of the new, life settled quickly into harsh and familiar rhythms.

The Saturday after the first week of school Nick went over to see Spelk and found his dad sitting on the back step smoking and enjoying the morning sun. He had a bucketful of live crabs at his feet and seemed not to notice Nick but without looking up he said: "Ye lookin' fo' John are ye?"

"Aye, is he in?"

"He's doon the street wi's mam. He'll be back later the day."

Nick turned to leave when Mr. Gordon said: "Ye want to see somethin' funny?"

Nick looked into the bucket thinking he might be missing something but all he could see was a bucketful of crabs.

Mr. Gordon said: "Ah've been watchin' them noo fo' the best part of an ooah an' they dee the same thing owa an' owa again."

Slick and stony grey with streaks of amber the crabs scrabbled against each other in the bottom of the bucket.

"Aye," Nick said.

"Ye see that one on the top noo," Mr. Gordon gestured with his cigarette. "He's a detormined little bugga that one. Ah've watched him fight his way owa the others to get to the top at least a dozen times an' he nivah meks it oot but he keeps tryin', again an' again an' again."

Nick saw the crab Mr. Gordon meant, scraping the sheer metal sides of the bucket with its claws as it stretched upward to the rim.

Mr. Gordon sdaid: "Ye see they ahll want oot but the only way they can get oot is by climbin' owa each other and stannin' on the ones in the bottom so they can get high enough to reach the top. But each time one's just aboot to mek it oot the other ones pull him back doon."

Nick watched the topmost crab stretch up on its spindly legs and extend its claw almost to the top of the bucket. Just as it seemed about to hook onto the rim another crab came in from the side, pulled it down and scrambled to take its place.

"It nivah fails," Mr. Gordon said. "Ivery one o' them wants oot but they cannit work togitha so whenever one gets to the top the others keep pullin' him back doon. If any one o' them got owa the top ah'd tek him back to Newbiggin an hoy him back in the sea but in ahll the years ah've been crabbin' ah've nivah seen it yet." He smiled up at Nick. "Funny that, isn't it?"

*   *   *

The second Thursday in September Bright left work early to pull his leeks for the Netherton show. He eased them gently out of the ground, rinsed them, patted them dry and set them on a tea towel on the passenger seat of the Standard Eight for the drive to Netherton Club. He had a single pot leek as broad as his handspan with a flawless blanch and spotless flags he was sure would get him into the top hundred this year. And for the first time he was entering a stand of long leeks, identical twins that would establish him as a serious grower. At the club he parked the car, tucked his leeks under one arm and went inside thinking after he'd signed in he might have a pint with Ken Bossey.

The queue for entrants stretched from inside the main hall out into the corridor as far as the bar but Bright didn't mind waiting. There was a festive mood and he enjoyed a bit of back and forth with the other growers that made him feel like he belonged. Once he'd signed in, paid the entry fee and got his number cards he took his leeks to a receiving table and set them down with the others, making sure they were clearly identified. After almost nine months getting them to this point he was hesitant to leave knowing all it would take to spoil his chances was somebody to handle them a little too roughly out of carelessness or spite. He fussed with them, primped the flags and fanned out the beards to best effect before he was able to pull himself away. He took a stroll around the hall to see how the competition looked and came away feeling that mebbe he was right, mebbe this was his year. With Ken Bossey nowhere to be seen Bright stopped by the club secretary's office and asked Doreen if her boss had time for a pint. Doreen tapped on Bossey's door and opened it just wide enough to poke her head in so Bright couldn't hear what was said. Whatever it was it was brief. She closed the door and with an apologetic smile said Bossey was too busy to get away but would try to catch up with Bright over the weekend. Bright nodded, surprised. Bossey always had time to have a drink with him or at least to chat with him, however briefly. He paused on his way past the bar but there was no-one else he wanted to drink with and he didn't feel like drinking alone.

The night of the show he went back with his mate, Evan, both of them in civvies. They got a couple of pints at the bar and made their way to the main hall. Once again the hall had been transformed into its annual homage to the leek; emerald and platinum totems laid out for worship, the altar of the stage piled high with prizes. Bright searched the rows of display tables for his leeks but found none that matched his entry numbers. He made a second circuit of the hall examining the different categories more closely this time but still not finding his leeks.

"Tha's somethin' not right heeyah," he said to Evan.

He went looking for someone who could explain what had happened and found Ted Price from the leek show committee.

"Ah've taken a good look roond an' ah cannit find me leeks anywhere," Bright told Price. "Ah knah tha here somewhere cos ah signed them in mesel' yesterday."

Price looked unhelpfully back at him. "If ye don't see your leeks in heeyah it means they worn't accepted fo' show, Jimmy."

Bright shook his head. "That cannit be right. Tha was nowt wrang wi' them, tha the best leeks ah've ivah entered."

Price shrugged. "Tha's one way to find oot. The rejects go in the storage room for tha owners to pick up after. If ya leeks are in there, there's ya answer."

Price took Bright and Thompson to the storage room between the kitchen and the cellar and closed the door behind them, shutting off the din outside. There in the harshly lit coolness Bright found his leeks on a shelf second from the bottom along with their numbered cards. Puzzled, he looked around the other rejects stacked from floor to ceiling, some clearly undersized, some with obvious flaws like bent or broken flags. He picked up his single pot leek, turned it in his hands and found a thumbnail sized indent halfway up the barrel.

"That wasn't there when ah dropped it off yesterday," he said. "Some bugga's damaged it, that's why it's nae good noo."

Price met Bright's gaze. "Ah divvent knah owt aboot that, Jimmy," he said. "Ah'm sorry, ah divvent knah what else to tell ye. Ya not the forst to get upset when somethin' like this happens."

"Upset?" Bright repeated. "Aye, ye might say ah'm upset." He handed the spoiled leek to Evan and picked up the remaining pair, one in each hand. "Look at them, tha's nowt wrang wi' them two. Noo look at the other leeks in heeyah an' ye tell me…tha's nae comparison. Ye can tell by just lookin' at them, it's that obvious."

Price hesitated before answering. "Ah divvent hae owt to dee wi' selection, Jimmy. Naebody on the committee has any part o' the selection or the judgin'. Wi just organise the show. Ah cannit tell ye why ya leeks worn't accepted. Ya entitled to ya entry fee back an' if ye like ye can lodge a complaint wi' the committee and we'll tek it up fo' ye."

Bright struggled to keep his temper. He nodded once, short and sharp. "Ahlreet, ah think ah knah what's gannin' on here."

Without another word to he took his leeks and stepped back out into the corridor, Evan behind him. He worked his way through the crowd knowing there was nothing more he could do without making a fool of himself. On the way out he glimpsed Ken Bossey standing at the bar amidst a crowd of drinkers. He thought Bossey saw him too but the club secretary turned away before Bright could catch his eye.

* * *

The worst thing about her moods was that they came on without any warning. There was no obvious cause, just a shift in her meteorology, a spike or a slump in the flow of hormones, a chemical imbalance in the brain and she would go off on a tangent that made no sense to anyone but her. She should have been in a good mood. It was a Friday night, the end of the work week, Nick's dad was home for tea and she'd stopped at the fishmongers on the way home to buy him a treat for dinner, Craster kippers. She had plenty of reason to be happy, but she wasn't. Soon after they sat down to eat at the kitchen table she started on Nick.

"Nicholas doesn't love is anymore," she said to his dad. "Isn't that right, Nicholas?" She smiled at him. "Ye don't love ya mother anymore."

It was true that he didn't like her touching him but he didn't think it should come as a surprise to her.

"He won't say so but he loves ye more than he loves me," she told his dad. To Nick she added: "Isn't that true, Nicholas? Ye love ya dad more than ye love ya mutha?"

Nick wouldn't be drawn.

"It's only cupboard love, though, isn't it?" she continued. "Ye love whichever one o' wi gi's ye the most, don't ye?" She turned back to Bright. "He loves money, ye knah, wor Nicholas. He loves money more than he loves either one o' us."

Nick eyed his father across the table working on his kippers. Were other families like this when nobody was there to see them, he wondered?

"He loves ye more than he loves me but ah bet if ah offer him money ah can get him to say he loves me more," she added. "Won't ye, Nicholas? Ah'll gi' ye haff a dollar if ye say ye love me more than ye love ya dad."

Only two and six, Nick thought. She'd have to do better than that.

"Ah'll gi' ye five shillin'," she said. "Ah'll gi ye five shillin' if ye say ye love me more than ya dad."

Nick had to stifle a laugh and the effort made his face redden.

"See, he's gettin' mad," his mam said triumphantly. "He wants the money. Don't ye, Nicholas, ye want the money? But ye don't want to prove is right either de ye? Ah tell ye what, ah'll mek it ten shillin'." She picked up her purse, took out a ten shilling note and put it in the middle of the table. "There ye are, Nicholas, ten shillin'. An' ahll ye hae to dee is say ye love me more than ye love ya dad."

Nick wondered what his father would do if he took it. Whether there'd be any reaction at all.

She leaned down trying to see into Nick's eyes. "Go on, tek it, Nicholas, ah know ye want to. Ahll ye hae te dee is say ye love me more than ye love ya dad."

He was nearly finished, just a few more mouthfuls.

"Ahlright then…" She put the 10 shilling note back in her purse and Nick felt a pang of regret.

"Ah'll gi' ye a pund," she said.

She spread a one pound note on the table between them, flattening it with her hands. Nick eyed the elegantly filigreed banknote with its picture of Britannia on her island throne. A whole pound. It would be so easy to reach out and take it, he really didn't care what she thought anymore.

"There ye are," his mam said. "Just say ye love me more than ye love ya dad an' ye can have it."

"Pat, that's enough," Nick's dad said.

It was as if she hadn't heard.

"This is ya last chance, Nicholas," she said. "Ye can hae that pund note if ye say ye love me more than ye love ya dad."

Nick put the last forkful in his mouth and got up from the table. "Ah'm finished," he said. He scraped the skin and bones into the bucket by the back door, put his plate in the sink and left to go up to his room. His mother smiled as she watched him leave and put the pound note back in her purse. She turned her attention to her husband.

"Is that good, hinny?"

Nick repeated his father's words to her as he went upstairs. 'Pat, that's enough.' What a joke. They had no idea, the two of them. No idea.

*   *   *

Christmas lights daubed the cold wet streets of Newcastle with a watery patina of colour when Shep's assault case went to trial the first week of December. On the quayside a blustery wind flecked the River Tyne with spume making Bright glad of his police greatcoat as he climbed the front steps of Moot Hall. The mood of the group from Bedlington was as bleak as the weather. Bright had come in the Wolseley with John Robson, Evan Thompson and Alec Newell. Shep had driven himself, his wife, Audrey, and their eldest daughter, Beryl. It wasn't yet nine-o-clock and the Assizes wouldn't start till 10 but Shep's barrister, Morrie Pickering, had told them to be there early. There were four courts in session and Shep's case was first on the docket in Courtroom 4 at the furthest end of Moot Hall.

In the preceding months Bright had been interviewed twice by Pickering and each time the old warhorse had reminded him of the importance of his testimony. Not that Bright needed reminding. Ever since his confrontation with Shep at the Top Club the relationship between the two of them had been strained. Shep believed his judgement was superior to that of any judge or jury. Police work was never as neat and tidy as the courts tried to make it. Messy situations arose all the time for which the rarefied climes of the courtroom had no answer. If the role of the police was to keep order, without which there could be no law, then keeping order came down to the judgement of the polis at the scene. And sometimes that meant somebody had to get a smack in the gob. Picking apart that decision in a courtroom months later, far removed from the excitations of the moment, was more often than not a parody of the truth. Except this time everybody but Shep believed he'd gone too far. Under pressure from all sides Bright had thought hard about his obligation to Shep and decided it was his duty to do what was right, no matter what the cost.

In the central lobby at Moot Hall pinched white faces rode on waves of winter woollies and the air was thick with cigarette smoke. Corridors in both wings were thronged with barristers, policemen, witnesses and defendants whose wives, husbands, mothers and fathers had come to show their support. But there was little noise, only the murmur of conversation conducted in the same muted tones heard outside an intensive care ward. The same principle applied; lives were broken, some would get another chance, some had used up all their chances.

Bright, Robson, Thompson and Newell made their way to Courtroom 4 where they found Shep and Pickering huddled in conference on a bench outside the closed courtroom doors. Shep wore the same brown raincoat he always wore, hat clutched in his big red paw. Audrey and Shep's daughter, Beryl, sat nearby. Beryl had come up from Darlington to support her mother more than her father. Bright caught Audrey's eye but she looked right through him. Pickering, a twig of a man with a cascade of lizard scales under each eye, was robed, wigged and ready for battle. With him was his legal assistant, a slight young man who needed both arms to hold Pickering's leather satchel. Similar tableaus were to be seen up and down the corridor. Moot Hall offered little privacy and last minute dramas were enacted for all to see.

The four police officers from Bedlington passed the time with the same awkward small talk they'd made during the drive from Bedlington. Bright scanned the crowd for McMahon but didn't see him. A couple of months earlier McMahon had pleaded guilty at Bedlington Magistrates Court to refusing to take a sobriety test and not guilty to driving while intoxicated. Bright, Thompson and Newell gave evidence against him. Chief Magistrate Phyllis Ritchie fined him 20 pounds for refusing to take the sobriety test, found him guilty on the drunk driving charge and fined him 40 pounds, suspended his licence for six months and lectured him on the evils of drink. A third charge of causing injury while driving under the influence was dropped because Mickey Dodd escaped with bruises and a sprained ankle and the doctor who saw him wrote in his report that Dodd was "intoxicated and incoherent." Bright had since heard that McMahon was appealing his drunk driving conviction.

After a while Pickering and Shep concluded their discussion and Pickering got up to join the waiting officers while Shep slid along the bench to speak with his wife and daughter.

"We've got Quentin Bannister on the bench," Pickering said. "He can be difficult when he chooses. Depends on his mood when he got out of bed this morning. If his piles are acting up he could send Jack down for 20 years."

It was impossible to tell if Pickering was joking. But behind his droll manner was an agile mind and he not only knew the quirks of every judge on the northern circuit he knew the law better than most of them too. At 9.30 the courtroom doors opened and the waiting crowds shambled in. Shep got up, shrugged off his raincoat and gave it to Audrey to hold for him. Underneath, instead of his usual baggy olive suit, he wore a blue blazer and grey slacks with creases sharp enough to slice bread. His tie was the red and grey stripe of the Royal Northumberland Fusiliers and on his breast pocket was the regimental crest, which depicted St. George slaying the dragon, and the regimental motto 'Quo Fata Vocant.' But it was the starburst of colour above his breast pocket that captured every eye. Shep's left shoulder was ablaze with campaign medals, ribbons and battle honours he'd earned from North Africa to Italy, France and Germany. Most prominent among them was the Military Cross he'd earned for gallantry at Monte Cassino. He pulled himself up to his full height and accompanied Pickering into the courtroom to surrender himself to the bailiff. Audrey and Beryl followed and took their seats in the front row of the public gallery, Audrey clenching her husband's coat as if she needed it to keep warm. Robson, who'd come in civvies, waited till they were settled then took a seat in the public benches across the aisle and a few rows back. In the corridor Bright, Thompson and Newell took off their greatcoats and made themselves comfortable on the newly cleared benches to await their turn on the witness stand.

Inside the courtroom the bailiff escorted Shep to the dock, a rectangular booth raised above the well of the court and facing the judge's bench. The courtrooms had changed little since they were built in the 1850's - the only touch of modernity being the addition of electric lights - and were intended to convey all the majesty of the law. The ceilings were 20 feet high, the furniture and fittings baronial. The judicial bench reared up like the ramparts of a castle and behind the bench a throne-like chair thickly padded with red leather was inlaid with the royal coat of arms.

In the dock Shep sat with his considerable bulk tilted forward, the heels of his hands on his knees, like a sumo wrestler readying himself to charge. It was the first time he'd known the isolation of the dock and he didn't much care for it. His fate was in the hands of others who busied themselves around him with practiced indifference. In the floor of the dock was a closed trapdoor that opened onto a spiral iron staircase which led to the holding cells underneath where Shep would be taken if convicted. In the press gallery, high on one side of the court, he saw a couple of reporters with their notebooks ready. Whatever happened to him here today the world would know.

Outside Peter McMahon had arrived accompanied by his solicitor, Walter Makepiece, and his barrister, Geoffrey Jervis Q.C. None of them acknowledged the police contingent from Bedlington. McMahon, in a smartly tailored black overcoat, stood briefly in the open doorway and looked around the courtroom, his eyes settling on the back of Shep's creased red neck. He turned and spoke softly to Jervis and Makepiece but not so soft Bright couldn't hear him.

"That's what I've been waiting to see," McMahon said. "That big bastard right where he belongs."

They exchanged a few more words then Jervis went into the courtroom and sat in the public benches, leaving McMahon and Makepiece outside to be called as witnesses. There was no doubt in anyone's mind that if Shep was found guilty a civil suit against him and the Northumberland Police would follow. McMahon was slimmer than Bright remembered, his fair hair swept back from a tanned face that suggested a recent holiday far from the frozen twilight of the northeast. There were no facial scars that Bright could see and his nose had been restored to its proper shape. His overcoat was unbuttoned and revealed a lining of blue silk. Underneath he wore a grey pinstripe suit with a high collared shirt and a red paisley tie. His shirt cuffs were fastened with gold cuff links that sparkled in the fluorescent light. McMahon almost certainly came from Irish Protestant stock, Bright decided. Not that it mattered: Protestant or Catholic the Irish were a nuisance wherever they went.

A few minutes before ten the bailiff came out into the corridor with a clipboard, called out the name of each witness and told them to wait until they were summoned. After they had given evidence, he said, they could remain in the courtroom unless otherwise ordered. Moments later the doors closed, Mr. Justice Bannister took his seat. The clerk of the court called the court to order and Courtroom 4 was in session.

Shep knew Barry Coleman, the assistant Crown Prosecutor, but not well. Coleman had been with the Crown Prosecutor's office little more than two years and they'd spoken on the 'phone a few times about cases remanded from Bedlington to the Assizes. But, from the tenor of Coleman's opening remarks, none of that was going to be of any help today.

Coleman was milky pale with a haze of dark stubble on his jaw. And he liked to pace. He paced back and forth across the well of the court, using the centre stage, punctuating his statements in the air with his right forefinger as if chalking up each point on an invisible blackboard.

In his opening remarks he told Judge Bannister they were there for the "regrettable purpose of prosecuting a senior police officer for the unprovoked and brutal assault of a man of impeccable character while in police custody." He said the Crown would prove that when McMahon was taken to Bedlington Police Station the night of his arrest he was denied access to his solicitor and when he insisted on his right to have his solicitor present before he answered any questions he was assaulted by Detective Inspector Shepherd, not once, but twice. He said McMahon was treated at the Royal Victoria Infirmary for injuries that included a broken cheekbone, a broken nose and a cut to the bridge of his nose that required five stitches. He also suffered a concussion caused by blows to the face and the back of the head.

In his measured response Pickering said McMahon was intoxicated the night of his arrest, that he was obnoxious and uncooperative with the police, that there was no delay by the police in contacting his solicitor and that D. I. Shepherd acted in self defence when McMahon attempted to strike him.

For his first witnesses Coleman called Evan Thompson and Alec Newell. Both testified that McMahon had surrendered his car keys, licence, insurance and motor vehicle registration on demand, that he had not resisted arrest and he was uninjured when turned over to the custody of Bright at the police station.

On cross-examination Pickering elicited the information from Thompson and Newell that McMahon's speech was slurred and his gait unsteady but he had denied that he was drunk and refused to take a sobriety test. Asked about McMahon's general demeanour in response to his arrest Thompson described him as "obstreperous," and Newell said he appeared "angry."

On the bench Judge Bannister sat hunched forward, one hand propping up his chin, the other holding a pen while he took notes, except his pen wasn't moving and behind his glasses his eyes were either cast steadfastly downward or he was sleeping.

Coleman's next witness was McMahon who took the stand looking relaxed and confident. Coleman began by emphasising McMahon's good standing in the community, that he was the founder and general manager of a successful architectural firm and served on the boards of several charitable foundations. He took McMahon through the events of December the 21st the previous year, his drive to Ashington to deliver Christmas presents to his sister's family, how he had stayed for dinner and had two glasses of wine and one after dinner brandy before starting home. When Coleman got to the point where McMahon was stopped at the zebra crossing in Bedlington while a group of young men crossed the road he asked McMahon to describe the events that followed.

"Well, there were five or six of them," McMahon said. "They were shouting and carrying on. They were obviously very drunk…"

"Speculative, m'lord," Pickering objected.

Without looking up, Bannister said: "Mr. McMahon, please confine yourself to the facts as you know them."

"Yes, my lord," McMahon responded. "They were behaving in a… rowdy, a very rowdy manner. They were larking around in the middle of the crossing, blocking traffic and I couldn't get past. I waited several minutes but when they showed no sign of moving I sounded the car horn to get them to move."

"And then what happened?" Coleman asked.

"They crowded around my car banging on the windows and kicking the doors. They were swearing and shouting and threatening me."

"And what was your response to this?"

"I was afraid, I was afraid for my safety," McMahon answered. "I kept sounding the car horn. I was hoping they would move or the police would come but nobody came and they were getting worse. They were trying to break into the car to get at me."

"M'lord," Pickering interjected, "we do not contest the details of Mr. McMahon's arrest so I fail to see what relevance any of this has to the charge before us."

Judge Bannister's slablike eyelids lifted and he peered through his glasses at the assistant crown prosecutor. "Are you going anywhere with this line of questioning, Mr. Coleman?"

"Indeed I am, m'lord," Coleman answered. "According to the testimony of Constable Thompson and Constable Newell Mr. McMahon was intoxicated and this bears directly on his subsequent behaviour. It is our contention that Mr. McMahon was not intoxicated and the encounter between himself and the youths on the zebra crossing was not due to any provocative action by him at all."

"M'lord," Pickering responded, "two police officers have testified under oath that Mr. McMahon smelled heavily of drink and was unsteady on his feet and that he refused to take a sobriety test."

"Quite," Judge Bannister responded. "Mr. Coleman?"

"M'lord, the known facts are that when the police arrived on the scene there were several young men around Mr. McMahon's car who were intoxicated. The strong smell of alcohol the police officers attributed to Mr. McMahon could quite as easily have come from them. Indeed, Mr. McMahon was under the impression the police had come to assist him, he had every reason to welcome their arrival, not resent them."

Pickering got to his feet. "M'lord, the *indisputable* facts are that Mr. McMahon used his motor car to bulldoze his way through the crowd on the zebra crossing and in doing so knocked one of the young men to the ground. Furthermore, the contact Constable Thompson and Constable Newell had with Mr. McMahon extended beyond that initial encounter. Certainly Constable Newell was alone with Mr. McMahon for several minutes when he took him to the police station. And Mr. McMahon could have dispelled all doubt about his sobriety if he had consented to a sobriety test, which he refused. It is the collective judgement of three police officers, including the duty officer at Bedlington Police Station that night, that Mr. McMahon was under the influence of alcohol. Since then Mr. McMahon has been convicted of driving while under the influence of alcohol according to the facts just described."

"Mr. Coleman," Bannister added, "the witness has admitted that he consumed alcohol that evening. And when Mr. Pickering says Mr. McMahon has been convicted of driving under the influence it would be reasonable to accept, would it not, that..."

"A conviction that is under appeal, m'lord," Coleman interjected.

"No matter, it is the facts before us that concern us today," Judge Bannister said. "And, Mr. Coleman, it would please the court if you would not interrupt me again. Now please, move this along."

"I do beg your pardon, m'lord," Coleman said with a deferential bob of his head.

In the dock Shep's Sumo stance was unchanged but he was pleased at the way Pickering was playing the Crown Prosecutor against the judge.

Coleman turned back to the witness stand and said: "Mr. McMahon, would you please tell the court in your own words what happened after Constable Newell escorted you to the police station."

McMahon nodded but his posture had changed, he no longer looked quite so assured.

"I was handed over to another police officer at the police station and I told him straight away that before we went any further I wanted my solicitor present. I wanted him to call my solicitor."

"And who was the officer at the police station?"

"Constable Bright, I believe."

"And you asked Constable Bright to call your solicitor, Mr. Makepiece?"

"Yes."

"Immediately?"

"Yes."

"And what time was that?"

McMahon hesitated. "It was around half past ten I believe."

"And how would you describe the manner in which you asked Constable Bright to call your solicitor?"

"I was civil, perfectly civil," McMahon said.

"Anything else?"

McMahon seemed momentarily perplexed. "I was very clear that before things went any further I wanted my solicitor present."

"So you insisted..."

"M'lord, my learned friend is leading the witness," Pickering interjected.

Bannister glanced up. "Mr. Coleman, kindly do not put words into the witness's mouth."

"Mr. McMahon, why was it so important to you to have your solicitor present?" Coleman continued.

"I was worried about the way things were going," McMahon said. "I didn't believe the police had any reason to arrest me. I wasn't drunk. The kids on the zebra crossing were the ones who were drunk. They're the ones who caused all the trouble. I thought the police were taking the side of the locals against me…"

"M'lord…" Pickering began but Coleman raised his voice to speak over him.

"M'lord, the state of Mr. McMahon's mind and his apprehension as to the motives of the police in arresting him have a direct bearing on his actions at the police station that night," Coleman said.

Bannister pondered it a moment then said: "I'll allow it."

Pickering sat down with a grimace.

"Would you say you asked the duty officer at the police station clearly and unequivocally to call your solicitor?" Coleman continued.

"Yes, very much so."

"And what happened next?"

"He ignored me," McMahon said. "They all ignored me. It was as if they weren't interested in anything I had to say except what…"

"M'lord," Pickering said, exasperated.

"Mr. McMahon, you cannot testify as to what others may or may not have been thinking," Judge Bannister said. "I must remind you to confine yaself to the facts as you know them."

"I'm obliged, m'lord," Coleman said: "Mr. McMahon, please tell the court what happened next."

McMahon nodded. "Constable Thompson came in after driving my car to the police station then he and Constable Newell left. Then Constable Bright told me to turn out my pockets."

"And what did you do?"

"I did as he said. I wasn't trying to be difficult."

"So you complied?"

"Yes."

"Did Constable Bright call your solicitor before he asked you to turn out your pockets?"

"No."

"Did you ask him to call your solicitor?"

"I did, repeatedly."

"And what was Constable Bright's response?"

"He ignored me. He kept asking where I'd been and how much I'd had to drink."

"Did you tell him?"

"No. I wanted my solicitor there before I said anything more."

"And where did all of this take place?"

"In the police station, at the front counter."

"And where were you and Constable Bright in relation to each other?"

"We were facing each other. I was standing in front of the counter and Constable Bright was standing behind the counter."

"So the counter was between you?"

"Yes."

"And what happened next?"

McMahon paused a moment. "Constable Bright asked me if I would consent to a sobriety test and I told him again I wouldn't do anything without my solicitor present."

"How many times would you say you asked Constable Bright to call your solicitor?"

"Many times…a dozen times at least."

"Did Constable Bright ever call your solicitor?"

"Yes, he did."

"When was that?"

"After Detective Inspector Shepherd hit me."

Coleman paused, allowing McMahon's words to hang in the air.

"And what time was this?"

"Eleven-o-clock I think. Close to 11-o-clock."

"So, at least half an hour had elapsed between your arrival at the police station, when you first asked Constable Bright to call your solicitor, and when he actually called your solicitor? And during that time you say you were assaulted by Detective Inspector Shepherd?"

"Yes."

"Mr. McMahon, would you describe for the court the events that immediately preceded the assault?"

McMahon took a breath. "It was unexpected, to say the least," he said. "Constable Bright kept pressing me to make a statement without my solicitor present and I kept refusing. Then Detective Inspector Shepherd came in."

"Came in from where?"

"Came in the front door, from the street."

"And what happened then?"

"He walked past me. I remember he gave me a dirty look as he passed me."

"What exactly do you mean by a dirty look?"

"M'lord," Pickering said.

"Upheld," Judge Bannister said. "Mr. Coleman, you know better."

"I do beg your pardon, m'lord," Coleman said. Then to McMahon: "Do you see Detective Inspector Shepherd in the court today?"

"Yes," McMahon said.

"Would you point him out please?"

"That's him over there," McMahon said and pointed to Shepherd in the dock.

"Let the record show that Mr. McMahon identified the prisoner, Detective Inspector Shepherd," Coleman said. "Please go on, Mr. McMahon, what happened next?"

"He went behind the counter and spoke to Constable Bright."

"Did you hear what was said?"

"No, they had their backs to me and they were talking quietly so I couldn't hear."

"Then what happened?"

"Inspector Shepherd came back around the counter and stood in front of me, stood right in front of me, staring at me."

"Did you know his identity at that point, that he was in fact a Detective Inspector?"

"No, not at the time. He was wearing ordinary clothes but because of the way he conducted himself I assumed he was something to do with the police."

"Did he identify himself to you then?"

"No, not at all."

"Did he say anything to you?"

"He said something to the effect of 'what's your game?' or 'what do you think you're playing at?'"

"And how did you respond?"

"I told him the same thing I'd been telling Constable Bright, that I wanted to see my solicitor."

"And then what happened?"

"He punched me…in the face."

"He punched you in the face?"

"Yes."

"Without warning?"

"Completely without warning."

"Did you do anything to provoke him?"

"No, of course not."

"You're quite sure about that?"

"I'm absolutely positive. I've never hit anybody in my life."

"Did you raise your hands or make any sudden movement that might have been perceived as a threat?"

"No, none at all."

"So, you made no sudden movement of any kind toward Detective Inspector Shepherd?"

"Absolutely not."

"Did you threaten to strike Detective Inspector Shepherd?"

"No, that's not something I would do."

"So, it is your testimony that while you were in police custody you said nothing and did nothing that could be considered aggressive - towards anyone?"

"That's correct."

"Go on, Mr. McMahon, please tell the court what happened next."

"When Detective Inspector Shepherd hit me I fell back onto a bench, a wooden bench. I was dazed and blood was pouring out of my nose."

"And what did Detective Inspector Shepherd do then?"

"He walked away. He said something to Constable Bright then disappeared out the back of the police station somewhere."

"Did Detective Inspector Shepherd or Constable Bright come to your aid?"

"No."

"Did either of them offer to help you in any way?"

"No."

"Then what happened?"

"That's when Constable Bright called my solicitor."

"Was he able to reach your solicitor?"

"Yes."

"Did Constable Bright let you speak to your solicitor?"

"No, he did not."

"Are you quite sure about that, Mr. McMahon? He called your solicitor, Mr. Makepiece, but wouldn't let you speak to him?"

"That's exactly what happened."

"Did Constable Bright say why?"

"He said I couldn't come to the phone. He said I was under the weather or some such thing." McMahon gave sarcastic emphasis to 'under the weather.'

"Please, go on."

"Well, Constable Bright disappeared out the back then came back after a minute or so and then Detective Inspector Shepherd came back."

"And where were you in relation to them?"

"I was still at the counter. I didn't move from there."

"You didn't attempt to leave the police station, even though you were on your own and you'd just been assaulted?"

"No, I was under arrest."

"Were you sitting or standing by then?"

"I was standing. I was holding my handkerchief to my nose to stop the bleeding."

"And what happened next?"

"Detective Inspector Shepherd came up to me and said my solicitor was on the way and I should go into the toilet and get myself cleaned up."

"And what was your response to that?"

"I told him I wanted my solicitor to see me the way I was."

"And then what happened?"

"He hit me again, he punched me in the face again."

"Again?" Coleman said raising his voice for emphasis. "Detective Inspector Shepherd punched you in the face a second time?"

"Yes," McMahon said. "He punched me a second time."

"Did you say or do anything that would cause him to strike you a second time?"

"Of course not," McMahon said. "Nobody goes into a police station looking to get beaten up."

"My lord," Pickering called out.

"I'll allow it," Judge Bannister said.

"And what happened when Detective Inspector Shepherd struck you that second time?"

McMahon took a breath. "I fell back against the bench again. I was stunned. I couldn't believe what was happening. I was bleeding all over the place."

"You were bleeding all over the place?" Coleman repeated slowly.

"Yes," McMahon said.

"And what did Detective Inspector Shepherd do?"

"He was leaning over me, shouting, carrying on like a madman. I put my hands up to protect myself, I thought he was going to hit me again."

"So, both times you were assaulted the only time you put up your hands was after you'd been punched for a second time and that was to defend yaself?"

"Yes, absolutely."

"Mr. McMahon, would you demonstrate for the court the way in which you put up your hands to defend yaself against Detective Inspector Shepherd?"

McMahon lifted his hands, keeping them open with the palms outward.

"So, you held up your hands in what was unmistakeably a defensive posture?" Coleman said. "You didn't clench your fists at any time?"

"No, never."

"And what did Detective Inspector Shepherd do then?"

"That's when he said his name. He told me his name and his rank so I would know who he was."

"M'lord…" Pickering protested.

"I'll allow it," Bannister said.

"How would you describe the manner in which he told you his name?" Coleman asked.

"He was taunting me, daring me to do something about it."

"M'lord, I really must protest," Pickering objected again.

"You've made your point, Mr. Coleman, please move along," Bannister said.

"I'm much obliged m'lord," Coleman said. To McMahon he said: "Then what happened?"

"He went away, he left the police station."

"Detective Inspector Shepherd left at that point?"

"Yes."

"And Constable Bright?"

"He was still there."

"And how would you describe your physical appearance at that point?"

"I was a mess. I felt as if my face had been split open, there was blood all over my clothes."

"Did Constable Bright offer you any assistance?"

"He asked me if I wanted an aspirin."

"He asked if you wanted an aspirin?"

"Yes."

"Your nose was broken, your face was cut, you were bleeding profusely and Constable Bright asked if you wanted an aspirin?"

"Yes."

"M'lord, I protest," Pickering interjected. "Try as he may, my learned colleague cannot turn this into the Massacre of the Innocents."

"Noted, Mr. Pickering," Bannister said. "Mr. Coleman, the court would thank you not to embelish the testimony of the witness."

"No embelishment intended, m'lord," Coleman said. "Mr. McMahon, would you detail for the court the medical treatment you received as a result of the injuries you suffered at the hands of Detective Inspector Shepherd."

McMahon took a breath. "It took five stitches to close the wound on my nose but my face was so badly bruised they couldn't do anything to reset my nose until after the swelling had gone down."

"How long did that take?"

"About six weeks."

"And how did you manage your everyday affairs in that time?"

"Not very well. It caused a great deal of upset to my wife and daughters. It ruined Christmas for us. It's not a memory you want stuck in your children's heads."

"Were you able to work?"

"I was prescribed painkillers and sedatives, which left me feeling rather groggy. Because of that and my appearance I couldn't go into the office and meet with clients. I had to do what work I could at home."

"Did your business suffer due to your absence?"

"M'lord," Pickering said.

"Upheld," Judge Bannister said.

"What treatment did you receive for your broken nose?" Coleman asked.

"They couldn't do anything until the stitches were taken out and the cut had healed properly, that was another three weeks."

"And after that?"

"The broken bones in my nose had begun to set so they had to break my nose again and reset it with a splint."

"So, you had to undergo a rather painful operation to have your nose repaired?"

"Yes."

"And how long did all of that that take?"

"The operation was about 90 minutes, I was in hospital two days and I had to wear a nose splint and bandages for four weeks after that."

"And how long was it after the assault before you were completely healed?"

"Close on four months."

"So, as a direct result of Detective Inspector Shepherd's unprovoked assault on you, it was four months before you recovered sufficiently to resume anything like a normal life?"

"Yes," McMahon said. "It was the beginning of May before I was back to normal."

Coleman turned to the prosecution table, picked up a file and handed it to the Clerk of the Court.

"M'lord I enter into evidence these photographs of Mr. McMahon, which were taken approximately 10 hours after the assault. There is also a medical report by Dr. Dawson from the Casualty department at the Royal Victoria Infirmary in Newcastle, which confirms that Mr. McMahon was treated for a broken nose and extensive facial cuts and bruises in the early hours of December the 22nd …three days before Christmas of last year."

"M'lord, I really must object…" Pickering began.

"There are also photographs of Mr. McMahon after the operation to repair his broken nose and a medical report from the surgeon who performed the operation."

"M'lord…" Pickering tried again but Coleman raised his hands in a gesture of submission and said: "I'm finished with this witness, m'lord."

"Your witness, Mr. Pickering," Judge Bannister said somewhat wearily.

Pickering got to his feet, walked slowly to the witness box and stared at the floor for a long time, seemingly deep in thought. When people began to get restless he turned to the bench and said: "M'lord, I see we are coming up to noon time. Might I suggest we adjourn for lunch and I will begin my cross-examination of this witness when the court resumes?"

"Very well, Mr. Pickering," Judge Bannister said without demur. "This court is adjourned until two-o-clock this afternoon."

As the court emptied Pickering went over to the dock and spoke confidentially to Shep. "Mr. Coleman seems to think he's playing to a jury. I hope he's antagonising the judge as much as I think he is."

"Aye, that's what I thought at first," Shep said. "But the way he's goin' on ye'd think ah was Jack the Ripper."

"Well, you can take heart then can't you," Pickering smiled. "Jack the Ripper was never convicted of anything."

Shep leaned back, unamused. Watching from the public benches John Robson assumed Pickering was trying to bolster Shep's confidence though he didn't think Shep had much to be confident about. Coleman might have pushed his luck with the judge here or there but he had painted a vivid picture of not one but two unprovoked assaults on McMahon while he was in police custody. If he was a betting man Robson would have bet on Bannister finding Shep guilty.

The court resumed at two-o-clock with a faintly beery smell in the air from those who had adjourned to the quayside pubs for lunch. McMahon returned to the witness stand and Pickering began his cross-examination by asking him how much he'd had to drink the night of his arrest.

"Two glasses of red wine and a small after dinner brandy," McMahon replied. "Over several hours with food."

"You seem very sure of that," Pickering said.

"I am," McMahon replied.

"How big were the glasses of wine?"

"Two or three ounces, no more."

"Less than half a bottle then?"

"Much less."

"With dinner?"

"Yes."

"And a brandy after dinner?"

"A small brandy. I was driving."

"So how do you explain the judgement of three experienced police officers that you were intoxicated?"

"They're lying."

"They're lying?"

"Yes."

"All three of them?"

"Yes."

"You seem very certain of that, Mr. McMahon."

"I am."

"And why would all three of them be lying?"

"To protect themselves, of course."

"So," Pickering rocked back and forth on the balls of his feet, his hands on his lower back as if easing an ache. "You were driving home the night of December the 21st, last year, minding your own business, perfectly sober and the police in Bedlington arrested you for no reason?"

"No good reason." McMahon said. "That's why I was so upset."

"You admit you were upset?"

"Yes, of course," McMahon said. "I think anyone in my position would be."

"And what exactly was your position, Mr. McMahon?"

McMahon hesitated. "An innocent man."

"An innocent man," Pickering repeated, nodding. "And how do you explain the behaviour of the young men on the zebra crossing that night?"

"They were drunk."

"Yes, as you have already said, it was your judgement that they were drunk?"

"They were yelling and shouting and falling over each other."

"And that was enough to convince you they were drunk?"

"Come, come, Mr. Pickering," Bannister said. "This is a coal mining community on a Saturday night. I think we might reasonably conclude that drinks had been consumed."

Laughter rippled softly through the courtroom.

"As m'lord wishes," Pickering conceded. "So, Mr. McMahon, in your estimation these young men were intoxicated?"

"Very."

"And you were in a position to judge because you were sober?"

"Yes."

"And when they wouldn't get out of your way you thought it was reasonable to drive through them?"

"I sounded my horn, several times. They wouldn't budge."

"In fact, the sound of your car horn only served to provoke them, did it not?" Pickering said. "It provoked them to attack your motor car, wasn't that your earlier testimony?"

"They did attack my car. They were banging on the doors and windows, trying to get at me. I was very frightened about what they would do."

"You were frightened because they were banging on the doors and windows?" Pickering stressed.

"Yes."

"They weren't tapping the windows or knocking on the doors, it was more violent than that?"

"Much more violent. They were punching the windows, kicking the car doors, banging on the roof with their fists, jumping up and down on the bumpers."

"And while they were doing this what sort of things were they saying to you?"

"They were shouting at the tops of their voices, threatening me, using foul language."

"Would you mind telling the court specifically what sort of threats they made and the language they used?"

McMahon paused a moment. "They were yelling at me to get out of the car, calling me names, saying they would kill me, kick my fucking head in, that sort of thing."

"They threatened to kill you?"

"They were out of control, they were capable of doing anything."

"And, naturally, you were alarmed?"

"Of course, anybody would be."

"Indeed," Pickering agreed. "An angry, drunken mob was attempting to break into your motor car and do you harm, of course you were alarmed."

"That's the way it was," McMahon said.

"But they didn't drag you from your car, did they Mr. McMahon? For all the alleged violence of their assault on your vehicle they never succeeded in breaking into your car. They never laid a finger on you, did they?"

"It wasn't for lack of trying."

"And that's why you stepped on the accelerator and drove into the crowd?"

"I didn't step on the accelerator…"

"Your car moved by itself?"

"If you'd let me finish…"

"Please."

"I stepped lightly on the accelerator, I eased the car forward. I wanted to push through them and be on my way, that's all I was trying to do."

Pickering nodded. "Mr. McMahon, would you tell the court what kind of motor car you were driving that night?"

"It's a 1955 Riley Pathfinder."

"A green 1955 Riley Pathfinder with leather upholstery and walnut faschia, seats six and has a top speed of 110 miles an hour?"

"Yes."

"A very nice motor car, wouldn't you say?"

"I think so."

"An expensive motor car, the kind of motor car you would want to look after?"

"Yes."

"And it's not the only motor car you own, is it, Mr. McMahon. Would you kindly tell the court what other vehicles you own?"

"Irrelevant, m'lord," Coleman objected.

"I also fail to see the relevance of this line of questioning, Mr. Pickering," Bannister said. "There is nothing improper about owning nice motor cars or having the means to enjoy them."

"Of course m'lord," Pickering responded. "As always I am much obliged for your lordship's invaluable insight."

In the dock Shep took a sharp breath. He didn't see how it would help him if Pickering went out of his way to antagonise the judge.

"Mr. McMahon," Pickering returned to his cross-examination. "You are aware, are you not, that when you regained possession of your motor car from the Bedlington police two days after your arrest there wasn't a mark on it? Not a dent or a scratch anywhere, not a cracked window or broken wing mirror, not a broken door handle, not a mark on the front bumper or the rear bumper after this violent encounter with a mob of alcohol crazed young men. In fact there is no evidence at all to support your version of events is there?"

"I can only tell you what happened," McMahon responded brittly.

"You signed off on the return of your car, Mr. McMahon. Didn't you inspect it?"

"I was just glad to have it back."

"So, you weren't overly concerned about a few dents and scratches on this beautiful and expensive motor car when you got it back?"

"I had other things to worry about."

"Of course you did," Pickering said. "But almost a year has passed since then, plenty of time to have any repair work done, wouldn't you say? Have you had any bodywork or repairs done to your car as a result of damage done to it during this violent incident, Mr. McMahon?"

McMahon shifted uneasily. "No."

"So, the encounter with the young men on the zebra crossing couldn't have been anywhere near as violent as you describe, could it? Unless, perhaps, the police at Bedlington, in a moment of sublime prescience, conspired to repair your car during the time it was in their custody for the sole purpose of contradicting your evidence here today?"

"M'lord," Coleman interceded. "Mr. Pickering is badgering the witness."

"Mr. Pickering you've made your point, kindly move along," Judge Bannister said.

"I'm obliged m'lord," Pickering said. Turning back to McMahon he said: "Let us look at the conduct of the police that night then shall we, which you say was so egregious?"

McMahon eyed Pickering warily.

"When were you aware of the presence of the police at the scene?"

"When they asked me to get out of my car."

"Was your car stationary at the time?"

"Yes, I stopped the car on the zebra crossing when I realised the police were there."

"So you felt safe enough to get out of the car?"

"Yes, I thought they were there to help me."

"And weren't they?"

"Not as it turned out, no."

"And why not?"

"Because I got beaten up by one of them instead of the crowd."

"Indeed," Pickering responded dryly. "But let's deal with one matter at a time, shall we. What happened to the mob of drunken louts, where were they at this time?"

"On the footpath I believe."

"So they were no longer on the zebra crossing blocking your car?"

"No."

"So the police had moved them on?"

"Yes."

"For your protection?"

"Supposedly."

"So it was the police, in fact, who rescued you?"

"That's what I thought at the time."

"Mr. McMahon, you just told the court that a mob of young men attempted to break into your car with the intention of doing you bodily harm and then the police arrived and moved them on. Did the police move them on or not? Yes or no?"

"Yes."

"And what happened when you got out of the car?"

"The older one of the two, Constable Thompson, asked if I was alright."

"And what did you tell him?"

"I told him I was a bit shaken up, that's all."

"Then what happened?"

"He asked to see my driver's licence, my motor vehicle registration and proof of insurance."

"And did you provide him with those documents?"

"Yes, I did."

"You were cooperative?"

"Yes, of course."

"And how close were you to Constable Thompson while this was taking place."

"I'm not rightly sure," McMahon hedged. "A few feet."

"Could you be more precise, Mr. McMahon? Were you speaking to him from a distance of two feet...ten feet?"

"No, it was less than that."

"What would you say it was?"

"Three or four feet."

"Three or four feet then," Pickering said. "And then what happened?"

"Constable Thompson asked if I'd been drinking."

"And what did you tell him?"

"I told him what I've said all along, that I'd only had a little to drink."

"Yes, two glasses of wine and a glass of brandy, wasn't it?"

"A small brandy."

"Yes, a small brandy. And then what happened?"

"Constable Thompson asked if I would consent to a sobriety test."

"And what did you tell him?"

"I told him I didn't think that was necessary."

"Is that all?"

"It was something to that effect. I wasn't drunk. I didn't see the point. It was late and I wanted to get home."

"Of course," Pickering said. "You've said all along that in your opinion you weren't drunk."

"I wasn't drunk," McMahon said firmly.

"Were you aware that refusal to take a sobriety test carries with it an automatic penalty?"

"I wasn't at the time," McMahon said. "I am now."

"Surely then, Mr. McMahon, if you were as cooperative as you say, it would have been easier for you to take a sobriety test than to refuse, wouldn't it? If you were sober you could have quite easily spared the few minutes it takes to administer the test and been on your way?"

McMahon hesitated. "In hindsight yes, that's what I should have done. But I was just so angry about the whole thing..."

"Oh, so you *were* angry?" Pickering said.

McMahon realised he'd made a slip.

"You weren't just upset, you were angry?" Pickering pressed him.

"Well, yes, of course. I'd been harassed and threatened by a bunch of drunken louts but it was me the police decided to arrest."

"You don't think it would have been helpful to take a sobriety test and be on your way, or if you were found to be intoxicated, to stay off the road for a couple of hours until you were safe to drive?"

McMahon grimaced. "That's not how I saw it at the time."

"Evidently not," Pickering said. "Would you tell the court what happened next?"

"I was placed under arrest by Constable Thompson."

"On what charges?"

"Driving while intoxicated and refusing to take a sobriety test."

"And what was the outcome of those charges?"

"I pleaded guilty to refusing to take the sobriety test and not guilty to driving under the influence, but I was found guilty and now it's under appeal."

"Yes," Pickering said, drawing the word out into a note of scepticism. He took a few steps away from the witness box then turned and fixed McMahon with a hard stare. "Mr. McMahon, I put it to you that you had considerably more to drink that night than you care to admit, that you knew you couldn't pass a sobriety test and that is why you refused. I further put it to you that your judgement was so severely impaired that night due to the level of your intoxication that you were nowhere near as cooperative with police as you claim."

"That's just not true," McMahon said.

"Mr. McMahon, it was the judgement of three police officers that you were intoxicated, are all three of them wrong and only you are right?"

"Yes, actually," McMahon said. "That's exactly the way it is."

"Oh, I see," Pickering folded his arms and contemplatively put a finger to his lips. "All three officers conspired against you to say you were drunk. No doubt the same three officers who conspired to repair your car after it was attacked by an angry mob."

"M'lord," Coleman objected. "Mr. Pickering is trying to belittle the witness, this kind of sarcasm serves no useful purpose."

"Mr. Pickering, you will refrain from baiting the witness," Bannister said.

"No baiting or belittling intended, m'lord," Pickering responded. "It is the position of the defence that Mr. McMahon's recollections of the events of December the 21st, last year are fatally flawed. That his testimony is unreliable due to his proven impairment from alcohol and an exaggerated sense of grievance against the police. I would respectfully remind the court that what is at stake here today is the career of a highly distinguished and long serving senior police officer."

"The court is obliged for your diligence, Mr. Pickering," Bannister said. "And there will be no more baiting the witness."

In the dock Shep stifled a grunt of exasperation. His career hung in the balance and now his barrister was sparring with the judge.

"I have only one final question for this witness, m'lord," Pickering said. "Mr. McMahon what would the police have to gain by charging you with driving while intoxicated…before any altercation you had with Detective Inspector Shepherd?"

"They're protecting one of their own," McMahon said, frustrated.

"Let me be perfectly clear about this," Pickering responded. "Mr. McMahon are you seriously trying to suggest that Constable Thompson and Constable Newell arrested you for driving under the influence and refusing to take a sobriety test because they could look into the future and see that you would be involved in an altercation with Detective Inspector Shepherd?"

McMahon's cheeks flushed. "No, of course not."

"Then what *are* you saying, Mr. McMahon? Do you even know what you are saying?"

"I know I wasn't drunk that night," McMahon said, struggling to keep his composure. "I think the two police officers made a mistake when they arrested me and things went downhill from there and now they're trying to cover it up."

"Well, we agree that things went downhill," Pickering said. "Where we disagree is the cause. What you seem to be saying, Mr. McMahon, is that the police have it in for you, is that correct?"

"It wasn't like that," McMahon said, frustrated. "When you put it like that it sounds…" he groped for the right words.

"How *do* you think it sounds, Mr. McMahon?" Pickering pressed him. "We'd all like to know."

"You're twisting the whole thing to make it sound ridiculous," McMahon said.

"Now *I'm* making it sound ridiculous, is that it?" Pickering said mockingly. "It's your testimony, Mr. McMahon."

Coleman started to object but Pickering cut him off with a dismissive wave of the hand. "No further questions, m'lord."

McMahon stepped down from the stand with the look of a man who'd been seized by the scruff of the neck and dragged unceremoniously through the looking glass. He took a seat next to Jervis in the public benches and the two of them whispered animatedly to each other.

For his next witness Coleman called Bright. As he crossed the well of the court Bright felt the hairs on the back of his neck prickle as if he were passing through an electrical field. When he took the oath he thought his voice sounded unnaturally loud in the stillness of the court and he was acutely aware of Shep's gaze. He sat down and stared fixedly to the front, determined not to be thrown off his evidence. The Crown Prosecutor wasted no time in telling Bright what was expected of him.

"Constable Bright, you are the only witness to what took place between Mr. McMahon and Detective Inspector Shepherd at Bedlington Police Station on December 21st last year," Coleman said. "This imposes upon you a responsibility to be particularly thorough in your recollection of events and to take great care with the testimony you give here today because the court is relying on you to shed some much needed light on what actually happened that night - do you understand?"

"Yes sir," Bright responded.

Coleman began by methodically walking Bright through the evidence, confirming Evan Thompson and Alec Newell's version of events until they left McMahon in Bright's custody.

"And after Constable Thompson and Constable Newell left, then what happened?" Coleman asked.

"Ah asked Mr. McMahon to turn out his pockets?"

"And did he comply?"

"Yes, after some objection."

"But he complied, nonetheless?"

"Yes."

"How would you describe his demeanour at this time?"

"He wasn't very happy."

"Would you expect him to be?"

"No, not especially."

"Let me put it this way, constable, in your experience how many people are happy to have been placed under arrest by the police?"

"Not many."

"Not many," Coleman repeated. "So, apart from some unhappiness that he was under arrest, he was cooperative?"

Bright paused. "To a point."

"What happened then?"

"I asked him where he'd been and how much he'd had to drink."

"And how did he respond?"

"He didn't. He refused to answer any questions unless his solicitor was present."

"Is that so unusual?"

"It is in Bedlin'ton."

"And why is that?"

"Because very few of the people we see can afford a solicitor who's willin'
to come down to the police station in the middle o' the night."

"How long have you been a police officer, Constable Bright?"

"Six years."

"Six years," Coleman repeated. "In your experience then, how many
people charged with committing a criminal offence have asked that their solicitor
be present when they've been charged?"

"In my experience - only Mr. McMahon."

Coleman nodded. "And because Mr. McMahon has the means to afford
a diligent solicitor who is prepared to come to his aid in the middle of the night
is that any reason to treat him differently from the way you would treat any other
suspect?"

"No."

"So there was no temptation to deal with Mr. McMahon a little more
harshly, perhaps, because he was perceived as a man of privilege?"

"Not at all."

"Not at all, constable?"

"We treated Mr. McMahon the same way wi treat everybody. In fact wi
bent over backwards to make sure wi treated him the same as wi treat everybody
else."

"And yet Mr. McMahon was assaulted and injured while in your custody,
Constable Bright. Is that the way you treat everybody else in Bedlington?"

"Really, m'lord," Morrie Pickering sighed.

"I'll withdraw the question m'lord," Coleman said.

It was exactly the way they treated everybody else in Bedlington, Bright
thought. And he saw where Coleman was going. He was going to make it about
class. He was going to make it about class and money and envy. He was going
to try and persuade the judge that Peter McMahon was a victim of the casual
brutality of police officers unable to rise above the working class mire. And he
was right. That was exactly the way it was. But it was a victory Bright couldn't
let him have. Because Shep was right too. And in that moment Bright saw two
futures. In one future McMahon would win and return, vindicated, to his life
of privilege and luxury. In the other he would lose and return, frustrated, to
his life of privilege and luxury. But if McMahon won the effects on Bright and
Shep would be devastating. Shep would lose his job and his pension. And, if
Bright wasn't sacked, a cloud of suspicion would hang over him for the rest of
his life and his prospects of advancement in the police force would be nil. And
if McMahon were to lose, Shep and Bright would go on with their lives as usual.

That was the most they stood to gain. They would get to keep what they had. Fuck Coleman, Bright thought. Fuck Coleman and McMahon and Jervis and Makepiece and their lives of security and comfort. Fuck the lot of them. He had a life to live too. He knew his place.

"Constable, at what time did you call Mr. McMahon's solicitor, Mr. Makepiece?" Coleman asked.

"Between twenty to and a quarter to eleven."

"And how much time would you say elapsed between Mr. McMahon's arrival at the police station and you calling his solicitor?"

"No more than 10 minutes."

"Are you sure about that, constable?"

"Quite sure," Bright said calmly. He opened a tunic pocket and took out the notebook he had prepared in case he had to cover himself. "Ah made a note o' the time he was delivered to the police station and the time ah made the call."

Coleman seemed taken aback.

"And what time was it you say you placed the call?"

"10.42 p.m."

"You wrote that in your notebook?"

"Yes sir."

Coleman went back to the defence table, took a moment to sort through some papers and returned to his examination of Bright with a copy of Bright's incident report in his hand.

"Constable Bright, can you explain why the time you've just given the court of your phone call to Mr. McMahon's solicitor is at odds with the time you gave in your incident report?"

"Ah believe ah gave an approximate time in the incident report, some time between 10.30 and 11. Me superior officer, Inspector Robson, told is to deliver me incident report as soon as possible the next day. Ah entered the precise time in me notebook after ah filed me incident report. Ah think you'll find that's right, Mr. Coleman. If ye like ye can verify it with the GPO and with Mr. Makepiece."

Coleman frowned. "So you're testifying that only 10 minutes elapsed between the time Mr. McMahon arrived at the police station and the time you called Mr. Makepiece?"

"That's correct, sir."

"Constable, would it surprise you to learn that Mr. McMahon testified earlier to this court that he was at the police station at least half an hour before you called his solicitor and, furthermore, that you did not call his solicitor until after he was struck by Detective Inspector Shepherd?"

"No, it doesn't surprise me."

"Why not?"

"Because Mr. McMahon was drunk. He didn't know what he was sayin' or doin'."

"And at what time did Detective Inspector Shepherd arrive?"

"10.42 p.m. The same time ah was callin' Mr. Makepiece."

"You say you were on the telephone when Detective Inspector Shepherd arrived?"

"Yes."

"What happened then?"

"While ah was waitin' for the call to go through D. I. Shepherd asked if ah needed any assistance with Mr. McMahon."

"And what did you say?"

"Ah asked if he would keep an eye on Mr. McMahon while ah made the call."

"Then what happened?"

"D. I. Shepherd went over to Mr. McMahon and spoke to him."

"Did you hear what D. I. Shepherd said?"

"Not precisely, the telephone was ringin' in me ear."

"And then what happened?"

"Ah heard Mr. McMahon raise his voice."

"When you say you heard Mr. McMahon raise his voice, was that in response to something that D. I. Shepherd said?"

"Ah don't know what D. I. Shepherd said."

"So you didn't hear what D. I. Shepherd said but you heard what Mr. McMahon said? That's rather convenient, isn't it constable?"

"M'lord…" Pickering began but before he could voice his objection Judge Bannister said: "I'll allow it."

"D. I. Shepherd was speaking in a normal voice," Bright responded. "Mr. McMahon had worked himself up into a state."

Coleman looked unhappily at the floor before looking back up at Bright.

"Constable, are you aware that not only does your testimony bear little relation to the testimony given here today by Mr. McMahon, it bears little relation to your incident report from that night and little relation to any prior statement you made in interviews with myself or Mr. Pickering?"

"M'lord," Pickering protested, "my learned colleague is taking gross liberties with this witness."

"Constable Bright seems to be up to it, Mr. Pickering," Bannister said. "I'll allow it."

Bright met Coleman's sceptical gaze.

"Ye asked is to be thorough, Mr. Coleman," he said. "Ah'm tryin' to be as thorough as ah can."

Irritation flared in Coleman's eyes.

"Constable Bright, how far away from Mr. McMahon and Detective Inspector Shepherd were you when this exchange between them took place?" "About 15 feet, ah was usin' the phone at the duty desk."

"Do you recollect anything at all that Mr. McMahon said to Detective Inspector Shepherd?"

"It was the usual kind of drunken rant wi get all the time, 'what's wrong with you people…are you all thick here or somethin'…' that sort of thing."

There was a stir on the public benches and McMahon whispered agitatedly to Jervis.

"Are you all thick here or something?" Coleman repeated.

"Yes, somethin' like that."

"Constable Bright, that remark doesn't appear anywhere in your incident report. Would you care to tell the court why that is?"

"Ah didn't think much about it," Bright answered. "Like ah said, it's the kind of thing that gets thrown at wi by drunks all the time. That and a lot worse. As ah said before, Inspector Robson told is to file me incident report the next day because he wanted to see it as soon as possible. Ah tried to put everythin' in but there were some things came to is afterwards that ah wrote in me notebook."

"So there are some observations in your notebook that do not appear in your incident report?"

"Yes sir."

"Isn't it customary procedure to reference the incident report from the notebook, constable, and not the other way round?"

"It's not unusual at all, sir," Bright answered. "Wi often remember things afterwards that wi put in wa notebooks in case wi might need it to give in evidence."

Coleman allowed a note of scepticism to creep into his voice. "So, it's your testimony, Constable Bright, that Mr. McMahon was 'working himself up into a state' as you put it?"

"Yes sir. He was gettin' very agitated."

"Was it then that Detective Inspector Shepherd struck Mr. McMahon?"

"No sir. As far as ah could tell D.I. Shepherd was tryin' to reason with

Mr. McMahon. Tryin' to calm him down."

In the public benches McMahon had paled under his tan.

"So at what point do you say Detective Inspector Shepherd struck Mr. McMahon?" Coleman continued.

"Well, Mr. McMahon was carryin' on, shoutin' the odds about this an' that, and D. I. Shepherd put his hands up the way you would to calm somebody down, like that…" Bright moved his hands, palms outwards, in a calming motion. "And Mr. McMahon went to punch him."

"You bloody liar!" McMahon shouted across the courtroom. He was on his feet, fists gripping the back of the bench in front of him, his eyes darting between Bright and Judge Bannister. "Everything he's said is lies."

Bannister banged his gavel. "Mr. McMahon, you will restrain yourself or I will have you removed from this courtroom."

Jervis tugged on McMahon's arm and coaxed him back into his seat.

In the dock Shep looked down at his feet and exulted. If Bright's testimony wasn't convincing enough McMahon had just rvealed his temper for all the world to see.

Frustrated, Coleman turned away from Bright.

"No further questions, m'lord."

Pickering's cross-examination was brief and pointed.

"Constable Bright, you testified earlier that you have served with the Northumberland Police Force some six years, is that correct?"

"That is correct sir," Bright said.

"And how much of that time would you estimate has been spent dealing with members of the public in matters related to the consumption of alcohol?"

Bright paused only a moment. "About ninety percent."

"Would you say your experience has equipped you to know the difference between a man who intends to shake your hand and a man who intends to strike you with his fist?"

"Ah would say so."

"It is rudimentary police work is it not that a police officer, as a matter of self-preservation, has to assess each and every situation for the potential for violence?"

"It's drummed into wi durin' training that any situation can turn violent in an instant."

"And that assessment has to be made very quickly?"

"Yes."

"And in your judgement Mr. McMahon had, in an instant, adopted the posture of a man who was about to throw a punch?"

"He did."

"What happened then?"

"D. I. Shepherd punched him."

"How many times did Detective Inspector Shepherd strike Mr. McMahon?"

"Twice."

"And what was the effect of those two blows on Mr. McMahon?"

"He was immediately subdued."

"Immediately subdued you say?"

"Yes, that was the point."

"Then what happened?"

"Ah had Mr. Makepiece on the 'phone by then. Ah told him Mr. McMahon had been arrested on a charge of drivin' while under the influence and he wanted Mr. Makepiece to come over right away."

"Did Mr. Makepiece ask to speak to Mr. McMahon?"

"Yes, he did."

"Did you allow him to speak to Mr. McMahon?"

"Not at that time. Mr. McMahon was in no condition to come to the phone. Ah told Mr. Makepiece he should come to the station."

"So you weren' trying to keep Mr. Makepiece from seeing Mr. McMahon?"

"No, of course not."

"Where was Detective Inspector Shepherd at this time?"

"He was with Mr. McMahon."

"And what was he doing?"

"Standin', just keepin' an eye on him."

"Then what did you do?"

"After ah got off the phone ah went over to Mr. McMahon to see if there was anything ah could do to help him."

"And what was his response?"

"He told D.I. Shepherd and meself he didn't want any help from either of us."

"What did you and Detective Inspector Shepherd do then?"

"Ah asked Mr. McMahon if he would like an aspirin. Ah brought him a wet towel to use as a compress, ah offered to make him a cup of tea."

"And what was his response to these offers of assistance?"

"The same as he'd been since he was brought to the police station. He said he didn't want anythin' from us and he wanted his solicitor to see him as he was."

There was a burst of angry muttering from McMahon. Jervis put a restraining hand on his arm but McMahon pulled away and pushed along the bench to the center aisle. The bailiff at the front of the court and the usher at the rear started to converge on McMahon but instead of making for the front of the court he turned toward the exit shouting and gesturing as he went: "I will not sit here and listen to these lies…this whole thing is a disgrace…this is an absolute travesty of justice…"

Jervis got to his feet, apologised to Judge Bannister on McMahon's behalf and hurried out after his client. The interruption over, Pickering told Judge Bannister he'd concluded his cross-examination, Bright stood down and in the dock Shep struggled to contain his delight.

For his final witness Coleman called McMahon's solicitor, Walter Makepiece. But Makepiece had nothing new to add and after McMahon's outbursts there seemed little doubt which way Judge Bannister's decision would go. Pickering called Shep to the stand to testify on his own behalf and had him identify his campaign ribbons and medals from the war including the action that won him the Military Cross at Monte Cassino. He also went through Shep's five commendations for outstanding police work, two of them for bravery. It was a process that took some time and when Pickering was finished it seemed all that was left for the court to do was for Bannister to apologise to Shep for the way he'd been inconvenienced by having to go to court at all.

Both Coleman and Pickering made short work of their closing arguments and Judge Bannister didn't bother to adjourn before ruling the charges against Shep 'Not Proven.' For good measure he admonished Coleman with the remarks: "Given that three experienced police officers were able to corroborate the evidence on behalf of such a distinguished and highly decorated senior police officer as Detective Inspector Shepherd against the word of a disgruntled citizen convicted of driving while intoxicated, the court is astonished that the Crown Prosecutor's office would see fit to bring such a weak case to trial at all."

When the court rose Pickering went to shake Shep's hand as he stepped down from the dock. With Bright, Robson, Thompson and Newell looking on Shep embraced Audrey and Beryl, who were unable to hold back their tears. Then Shep clasped Bright's hand, shook it vigorously and squeezed his shoulder.

"Ah won't forget this, lad," he said.

When they'd all moved outside into the corridor Pickering told them: "Quentin Bannister has never been a good morning man. He can be a bit discombobulated and it's easy to get on his wrong side during the morning session so I like him to get a good lunch under his belt before he comes back for the afternoon session so he's in a better mood and more inclined to remember the evidence." With a nod to Bright he added: "I have to say Constable Bright came through for you in spades today, Detective Inspector. And we can't overlook the contributions of Mr. McMahon to our victory can we? He could hardly have done more on our behalf."

Robson was first to leave. He stood at the top of the courthouse steps buttoning his coat against the wind, waiting for the others to catch up. When Bright came out Robson observed wryly. "Well, you've made your bed, now you're going to have to lie in it."

Bright met his gaze. "Ahll ah did was tell the truth, boss."

The four Bedlington police officers hurried across the windswept car park for the shelter of the Wolseley and the consolation of a smoke. Behind them Shep led Audrey and Beryl to their car. On the way he glimpsed McMahon with Makepiece and Jervis in a basement doorway, out of the wind, deep in conversation. Shep got his wife and daughter settled in the car and told them he'd be back in a minute. A dozen parking spaces away Robson turned on the headlamps and in the twin cones of light saw Shep walking back across the car park toward the three men sheltered in the doorway. There was just enough light to illuminate their faces.

"Ahh Jack," Robson groaned. "Don't say anything."

Bright, Thompson and Newell followed Robson's gaze.

Shep crossed the car park, hunched against the wind, holding his hat down over his face. As he came close the men in the doorway recognised him and stopped their conversation. When Shep was close enough to be out of the wind he smiled at McMahon and said: "Merry Christmas, ye cunt."

1958

Manchester United loses seven of 'Busby's Babes' in an air crash at Munich airport; race riots erupt in London's Notting Hill. Top TV hit is The Black And White Minstrel Show. Box office hits are South Pacific starring Mitzi Gaynor and Rossano Brazzi; A Town Like Alice starring Virginia McKenna and Peter Finch; Ice Cold In Alex starring John Mills and Anthony Quayle. Top record hits are Jailhouse Rock by Elvis Presley, Move It by Cliff Richard, Rave On and Maybe Baby by Buddy Holly and The Crickets.

Inside Job

In an enlightened effort to build social harmony the Northumberland Department of Education built Westridge Secondary Modern School back to back with St. Bede's Catholic School, which meant instead of the protestant kids and the catholic kids fighting each other some of the time they could fight each other all of the time. The only separation between the two schools was a hedge about ten feet high with a small field on each side. In spring and autumn kids went into the fields to lob stones over the hedge at each other and in winter they would fill the air with volleys of snowballs. Battles involved as many as a hundred kids on each side and schoolyard strategists emerged to deploy forces and lead attacks. One of the most successful actions in the winter of 1958 was a raid led by Bumper Barrett whose love of violence was enhanced only by the opportunity to implement it on a large scale. Nick was one of a dozen or so kids who volunteered to go with him because it never hurt to be on Bumper's side. A country path skirted the perimeter of both schools and came out behind St. Bede's. The plan called for the main Westridge force to give Bumper ten minutes to get around St. Bede's unnoticed and come up on the catholic rear. The Westridge kids would then launch a sustained bombardment intended to drive the St. Bede's kids back into the confines of their schoolyard where Bumper would be waiting. Clausewitz couldn't have executed it better. When the barrage from the Westridge side of the hedge intensified the catholic kids retreated into the safety of the schoolyard only to have Bumper's Bombers pop up from behind a wall and unleash a series of volleys into them at point blank range. Snowballs smacked into startled faces only a few feet away, the catholic kids scattered in panic and Bumper's Bombers scampered back to Westridge whooping with laughter.

It was this ambush that set the stage for an incident later that day that was to stay with Nick for the rest of his life. Among Bumper's Bombers was his cousin, Shorty Short, from 2C. Shorty came to Westridge when his family moved from Stakeford to Bedlington and was taken under Bumper's protection. A weasely little sod he was always picking fights with kids who would have given him a thumping had they not been afraid of Bumper. When the schools got out that afternoon some of the bigger catholic lads waited to take their revenge on Bumper and his mates. A series of running battles broke out along Ridge Terrace and spilled onto a patch of wasteland where scores between the schools were often settled. When Nick, Spelk and Dave got there they found several fights underway, vortices of violence amid a roaring mass of kids. They were quickly caught up in the surge of the crowd and found themselves among a circle of kids watching Shorty getting a hiding from a catholic kid. The kid straddled Shorty's chest and rained down blows on him as kids from St. Bede's and Westridge urged him on. A chorus of cheers signaled the end of a fight nearby followed by a commotion in the crowd as the victorious Bumper pushed his way through to his cousin. Bumper, straw coloured hair hanging down over his welted face, strode into the circle where the catholic kid sat astride Shorty, swung his foot back and kicked the kid in the head as if it was a football. Nick expected to see the kid's head lift off his shoulders and soar over the nearby rooftops. But it didn't. The impact lifted him off Shorty and flung him backwards onto the trampled snow where he lay dazed, an oozing cut on his forehead amid the imprint of Bumper's boot. Bumper hoisted Shorty onto his feet and dragged him off through the crowd. Nick remained with the suddenly hushed circle of kids staring at the kid on the ground. Just like that Bumper booted a hole through the fabric of civilisation. He'd kicked that kid in the head and thought nothing of it - even though he could have killed him. Was that what it took to get by in the world? Because if it was Nick didn't think he had it in him.

* * *

Change came in a hurry that spring. After a long period of stability at Bedlington Police Station, a sudden confluence of events changed everything. Bert Fry, the station sergeant for the past 11 years, was diagnosed with pancreatic cancer and went on medical leave from which he was not expected to return. John Robson was transferred to Ponteland and replaced by Ted Dunlop from Ashington, one of Shep's old police mates from before the war. If the chiefs up at Morpeth had set out to create the most favourable environment possible for Shep they couldn't have done better. The appointment of Ted Dunlop as inspector in charge of uniform branch enabled Shep to turn Bedlington into his personal fiefdom. Robson had barely cleaned out his office when Shep took a bottle of Cutty Sark from his filing cabinet and invited Bright in to celebrate. He splashed whisky into a couple of tea mugs and said: "This'll work out well for ye, Jimmy. Ah'll tell Ted you're to be the acting duty officer till ye get your stripes. Take the sergeant's exam this summer and I'll see you're confirmed as station sergeant afore the end of the year."

Things had been better for Bright since he'd lied for Shep on the witness stand. Shep's memory of the night he bloodied Peter McMahon was hazy but all he cared about was that Bright had done right by him when it mattered. Bright was also happy to see John Robson go. Robson hadn't bothered to hide his suspicion that Bright had perjured himself for Shep. But that was all it was - suspicion. And Shep had been proven right. Even inside the police force suspicion wasn't worth a shovelful of sheep shite.

The following week, as Shep promised, Ted Dunlop sent out a memo announcing that Bright would be acting daytime duty officer, effective immediately. There was no reason why he shouldn't. He'd stood in for Bert Fry often enough when Bert had taken more and more sick days over the past year. He accepted the congratulations of his colleagues modestly. And on his second day as acting duty officer he took a phone call from Ian Cuthbertson, the young polis who ran the one-man station up at Wooler in the Cheviot Hills.

"Ah wanted to let ye knah ah'll be needin' some assistance from ye blokes owa the next few weeks," Cuthbertson said.

Bright knew Cuthbertson's wife had just had a baby and asked: "Ye want some leave to spend with the wife an' bairn?"

"Ah wish that's ahll it was," Cuthbertson answered. "Ah've spent owa many nights up on the fells these past few weeks tryin' to find oot wee's stealin' ahll wa sheep."

The wind scoured Cheviot Hills sprawled across the borderlands between Northumberland and Scotland and were inhospitable and empty except for thousands of sheep raised for their wool.

"Ye've got a bit o' sheep stealin' goin' on then?" Bright said.

"Mair than a bit," Cuthbertson said. "Folk up here expect to lose a few sheep each year to one thing or another but by wor reckonin' we've lost between 60 an' 70 heed since January an' it wasn't because o' bad weather. And that's on top of the two dozen we lost through the tail end o' last year."

"Soonds like somebody's gettin' greedy," Bright said. "What do ye need from us?"

If Cuthbertson needed extra manpower there were police stations at Alnwick, Morpeth and Berwick-On-Tweed, all of them closer to Wooler than Bedlington.

"Weeivah's tekkin' them has been comin' on weekends closest the full moon," Cuthbertson said. "Ah finally clapped eyes on the buggas aroond two-o-clock yisterday mornin'. Tha was four or five o' them and tha weel organised. They've got a good sized lorry an' they left their lights off so they wouldn't attract attention. They took nine or ten sheep that ah coonted. Ah got close enough to get the licence number o' the lorry an' ah cahlled it in to Morpeth this mornin'. It's registered to the Doctor Pit in Bedlin'ton, so it looks like it's some lads from doon your way."

"That doesn't surprise is," Bright said. "Ye want wi to tek a look owa the Doctor Pit fo' ye?"

"Actually, no, ah don't," Cuthbertson said. "After ahll the trouble they've put is tee ah'd rather nail ahll o' the buggas at once an' that means catchin' them in the act. Ah divvent want them to get wind wa onto them or they'll gan to grund an' it'll be that much harder to catch them when they start up again. Ah've put a request in to Morpeth for extra manpower but ah'm thinkin' we should hae somebody from Bedlin'ton to identify them."

Bright remembered what Shep had told him about Tommy Locke, the foreman at the Doctor Pit transport depot.

"Ah'll pass it on to D.I. Shepherd an' one o' wi will get back to ye," he said.

"Ye knah what's funny?" Cuthbertson added. "It's not that lang since they stopped hangin' buggas fo' sheep stealin.'"

"Aye an' mair's the pity," Bright said. "Tha's a few buggas doon here that want hangin'."

Bright talked to Shep that afternoon and Shep wasn't pleased.

"Ye let them mek a few quid on the side an' it's nivah enough, they always want more," he grumbled. "Hoo lang's this been gannin' on, did he say?"

"He says tha was aroond two dozen tekin the tail end o' last year an' between 60 and 70 so far this year."

"Bloody hell, that's nearly a hundred sheep in what, nine, ten months?" Shep said. "What are they deein' wi' them ahll?"

"They'll be sellin' them to leek growers more than likely," Bright answered. "Ye cannit get blood an' bone nae mair lessin' ye knah somebody, so tha's nivah enough to gan roond fo' ahll that wants it. They'll be tekin' orders an' droppin' them off the same night tha stealin' them."

"There's enough money in it fo' them to go to that much trouble?"

"Whey aye, man," Bright said. "Ye've seen the prizes tha givin' away these days haven't ye? Livin' room sets, kitchen sets, televisions an' the like. Top prizes worth fifty, sixty pund. Last year Netherton Club put up nine hundred pund worth o' prizes, the Top Club was owa a thoosand."

Shep lit a Capstan Full Strength and pondered what Bright was saying.

"An' it doesn't just stop at the prizes," Bright continued. "Ye can sell the seeds from a prize winnin' leek for two bob apiece these days. If a grower pays

10, 15 quid a sheep an' has a good year he'll get that and mair in nae time."

"They'll be gettin' some money for the meat an' all then," Shep said. "They cannit be hoyin' it oot."

"Oh, there'll be nowt goin' to waste," Bright agreed. "If the buyers divvent want it they'll be usin' it fo' dog food or sellin' it to some chinky restaurant in the toon."

"When does Cuthbertson say he thinks they'll be back?"

"He says they ahlways come the weekend closest to the full moon. He's fund where they've been operatin'. He wants to catch them in the act, get ahll o' them at once. He's put in a request to Morpeth fo' the men."

Shep made up his mind.

"If Tommy Locke is behind this ah'll handle it from this end. Tell Cuthbertson ah'll be tekin' it over."

"He asked specifically that wi don't go to the Doctor Pit," Bright said. "He's afraid we'll tip them off an' wi won't get ahll o' them."

"Ye can tell young Cuthbertson we'll get ahll o' them," Shep said. "Tell him he can mark mah words, we'll get every last bloody one o' them."

*   *   *

The day had cooled and there were only a handful of kids left at the baths. Humford Mill Open Air Swimming Baths sat in a hollow in Hartford Woods next to the River Blyth and was popular with kids throughout the summer. Nick had come late in the day with Spelk and Dave despite overcast skies and a cold wind that had driven everybody else home. The three boys seemed not to feel the cold as they bombed each other from the high diver, showing off to a couple of girls who paddled, giggling, around the middle of the pool. One of them was the lovely Norah Cox, the other her friend, Lorraine, a pudgy blonde who served to make Norah look even lovelier. Norah was a couple of years ahead of Nick at school and, like all the younger lads, he lusted after her from a distance. But, encouraged by her reaction to his antics off the high diver he'd spoken to her a couple of times as he swam past. He couldn't believe his luck in having unobstructed access to one of the sexiest girls in school but he had no idea how to follow it up so he did what most boys did in the presence of overwhelming sensuality - nothing.

When they could stand the cold no longer the two girls got out to get changed. Deprived of their audience the boys soon followed. The women's changing rooms were a row of rickety wooden cubicles along the side of the pool with the men's changing rooms on the far side of the baths by the filtration pool. Spelk and Dave disappeared into their cubicles and Nick was on his way to his when it occurred to him that he had an opportunity now that might never have again. He was alone in the amphitheatre of the baths, the only sound the slapping of the water against the sides of the pool. Even the caretaker, Wilf, who was always around, was nowhere to be seen. Nick padded back around the pool to the women's changing rooms and the cubicle where Norah and Lorraine were getting changed. The old wooden boards were warped and cracked, leaving chinks that made it possible to see inside. Most of the time there were people around to prevent the boys peeking into the girls' changing rooms but not today.

Nick squinted between the boards and was rewarded immediately with a glimpse of skin. He felt a tingle of excitement. Norah Cox was on the other side of the door, naked. The two girls, shivering and breathless, were toweling themselves to get warm. Nick twisted his head around to put the sliver of skin into some sort of context. There was a blur of towel, the skin trembled and he realised it was her tit. He was looking at Norah Cox's tit in the flesh. His blood rose banishing all vestiges of cold. But then it occurred to him that it might not be her tit at all, it could just as well be her arm. What if it was her arm moving up and down with the towel? There was all the difference in the world between tit skin and arm skin. Tit skin was a rare and elusive object of desire. Arm skin was just skin. Norah Cox could be naked from head to toe on the other side of the door and it didn't matter in the slightest if all he could see was a piece of her arm. He shifted around trying to find different angles but she was too close to the door for him to see anything more. He glanced around the baths but there was still nobody to stop him. He pressed his eye hard against the crevice hoping for a glimpse of bra strap, something lacy or, god help him, a single delectable nipple to tell him he was looking at Norah's tit. Then he had an unsettling thought. What if it wasn't Norah, what if it was Lorraine? What if it was Lorraine's flabby tit he was looking at? Norah's tits stood up like headlamps, Lorraine's tits hung down like a couple of shopping bags. Just the thought made him queasy. But the girls' voices were too close to separate one from the other. Frustrated, he gave up and went back to the men's cubicles. He blamed god. God was always making things more complicated than they needed to be and Nick was tired of it. There was nothing funny about sex with its importuning erections and the inability to do anything about them. There was no sense to them, no logic. It didn't matter where he was; sitting in class, riding on the bus, watching television, buying lollies at the sweet shop, without warning his prick would leap in his pants like a salmon fighting its way upstream. His first concern was to hide it so nobody would know.

He'd found that by groping around in his trouser pockets he could pin his nob end under the waistband of his underpants which would hold the shaft against his lower belly where it would impress itself into his skin like a prick shaped hot water bottle. But it wasn't always possible to work it into a discrete position. Especially on a crowded bus when he was standing in the aisle and needed both hands to keep his balance while his prick struggled to get free and latch onto the back of some unsuspecting lass's neck like a lamprey eel. At those times he tried to keep his school bag between his prick and the rest of the world but it seemed so obvious that whenever he saw another lad carrying his school bag in front of him Nick assumed he was hiding a hard-on.

What was the point he wanted to know? Why were there so many of them? What was he supposed to do with them all? Actually, he knew what he was supposed to do, he just didn't know of any girl who'd be alright with it if he was to walk up to her, pull it out and ask her to give him a hand. So why? He was a kid not a man. What did he need with a man's prick? A great walloping wally wagging around like a divining rod sniffing for tash? According to the lads at school the answer lay in his own hands; he should be wanking regularly to siphon off the inexhaustible supply of semen his knackers were churning out morning, noon and night. It didn't help that they referred to it as 'tossing off" as if it was some kind of plumbing job. He'd tried it a few times but it left his prick sore and puffy like the Michelin Man's prick. And besides, it made him feel ridiculous. Surely, he thought, there must be a more dignified way to relieve the ache in his scrotum caused by the over-production of spunk that had nowhere to go. He wondered if he should see the doctor, if there were pills that would at least dry his goolies up a bit. It just seemed inherently wrong that the only recourse for boys all over the world was to wank themselves off every night like monkeys in the zoo.

And then Brigitte Bardot came to his relief. Somehow in the gauzy dimension of sleep she found her way to West Lea and slipped into bed beside him. In some remote crevice of his mind he knew it was a dream but it didn't matter because he could see her and feel her in such exquisite detail. She nestled beside him under the covers, naked, soft and warm, her pouting lips on his neck, the tendrils of her hair tickling his face, her slender fingers on his cock. And he knew just what to do. With uncharacteristic confidence he rolled over on top of her and felt her receive him deeply into her soothing loins. It was a pleasure unlike anything he'd imagined and he wanted it to last forever. He wanted her to stay with him, so tender, so generous in her knowingness. And then he came. A rapturous pulsing stream that emptied him of all need and within seconds he was lost in blessed, relaxing sleep.

*　　　*　　　*

Tommy Locke was a man of habit and one of his habits was to play dominoes at The Howard Arms on a Monday night. Shep made sure to arrive shortly before closing time and had a pint at the bar while he kept an eye on Tommy at a corner table with his dominoes partners. When Tommy got up to go to the toilet he didn't notice Shep. He had no idea Shep was behind him as he limped down the corridor and went to push open the door to the men's toilet until a hand seized his collar and thrust him out the fire door. He stumbled into the darkened lane swearing and spun around to defend himself until, in a narrowing shaft of light from the closing door, he recognised Shep.

"Bloody hell," he said and relaxed his posture. "What are ye tryin' to dee, gi's a heart attack?"

"Ah'll gi' ye a heart attack ahlreet if ye don't tell me what ye've been up to," Shep said.

The two men rarely spoke directly to each other and when they did it was in places like this where nobody could see them together.

"Ah hae nae idea what ya tahkin' aboot," Locke said.

"Ye've been workin' a new fiddle without telling is haven't ye, Tommy?"

"Are ye ganna gi's a clue what ya on aboot or am ah supposed to guess?"

"Don't get cheeky wi me," Shep said warningly. "Ye an' me are supposed to have an understandin'."

"Ah've been sendin' ya commission," Locke protested. "Did ye not get it last month? Is that what you're on aboot?"

The last Friday of every month Locke put a few pounds from his bookmaking business in an envelope and posted it to Shep's home.

"Ah'm not tahkin' aboot that," Shep said. "Ah'm tahkin' aboot ye deein' a bit o' business on the side without tellin' me."

Locke ran a quick mental check on everything that brought him in a few extra quid each month but he didn't know which one Shep meant and he didn't want to give any of them away.

"Just tell is, Shep," he said. "Ah'm not tryin' te be funny. Just tell 'is an' ah'll tell ye what ah knah."

"Ye've been workin' a dodge wi the pit lorries, haven't ye?" Shep said. "An' ye thought ah wouldn't find oot."

Locke took a breath. So that was it, the arrangement with Danny Mullen. He could easily resolve that.

"It's purely temporary," he said. "An' tha's definitely not much money in it. Ah can put a stop te it, nae bother, if that's what ye want."

"Oh, it's gone way past that," Shep said. "Morpeth knahs aboot it noo an' that means somebody has to get his arse kicked."

Locke was puzzled. They were talking about sheep shite. How much money did Shep think there was in sheep shite?

"It's a few loads o' sheep shite, that's ahll," he said. "Tha's nae need for Scotland Yard te get involved."

"De ye think ah'm stupid, Tommy?" Shep said. "De ye think ah don't know what ye've been up te? Ah want to knah ivery bugga wee's in it wi ye, ivery name, ivery last one o' them. If ye cooperate ah'll see what ah can dee fo' ye, but if ye keep buggerin' is aroond ah'll run ye in an' ahll an' don't think ah won't."

Locke knew now that whatever Danny Mullen was up to had to involve more than sheep shite.

"Fuckin' Danny Mullen," he said. "Ah telt him he could use one o' the lorries noo an' again an' the deal was he'd pay is a fiver each time he took one oot. He said he was gannin up te the Cheviots te collect sheep shite te sell to leek growers. That's why ah only charged him a fiver."

"He's been collectin' mair than sheep shite," Shep scoffed. "He's been collectin' sheep. He's stolen nearly a hundred we knah aboot. An' you're tryin' to tell me ye knah nowt aboot it?"

Locke was genuinely shocked.

"Ah Christ, ah should hae knahn. Iverybody wee does business wi' that family lives to regret it. Ah should hae knahn."

"Ye should hae knahn…" Shep repeated sarcastically.

"On me mother's life, Shep, ah didn't knah what he was usin' the lorries for."

"Wee's in it wi'm?"

Locke shook his head. "Mah arrangement was wi' Danny. He said his brutha would help him oot. Ah thowt they were collectin' sheep shite. Ah didn't think it was much of a fiddle at ahll."

"Aye weel it'll be the whole family that's in it and those thievin' buggas next door to them at West Lea, the Learys - if you're tellin' me the truth," Shep said.

"It's the god's honest truth, Shep. What do ye want is to dee? Tell is what ye want is to dee an' ah'll dee it."

"I divvent want ye te dee owt for noo," Shep said. "Divvent let on te Danny Mullen aboot anythin'. Act like it's business as usual. The next time he asks te borrow a lorry, ye tell me aheed o' time. Ah want te knah as far in advance as possible."

"As soon as ah knah, ye'll knah." Locke said.

"Ah bloody better," Shep said.

*   *   *

The waiting room at Dr. Ritchie's surgery was a reflection of his personality; florid and a bit dowdy. The walls were decorated with flowery wallpaper and hunting prints in which scarlet jacketed men in black caps and tight breeches galloped across an idyllic countryside a long way away from Bedlington. Rose patterned linoleum on the floor was covered with worn floral carpets and the chairs were creaky parlour chairs that had seen better days. A corner table was piled high with back issues of Country Life and The Illustrated London News, which served as reminders to Dr. Ritchie's patients of their place in the world.

Friday afternoons were Dr. Ritchie's time to wind down after a week of treating the sick, the lame and the miserable and he had his receptionist, Agnes, hold his easier appointments till after lunch. This afternoon there were only two patients in his waiting room: Mrs. Broadbent, whose incurable loneliness cost the National Health a weekly visit to the doctor, and Nellie McBride with her youngest son, Keith.

Dr. Ritchie had a jolly manner and pink cheeks nourished by a lifetime of good living. His bouffant white hair was complemented by a pencil line moustache that had given him a rakish look in the 1920's when he and the former Phyllis Adler had embarked on a marriage of convenience predicated on separate bedrooms and no children. His wife took more interest in her golden retrievers than she did in children and it was left to her husband to indulge the kids who came into their lives with sixpenny pieces and mint humbugs from a bag he carried in a jacket pocket of his whiskery tweed suit. At the end of the day, after he'd poured Mrs. Broadbent a glass of medicinal sherry, Dr. Ritchie would pour himself a whisky, light his pipe and settle back for a bit of a gossip. It was for this reason he saved Mrs. Broadbent till last.

Agnes showed Nellie and Keith into Dr. Ritchie's office and closed the door behind them. Ritchie greeted them warmly and gestured them to a couple of empty chairs. As she sat down Nellie glanced around at shelves stocked with imposing medical textbooks and photographs of the Ritchies' prizewinning bulls at the Northumberland Agricultural Show. Keith was interested in none of it.

"So, young Keith's been a bit under the weather then, has he?" Ritchie said. He'd seen Nellie McBride through three pregnancies - one of which ended in a miscarriage - and her two boys through the usual childhood ills but he hadn't seen Keith for nearly two years.

"He's ahlways been quiet," Nellie said. "But as he gets older it's like he has no interest in anythin' that goes on around him. He's nivah been like other kids his age an' now he's nine ah'm worried there might be something wrong wi'm." She'd removed her headscarf and she twisted it restlessly in her lap. "Ah took him out o' school this week because he's ahlways gettin' picked on - ye know what kids can be like - an' he cannit stick up for hissel'."

Keith was slender as a blade of grass with fair hair, milky blue eyes and skin pale to the point of translucence.

"Dear oh dear, we'll have to see what we can do about this then," Dr. Ritchie responded sympathetically. "How's his appetite?"

"He eats like a spuggie," Nellie answered. "He'll eat a teeny little bit then poke his dinner around the plate like tha's somethin' wrong wi't. He doesn't hae any energy, he'd lie in his bed ahll day if ah let him."

Ritchie nodded. Despite the best efforts of the National Health Service he still saw children with rickets caused by chips with everything. Vegetables served at Sunday dinners had all the goodness boiled out of them, the only time kids got an orange was at Christmas and he had yet to meet the miner's family that would sit down to a salad at dinner time.

"What about you, Keith?" Ritchie inquired gently. "What do you have to say about this - don't you like your mother's cooking then?"

Keith wouldn't meet Dr. Ritchie's eye.

"Ah don't know," he said, his voice barely audible.

"He gets the same food as the rest o' wi an' there's nowt wrong wi' us," Nellie said.

"That's alright, Keith," Dr. Ritchie tried again. "You can trust me. Nobody's going to make fun of you here."

Keith stared at his feet.

"Ye mind ya manners when the doctor's speakin' to ye," his mam said. "Ye tell him what's the matter wi' ye."

Dr. Ritchie smiled. "I don't think he knows, Mrs. McBride. That's what we're here to find out."

Nellie shook her head. "Ah'm worried he's got somethin' really wrong wi'm, Dr. Ritchie. Ah think he might hae somethin' wrong wi's blood."

Ritchie knew that, like any mother, Nellie McBride feared the worst, that her son might have something incurable like leukemia.

"I don't know if that's something we have to worry about quite yet," he said. "But there might be something missing from his blood." Ritchie addressed himself directly to Keith again. "Do you ever feel dizzy, Keith? Do you feel as if you're going to faint sometimes?"

Keith looked uncomfortable. Fainting was something girls did, not boys, unless they were puffs. And he was tired of the boys at school calling him a puff. He kept his eyes averted and said nothing. His mother tutted her frustration.

Ritchie said: "Come over here beside me, Keith, where I can take a closer look at you."

Keith hesitated but his mother prodded him and said: "Go on then, do what the doctor says."

Keith got out of his chair and stepped listlessly around Ritchie's desk. Ritchie swiveled his chair to the side, took Keith's hands in his and studied them closely: the fingernails were soft and opaque and fraying at the tips. Along with everything else it was all Ritchie needed to make a diagnosis.

"You know what I'm thinking, Mrs. McBride?" he said. "I'm thinking that Keith probably doesn't have enough iron in his blood, that's all. I'm thinking that what we have here is a case of anaemia. That would explain his pale complexion, his poor appetite and overall lethargy."

"Anaemia?" Mrs. McBride repeated. "Ah thought it was only women got that."

"It's more common in women than men," Ritchie confirmed. "But it can present in men too, especially if it runs in the family."

"Nobody ah know of has it in our family," Nellie said defensively.

"It can jump a generation or two and present itself in only one member of a family," Ritchie said. "If you look back on both sides of your family tree you'll probably find somebody who was anaemic, though it was often misdiagnosed in the past or mistaken for idleness."

Nellie looked thoughtful. "Now ye come to mention it, me mam's sister, Mavis, was always poorly, always catchin' whatever was goin' around."

"She might well have been anaemic then," Ritchie said.

"Well ah never," Nellie said, looking relieved. "Our Keith anaemic, ah would never hae thought o' that."

"He's too young for me to prescribe iron pills," Ritchie added. "But there are things you can add to his diet."

Nellie looked confused. "He's not on a diet. Nobody ah know has ivah been on a diet."

Ritchie smiled: "Just make sure he gets a good supply of iron rich foods like beef liver, broccoli, Brussels sprouts, that kind of thing." He picked up a pencil and made a list on his notepad. "Here, I'll write a few things down for you. Try to see that he gets three or four meals a week that are rich in iron and don't overcook the vegetables. It won't cost you anything extra and you should notice a difference in a month or two."

"Ah don't like liver," Keith said.

"Ye'll just have to get used to it then won't ye," his mam said. "Ye'll eat what the doctor says ye'll eat…doctor's ordahs."

Ritchie tore off a sheet of notepaper and handed it to Nellie.

"While you've got him here I may as well give him an examination," he added. "That way we won't miss anything. If you wouldn't mind waiting outside perhaps Keith and I can have a talk man to man as it were. He might find that a bit easier." Ritchie turned his attention back to Keith and said encouragingly: "Would that be better, Keith? I can give you an examination and you can tell me anything you want and you don't have to be the least bit embarrassed."

Keith showed no reaction. Nellie got up from her chair.

"Ye mind ye do whatever Dr. Ritchie tells ye to do," she told her son. "He's tryin' to help ye get better."

She stepped outside and when the door closed behind her Ritchie got up and quietly turned the key in the lock.

"Now then…" Ritchie returned to his chair and looked directly into Keith's eyes. "First thing you need to do is get undressed. Take all your clothes off so I can get a good look at you. There's no need to be embarrassed, we're both men aren't we?"

Keith hesitated then, remembering what his mother said, pulled half heartedly at his shirt buttons.

"Here, let me help you," Ritchie said. "We'll get it done in half the time."

Ritchie quickly unfastened the buttons and removed Keith's shirt. Next he pulled off the thin vest Keith wore underneath then helped him with his socks and sandshoes. Finally he helped Keith out of his pants and underpants until the boy stood naked before him. Self-consciously Keith clenched his hands together over his groin and stared at the floor.

"There, there, Keith," Ritchie said soothingly. "There's no need to be embarrassed, you've got nothing to be ashamed about. God made us all the same you know."

Keith continued to stare mutely downwards. Ritchie gently took the boy's hands, unclenched them and placed them at his side so he had an unobstructed view of Keith's delicate white body. He stared for the longest time until the room filled with a suffocating silence. Abruptly, Ritchie retrieved his stethoscope from his desk and put it on.

"I'm going to use this to listen to what's going on inside your chest," he said. "It's a bit cold so I'll warm it up for you." He breathed on the head of the stethoscope, making a little game of it, then held it against Keith's narrow chest. "There, that's not so bad is it? Now, breathe in as deeply as you can and hold it till I tell you to let it go."

Keith did as he was told and Ritchie moved the head of the stethoscope around, repeating the process several times, then had him turn around so he could do it again to the boy's back.

"Well," Ritchie turned Keith to face him again, "your heart is good and strong and there doesn't seem to be anything wrong with your lungs." He let the stethoscope hang from his neck then held the tips of his fingers to Keith's chest and tapped them with his other hand while leaning his head against Keith's chest to listen, trying to get Keith comfortable with his closeness and his touch.

"Jolly good." Ritchie sat up and smiled approvingly. "Doesn't seem to be anything much wrong with you at all, Keith. You're a lovely little boy…a lovely little boy."

Ritchie thought he saw the flicker of a smile on Keith's face.

"It's not nice to be picked on at school is it?" Ritchie said. "Do you know the same thing used to happen to me when I was your age. I hated school and it was all because of the bullies. They're horrible, horrible people who come from horrible, horrible homes. They hate anybody who's the slightest bit different to them and they pick on you and pick on you until after a while you start to think that perhaps they're right, there is something wrong with you. Is that how it is for you at school, Keith, is that how it is?"

For the first time Keith met the doctor's gaze and Ritchie saw his opportunity.

"I wasn't like the other boys at school and you know what, Keith? I was glad. I didn't want to be like them. I didn't like the things they liked. I didn't like sport. I didn't like the rough games they played. I was different and I was glad to be different. Do you ever feel like that, Keith? Do you ever feel that you're different to the other boys?"

Keith hesitated then said shyly: "Sometimes."

"Yes, of course you do," Ritchie said reassuringly. "You are different. You're better than they are and you should be proud of it."

Keith seemed to have grown more comfortable in his nakedness.

"Now, I'm just going to check your reflexes," Ritchie said. "Tell me how this feels."

Ritchie trailed his fingertips slowly from Keith's right shoulder, down his arm to his hand then did the same again with his left arm.

Ritchie paused. "How did that feel?"

Keith shook his head. "Nothing."

"Mmm," Ritchie paused thoughtfully. Then he started at the instep of Keith's right foot and traced his way slowly up the inside leg till he came to the groin then moved his hand to the back and cupped Keith's right buttock in his hand.

"What about that?" Ritchie asked. "Feel anything that time?"

Keith paused. "It tickles a bit."

"Good, very good," Ritchie said. He did the same with Keith's left leg, this time staring keenly at the boy's groin only inches away, looking for some kind of reaction.

"I'm just going to go downstairs for a minute," Ritchie said. "Make sure everything's alright there."

Downstairs, Keith thought. Was Dr. Ritchie leaving now?

"I'll be as gentle as I can and I want you tell me exactly how it feels, alright?"

Keith didn't respond one way or the other as Ritchie cupped the fingers of one hand under his undeveloped scrotum.

"Now, I want you to cough for me," Ritchie said.

It seemed like some kind of game the doctor was playing but Keith did as he was told and coughed, then two more times before Ritchie withdrew his hand.

"Did that hurt at all?" Ritchie asked.

Keith shook his head.

"There, I told you I would be gentle," Ritchie said. "You know you can trust me now don't you, Keith, you know that?"

Keith took a breath and nodded.

"And what about your little winkle?" Ritchie said and lightly tickled Keith's penis with his fingers. "Any feeling there?"

Keith flinched and drew away.

"Did that hurt?" Ritchie asked, concerned.

Keith hesitated. "Not really." he said. "It feels…sort of funny."

"Funny? "Ritchie smiled. "Funny how?"

"Ah don't know."

"Come on, Keith, you can do better than that," Ritchie chided him gently. He took Keith's tiny penis again and rubbed it lightly between his thumb and forefinger. "How about that? What would you say about that, good or bad?"

Keith seemed to think about it. "It sort of…tickles," he said.

"Well there you are then," Ritchie said enthusiastically. "It's supposed to tickle. It's supposed to feel quite nice. Your winkle is a very important part of your body. It's not just for peeing, you know. It's very sensitive to the touch, it's supposed to be, it means you're perfectly normal."

Keith looked unsure but his mam had told him it was alright and Dr. Ritchie wouldn't do anything to hurt him. He swallowed and nodded his head.

"Now, let me try something else," Ritchie said. His face had become flushed and there was a thickness in his voice that wasn't there before. "It's perfectly normal but it is something we keep to ourselves, do you understand? It's something boys can do for each other when they're special friends. But it's not something we talk about to others. It's one of life's little secrets between men so you have to promise you'll never talk about it to anybody else, do you understand? It's our special secret, just between you and me."

Ritchie put his hands on Keith's hips and held him there, then he ducked his head and took Keith's penis in his mouth. He sucked it gently, swirling it around in his mouth, running his tongue lightly over it. He did it for a full minute before he released it and sat up and wiped his lips with his fingers. His face was bright pink and he was breathing heavily.

"There now, how did that feel?" he asked.

Keith stared uncomprehendingly back at Ritchie.

"Ah don't know," he said.

"Well, would you say it was a good feeling or a bad feeling?" Ritchie pressed him.

For the longest moment Keith seemed not to know how to respond. Then he said: "It was…alright."

"Well that's good then isn't it?" Ritchie said. "And you know what, it will get better as you get older, I promise you that. It's something you can look forward to when you're grown up, when you're a man."

Ritchie realised they had been alone for longer than he intended. He told Keith he could get dressed and helped him put his things back on. When Keith was fully dressed and Ritchie's colour had returned to normal he took a half crown from his trouser pocket and held it up to Keith.

"You know how much this is?"

"Two and six," Keith replied.

"That's right, two shillings and sixpence," Richie said. "You're a very clever boy and you're a good boy and it's yours to keep. You have to remember now, this is a secret between us so nobody else thinks they can come and get two shillings and sixpence from me. And next time I see you, if you've been a good boy - and I'm sure you will be - I'll give you another two and sixpence. I'll look after you, Keith. As long as you're a good boy I promise I'll look after you."

He tucked the big silver coin into Keith's trouser pocket.

"And don't let your mother know I gave you this either or she'll get angry at me and I'm sure you wouldn't want me to get in trouble with your mother now, would you? Or nobody in your family would ever be able to come back and see me and you wouldn't like that either, would you?"

Keith slowly shook his head. Ritchie got up, unlocked the office door and called Nellie back in.

"No need to worry, Mrs. McBride," Ritchie said. "Despite the anaemia he's a very healthy boy. Heart, lungs, reflexes all perfectly normal. All he needs is a little more iron in his blood and you'll notice an improvement in no time. Bring him back in six months and we'll see how he's doing then."

Ritchie watched them go then reached into a jacket pocket, took out a mint humbug and popped it into his mouth.

*   *   *

Tommy Locke called Shep the Wednesday after the August Bank Holiday and told him Danny Mullen had asked to borrow a lorry for that Saturday when there would be a full moon. At Shep's request Bright had recruited some 'handy lads' and told them to be ready at short notice. On Saturday afternoon Shep drove the Wolseley up to Wooler with Bright in the passenger seat, both of them dressed for a night on the fells. On the way they stopped at Morpeth to pick up a couple of volunteers. Ian Cuthbertson was to be joined at Wooler by two more from Ashington and another from Berwick-Upon-Tweed, which would give Shep eight men, including himself, more than enough to handle Cuthbertson's estimate of four to five sheep thieves.

There was little traffic and the drive from Morpeth to Wooler took barely an hour. Shep parked outside the one-man police station on the high street and the four of them went inside. The station had room for a counter, a bulletin board, a desk with a typewriter and phone, and a single filing cabinet. Another door led to the private quarters out back. Cuthbertson was waiting with his reinforcements in a fog of cigarette smoke. The younger lads knew each other from playing rugby for the police team and those who didn't know Shep first hand knew him by reputation. In their dark clothing and heavy boots they could have passed for a gang of villains themselves.

"Right," Shep said, "it's goin' to be a long night so, first order of business, let's get some beer an' grub into wi."

They walked down to The Black Bull in the buttery summer light, their voices echoing around the empty street. The pub had only a few drinkers and the policemen took over a corner of the bar and drank beer and ate sandwiches and crisps while Shep briefed them on the job ahead. They passed the rest of the evening playing darts and dominoes and drinking the way rugby players drank. Shortly before ten with the light fading Shep decided they should go to work. Cuthbertson in the police Land Rover led the way back down the A697 with Shep behind in the Wolseley. After a few miles they turned off the macadam onto a narrow unmarked track that led to Langlee Crags where Cuthbertson had last seen the sheep thieves. The two vehicles bumped along a badly rutted track for a quarter of a mile till it ended in a rock strewn bowl with steep hillsides on three sides. Bright saw there was barely enough room to turn the cars around, which would make it that much harder for the thieves' lorry to manoeuvre. It was just getting dark and the headlamps of the two vehicles swept the hillsides illuminating scores of grazing sheep. It was the perfect place, Bright thought. Nobody would see or hear anything from the road and the sheep could easily be herded down into the bowl where there was a water trough and a stand pipe in the middle of a patch of churned up mud.

"Like robbin' eggs from a nest," Shep said.

It took only a minute to assign everyone their places. Bright and the five burly young coppers would conceal themselves about the hillsides while Shep and Cuthbertson drove the two cars back out to the road and hid them off to the side in a stand of trees. When the lorry turned onto the track Shep would give them a few minutes to reach the rocky bowl then he and Cuthbertson would follow in the Land Rover, leaving the Wolseley behind to block the way out. Once the lorry was loaded with sheep Bright would sound his whistle, the Land Rover would speed in and Shep and Cuthbertson would help round up the thieves.

"Like ah said earlier there's a good chance it'll get lively," Shep said. "These aren't the cliverest lads we're dealin' wi so don't worry aboot bein' too heavy handed wi them, it's the only language they understand."

There was an anticipatory chuckle among the volunteers.

Shep and Cuthbertson turned their cars around and drove out while Bright dispersed his men. A few wisps of cloud drifted across the pockmarked face of the moon but there was enough light to see short distances. Bright told the young coppers not to spread out too far so they could confine the thieves to the bottom of the bowl and keep them from escaping onto the fells. The Cheviots were no place to go charging about at night in pursuit of some villain no matter how bright the moon. There were drop-offs, ledges, gullies and streams that drained into bogs so deep they could swallow a man. Bobbing torchlights marked the progress of the young coppers across the hillsides till they were all settled. Bright picked his own spot about fifty yards up the nearest hill and sat down on the springy grass. The night air was warm, they'd had plenty to drink and it wasn't long before he heard the sound of somebody snoring.

"Weivah that is, wake up ye dozy bugga," Bright shouted and flashed his torch in the direction of the culprit. The snoring stopped followed by an embarrassed "sorry boss" amid scattered laughter.

Time passed slowly, the only sounds the bleating of the sheep and the tearing of their jaws at the grass. The waiting seemed longer because nobody was allowed to smoke so the glow of cigarettes wouldn't give them away. Around midnight Bright found himself hoping they wouldn't have to wait much longer or he too might nod off. About one thirty he heard the rumble of a lorry engine on the track. The driver had switched off his lights but as the lorry drew closer Bright heard singing. He watched the dark bulk of the lorry take shape on the moonlit track and heard voices singing to the tune of Mademoiselle From Armentieres.

"The Jarman Officers crossed the Rhine, parlee-voo,

The Jarman Officers crossed the Rhine, parlee-voo,

The Jarman Officers crossed the Rhine, fucked the women and drank the wine,

Inky-Pinky parlee voo."

Whoever they were they weren't worried about anybody hearing them. That told Bright something else; they were pissed too. Like the coppers waiting in ambush they'd spent the night drinking before going to work. Bright watched the lorry pass below him and saw the initials 'NCB' on the cab door reflected in the moonlight. Farther back on the track Shep and Cuthbertson would be moving in behind.

"They came upon a wayside Inn, parlee-voo
They came upon a wayside Inn, parlee-voo
They came upon a wayside Inn, pissed on the door and wahlked streyt in,

Inky-Pinky parlee-voo."

The lorry jolted to a halt amid a rash of curses. The driver switched off the engine, the tailgate slammed down and several dark figures spilled out onto the track. The cab doors opened and a dim yellow light shone briefly but the driver and passenger were too far away for Bright to make them out. They gathered at the back of the lorry and matches flared as they lit cigarettes, making no effort to keep their voices down. Bright heard the clink of glass as they passed a bottle or two around. Amid the drinking and laughing Bright heard Paddy Mullen's phlegmy cackle. After another pass of the bottle it occurred to them that they should get on with it and steal a few sheep. They didn't have to go far. Using the light of the moon and stars they rounded up the sheep nearest the track, herded them over to the water trough and tethered them to the stand pipe. By Bright's estimate it took no more than ten minutes to round up a dozen sheep. They then led the sheep to the back of lorry one at a time where two men threw the animal to the ground and held it still while a third man swung a mell and crushed its skull. They heaved the dead sheep into the back of the lorry where another man dragged it to the back while they returned to the trough for another sheep. They went about their work in a relaxed and unhurried manner, smoking, drinking and cracking jokes. It was all too easy. Another half hour and they'd be on their way back to Bedlington. If they got ten pound for each sheep they'd make 120 quid. After Tommy Locke got his fiver that would leave 115 pounds to be divided five ways - 23 pound a man. A week's pay for a night's work.

Bright waited till they'd thrown the last dead sheep into the back of the lorry before he got to his feet. Below him two figures got into the cab and the three who were to ride in the back with the sheep carcasses climbed up and slammed the tailgate shut. Before the driver could start the engine Bright stood up and blew three piercing shrieks on his police whistle. Torches lit up around the hillsides all trained on the lorry below. The driver switched on the engine and pitched the lorry back and forth as he tried to get it turned around. The men in the back swore and held onto the sides. The driver had the lorry sideways across the track when the Land Rover came charging in, its high beams trapping the lorry in a blinding white glare. Cuthbertson stopped 20 or 30 yards from the lorry and Shep got out and yelled: "Ahll ye buggas stay right where ye are. You're all under arrest, the bloody lot o' ye."

The three men in the back of the lorry vaulted over the sides, the passenger door flew open and another jumped out and the four of them bolted in different directions.

"Get after them lads, don't let 'em get away," Bright shouted and started down the hillside as fast as the steep and uneven surface would allow. Torch beams danced a wild jig as the waiting police officers tightened their noose. Scissors of light sliced across panicked faces and the night filled with curses. Inured to caution by alcohol the young coppers hurled themselves down the hillsides eager to get to grips with the fleeing thieves. Bright heard the crash of colliding bodies accompanied by heavy grunts and shouts of pain. Then the sheep stampeded. To the din of battle was added the bleat of frightened animals and the thump of hooves as the sheep swarmed across the hillsides. Torch lights blinked out as men came into hard contact with each other. Fists and boots flew in the dark but nobody knew who was hitting who. Men were bowled over by fleeing sheep. Bright heard giddy laughter. Everybody was fighting everybody and only the sheep knew what they were doing. A shambles, Bright thought. An absolute bloody shambles.

Below him on the track the lorry pulled around, the driver revved the engine and lurched toward the Land Rover. The track was about 12 feet wide with shallow ditches on each side. The only way out for the lorry was to shove the Land Rover into a ditch, which the driver seemed intent on doing. Bright watched the confrontation unfold like a drama on a brightly lit stage. The distance between the two vehicles closed quickly, the lorry driver turned on his headlights catching Shep in the interlocked brilliance of both vehicles' lights. Whether it was the drink or Shep's confidence in his own invincibility was impossible to know. But instead of getting out of the way Shep stepped in front of the oncoming lorry, put up a hand and commanded: "Stop! In the name o' the law!"

Under other circumstances it would have been funny - but the lorry kept coming and Shep wouldn't budge. Another few feet and he would be crushed between the lorry and the Land Rover.

"Shep, he's not stoppin'," Ian Cuthbertson yelled. Bright yelled too but Shep wasn't listening. Above everything Bright heard Shep's voice goading the driver: "Come on Paddy, ye mad bugga, ye want to kill a polis, come on!"

Paddy Mullen couldn't have heard what Shep said but he could see the stubborn old polis wasn't going to budge and he had to fight down the murderous impulse that burned inside him and stamp on the brake. The engine stuttered and stalled, the lorry skidded forward under its own momentum and still Shep wouldn't move. Instead he put out his hands as if he could stop the lorry with his superhuman strength. And that was how it looked. The lorry shuddered and stopped as it reached Shep's hands. He leaned forward and looked up at Mullen behind the wheel.

"Aye, ye better bloody stop an' all."

Shep stepped out from between the two vehicles, went to the driver's side of the lorry, yanked open the door and pulled Mullen out.

"Ye want to hang, Paddy?" he shouted as Mullen hit the ground and stumbled back to his feet. Shep held him by the shoulder and shouted into his ear: "Is that what ye want? Ye want to hang for killin' a polis?"

Mullen looked away and Shep slapped the back of his head as he would slap an unruly kid. Mullen flinched but said nothing. Shep took out a pair of handcuffs and cuffed Mullen to the lorry.

"You're a fool of a man, Paddy," Shep said. "You're a fool of a man."

It was an hour or so before Shep, Bright and Cuthebertson were able to draw any order out of the chaos. They caught three of Paddy Mullen's accomplices; his eldest sons Danny and Stephen and Michael Leary's son, Brendan. But it seemed the senior Leary had got away onto the fells. Shep wasn't worried. With nowhere to go he would be picked up the next day. Still, the cost to the police was higher than Bright liked. He, Shep and Cuthbertson were the only ones unhurt. The five younger lads, in their zeal, had fared worse than the thieves they'd come to apprehend. One of the lads from Morpeth collided with the lad from Berwick, leaving both of them concussed and unable to take any further part in the operation. The other lad from Morpeth broke his leg tripping over a panicked sheep and one of the lads from Ashington had his nose broken subduing Danny Mullen.

Bright and Shep spent the rest of the night shuttling their captives and the lorry load of dead sheep to Wooler. The local doctor administered first aid to the injured and afterwards Bright drove the injured coppers to the hospital at Berwick. When the sun came up Cuthbertson took the Land Rover out on the fells to pick up Michael Leary who he found nine miles from the ambush site and too exhausted to resist.

Cuthbertson's wife, Avis, made tea for everybody until Alec Newell arrived in the Black Mariah to take the prisoners to Bedlington. Shep spent the time trying to decide what charges to bring. In the end he charged all of them with theft of livestock, drunk and disorderly and resisting arrest. To protect Tommy Locke he charged Danny Mullen with theft of a motor vehicle. He considered a charge of attempted murder against Paddy Mullen but changed his mind because there were too many witnesses who saw Mullen stop the lorry in time. He settled instead for a charge of driving to endanger.

As disastrous as it almost was the operation went on to become a public relations triumph for the Northumberland Constabulary. Bright, Shep and Cuthbertson received commendations for outstanding police work. A picture of them with the Chief Constable, smiling and holding up their certificates of commendation, appeared in The Evening Chronicle with Bright in his newly awarded sergeant's stripes. At Bedlington Magistrates Court, after viewing photographs of the sheep with their brains bashed out, Phyllis Ritchie convicted the Mullens and the Learys on all charges. They were fined twenty pounds for each sheep, ordered to pay restitution and bound over to keep the peace for three years with suspended sentences of six months. On the drunk and disorderly charges they were each fined an additional ten pounds and on resisting arrest they were sentenced to 90 days in jail. Danny Mullen got an extra 90 days for theft of a motor vehicle and was sacked from the Doctor Pit. For driving to endanger Paddy Mullen had his licence suspended for three years. And soon after the pictures of the evidence were taken the dead sheep disappeared. In the days that followed several leek growers were approached discretely by Tommy Locke and he and Shep came into a few extra pound.

1959

Buddy Holly, The Big Bopper and Ritchie Valens are killed when their small plane crashes during a snowstorm in Iowa; Fidel Castro seizes power in Cuba. Quatermass And The Pit draws a record 11 million TV viewers; Juke Box Jury makes its TV debut. Top draws at the pictures are I'm All Right Jack with Peter Sellers; Room At The Top with Laurence Harvey; Ben Hur with Charlton Heston and Jack Hawkins; Some Like It Hot with Marilyn Monroe, Jack Lemmon and Tony Curtis. Top song hits are Living Doll by Cliff Richard and Mack The Knife by Bobby Darin.

Imparted Wisdom

With the extra pay that came with his promotion to sergeant Bright bought a new car. He traded in the Standard Eight with its draughty canvas roof for a black 1957 Ford Consul. To Nick the Consul was the first real car they owned and he was proud to see it in all its bulbous black shininess outside their house. With his dad's extra pay and his mam's job at the pit canteen he had to get used to the idea that they were now comfortably off. But the most thrilling proof of their newly attained affluence wasn't the Consul, it was the bike his parents gave him for Christmas, a fire engine red Raleigh with Sturmey Archer three speed gears. It came with high handlebars that made you look like a wanker but Nick replaced them with a set of straight handlebars Spelk gave him. There were only two types of handlebars worth having, straights or racers and Nick thought straights looked better. He was 13. Image mattered.

For the first time in his life Nick could go where he wanted when he wanted without having to rely on the bus or his parents. With distance no longer an obstacle Nick, Spelk and Dave went everywhere on their bikes. In a matter of minutes they could be at the Top End, the Market Place or Humford Baths. They could visit their schoolpals wherever they lived and when they got bored with one place they could swap it for another. And getting there was half the fun. They hurtled around the roads, lanes and back streets of Bedlington, eyes narrowed, hair writhing in the wind, swooping down hills, jumping streams, sliding and skidding, throwing showers of gravel into the air just for show. Some Sundays they'd ride to Blyth sands and dart along the prom past carloads of folk who'd come for the sea air and sat bundled in their cars with the windows up, smoking and reading the papers.

Another event of earth shaking importance was the arrival of independent television. Tyne Tees began broadcasting in January, doubling the number of TV channels available in the northeast from one to two. TV had lost some of its novelty, ruled as it was by the BBC whose programming was dictated by grey men in grey suits in faraway London. The BBC had some good programmes like Hancock's Half Hour and Sergeant Bilko but they were grossly outnumbered by programmes like Come Dancing, The Good Old Days and The Black And White Minstrel Show. On cold and dreary Sunday afternoons the house could feel like a prison and all the BBC could offer was Flying Down To Rio with Fred Astaire and Ginger Rogers, made in 1933. At six-o-clock on Sunday nights the TV went off altogether because there was nothing but religious sermons and hymns till What's My Line came on at 7.30., which was only worth watching to see Gilbert Harding insult the contestants. Into this parched desert Tyne Tees Television came as a cloudburst of variety with programmes kids wanted to see like The Adventures Of Robin Hood, The Army Game, The Buccaneers, The Invisible Man and Whacko! But the best TV was American TV. American comedy shows like Burns and Allen and The Jack Benny Show were brighter, glossier and funnier. Westerns like Cheyenne, Wagon Train and Bronco were set against spectacular landscapes with forts, cavalry soldiers and hordes of marauding Indians while British shows had a cast of five and looked like they'd been made for ten bob in a suburban garage.

It was around this time Nick's mam decided what was missing from their lives was a pet. Not a cat or a dog, which would be too much trouble, but something easy like a budgie. Budgies were colourful and cheery and didn't need much more than a sprig of millet, a cuttlefish bone and a sheet of newspaper in the bottom of the cage. The first Nick knew about it was when his mam came home with a cage and a green and yellow budgie she called Mickey Drippin'. They hung the cage in the bay window where it glittered like a mirror ball while Mickey Drippin' bashed his head against a little brass bell.

The first sunny weekend of spring Nick, Spelk and Dave took off on their bikes with another couple of lads from school, the droll and sleepy eyed Alan Wise and the sex obsessed Derek Mott who everybody knew as Minge. They met at the Top End around nine on Saturday morning and followed the A1068 north to Druridge Bay, stopping along the way to buy pop and sweets to go with the sandwiches they'd packed. Despite brilliant sunshine a brisk onshore wind gave the day a chilly edge and when they reached Druridge Bay there were only a couple of cars in the grassy parking area. They shouldered their bikes and carried them through massive, grass tufted dunes to a pillbox left over from the war. From the pillbox they could see the scimitar sweep of the bay from north to south. A dotted line of cement cube tank traps and scribbles of rusty barbed wire separated the dunes from the open sands; remnants of Britain's shoreline defences from World War Two that the government still couldn't afford to remove. On the beach an elderly couple walked their Scottish terrier and a father and his young son fought the wind for control of a long tailed kite. The boys stripped down to their swimming trunks and raced down to the water only to be driven out howling by the cold. They scampered back to the dunes stung by wind driven flurries of sand and turned their energies to seeing who could jump the furthest from the highest dune. When they were ready to eat they went back to their bikes and took refuge from the wind in a hollow behind the pillbox. Nick had made cheese and tomato sandwiches with lettuce and salad cream and thought nothing had ever tasted so good. He drank half his lemonade, saved the rest for the ride home, and ate the Kit-Kat he'd bought for dessert.

Sated and sheltered from the wind the five of them lounged in the sun while their minds, pulled by the gravity of adolescent hormones, turned to the matters that most interested thirteen year old boys: farting and fucking. All of them had a fascination that bordered on reverence for the amazing noises that could be generated by the human body. Nick had taught himself to belch by swallowing air and forcing it back up and in a very short time he was able to produce belches of impressive volume and duration. He had to be careful because if he did too many he would retch, which was also funny, but made his throat burn. But, the acoustics of the arse were king. There was nothing so funny in the world as a fart. Small farts, loud farts, watery farts, loud dismissive farts, short nasty farts, long rasping farts and those awe inspiring monster farts that sounded like twenty feet of sailcloth tearing. The art of the fart had even acquired its own vocabulary and ratings system. A deliberate fart could be funny, especially when deployed to offend girls in the schoolyard, but not as funny as an accidental fart in a hushed classroom. A deliberate fart that resulted in the exponent accidentally shitting himself was much funnier. Farts that might in themselves not be particularly memorable among a bunch of boys horsing around could be rendered immortal by an inspired verbal response such as: 'Is there blood?' 'Get it while it's hot!' and 'Flirt!'

Context was critical. Dave once let rip with a boomer in a crowded picture house that prompted hysterical laughter from a girl in the dress circle and sent Nick and Spelk running for the exit. The only fart that came close to trumping it was an anonymous contribution during morning assembly when somebody tried to sneak one out only to have it turn into a long, high-pitched keening, a tremulous, escalating plaint that ended on a forlorn note, as if questioning the meaning of life, and set shoulders shaking throughout the hall. For boys these were the precious memories of youth.

The only subject that interested them more than farting was fucking. Not that any of them knew what it was like to fuck but they liked talking about it as if talking about it would somehow bring them closer to it. The latest object of their indiscriminate lust was Miss Matthews, the new B-stream English teacher. Miss Matthews had come straight from teacher's college and her dark and sultry beauty combined with a natural demureness made every day for her an ordeal.

"She's made for fuckin'," Dave said.

"Aye but she acts like she doesn't knah," Spelk said.

"Acourse she knahs," Minge said. "They ahll knah."

"Hoo could ye hae a body like that an' not knah what it's for?" Alan Wise said.

"Ah'd like to fuck her pink."

"Ah'd give ah a touch o' the tusk."

"Ah'd be happy just to be a pair of ah knickers."

"Stick a paddle up ah arse an' lick ah like a lolly."

And the five of them cackled like parrots.

"If ye could fuck any woman in the world," Spelk said. "Wee would it be?"

"Doris Day," Nick said immediately.

"Doris Day?" the others jeered.

"Ah think she's fuckin' lovely," Nick said.

"Doris Day," Dave scoffed. "Ya off ya fuckin' heed."

"She's in top nick, but," David Wise said.

"Fuckin' Doris Day would be like fuckin' ya mutha," Minge said.

"Ye must hae somebody better than Doris Day," Spelk said.

Nick paused. "Tinkerbell."

"Tinkerbell?" Dave echoed as the others guffawed. "She's not even real fo' fuck's sake."

"She's a fuckin' drawin'," Minge said. "Ye cannit fuck a fuckin' drawin'."

"Ye could draw a picture of ah, poke a hole in it an' fuck that," David Wise said.

"Ah nivah thought o' that," Nick said.

"Look, he's thinkin' aboot it noo," Dave added.

"Hoo can ye fuck somebody wee's not real?" Spelk asked.

"Ah wish she was real," Nick said. "Ah wish ah could fuck ah."

"Aye an' hoo do ye think ya ganna dee it?" Dave asked. "If'n she was real she'd be aboot the size o' ya nob."

"Ye could practice forst on a claes peg."

"Ya fuckin' demented."

"Police are lookin' for a mad Geordie wee fucked Tinkerbell te death."

"She'd hae to be life size," Nick protested.

"Tinkerbell," Minge sniggered. "He's got a hard-on fo' Tinkerbell."

"Get nicked."

"Wee de ye wank owa?" Dave asked. "Fuckin' Bambi?"

"Get bent."

"Get knotted."

"Ah stand as much chance as ye lot gettin' weeivah ye want," Nick said.

"Do ye not want to fuck somebody real, but?" Minge asked. "Ah mean, like Brigitte Bardot or somebody?"

"Ah fuck hor ivery neyt."

"That's not Brigitte Bardot, that's the five fingered widah."

Dave turned to Spelk: "Wee would ye choose, like?"

"Ah wouldn't mind a lash at Joan Stokoe."

"Ya jokin'," Dave said amid a chorus of groans.

"Ah body's ahlreet but she's got a heed on ah like a cuddy," Minge said.

"Ye divvent look at the mantelpiece when ya pokin' the fire."

"Aye but ye hae to look at the clock to see what time it is."

"Ah mean famous women, like film stars," Dave persisted.

"Ah divvent knah," Spelk said. "They're ahll aad."

"Marilyn Monroe's not aad," Minge said.

"What aboot Diana Dors?" Dave asked.

"That fat hooah?"

"She's not fat."

"See, yours are nae better than mine," Nick said.

"At least Diana Dors is real," Dave said.

"Jayne Mansfield," Minge said. "Ah could shag the arse right off o' hor."

"No ye couldn't, cos she'd break ya fuckin' back forst." Spelk said.

"Aye but ah'd die happy."

Spelk turned his attention to Alan Wise. "So wee would ye choose?"

Wise pondered the question as though hearing it for the first time.

"One o' the Vernons Girls."

His answer gave them pause.

"Which one?" Spelk asked.

"Ah divvent knah," Wise said. "Ah'd hae to fuck ahll o' them so ah could mek me mind up."

Confronted by such logic the rest of them could only murmur their assent.

Nor was there to be any mercy for Miss Matthews. The end came the day Kevin Burney in 4C brought a Doctor White's to school, doused it with red ink and draped it over the rim of the wastepaper basket beside the teacher's desk. Miss Matthews taught for about 10 minutes, passing the wastepaper basket several times before the sniggering among her pupils told her all was not as it seemed.

"Alright, what's…" she began and then she saw the stained sanitary towel on the wastepaper basket. Those who were there said she froze where she stood for a good long while till at last she burst into tears and ran from the room followed by the pitiless laughter of the boys and girls of 4C. And she was never seen at

Westridge again.

*   *   *

Saturday morning Nick was resting on his bike outside the Top End newsagent's shop waiting for Spelk when he overheard a conversation between two women who'd met while out shopping. One of the women, small but sturdy and pugnacious, was telling her friend how she dealt with a neighbour who'd spread some gossip about her.

"Soon as ah hord, ah says, ah says, 'right, ye bugga,' ah says. An' ah says te mesel', ah says, ah says, 'she'll keep,' ah says. Ah says 'ye just bide ya teym,' ah says, 'hor torn'll come, an' it did.'"

"So ye've seen ah?"

"Oh aye, ah've seen ah ahlreet. She was tryin' te avoid is, like, but she could only dee that fo' sae lang. Ah was comin' up the shortcut from the rahs last Wen'sday an' wee dis ah see comin' tappy lappin' doon the lonnen like she doesn't hae a care in the world but lady muck ahsel?"

Nick knew the shortcut from the pit rows to Front Street, a long uphill path with high fences on both sides that made it impossible for two people to avoid each other.

"Eeh, what did ye say?" the friend asked.

"Ah waited till wi were reyt on top o' each otha, like, an ah says, ah says, 'hey' ah says. Ah says 'ah've got a bone te pick wi' ye.'"

"An' what did she say?"

"Whey at forst she disn't want te say nowt, like. She tries te act ahll innocent like she haes nae idea what ah'm tahkin' aboot. She just gi's a dorty look an' gans te gan streyt past is."

"Eeh, what did ye dee then?"

"Ah says, ah says, ah says 'hey,' ah says. 'Ah'm tahkin' te ye,' ah says. Ah says, ah says, ah says, 'divvent ye crack on like ye hae nae idea what ah'm tahkin' aboot neither.' An' she says, she says, 'ah hae nowt te say te ye,' she says."

"Eeh, she nivah did?"

"She did. True as ah'm standin' here, that's what she did."

"The cheek of ah."

"Ah knah, the way she gans on ye'd think buttah wouldn't melt in ah mooth."

"So then what did ye dee?"

"Ah says, ah says, ah says…" And she prodded her friend in the chest, mimicking how she'd prodded the other woman. "Ah says ye might not hae nowt te say te me but ah hae plenty te say te ye an' ya ganna listen whether ye like it or not'."

"Eeh, mind that's tellin' ah," the friend said, relishing the tale.

"Ah knah, ah knah…the narve o' ah, the bloody narve o' ah. She tells the whole world me man is off galivantin' somewhere wi's fancy woman an' she thinks she's just ganna wahk right past is on the street like ah'm not ganna say nowt."

"She needed tellin'," the friend said. "It's aboot teym somebody telt ah."

"Oh, she needed tellin' ahlreet an' ah telt ah."

"Ah bet ye did."

"Ah haven't telt ye the best part yet." the first woman said. "So, she gans te keep on gannin' like, an' ah says 'hey,' ah says. Ah says, ah says, ah says, 'divvent ye torn ya back on me,' ah says. An' ah grabbed ah bi the arm an' yanked ah back, an' ah yanked ah that hard ah nearly pulled ah off ah feet. An' ah says, ah says, 'ah'm not finished wi ye yet by a lang chalk.'"

"Eeh, ye nivah did."

"Ah did, ah did. True as ah'm stannin' heeyah. Ah divvent knah what she was thinkin' but she picked the wrang one te cross this time."

"Ah wouldn't want te get on the wrang side' o' ye."

"She thowt ah was ganna hit ah. She nearly shit ahsel."

"Ah bet she did."

"An' ah says, ah says, 'next time ye want to tell tales aboot me an' mah man try tellin' is te me face.'"

"An' what did she say?"

"Tha was nowt she could say. So ah yanked ah reyt up close t'is, closer than ye an' me are stannin' heeyah noo, an' ah says 'just so ye knah, mah man has nae need te stray - he gets ahll he wants at yem.'"

Her friend put her hand to her mouth. "Mind, ye didn't haff show hor didn't ye? Ye showed hor ahlreet."

"Oh, ah showed ah."

"Ye telt ah, ahlreet."

"Aye, ah telt ah."

"She'll think twice afore she says owt aboot ye again."

"She betta, cos if tha's a next teym ah'll dee mair than tell ah, ah'll tek ah bloody face off ah."

*　　　*　　　*

Nick's mam decided now she was a sergeant's wife she should be respectable and do respectable things like go to St. Cuthbert's annual garden fete. It was a staid affair with hoopla, bean bag tosses and jumble sales that raised money for the upkeep of the vicarage. Nick hadn't known there was anything quite so posh as a garden fete in Bedlington but he knew the vicar, the Reverend Francis Pevensey, because pupils at St. Cuthberts' Infant School and Whitley Memorial Junior School were required to attend church services at Whitsun, Easter, Harvest Festival and Christmas. He liked Harvest Festival because the church was filled with the delicious aroma of donated fruit and vegetables piled high around the pulpit to be packed later into cardboard boxes and distributed among local pensioners. It was the only time Nick knew charity to be even faintly cheerful; most charities had the aura of the forlorn about them. And there was nothing cheerful about the Reverend Pevensey. Short, fat and bald with wet lips and pointy little teeth the kids hated him because he was a pincher. Whenever a kid did something he didn't like he would take hold of them and pinch them behind the knee hard enough to leave a welt.

The day of the fete Nick's mother made him wear his new school blazer with a pair of grey short pants and a white open neck shirt. She wore a pale blue frock with white shoes and a feathery white hat that looked like broken eggshell. On a silver foil plate wrapped in a tea towel she carried a dozen chocolate buns with icing sprinkled with little silver balls. She'd made them herself and taken extra care with the decoration and Nick thought they looked as good as anything that came out of a cake shop. Nick's dad dropped the two of them at the vicarage gates before going to the Bottom Club with instructions to come back for them at three-o-clock.

The vicarage sat in its own walled enclosure behind the church, an imposing freestone manse with a descending three tiered garden. The first tier was an expanse of open lawn, the second tier flowerbeds traversed by mossy stone pathways and the bottom tier hedges and trees that formed a bower with a wooden bench. Church ladies supervised children's games on the lawn and in the topmost corner of the lawn, under a green and white striped shade umbrella, the Reverend Pevensey and his wife, Hilda, entertained a doting cluster of women who bobbed and cooed around them like plump little pigeons. It was Englishness at its most benign, a crystalline sky, vivid flower beds, tea on the lawn and not a breath of wind to ruffle the ladies' dresses.

Nick's mam went up to the kitchen to deliver her iced buns leaving Nick to seek out familiar faces among the crowd. He wandered around seeing nobody he knew, feeling out of place and wondering who all these people were until at last he came across Mary Beecroft. He hardly saw her anymore since she'd gone to the Grammar school but she seemed pleased to see him, if surprised. The first words out of her mouth were: "What are you doin' here?"

He told her the truth - he didn't know. Which amused her because she knew Nick's mother as a proud, self-declared 'heathen.' But she couldn't talk for long because she was on her way to help her mam at the jumble sale stall, which left Nick on his own again till his mam returned from the kitchen. Together they made the rounds, taking a turn at the hoopla and the bean bag toss, neither of them winning anything, neither of them enjoying themselves. Nick's mam chatted briefly with Mary's mam but it only emphasised how odd it was for them to be there at all. Nick's mam decided the two of them should have something to eat and took him up to the refreshments tent where she bought a cup of tea and a slice of swiss roll for herself and a glass of lukewarm orangeade and an Eccles cake for him. She looked among the cakes and pastries and didn't see her chocolate buns anywhere but she knew how busy the church ladies were.

When they came out of the tent she looked for a seat in the shade. There were a couple of empty seats under the vicar's umbrella but when she and Nick went to sit down Hilda Pevensey, inscrutable behind her kabuki make-up, said the seats were taken. So Nick followed his mam down to the second tier where they found room on a wall under an elm tree. They weren't there long when he saw a woman approach the group under the umbrella and be offered one of the vacant seats. He realised his mam had seen it too and watched her whole demeanour change.

She put her cup down on the wall a little too hard and said: "Wait here, ah'll just be a minute."

Nick waited, his stomach turning.

She went back up to the kitchen where a trio of church ladies in aprons washed cups and plates and kept the tea and pastries flowing out to the refreshments tent. It took her a moment but she found her chocolate buns pushed to the back of a counter behind dirty cups and plates waiting to go into the sink.

"Do ye not want those buns?" she said, pointing to her plate. None of the women responded so she asked again, louder: "Is there somethin' the matter wi' those sticky buns over there?"

One of the women picked up a plate of sliced cake to take out to the tent. She had to step around Nick's mam to get past but wouldn't look her in the eye. The woman at the sink glanced up nervously while the third woman wiped her hands on her apron and, in a strained voice, said: "Ah was goin' to put them out but Mrs. Pevensey told is not to."

"Did she say what's the matter wi' them?"

The woman looked uncomfortable. "No…she didn't."

"Are they not good enough, is that what's the matter?"

A pained expression appeared on the woman's face but she was lost for an answer.

"Ahlright, ah'll make it easy fo' ye then, will ah." Nick's mam crossed the kitchen, picked up the plate and threw the buns into an open bin inside the door. "There, ye divvent hae to worry aboot them at ahll noo de ye." She left with her plate and tea towel and went back to where Nick waited.

"Come on, wa goin' home," she said. "Tha too good fo' wi heeyah." The two of them walked back up to the lawn, past the stalls and playing children, out the vicarage gates onto Church Lane and felt every step of the way they might as well have been invisible.

*   *   *

The house was empty when Nick got home on the last day of the summer term so he dumped his rucksack in the hall and ran over to the grassy hill where the kids had made a slide using sheets of plywood and cardboard. One after another they launched themselves down a dirt strip they'd worn into the grassy slope that overlooked a turnip field. The slide bottomed out sharply and ended a few feet further on in the thorny embrace of a hedgerow so each slider had to throw himself off to the side before reaching the hedge.

Nick borrowed a cardboard sheet from Spelk and took a turn on the slide, hurtling down the slope in a giddy rush and diving for safety at the last moment. Laughing he climbed back up the hill, returned the cardboard to Spelk and waited for his next turn. He got a better push off this time and flew, grinning, down the slide until near the bottom he felt a jarring pain in his buttocks. He threw himself to the side and, to the amusement of the watching kids, tumbled the rest of the way in a blur of arms and legs. When he stopped rolling he lay still for a moment to catch his breath. The other kids fell silent, thinking he might be hurt. He got slowly to his feet and looked around. The sheet of cardboard was a few feet away with a rip in it. He felt around the seat of his trousers and found a ragged tear. There was no pain, just a sensation of pins and needles. Then he felt something warm and wet on the back of his leg.

"Ye didn't shit yasel' did ye?" Spelk called from the top of the hill and the other kids laughed.

Nick shook his head. "No, but ah've done somethin'. Ah think ah better gan yem."

He limped away and behind him one of the kids yelled: "He's wrecked his arse bone," followed by more laughter and they went back to their sliding. By the time Nick got home his left buttock was burning and his sock was soggy with blood. Fortunately his dad was home early. Nick told him what happened and his dad had him drop his trousers and bend over. The wound, whatever it was, must have been close to his rectal opening because his dad had to prise his buttocks apart to see it properly. His dad's next words were not what Nick wanted to hear.

"Ye've done a good job on yasel', lad," he said. "Ah think ya ganna need stitches."

Nick rode with his father in the Consul to Dr. Stone's office on Front Street, a towel underneath him to protect the seat and him leaning to one side so as not to aggravate the wound. It was half an hour before Dr. Stone closed for the day and the waiting room was empty. Nick knew the receptionist at the front desk. Her name was Carol and she'd been in 4B before leaving school the previous year. A chatty brunette she was only three years older than Nick and he was mortified that she would soon find out why he was there.

"Ah'm sorry to turn up wi'oot an appointment, pet, but me lad here's cut his backside quite badly," Nick's dad said. "Ah was hopin' Doctor Stone could save wi' a trip to the General in Ashin'ton."

Carol gave Nick a sympathetic look. "Ah'll just ask him, Mr. Bright."

She poked her head around the door to Dr. Stone's examination room and there was a murmured exchange. Nick had never paid much attention to Carol before but as she stretched around the door on one toe, her white blouse taut against her breasts, her dark pleated skirt clinging to her legs he saw how pretty she'd become. Horrifyingly, his willy agreed.

"Ye can go straight in, Mr. Bright," she said and stepped away with a smile. Nick limped in after his father, his face reddening.

"Thanks for seein' wi' wi'oot any notice, Bob," Nick's dad said. "It is an emorgency but ah doot it'll need mair than a few stitches."

A few stitches. The words rattled around Nick's head. It was his bum and he wanted it to be something that could be fixed with a dab of antiseptic and a sticky plaster.

"Don't you fret yourself, man," Dr. Stone said affably. "So your young lad's had a bit of an accident has he?"

Dr. Stone was a compact grey haired man in his late 50's who'd practiced medicine in Bedlington for donkeys' years and had the assurance of someone who'd cured everything from shingles to syphilis.

"Just get up on the examination table there on your hands and knees young lad and let's take a look at you," Dr. Stone said.

Nick prised off his shoes, climbed up on the exam table and self-consciously pushed down his ruined trousers and underpants.

"Lean forward on your elbows so I can get a good look at you in the light," Dr. Stone said.

Nick leaned on his elbows so his wounded bum was tilted towards the ceiling. Dr. Stone and his father leaned in close and studied the injured area. Dr. Stone wore glasses but his eyesight couldn't have been good.

"I can see it but I can't see all of it," he said. "Jimmy would you mind holding his cheeks apart so I can see it properly."

Bright took hold of Nick's buttocks, one in each hand, fingers toward the crease and pulled them apart. Nick winced and his willy shriveled.

"Just the job," Dr. Stone said. Nick felt the doctor's fingers poking around the wound and was dismayed at how close it was to his sphincter.

"Ya bloody lucky it's not another haff inch owa," Nick's father said. "If ye'd torn ya arsehole oppin then ye'd be in real trouble."

"Aye, well, I think we can take care of that," Dr. Stone said. "I'll stitch it up and give you some ointment to put on it. You'll have to be careful about keeping the area clean so there's no infection but I think you'll live."

"How many stitches are ye goin' to put in?" Nick asked.

"As many as it teks," his father said.

"Probably no more than five or six," Dr. Stone added. "Just stay where you are and we'll have you done in a jiffy."

No more than five or six, Nick said to himself. Sweat formed on his forehead and dripped onto the worn leather surface of the examination table. He heard the door open and was gripped by terror.

"Carol, could you come in here and lend me a hand please?" Dr. Stone said.

Nick thought his heart was going to stop. Surely they weren't going to bring in a girl only a few years older than him to see his mangled arse.

"Dad, ah don't want…"

"Ye just haad ya whisht an' let the dog see the rabbit," his father interrupted. "Folk are tryin' to help ye heeyah."

Nick felt a cold dread wash through him.

"I'll need you to assist while I clean and suture the wound," Dr. Stone told Carol. Nick glimpsed a passing shadow. He heard drawers open, the clink of metal instruments on a tray. Then footsteps and Dr. Stone was behind him again. With Carol. Not only was she getting a close-up of his mangled arsehole but a perfect rear view of his plums and his willy.

"You might feel a little bit discomfort," Dr. Stone said. Nick felt a cold wet swab in and around the wound that turned to fire as soon as the antiseptic bit. He grimaced and more sweat dripped onto the examination table. There was a pause and Nick braced himself for the sting of the needle.

He heard Doctor Stone say: "Jimmy, hold his cheeks as far apart there as you can, will you. I need as much room to work in there as I can get. Carol, just put that down would you, pet, and bring that lamp from over there and shine it on the wound would you, please, so I can see what I'm doing."

Why not invite Carol to shine a light on his arse, Nick thought? Why not invite a few folk in off the street while they were at it? He counted each time the needle pierced his skin. It came to 10, which meant five stitches. If they were anywhere else on his body he'd have been proud to show them off.

"Alright, young-fella-me-lad, that should do you for now," Dr. Stone said. He went to a wash basin and washed his hands while Nick's dad let go of his son's aching buttocks and Carol replaced the lamp. "You can get down and get yaself dressed," Dr. Stone said. "I've put a dressing on the wound and I'll give you some sterile pads to take home with you. I'll give your dad a prescription for some penicillin tablets and ointment. You'll have to take the tablets for five days and make sure you take all of them and apply the ointment every time you change the dressing, which should be every 24 hours. Probably before you go to bed so you can give your backside a good clean."

Aye, give his arse a good clean, Nick thought. Why not say it louder in case Carol hadn't heard? She finished what she was doing and left the examination room without looking at him. He got down from the table and pulled up his torn trousers.

"Thank ye, Bob," his dad said. "Ah appreciate ya tekkin' wi wi' nae notice."

"No bother at all, man," Dr. Stone said. He looked at Nick and added: "And you, young man, be careful what you're doing the next few weeks, you don't want those stitches to open."

"Aye," Nick's dad said. "Nae mair slidin' doon hills on ya arse."

"Ah wasn't…" Nick began and Dr. Stone chuckled.

"Come back in two weeks," he said. "Make an appointment with Carol on the way out. All being well those stitches can come out then."

Of course, Nick thought. Stitches had been put in, stitches would have to come out. Carol could assist again, perhaps bring a few of her girlfriends to watch. He hobbled across the waiting room and stood by the door while his dad made the appointment. He couldn't look at Carol. He was beyond physical pain, bound in the rags of humiliation for which there was no relief.

He and his dad rode home in silence, Nick listing to one side like a stricken ship. It had started to rain and the black wet streets matched his spirits. When they got home Nick saw the lights were on, his mam was back from work. His dad switched off the engine and the only sound was the rain drumming on the car roof. "Well son," his dad said, "ah'll say one thing fo' ye…"

Nick waited while his dad searched for a few words of consolation.

"Ye've got a really hairy arse," he said.

*   *   *

Big Mac was lying on his side on a rope pulled bogey using a pick to hack lumps of coal out of a darkly glistening seam when he heard a hiss behind him followed by a claw reaching out of the shadows to seize him by the shoulder. He shouted in alarm, tried to pull away and woke up in bed with Nellie shaking him and whispering urgently in his ear.

"Ah just heard somethin' in the garden," she said. "Ah think somebody's havin' a go at ya leeks."

Mac threw the bedclothes off and hurried downstairs in his pajama pants and vest.

"Be careful, hinny," Nellie called after him.

He grabbed the poker on his way past the fireplace, threw open the back door and charged out into the night. Nellie was right, there was somebody in the garden, a man thrashing around in the web of chicken mesh and barbed wire Mac had set up to protect his leeks.

"Got ye, ye bugga," Mac said, hastening down the garden path, the poker raised in his hand. "Stay reyt where ye are or ah'll tek ya fuckin' heed off."

"It's me, man," a familiar voice said.

The upstairs light in Jimmy Bright's house went on then the downstairs light and Mac heard their back door open.

"Ah'm not, it's not…it's not what ye think," the voice from the leek trenches said. "Get is oot o' here will ye, man. Ah was tryin' to help ye."

Nellie opened the back curtains and light flooded into the garden. Bright, in his dressing gown with his police torch in hand, stepped over the back fence. He saw Mac with the poker poised over somebody on the ground struggling in a tangle of gleaming wire.

"Get is oot o' here will ye," the man grunted. "Ah'm gettin' cut to bloody ribbons."

"De ye see wee it is?" Bright asked.

"It's the bastard wee's been slashin' me leeks," Mac said.

"For fuck's sake, the two o' ye…"

Bright aimed his torch and saw the scratched and bloodied face of Joe Gordon.

"Ah no," Mac groaned and turned away. "Ah don't believe it. Ah don't bloody believe it."

Bright shone his torch around and saw that Gordon was hopelessly ensared in the wire and the leeks around him crushed and broken.

"Stop strugglin' Joe, ya just mekkin' it worse," Bright said.

Gordon stopped and slumped back onto the ground.

"It's not what it looks like, Jimmy, honest, it's not what it looks like."

"Mac, hae ye got a pair o' snips?" Bright asked.

Mac looked dazedly at Bright. "Aye."

He went into the washhouse, returned with the wire snips and handed them to Bright.

"Ah cannit believe it's him," he said. To Gordon he said: "Ya the last porson on orth ah would hae expected, Joe. The last porson on orth."

"Ah'm tellin' ye it's not hoo it looks," Gordon protested. "Ah was lookin' oot fo' ye, man. It wasn't me, it was somebody else."

"Aye an' where is he noo?" Mac asked.

"He was ahlready in heeyah when ah tackled him but he got away an' ah got stuck."

"Did ye see wee it was?" Bright asked.

"No, ah didn't," Gordon answered despairingly. "But it wasn't me. Ah was tryin' to stop the bugga."

"Just haad yasel' still a minute," Bright said and snipped at the wires that held him.

Nellie McBride came out and when Mac told her who it was her hands went to her face. The neighbours were awake, silhouettes in the open doorways of nearby houses. Word went door to door that Joe Gordon had been caught slashing Big Mac's leeks.

Bright cut Gordon free and helped him to his feet. His clothes were torn and there were cuts on his arms.

"Noo are ye ganna behave yasel'?" Bright said. "Or do ah hae to put handcuffs on ye?"

"Surely, ya not ganna tek is in, Jimmy," Gordon said disbelievingly.

"That depends on ye'," Bright said. "Ye might want to get them cuts looked at though."

"Tha nowt," Gordon said. "Just scratches." He went over to Mac and in a pleading tone said: "Surely ye divvent think ah would dee owt like this, Mac. Ah was oot the back havin' a tab when ah thowt ah saw somebody comin up the back o' your place so ah come owa to see wee it was. When ah saw what he was up te ah sneaked up ahint him an' grabbed ahaad of him but he was quick as a bloody fox an' ah couldn't hang onto him."

Mac shook his head and turned away while Nellie stared at Joe in dismay.

Bright walked around the smashed leek trenches scanning the ground with his torch. He saw something in the shining tangle of wire, a knife or a blade of some kind, and bent down to pick it up. But it wasn't a blade, it was a syringe. He shone his torch on it and saw it was too big for human patients and was more likely a veterinary syringe. There was something else, it held a few drops of fluid and smelled of urine.

"Is this yours, Joe?" he asked, turning to Gordon.

Gordon came back and stared at it. "It's a hypodermic needle," he said as if surprised. "That must be what ah thought was a knife. Ah saw somethin' shinin', like, an' ah grabbed it off him an' he put up such a fight but ah stuck the bugga with it afore he got away…ah knah a stuck him cos ah felt it gan in."

"Ye sure ye worn't usin' it to inject Mac's leeks wi' piss?" Bright said.

Mac rushed up before Joe Gordon could answer. "See, ah knew it wasn't me. Ah telt iverybody it wasn't me. It was him ahll the time injectin' piss into me leeks."

"Mac, ah wasn't, honest." Gordon insisted. "Ah would nivah dee owt like that."

"Aye, that's what ah would hae said till the night," Mac added.

Bright said: "Ah hae to place ye under arrest, Joe."

Joe looked stunned. "Jimmy, ye cannit be serious…"

"Oh aye ah am," Bright said. "We'll sort it oot doon the police station. Ye can mek a statement doon there an' we'll get them cuts looked at at the same time."

"Ahh no, Jimmy," Joe said despairingly. "Ye cannit seriously think it was me, ah'm tellin' ye the god's honest truth, man."

"Ah hope ye are for your sake," Bright said. "But you're ahll we've got for noo."

"Ah cannit go to jail, Jimmy," Joe said and backed away. "Ah cannit go to jail."

"Joe, don't mek this any…" But before Bright could finish Joe turned and ran. He ran down the garden, vaulted the back fence and disappeared into the darkness in the direction of the cemetery.

"Bloody great," Big Mac said. "We'll nivah find him in there."

"Silly bugga," Bright said. He knew about Joe's history as a prisoner of war and would never have put him in a cell.

The next morning all West Lea knew Joe Gordon had been caught destroying Robbie McBride's show leeks but he'd run away and was now hiding in the old cemetery. People said the police were organising a manhunt, they were just waiting for extra men with police dogs to sniff Joe out. But a couple of days went by and there was no manhunt and no sniffer dogs. Bright took a statement from Mac, wrote out a report and told Jean Gordon that when her husband came to his senses he should come up to the station so they could sort things out.

But when a week passed without any sign of him, Joe's disappearance acquired sinister new dimensions. He was the fugitive madman in the old cemetery behind every gravestone, he was living off rabbits and hedgehogs, he would kill and rob anybody who went into the cemetery to get money for his escape. And that was how it might have stayed were it not for news from Ashington ten days later.

Shep called Bright into his office and said: "Ah hae somethin' ah think'll be of interest te ye."

Bright sat down and lit a cigarette.

"Ah just got word from Ashin'ton that Danny Mullen died last night at the General."

Bright nodded, unsurprised. "Caught sneakin' oot the wrang bedroom?"

"Not accordin' to the inquest report," Shep said. "Septicaemia."

Bright's eyebrows arched. "Blood poisonin'?"

"His family took him in yesterday mornin' but he'd been in a coma for nigh on 48 hours an' it was owa late," Shep said. "There was nowt could be done for him an' he died last night. A Dr. Lovell over there didn't buy the load o' tosh Paddy Mullen tried to give him aboot an accident so he let Ashin'ton police know and the medical examiner did a post mortem first thing the day. It looks like the infection was introduced to Danny's body in the form of a puncture wound to his arse. It turned into blood poisonin' an' when they did their tests they found the infction was caused by human urine."

"So Joe Gordon was tellin' the truth," Bright said.

"Looks that way, doesn't it."

"Human urine can dee that te a man?"

"Apparently," Shep said. "It's safe when it's passin' through your body in the normal fashion but if ye introduce it into the bloodstream in any quantity at all, even if it's your own, it'll kill ye. It might take a while but if you're not treated it'll kill ye."

"Bugga mah," Bright said. "An' Paddy would be scared te tek him in so they let it go till it was owa late."

"Ye knah what the family's like," Shep said. "Paddy would let his ahn son die rather than risk owt comin' back on him."

"Would he hae lived if they'd taken him in sooner?" Bright asked.

"He'd hae had a chance. They coulda filled him full o' penicillin if they'd tekkin' him in earlier an' he might hae fought it off, but they waited more than a week an bi then he was too far gone."

"Looks like ah'll be havin' a tahk wi' Jean Gordon then."

"Ye can tell ah it's case closed as far as we're concerned," Shep said.

When Bright got off work he went first to the Gordons' house where Jean eyed him warily from behind the half opened door.

"Joe comin' yem fo' his dinner the night then?" Bright asked.

"Ahh, ah don't know," Jean said, flustered.

Bright smiled. "Weel ah hae some good news for the both o' ye. Tell him when ye see him naebody's lookin' for him an' tha's not goin' to be any charges against him."

Jean's eyes widened. "Fo' real?"

"As real as ah'm standin' here," Bright said. "Tell him we knah he was tellin' the truth. It was Danny Mullen he saw sneakin' into Mac's garden, that's wee he was fightin' wi'."

"So are ye goin' to charge Danny Mullen noo?" Jean asked.

"Be a bit difficult, pet," Bright said. "He's as dead as a maak. Seems he came doon wi' a bad case o' blood poisonin'."

Jean put her hand over her mouth but at the same time Bright saw relief in her eyes.

He whistled as he walked down to the McBride's house where he gave the same news to Big Mac. Mac was stunned.

"So it wasn't Joe after all. He was tellin' the truth?"

"Aye he was," Bright said. "He was tryin' to dee ye a good torn, an' at some risk to hissel' ah might say. Ah think ye an' me owe him an apology."

Mac nodded. "Ah'm glad it wasn't Joe, ah feel better knahin' it wasn't him."

Bright turned to go but Mac called after him: "Does this mean Joe's ganna be charged fo' what happened to Danny Mullen?"

"No, it does not," Bright said. "As far as the police are concorned the case is closed. The Mullens haven't lodged a complaint an' ah don't expect they will because they knah what Danny was up te when he got caught an' they knah they're to blame for waitin' owa lang to tek him to the hospital. So if anybody's guilty o' lettin' Danny die it's them. An' when ah see Joe ah'm ganna shake his hand for deein' wi' ahll a good torn."

"So ye can arrest Joe Gordon fo' damagin' me leeks," Mac said. "But ye cannit arrest him for killin' Danny Mullen?"

"Aye weel," Bright shrugged, "champion leeks are hard te come by. Blokes like Danny Mullen are two a penny."

1960

John F. Kennedy is elected the first Catholic president of the USA; in South Africa 70 blacks are massacred protesting apartheid; after an obscenity trial Lady Chatterley's Lover by D. H. Lawrence is published for the first time in Britain. Coronation Street debuts on ITV. Biggest Box Office hits are Alfred Hitchcock's Psycho; Spartacus starring Kirk Douglas, Laurence Olivier, Peter Ustinov, Charles Laughton and Jean Simmons; Sink The Bismarck starring Kenneth More; The Magnificent Seven starring Yul Brynner and Steve McQueen. Top song hits are Kon-Tiki by The Shadows; What Do You Want To Make Those Eyes At Me For by Emile Ford and The Checkmates; Shakin' All Over by Johnny Kidd and The Pirates; My Old Man's A Dustman by Lonnie Donegan; Goodness Gracious Me by Peter Sellers and Sophia Loren.

Hard Knocks

Nick was due for a fight. He'd had countless play fights and a few real fights but nothing serious. Until now. He'd grown taller and heavier over the last year and his voice had deepened, which was a clear provocation to the bad lads. He quite enjoyed the physical challenge of a fight, it was the viciousness he didn't much care for and he'd seen abler kids than him scarred for life in fights. But you couldn't duck a fight without being labeled a coward and if you were a coward you'd be tormented all the more. Nick thought he'd been lucky to avoid any serious fights so far. Throwing stones and snowballs didn't count, it was easy to be brave at a distance. Coming to grips with a kid who wanted to kick the living shit out of you was something else. But this was the year Nick went from Third Remove to Fourth Remove and for the kids who went into 4C it was the last year of school and their time to do whatever they liked.

Nick had seen most of his school pals get into confrontations with one or other of the bad lads. There was no walking away. No talking your way out of it. Try as you might to avoid them, when they wanted you they got you, nutting you as you passed in the hallway, coming after you in the schoolyard or waiting for you outside school. At the end of the last summer term Nick had seen the utterly harmless Alan Wise knocked unconscious just outside the school gates by Billy Finch from 3C for no other reason than Finch thought Alan liked himself too much. And, like everybody else, Nick had done nothing.

In their final year Finch and his mates, Rocky Banks and Blackie White were impossible to deal with. There was no reasoning with them and apparently no taming them. They'd grown up believing a reputation as a hard lad was more important than anything else in life. Wherever they went they were preceded by the propaganda of fear, the knowledge that they loved violence and used it often. In another time they'd have been pressed into military service and sent off to some faraway land to fight fuzzy wuzzies and do something useful by dying for their country.

Somehow Nick had managed to avoid a serious confrontation but it was only a matter of time and the odds caught up with him on a Monday night at the Clayton Ballroom at Bedlington Station. The Clayton hosted rock and roll skating on Saturday afternoons and a teen dance on Monday nights. On any given Monday there were half a dozen fights inside the ballroom and more outside. It took very little to start one; a bumped shoulder, a word, a look, anything. There was nothing fancy about the Clayton, it had a stage, a dance floor, cinema style seats against the walls and a snack bar, but it brought three or four hundred teenagers together in a cloud of hormonal static. The girls danced while the boys, brimming with a furious energy they could neither comprehend nor contain, prowled the fringes looking for the release of sex or violence.

The fight came on as fights often did, in a blur. One minute Nick was standing by the dance floor with Spelk and Dave watching the girls, the next he had half a dozen bad lads around him. He recognised Rocky Banks and Blackie White but it was a kid he'd never seen before who grabbed him by the shirtfront.

"Keep away from Patsy," the kid said, and even though it made no sense Nick knew immediately what had happened. Some girl at school had used his name to make her boyfriend jealous. But what surprised Nick was his reaction. Whatever fear he might have felt was banished by a fierce indignation. The kid punched Nick in the face but Nick barely felt it. His assailant was shorter than him and lighter but his mates were goading him and he had strength in numbers. Nick grabbed the kid and hit him back and the two of them launched into a manic waltz across the dance floor, a series of staccato images in the mottled light. Girls screamed and scattered. The two boys lost their footing and fell to the floor with Nick on top, one hand around his attacker's throat, the other balled into a fist hitting him in the face as fast and as hard as he could. Then he sprouted wings and flew away. An irresistible force clamped onto his shoulders, he felt himself hoisted into the air and propelled toward a pair of fire doors. He put his arms up to protect his face just as he hit the doors. They opened with a bang, the clamp on his shoulders released him and he arced through the darkness and hit the ground in a heap. He scrambled back up to confront his opponent but the doors swung shut and he was alone in the alley, panting, elated. He took stock of himself and seemed not to be hurt. More importantly he hadn't backed down. He'd fought and he would have won if the fucking bouncer hadn't grabbed him and thrown him out. And he'd learned something - fighting didn't hurt. You didn't feel anything when your blood was up. All you had to do was awaken the beast inside you that was ready and waiting to be unleashed. There was no fear, no pain, no thought to complicate things, just the white hot purity of rage.

*   *   *

"Ye given much thought to your future?" Shep asked.

"Ah divvent hae te when ah've got ye te dee it for is," Bright answered.

Shep smiled, unconcerned. The two of them had taken refuge from a stiflingly hot day in a corner of the bar at the Top Club. Until a minute ago they'd been kept company by the manager, Col Beatty, a heavy set man in a black waistcoat and starched white sleeves who'd been called to attend to a newly tapped barrel that had too many floaters.

"Ye don't care where ye go from here?" Shep queried. "Or are ye content to be the station sergeant at Bedlington for the rest o' your life, like Bert?"

"Christ, ah haven't been in the job two year yet," Bright said.

"Ah was tahkin' to Ted the other night," Shep continued. "He plans on retirin' as soon as he turns 65 the year after next. If ye were to get ya inspector's exam afore then ye'd be a strong candidate to replace him."

Bright tried to change the subject. "What aboot ye? Ya not that far off retirement age yasel are ye?"

Shep and Ted Dunlop had joined the police force around the same time but Shep was cagier about his age.

"Oh, ye want my job noo de ye?"

"Nae thanks," Bright said. "Ah've got ahll the aggravation ah need where ah am."

"Ah'll retire when ah'm good an' ready," Shep said. "Things are goin' var' canny the way they are an' ah'd like them to continue that way. When Ted retires ah want somebody ready to take his place that ah can trust, somebody ah knah ah can rely on."

"Ye think Morpeth would promote is to inspector just after ah got me sergeant's stripes?"

Bright had never been particularly ambitious. All he'd ever wanted after the war was a comfortable life but however much he tried to work his way into a cosy little rut it seemed there was always somebody who wanted to prod him out of it.

"It's happened before," Shep said.

"Aye, durin' the war when anybody could get promoted."

"It wouldn't be that soon," Shep added. "Take ya inspector's exam next summer and as soon as Ted puts in for his retirement ah'll put your name in to take his place, that's still a couple of years from noo."

"An' ye think Morpeth'll gan along wi' whatever ye want?" Bright said and finished his pint. "De ye not think they could mek is an inspector and post is somewhere they wanted?"

"It's possible," Shep said, though his manner suggested he knew otherwise. "If ye request specifically to stay in Bedlin'ton an' if Ted recommends ye for his replacement an' you're supported by a strong recommendation from me ah think they'd be inclined to see it wor way. As lang as iverythin' in Bedlin'ton is runnin' like clockwork why wouldn't they?"

"Let is think aboot it," Bright said. "It just seems a bit sudden to me."

"Tek ahll the time ye want," Shep said. But Bright had heard those words before.

"Do ye want a short?" Shep said. "Ah think ah'm ganna have a short, de ye want a short?"

Bright thought about it and decided why not. Ted knew where to find him if there was an emergency and what little paperwork he had to do could wait until tomorrow.

Col had returned to the bar and Shep called over to him: "Couple o' whisky shorts owa here, Col, if ye don't mind."

*   *   *

In the gauzy warmth of a summer evening Nick caught the 10A for Newcastle at the Top End. He went upstairs and took a seat in the front row where he could put his feet up on the window ledge. Spelk had gone shopping with his mam in Newcastle and the plan was that she'd come home by herself and he would meet Nick in the Haymarket and they would go and see The Magnificent Seven.

Nick took a tab from a new packet of 10 Gold Leaf and lit up. He and Spelk and Dave had been smoking on the sly for a few months. It was another reason they liked going to the pictures because they could smoke in the dark. Nick was taking a chance that somebody on the bus would see him and tell his dad but he didn't much care. A lot of lads were smoking by the time they were 14. Besides, he was getting 15 bob a week doing a paper round and it was his money to do as he wished.

The bus stopped at the bottom of Hartford Road across from the entrance to the Hartlands council estate and Nick's spirits sank when he saw Rocky Banks and Blackie White among those waiting to get on. They came upstairs, sat next to Nick and put their feet up on the ledge beside his. Banks reached into a jacket pocket, took out a couple of loose Woodbines and passed one to White. On impulse Nick offered them a Golf Leaf. Banks hesitated then took one followed by White.

"Ta," Banks said.

He and White both wore the hard lad uniform; black jacket, drainpipe jeans and winklepicker shoes with buckles. White was Nick's height but thinner with sharp features and blonde hair and he liked to wear black shirts with white bootlace ties. Banks was a little taller than Nick, raw boned with bad skin and hair the colour of mud. He wore a studded leather belt and his shirt collar turned up at the back like a cornet holding a pile of greasy hair.

"Ye pinch these off ya fatha?" Banks said, gesturing with his tab.

"No, ah paid fo' them," Nick said.

White smoked and watched the passing scenery, the planes of his pasty white face immobile.

"Where ye gannin in the toon?" Banks asked.

"The pictures," Nick said. "Where ye gannin'?"

Banks shrugged. "Naewhere."

It could mean anything. They were like outlaws in the old west, wandering aimlessly, taking whatever they wanted, always ready for trouble.

The three of them travelled in silence for a while then Banks said: "Ya fatha larn ye to fight?"

Nick shook his head. "Me fatha nivah larned is shite."

Banks seemed amused. "From what ah hear he's not scared of a fight. Me fatha says he saw him tek on three blokes at the Top End once."

Nick thought it was funny. If they only knew. His father might be a hard man on the street, not afraid to stand up to anybody. But not in his own home. In his own home he couldn't stand up to his own wife.

"Ah divvent gi' a shite aboot me fatha an' he doesn't gi' a shite aboot me," Nick said. "Tha's nowt good aboot havin' a polis fo' a fatha."

The words of betrayal spilled easily from his lips. They'd been there for a while, just waiting for the right moment. His parents had betrayed him in a thousand ways without knowing it; at least his betrayal was deliberate. When the bus reached the Haymarket the three of them went their separate ways without another word.

The next time Nick saw Rocky Banks was when Banks tried to drown him at Humford Baths. A mid-afternoon rainstorm had sent most swimmers scurrying but Nick took the opportunity to swim lengths in the uncrowded pool. He loved to swim. He could feel his strength and endurance growing every time he was in the water. Fifty laps was a mile and he knew he could swim that and more. He was on his twentieth lap when a terrific shock to his head and shoulders drove him under the water. He struggled to the surface choking and saw Rocky Banks swimming away, laughing. When Nick, Spelk and Dave played Bombers the idea was to come as close to your target as possible without actually hitting him. Apparently Banks's idea was to start with a direct hit.

"Ye fuckin' bastard," Nick coughed. He swam to the side, heaved himself out of the water and ran around the edges of the pool looking for a good jump off point while Banks kept to the middle. Nick scampered up the high diver and leaped off the top, knees clenched to his chest in a cannonball. Banks hadn't realised how much distance Nick could get from the top step and lunged away at the last moment but Nick struck his shoulder, a glancing blow hard enough to push Banks under. Beneath the surface Nick kicked up at a wide angle and swam to the exit steps underwater so Banks couldn't catch him. When Nick climbed out Banks was hanging onto the side rail rubbing his left shoulder.

"Ye hit me bad shoulder ye cunt," he said. "Ah'll fuckin' get ye for that." He hauled himself out and for the next half hour he and Nick chased each other all over the baths, in and out of the pool trying to get in one more hit. They called a truce only when stopped by cold and exhaustion. As they dried themselves off Nick saw close up what Banks meant by his bad shoulder. His left shoulder and much of his upper arm was waxen and pitted and where his armpit should have been was a hairless web of skin.

"Hoo'd ye get that?" Nick asked.

"Me brutha," Banks said. "He pulled a chip pan doon on 'is when ah was ten." Nick remembered Banks's older brother, Johnny, from school three years ago. Johnny Banks was at the Doctor Pit now, tending pit ponies underground.

"Was it an accident?" Nick asked.

"Ah think sae," Banks said with a half smile. "Ah was in the hospital nearly six month, but. Ah had to keep gannin back fo' skin grafts." As an aside, he said: "Tha was one time ah was hangin' off the back of a horse an' cart an' the skin under me arm ripped."

Nick felt a twinge of sympathy, something he'd never expected where Rocky Banks was concerned.

Afterwards, when Nick was removing the lock from his bike outside the baths, Banks asked if he wanted to go for a smoke. Nick hesitated then snapped the bike lock shut and walked with Banks down to the river. They crossed a string of cement slab stepping stones and sat at the top of a steep bank on the other side worn bare by kids playing on a rope swing. The river was sluggish and skeined with dust. Too low now for kids jumping off the swing. Banks opened a frayed khaki shoulder bag he used to carry his towel and trunks and took out a packet of Players Navy Cut, a box of matches and a bottle of Newcastle Brown Ale. They lit up and Banks used a sheath knife to prise the cap off the brown ale. He took a few swallows and handed the bottle to Nick. It was the first time in his life Nick had tasted beer and he thought it so amazing it took all his self control to pretend he'd never had it before. They finished the bottle quickly and the coil of warmth it instilled along with an overall feeling of well being made him receptive when

Rocky said they should get some more.

"Pam's haein' ah borthday party the night," he said. "We'll get some mair there."

He meant Pamela Ellis from 4C, a skinny brunette who wore tight skirts, high heels and had breasts that reminded Nick of ping pong balls. So, he walked his bike up to Hartlands with Rocky Banks and left it down the side of Rocky's house. He met Rocky's mother, a hard eyed woman with a deeply lined face who chain smoked and seemed surprised to have the polis's son in her house. Nick and Rocky smoked and watched The Flintstones on the TV till Rocky decided it was time to go. They didn't have far to walk. Rocky lived at the top of the estate and Pam at the bottom. As they crossed the grassy oval it occurred to Nick that neither of them had a present for Pam. They went to the back door where they could hear Billy Fury singing at top volume on the record player.

"She's fuckin' mental aboot Billy Fury," Rocky said

He hammered on the door to make himself heard. One of Pam's girl friends came to the door, face flushed, eyes excited, but her expression changed when she saw who it was. Nick guessed Rocky wasn't invited. From what Nick could see there were eight or nine girls inside, dancing, talking and laughing. Pam's friend went back in and everybody except Billy Fury shut up. Pam came to the door, a look of apprehension on her face. She shot Nick a curious glance then said to Rocky: "Ye cannit come in, Rocky. Me dad told is not to let ye into the house anymore."

"Hae ye any beer?" Rocky asked. "Ah'm just lookin' fo' summick to drink."

"Eeh, ah cannit gi' ye anythin' to drink," Pam said. "Me dad'll kill is."

Nick realised that Rocky expected Pam to give him any beer that was in the house, even if it was her father's.

"Ye must hae somethin'" Rocky insisted. As if doing her a favour he added: "Just gi's a couple o' bottles an' ah wunnit come in."

"Ah cannit Rocky, honest," she pleaded. "Ye hae to go, me mam and dad'll be back any minute."

Rocky looked frustrated. "Just gi's a couple of bottles, that's ahll ah want. Naebody's ganna tell ya fatha."

Pam seemed about to cry. "Ah cannit, Rocky, honest ah cannit."

"Ahh, ye stupid fuckin' hooah," Rocky said. He turned away in disgust and Nick followed him down the path to the front gate. In the amber light of a streetlamp Nick saw four small dark figures approaching the house. They reached the front gate at the same time and Nick heard a man's angry voice.

"Hey, what the hell de ye think ya deein' at mah hoose?"

It was two men and their wives and they smelled of drink. Nick guessed it was Pam's father who'd spoken. Rocky would have kept going if Mr. Ellis hadn't made the mistake of grabbing him by the arms. Rocky might only be 15 but he was a head taller than Pam's dad and strong. He broke Mr. Ellis's grip easily and threw him to the pavement where he landed with a gasp of pain.

"Divvent ye hort mah man," Mrs. Ellis screamed.

Rocky paused to see if the other man would have a go but the man said: "Just bugga off the two o' ye afore ye dee any mair harm."

Rocky strode across the darkened oval back towards his house. Nick hurried to keep up with him.

"Ah knah hoo wi can get some beer," he said. "Not the night mebbe, but ah knah hoo wi can get ahll the beer wi want."

"Hoo?" Rocky said gruffly, not slowing his stride.

"Me fatha has a skeleton key at yem," Nick said. "Ah knah where he keeps it, that'll get us in anywhere wi want."

*   *   *

That summer Nick's mam was offered a job as head barmaid at The Feathers, a country pub sagging under the weight of its own history. A former coaching inn just outside Morpeth it had ivy covered walls and bay windows with bottle bottom window panes. Inside it was all creaky floorboards, shabby furnishings and a whiff of mildew. Nick's mam and dad had become friends with the licensees, Percy and Dolly Harbottle, and when the head barman left Percy asked Nick's mam if she was interested. With her fun loving personality she was just the ticket to brighten the old place up, he said. With an extra couple of quid a month and unlimited free booze it wasn't a difficult decision. She could catch the bus to work from the bottom of the estate and Nick's dad would pick her up each night after he got off duty. She left the Doctor Pit canteen in July and took a couple of weeks off so she and Nick's dad could go to Austria with the Harbottles.

It was just the opportunity Nick needed to try out his dad's skeleton key. Long handled and steely grey it was like any other key except skinnier with fewer teeth and used properly it would turn any simple lock. His dad had showed it to him when he brought it home a couple of months earlier then put it in a drawer in the sideboard from where it had exerted a magnetic pull on Nick. He tried it on the back door to see if it worked and it did but he wanted to see if it would work where it mattered. He'd considered a few options and settled on a chemist's shop halfway between the Market Place and Bedlington Station. It closed every night at six, it was in a part of town where there were few pedestrians and little traffic after dark and it offered a ready escape into the Dene, a swathe of parkland beside the River Blyth. There was an alarm bell over the front door and an overhead light in the doorway but there was also an enclosed back yard and a back door with no alarm. The only deterrent was a rind of broken glass atop the wall. When he showed the key to Rocky, Blackie White and Billy Finch and told them what he had in mind they seemed impressed. So far he sensed they saw him as a bit of a novelty, a polis's son who hated his father, but that was all. This was a way to win them over.

They arranged to do it that Tuesday night and, at Nick's suggestion, went so far as to give themselves an alibi. They went to the Wallaw at Bedlington Station and kidded around with the lass in the ticket booth so she would remember them. Halfway through the picture they sneaked out through a fire door and hurried through the gathering dusk to the Dene. By the time they got to the chemist's shop it was completely dark and there was nobody around. Billy threw a sack filled with rags over the broken glass on top of the wall and the four of them were up and over it in no time. The back door was set inside a deep, unlit alcove and Nick had to feel around for the lock. When he found it he put the key in and immediately hit an obstacle.

"Tha's a key on the other side," he whispered.

"Push it oot," Finch urged. "Wark it aroond an' push it oot."

Nick tried but he couldn't get the key on the other side to budge.

"Gi's it here, ye cack handed cunt," Finch said. He elbowed Nick aside, squatted down and worked the key in the lock and Nick got the impression it wasn't his first time. He grunted and swore and then they heard the tinkle of a key landing on the floor on the other side.

"Got ye, ye cunt," he said. He pushed the skeleton key in all the way, eased it back and forth a couple of times, tried a few turns until it caught and the mechanism turned with a solid click. He stood up, tried the handle and the door opened inward with a slight creak.

"Open fuckin' sesame," he said.

"Fuckin' hell, it worked," Rocky said.

"Tek ahll ye can carry, lads," Finch said.

The four of them padded down the darkened hallway to the front of the shop, the only illumination coming from the overhead light outside the front door. They ignored a locked storeroom and an office with a safe and fanned out behind the counters grabbing whatever took their fancy.

"Wi shoulda brought fuckin' bags," Blackie said.

"Wi will next time," Finch said.

Any misgivings Nick might have had were submerged in the thrill of being able to take whatever he wanted, the kind of freedom known only to the rich. He didn't care that his was a fraudulent freedom, the spoils were real. Rocky, Billy and Blackie stuffed their pockets with packets of tabs then turned their attention to the beer and spirits. They plucked bottles of brandy, whisky and rum from the darkly gleaming shelves and when their pockets could hold no more they filled their arms with bottles of Newcastle Brown Ale. Nick took a few packets of tabs, a couple of bottles of brandy and a couple of bottles of brown ale. It was nowhere near what the others had taken but he was lacking their level of experience.

"It's time wi were fuckin' gone," Denny said. Nick saw that Finch had removed his jacket and tied the sleeves together to form a makeshift bag that clinked heavily as he hurried down the hallway to the back yard.

"The key," Nick said, "where's the key?"

"Ah've got it," Finch said. They threw the sackful of rags back over the broken glass and hauled themselves across, slower this time so they wouldn't drop any of their booty. Safely down the other side they scuttled into the enveloping blackness of the Dene. Nick felt as if he was walking on air. There was no guilt, no remorse, only the exhilaration of getting something for nothing. When they got deep into the Dene, where there was nobody to see or hear, they erupted in a chorus of exultant whoops. Finch led the way off the unlit path to a small copse, put down his jacket and struck a match so they could see what they were doing. They sat in a circle, lit cigarettes and laid out their loot. Each of them opened a bottle of brown ale so they could toast their success, their faces impish in the red glow of the cigarettes. Brothers in arms, Nick thought. Partners in crime.

Finch said to Nick: "Ye dee what ye say ya ganna dee, ah'll gi' ye that."

"Aye, but ah still need me key back," Nick said.

Finch took the skeleton key from a pocket and threw it to Nick.

"Mek sure ye hang onto it," he said. "Ah think wa ganna be needin' it again."

*   *   *

While his mam and dad holidayed in Austria with Percy and Dolly Harbottle Nick embarked on a crime spree with Rocky, Billy and Blackie, knocking over an off-licence one week and a furniture store the next. They took almost a hundred pounds from the furniture store, the first time they'd stolen money, and it infected them with the greed for more. Billy wanted to go to Newcastle and knock over bigger places where they could get more money. Nick had no objection to using the skeleton key for more jobs and he thought it a good idea to move beyond Bedlington but he was worried that increasing the number of break-ins would increase the odds of getting caught. That Friday night he had Rocky, Billy and Blackie come to his house so they could talk it over.

The four of them sprawled around the living room smoking, drinking and listening to Radio Luxembourg. Rocky, Billy and Blackie were tickled to be in the polis's house while the polis was away, just as Nick thought they'd be. He had access to things they couldn't get without him and as long as he controlled that access, to some extent he controlled them. To amuse them further he brought out his father's handcuffs and truncheon. They were especially impressed by the truncheon with its solid lead rod and ball encased in walnut.

"Ye'd knah it if ye got hit wi' this," Blackie said.

"Nah ye wouldn't," Billy said. "Ye wouldn't knah a fuckin' thing."

"Has ya fatha ivah used it?" Rocky asked.

"Sometimes," Nick said. "In emorgencies, like."

"Wi should tek it on wa next job," Rocky added. "In case some bugga gets in the way."

"Nah, ye wouldn't tek that," Nick said, "it's owa easy to lose, then iverybody would knah wee ye were." On impulse he added: "Ah'll show ye what'd work better than that." He went upstairs to his parent's bedroom, opened the wardrobe and reached to the back of the top shelf to see if the Colt 45 was still there. It was. He pulled it out in its blue webbing holster, took it downstairs and set it on the coffee table. Rocky, Denny and Blackie leaned forward to get a closer look. Nick popped the holster flap, took the pistol out and held it with the barrel pointed at the ceiling.

"Is it real?" Denny asked.

"Aye, it's real," Nick said. He thumbed the release button on the side, broke the pistol open and spun the six round cylinder. It turned easily and noiselessly. Apparently his father still kept it clean and oiled.

"Ah could put that to some fuckin' use," Blackie said.

"Aye an' wee would ye kill forst?" Rocky asked.

"Ye," Blackie said and they laughed.

"Heeyah, gis' a haad o' it," Billy said.

Nick snapped the pistol shut and gave it to Finch who passed it from hand to hand, feeling its heft and balance. He pulled the trigger a few times, watching the cylinder turn as the hammer rose and fell.

"Does it hae bullets?"

"Aye, it's got bullets." Nick unfolded the rag that held the cleaning rod and the six rounds in their shiny brass cartridge cases. Finch cracked the revolver open like Nick had done, picked up a bullet, put it in a chamber, closed it, spun the cylinder, pointed the gun at Nick and pulled the trigger. There was a sharp metallic click as the hammer fell on an empty chamber. Blackie sniggered.

"Just gan canny wi'd," Nick said, unable to fully comprehend what Finch had just done.

"It's ahlreet," Billy said. "Ah can see where the bullet is when it torns."

Nick took a swig of brown ale, Billy pointed the gun at him again and pulled the trigger. There was a loud crack and Nick jolted as if hit by an electric shock. The bottle fell from his hand, hit the corner of the coffee table and landed on the floor where it pulsed brown ale into the carpet. A bitter, burnt smell tainted the air and a knot of blue smoke uncoiled in the middle of the room. The only sound was Sam Cooke on the wireless singing "That's the sound of the men working on the chain ga-ah-ang." Nick waited for something to tell him where he'd been shot. Pain. Blood. All-consuming darkness. Something. The four of them sat rigidly, only their eyes moving.

"Fuuuck," Billy said.

"Fuuuck," Rocky said.

"Fuuuck," Blackie said.

Nick looked down at himself and saw nothing. No entry wound. No blood. He could move his head, his arms and legs, his fingers and toes. He could see and hear. He reached over to Billy, took the gun out of his hand and clenched it tightly to his chest feeling the heat of the barrel through his clothes.

"Fuuuck," he said.

He turned to Rocky next to him and the two of them looked each other up and down. Then they looked at Blackie and he looked down at himself but he had no sign of a bullet wound either. The three of them turned to Billy who slowly shook his head. Nick went to stand up but he had no strength in his legs. He put the gun, bullets and cleaning rod back in the holster and snapped it shut. The four of them looked around the room to see where the bullet had gone.

"Fuuuck," Rocky said looking in the direction of the hallway door. In the wall next to the door, about a foot below the ceiling, was a crater the size of a fist. The four of them stared at the bullet hole then back at each other, each of them thinking the same thing. Three of them were seated directly in front of Billy with only a few feet between them. How could the bullet have passed harmlessly between them in such a confined space?

Nick forced himself to get up, turned off the wireless and went over to the bullet hole gouged into the wall.

"Fuuuck," he said.

He peered between the curtains but the street was deserted, the only sign of life the flicker of television screens behind closed curtains. With the wireless off they could hear the TV next door; Sergeant Bilko and the laughter of a studio audience. Nick turned his attention back to the bullet hole. It was just above head height and looked like the kind of bullet hole you saw in the pictures, a ragged, powdery hole an inch or two deep and tree or four inches across with tendrils of torn wallpaper peeling around the edges. Nick turned and saw that from where Billy sat the bullet would have taken a steeply rising path between himself and Rocky.

"Fuuuck," Nick said.

He stared into the crater and realised something was missing. There was no bullet. He picked at the crumbly brickwork with a finger but the bullet wasn't there and it didn't appear to have gone through the wall. He looked back at the three of them.

"The bullet's not here."

They came over, looked into the bullet hole and then at each other. Then it dawned on them. The bullet must have ricocheted. They looked around the room for other signs of damage. Another hole in a wall, in the settee, in the chairs, in the sideboard, in the dining table. But there was none. The bullet, it seemed, had disappeared.

"Wi hae to find it," Nick said.

He took the revolver upstairs, locked it in the wardrobe and hurried back down to look for the missing bullet. They searched everywhere and found nothing. It didn't make any sense. None of it made sense.

"It has to be somewhere in this room," Nick said. "It couldn't just fuckin' disappear."

He stood with his back to the bullet hole and tried to calculate the bullet's trajectory from there. And then he realised…it must have ricocheted back across the room. But there was no bullet hole in the back window and no damage to the back wall. He got down on his hands and knees and hunted inch by inch under the back window and found the bullet wedged between the skirting board and the carpet, a scratched lead teardrop. He stood up holding it between his thumb and forefinger.

"It was ahll the way owa here," he said and thought how oddly distant his voice sounded.

Rocky, Billy and Blackie stared at Nick, then at the hole in the wall, then back at him. When Finch pulled the trigger the bullet had passed between three of them, climbing as it crossed the room, hit the front wall and ricocheted back across the room on a descending trajectory, somehow missing the four of them this time.

"Fuck me," Rocky breathed.

"Aye, weel, noo ye've fund it ah think ah've been here lang enough," Finch said and he scooped up his tabs from the coffee table. Blackie and Rocky exchanged smirks then they too left.

Nick stood alone in the shambles of the living room. However tipsy he'd been before the gun went off he was sober now. He cleaned up the easy mess first, the bottles and glasses and ashtrays, the spilled beer on the carpet, then turned his attention to the bullet hole in the wall. It seemed to get bigger every time he looked at it. How was he supposed to hide it? What would he tell his mam and dad? For a moment he thought he should just take off, pack a bag, hitch a ride to Liverpool and get on a tramp steamer to America. Instead, he hunted through the cupboard under the stairs where his parents kept the leftover wallpaper with a few half empty tins of paint and a box of distemper from when they'd papered the house. The wallpaper in the living room was Regency stripes; rust red with gold trim on a cream background. He took out the last remaining roll and held it against the bullet hole to see if it matched. It did, but there wasn't enough of it to hang a complete strip from floor to ceiling. Besides, his parents might notice if the whole roll was missing. He would have to fill the bullet hole, cut out a square of wallpaper and stick it over the top. But what was he supposed to use to fill the hole? Ash or clay wouldn't work, a wad of newspaper wouldn't do it. Then he remembered the Plaster Of Paris kit in his bedroom cupboard. He brought it down, mixed a cupful in the kitchen and patted it into the bullet hole. It set quickly and was almost dry by the time he cut out a square of wallpaper to match the pattern. He mixed up some distemper with water in a jar, smeared the back of the wallpaper and slid it over the patched hole, careful to align the stripes. When he stepped back to see how it looked he thought he could just as well have put up a neon sign that said 'Bullet Hole Here.' All he could do was hope that by the time it dried it would look better.

On the other side of the room there was a narrow furrow in the carpet where the bullet had ploughed a path a couple of inches long before stopping under the skirting board but unless you were looking for it you wouldn't know it was there. He would toss the spent bullet and the empty cartridge case but there was no hiding the fact that there were now only five bullets in the holster instead of six. Nick hoped his dad wouldn't check the revolver again for a long, long time, preferably after he'd left home.

By the time he went to bed he was drained and fell asleep quickly but when he woke up the next day his first thought was how the patched bullet hole would look. He hurried downstairs and while he knew where the patch was he was relieved to see that now it had dried it was no longer so obvious. To the incurious eye it mightn't be noticeable at all.

As his parent's return drew nearer the more nervous he became. The day they were due back he got up knowing they would likely be home by the time he got out of school and he would have to face them whatever the consequences. That afternoon he dragged his feet all the way home, past the old cemetery, across the playing fields, putting off the moment, not daring to contemplate the cost of failure. He felt a brief moment of reprieve when he saw the Consul wasn't parked out front and thought they might not be home yet but when the back door opened on the turn of the handle he realised they'd already unloaded the car and his father must have gone up to the police station. He saw the duty free bottles of rum and gin and cartons of cigarettes on the kitchen table and heard his mam upstairs unpacking. He thought about dumping his rucksack and taking off on his bike for a couple of hours but it was too late, his mam had heard him come in.

"Nicholas, is that you?" she called downstairs. Nick knew that tone. It was the tone she used that conjured up an image of a fuse burning. She came downstairs, her face set, an accusatory glow in her eyes. She stood in the doorway next to the bullet hole and said: "Wi cannit even go on holiday an' trust ye to behave yasel', can wi?"

Nick looked at the patch on the wall. From a few feet away, perhaps, it could be missed, but not close up.

"Why?" he said.

"What do ye mean, why?" she said disgustedly. "Did ye honestly think ye could get away wi' it?"

He wondered if he should tell her about Rocky and Blackie and Billy but instead of spreading the blame it would only make his mam and dad madder. Especially his dad.

"Ah've ahlways known tha was somethin' wrang wi' ye," she went on. "Ah think ye must be a throwback or somethin'. Hoo on orth could ye think wi wouldn't notice somethin' like that?" And she nodded at the patched bullet hole.

Nick felt himself sink into somewhere deep and dark within, the pit where all his fears and failings writhed like eels.

"Do ye think wi wouldn't care what happened t'im?"

Nick opened his mouth to say something then shut it again. Him? What the fuck was she talking about, him?

"Wee?" he asked.

"Wee de ye think ah'm tahlkin' aboot?"

"Ah divvent knah," Nick said.

"Mickey Drippin'," she said angrily. "Wee else would ah be tahlkin' aboot? What did ye dee to Mickey Drippin'?"

Mickey Dripping? The budgie? He followed his mother's line of sight from the hallway door, past the bullet hole to the cage suspended in the window, still and silent.

"Why, what's wrang wi'm?"

"Ye knah bloody weel what's wrang wi'm."

"No ah don't. Ah nivah touched him."

"Oh, so he just up and died on his own did he? Ahll by hissel fo' nae reason?"

Nick stepped over to the cage and saw a sad little cone of green and yellow feathers lying on the bottom, claws grasping emptily at the air.

"So are ye ganna tell 'is what happened?" his mam said. "He still has food an' wettah so ah knah he couldn't hae died o' hunger or thorst."

Nick met her gaze with complete confidence.

"He musta had a heart attack."

*   *   *

On a sodden Monday in October the only sound in the police station was the desolate patter of overflowing drains on rubbish bins along Catholic Row. Bright, at the duty desk, shuffled an endless succession of complaints, incident reports, arrest warrants, witness statements, licence renewals, memos and official correspondence while Ted Dunlop sat in his office and applied the same degree of concentration to that day's Sporting Life. At the back of the station Alec Newell gazed up at the streaming windows and thought of ships at sea while he stirred sugar into his tea. The sense of isolation imposed by the storm ended with a crash when Dr. Ritchie's receptionist, Agnes, burst through the front door. Her hair and clothes were soaked so she must have run through the storm without a coat and there was terror in her eyes. Her words came breathlessly, painfully. "He's killin' him…ye've got to come now…he's killin' Dr. Ritchie…"

Without reaching for his coat or helmet Bright ran for the open door and shouted back to Alec Newell: "Ye tek care o' hor."

As Bright vanished into the rain Ted Dunlop stepped out of his office and told Newell: "Ye get after him an' give him a hand, ah'll watch things here."

Newell dropped the spoon and followed Bright out into the downpour. Dunlop went over to Agnes, put an arm around her drenched shoulders and steered her to a bench. "Ye just sit yasel' down here for a minute, lass," he said. "Catch your breath an' tell is what's wrang."

It was about fifty yards down Front Street from the police station to Bernard Ritchie's surgery. Bright, in his police boots on slick pavement, made it in less than ten seconds. Three women formed an agitated huddle outside the surgery. As Bright rushed past one of them said: "He just came chargin' in an' attacked the doctor…"

The waiting room was empty and there was no sign of disturbance but the door to Ritchie's office was open and Bright heard a man's frenzied voice shouting: "Ah'll kill ye… ah'll kill ye…ah'll kill ye…"

Inside he found Ritchie on the floor and Robbie McBride kicking him ferociously. All Bright could see of Ritchie were his legs poking out from behind the desk, jerking under the impact of each kick.

"Mac, get off him," Bright yelled but Mac didn't hear. Coming up behind him Bright thrust his hands under Mac's armpits, locked his fingers behind his neck, hoisted him into the air and swung him away from Ritchie and out into the waiting room. Mac's feet flailed wildly.

"He's been interferin' wi' me little lad," he shouted. "He's been deein' it fo' years…ah'll kill him…ah'll fuckin' kill him…"

Alec Newell arrived as Bright threw Mac to the floor face first, knocking the air out of him. Together the two policemen held him down. Stunned, unable to move, Mac's rage crumbled into sobs. "He's been interferin' wi' Keith…me little lad…me little lad."

"Ye haad him heeyahe while ah see te Ritchie," Bright told Alec.

Bright went into Ritchie's wrecked surgery, stepped behind the desk and knelt down beside the doctor's still form. Ritchie's face was a mesh of destroyed flesh and there was a pool of blood under his head and shoulders. His white hair was soaked in blood and there were splashes of blood on the wall. Bright put an ear to Ritchie's mouth and listened for his breathing but there was nothing. Ritchie's chest wasn't moving and he had no pulse.

"Dr. Ritchie, can ye hear me…?" Bright shouted but there was no response. He rolled Ritchie onto his side, used his fingers to clear the doctor's mouth and throat but there was still nothing to say he was alive.

"Jesus Christ," Bright muttered. He rolled the doctor onto his back, put his hands on his chest the way he'd been trained and started pumping, counting each compression out loud. From far away he heard the urgent clanging of an ambulance and he kept pumping.

1961

The Soviets stun the world by launching the first man into space; the East Germans begin construction of the Berlin Wall; the National Health Service offers the birth control pill. Tops on TV are Thank Your Lucky Stars and The Dick Van Dyke Show. The Avengers, starring Ian Hendry and Patrick Macnee, makes its TV debut. Top films are West Side Story starring Russ Tamblyn and Natalie Wood; The Guns Of Navarone starring Gregory Peck and David Niven and Saturday Night And Sunday Morning starring Albert Finney. Top of the charts are Runaway by Del Shannon; Don't Treat Me Like A Child by Helen Shapiro and You're Driving Me Crazy by The Temperance Seven.

Young Love

Nick's dad once asked him what the role of the police was and Nick said: "To catch criminals."

"No," his father corrected him, "the role of the police is to prevent crime."

Well, Nick thought, ya not deein' a very good fuckin' job of it are ye?

Since then he'd seen no reason to change his mind. What sort of polis was it who didn't know his own son was a juvenile delinquent? Who didn't know his son was breaking into shops and stealing beer, whisky, rum and tabs? Who didn't know his son had been hanging around with some of the worst kids in town? Who didn't know his son had invited them over to his house for an underage drinking party? Who didn't know there was a bullet hole in the living room wall of his own fucking home? Nick needed his parents for food, shelter and clothing and that was all. For everything else he was on his own. Never more so than when he'd looked down the barrel of his father's Colt 45 and saw how easily, how stupidly, his life could have ended. He knew then that the way to save himself wasn't to become one of the bad lads, it was to leave them behind. He'd been given a second chance and he went back to school determined to make the most of it. He renewed his friendship with Spelk and Dave who'd joined a youth club at the Methodist Hall on Front Street West. It was run by volunteers young enough to connect with the kids; they listened to records, played games and discussed the important issues of the day. And it was a way to meet girls. To mix with them in a casual setting where there wasn't the pressure of the lonely walk across the dance floor with its inherent risk of an even lonelier walk back. Best of all he got to know Angie Wilks, the head girl at Westridge, a ravishing 16 year old with rosebud lips and coal black hair cut like Alma Cogan. Angie was someone he'd never otherwise have met because she was in Fifth Remove a year ahead of him. An older woman, mysterious and unattainable. Nick couldn't help but be drawn by her beauty and her vivacious personality. What he didn't expect was that she would be drawn to him, a discovery he placed on the same order of magnitude as Columbus's discovery of America. He had no idea where he belonged on the scale of attractiveness to the opposite sex, especially when compared to the young rakes around town who were all quiff and cock and drew girls like moths to a flame. At first he mistook Angie's interest for the same friendliness she showed to everybody and it wasn't till they played one of the club's most popular games he realised it was something more. It was a version of musical chairs that required the boys to sit in a circle while the girls walked around them till the music stopped, the lights went out and the girls had to scramble for an empty lap. And it was a game where everybody won because it always ended with a five minute lights out and a mass necking session. One night when the lights went out Nick found himself with Angie on his lap and she kissed him with an ardor he found startling and infinitely arousing.

Soon afterwards they started going out together. With little money to spend they joined the teenage diaspora that roamed the byways of Bedlington in all kinds of weather seeking out hidden places where they could have themselves a knee trembler. The old cemetery at West Lea was especially popular and it was said that the sounds of owls hooting in the night were actually the sounds made by young girls as their bare arses rubbed up against the cold gravestones.

It gave them time to get to to know each other, to confide in each other the insecurities of youth and to share the relief of knowing they'd found somebody who'd listen to them without sneering or laughing. When they could afford to go to the pictures they'd sit in the back row and snog for hours. Then the sex started. Real sex. She'd let him put his hand under her coat at the pictures and fondle her breasts and when kissing goodnight she'd welcomed the rigid outline of his prick through their clothes, feeling the urgency of his climax and leaving him to limp home with the effluence of his desire turning cold and clammy on his leg. The first time she let him take her clothes off was at his house on a Saturday night while his mam and dad were out at the pub. He told them they were going to watch television. No sooner had the Consul turned the corner than he and Angie went at each other like starving wolves. They lay together on the settee and his hands shook as he undid the buttons down the back of her blouse and threw it on the floor. He struggled with her bra and couldn't get it undone so he pushed it up around her neck and her breasts sprang out at him like a couple of blancmanges with nipples that stood up like jelly babies. He slid her skirt up around her waist, pulled her knickers off and played with her fanny for a while and from the way her eyes rolled back in her head she quite enjoyed it. Then she touched his cock and it was like being touched by the hand of god. Not exactly the hand of god because that would be a bit queer, especially if god was an old bloke with long hair and a beard. But it felt...*divine*. That was the word he was looking for. It felt divine to have her delicate fingers on his nob and its scaffold of engorged veins. Emboldened, she opened his trousers and pulled his cock out in time for him to spill a ridiculous amount of spunk over her and the settee. But there was plenty more where that came from. Their protracted fondling elicited three more ejaculations before his cock needed a rest. He used the dishcloth to wipe the spunk off the cushions and hoped the wet patches would dry before morning. Then he walked Angie home and she wanked him off again in the doorway.

After that they had sex whenever and wherever they could. When the weather was fine they'd go for walks in the countryside. He'd lean her against a stile and strip her from the middle outwards, pushing everything above her waist up over her breasts and rolling everything else down to her knees so she looked like a Christmas cracker. For all he knew he was in love with her because every time he saw her his heart leaped in his throat and his cock leaped in his pants. But they never had intercourse. She was too afraid of getting pregnant. They engaged instead in a kind of pseudo-intercourse where he'd put his prick between her upper thighs and rub the shaft against her fanny and that worked well enough. He was happy just to see her naked and she never seemed to tire of his admiring gaze on her body. He was astonished by the heat she gave off. She was so hot to the touch he reckoned if he slipped a slice of bread into her fanny about a minute later she'd pop it out as toast. It never occurred to them that what they were doing was wrong, that they should feel any shame or guilt. Just the opposite, it felt natural and necessary. All they knew was that they'd embarked on a voyage of mutual discovery and what they were experiencing was something that could only be experienced once.

One Friday night she came over to his house so they could watch her on television. As head girl she'd taken part in a tree planting ceremony that morning with the headmaster and some old pricks from the education department. A news crew from Tyne Tees had been there so it was going to be on the evening news. With the house to themselves they were soon on the floor peeling off each other's clothes. Nick had her spread out on the carpet like a starfish, her blazer, blouse, tie, skirt and underwear strewn around her when he happened to look up and saw her on the telly. She was wearing the same school uniform and smiling demurely as she sprinkled a spadeful of soil onto a newly planted tree while a bunch of bald old men in suits looked on. His eyes flicked back and forth between the prim and proper schoolgirl on TV and the wanton beauty underneath him and he knew that however long he lived there would never be another moment like this.

*   *   *

Bright decided to put in for his inspector's exam after all and a few weeks later he got a call that the Chief Constable wanted to see him. He asked Shep and Ted if they had any idea what it was about but they told him they hadn't heard anything. On the day of the meeting Bright drove up to Morpeth wondering what was so important that the most senior officer in the Northumberland Constabulary had to see him personally.

Former Chief Inspector Robert Heslop had succeeded Cyril Browning as Chief Constable. Bright had never met Heslop. All he knew about him was that he was capable, dull and had got where he was more by having the right connections than by any innate ability. It brought something else to mind too. John Robson, the former uniform inspector at Bedlington, had been promoted to Chief Inspector and moved from Ponteland to Morpeth. Bright wondered if Robson had confided to anyone at police headquarters his suspicion that Bright had lied under oath to save Shep in the McMahon case. Heslop struck Bright as a man who would not be as receptive to such information as the pragmatic Browning who was pleased to see the verdict go the force's way and didn't much care about the means. If Robson had spoken against Bright the purpose of the summons to the Chief Constable's office might be to tell Bright he should consider leaving the police force under his own initiative or be transferred to a one-man station like Wooler permanently.

Bright arrived twenty minutes early for the one-o-clock appointment and was kept waiting for nearly an hour. When the Chief's secretary finally sent him in there was no apology. It was Bright's first meeting with Heslop and he found a man with a peculiarly oblong head and eyes as flat as buttons. Bright stood to attention in front of the Chief's desk and saluted.

"Sir."

Heslop's desk was clear except for a couple of neatly stacked trays, a red telephone, a black telephone and a few loose papers on a big green blotting pad but he gave the impression of a busy man fitting Bright in between more important business.

"At ease, sergeant," Heslop said though he didn't invite Bright to sit down. "I understand you've applied to take the inspector's exam this year."

"Yes sir," Bright said and relaxed his posture, but only slightly.

"It has been brought to my attention that your wife works as a barmaid at The Feathers just outside Morpeth, is that true?"

"Yes sir, it's true."

"Then you have a decision to make," Heslop continued. "If you are to be promoted you must understand there are certain expectations of the wife of an inspector. She is expected to conduct herself in a manner commensurate with the importance of her husband's position in the community and if she is employed that also extends to the nature of her employment."

Bright was puzzled. He'd assumed most inspectors' wives didn't work because they didn't have to, not because there was some unofficial prohibition on the type of employment.

"Promotion to the rank of inspector brings with it all manner of responsibilities," Heslop continued. "Social obligations, formal occasions, presentations, public relations events, dinners, that sort of thing. The wife of an inspector represents the higher ranks of the police force just as much as her husband does and she is expected to carry herself accordingly. As Chief Constable I have to be confident that your wife is comfortable with those obligations." Heslop paused. "You may well pass the inspector's exam with flying colours, sergeant, and do not mistake me, I hope you do, but you also must understand that you cannot be promoted to the rank of inspector as long as your wife is employed as a barmaid. The wife of a police inspector in the Northumberland Constabulary does not work in a public house. If your wife wants to support your advancement in the police force she will have to give up her current job, it's that simple. But as I say, it is your decision to make. I am telling you this now so there can be no room for misunderstanding later on. Have I made myself clear?"

"Yes sir," Bright said, stunned.

"Good, then we understand each other," Heslop said finally. "Whatever you decide, I wish you the best of luck."

"Yes sir, thank you sir." Bright saluted, turned and left the Chief's office. He didn't acknowledge anyone on the way out but felt his colour rise with every step across the car park. He got into the Consul and his hands trembled as he lit a tab. The Chief had been very professional about it, very polite, and he'd made Bright feel like a piece of shite stuck to his shoe. He wondered how he would tell Pat. He knew what her reaction would be. The drive back to Bedlington would take him past The Feathers. She would be there now and the pub would be closed for the afternoon. It might be the best place, he decided. Besides, he could do with a drink.

Dolly Harbottle answered his knock at the back door.

"Hello stranger," she said. "This is a nice surprise."

"Aye, weel…" Bright made a face, "…it is and it isn't."

He followed Dolly through to the lounge where Pat sat at a table counting the day's take. A glass, almost empty, sat at her elbow. Behind the bar a young barman washed glasses and restacked the shelves. The lounge smelled of stale beer and cigarette smoke. When she saw him Pat began counting aloud with an escalating cadence so he wouldn't interrupt.

"Fifty three, fifty four, fifty five, fifty six, fifty seven!"

Finished, she wrapped an elastic band around the pound notes and went on to the ten shilling notes.

"What are ye deein' heeyah?"

"Ah've come straight from me meetin' with the Chief Constable," he answered. "Ah think wi could both use a drink afore ah tell ye what he said."

"What can ah get ye, Jimmy?" Dolly asked.

"Ahll hae a large whisky, love, if that's ahlreet."

"Nae bother at ahll, hinny," Dolly said.

Pat emptied her glass and said: "While ya there, Dolly, ah'll hae another G and T."

She finished counting the morning's take, put it in a cloth bag and took it to Percy in the back office. When she returned Bright and Dolly were seated at the table, each of them with a drink. She sat down and took a sip of her gin and tonic.

"So what did the Chief Constable hae to say fo' hissel'?"

Bright smiled abashedly at Dolly. "In a nutshell, he said ah might pass me inspector's exam but ah'll nivah be promoted te inspector as lang as me wife is workin' as a barmaid."

Pat and Dolly looked at each other in disbelief.

Dolly spoke first. "He said that? Those were his actual words?"

"They're his exact words."

"Can he do that?" Dolly added.

"He's the Chief Constable, he can dee what he likes," Bright answered. "An' if ah kick up a stink aboot it ah'll be sent to the back of beyond to see oot me days."

"Tha just a bunch o' snobs," Pat said. "That's ahll they are, snobs, the whole bloody lot o' them."

"De ye think they hae somethin' against the pub?" Dolly asked.

"No pet, it's nowt to dee wi' the pub," Bright assured her. "Ye couldn't get a nicer pub than this and cannier folk te run it in the whole o' Northumberland. It's the police force. An inspector's wife is supposed to set an example and apparently a barmaid isn't a good enough example."

"Ah have tried…" Pat said, her voice pitched shakily between hurt and affront. "Ah have done iverythin' ah can to please ahll the sae cahlled reyt folk an' nowt ah dee is ivah good enough. An' noo tha sayin' because ah'm a barmaid ah'm not good enough fo' the police force. Weel, bugga the lot o' them, that's ahll ah can say. Ah'm not givin' up this job, Jimmy. As far as ah'm concorned they can ahll hadaway an' shite because ah am not givin' up this job."

Bright was glad he'd decided to tell her at the pub. "Ah wouldn't expect ye tee, hinny," he said consolingly.

"Mind it's brazen, but, isn't it?" Dolly added. "Sayin' it right to ya face like that."

"Ah am not givin' up this job," Pat repeated.

"That's hoo it was presented t'is," Bright added. "If ah want to get any forther aheed in the police force me wife cannit work as a barmaid."

"Weel, it looks like ya finally ganna hae to choose between me an' the police force then, doesn't it?" Pat said.

"Divvent be sae soft," Bright said. "Ya me wife, it's not a matter o' choice."

Pat turned to Dolly. "This isn't the forst time they've tried to make him choose between me an' the job, ye knah. They've done it before."

Dolly shook her head. "Ye know, Pat, if ye want to take some time and think about…"

"No, no, no," Pat slapped her hand on the table. "Tha's nowt to think aboot. Ah am not givin' up my job just to please a bunch o' bloody snobs in the Northumberland police force."

Bright finished his whisky.

"Here, hinny, ah'll get another round in," Dolly said and went back to the bar.

Just then Percy came out from his office, smiling.

"Ah thought ah heard the polis's voice. Am ah in trouble again?"

"Pat and Jimmy have had a bit of bad news," Dolly interrupted before he could say anything more.

"Oh, ah'm sorry to hear that," Percy said. "Nothin' too serious ah hope."

Bright brought him up to date and he sat down at the table while Dolly brought fresh drinks including a whisky and water for Percy.

"Ye hear aboot this sort o' thing happenin' divvent ye, but this is just blatant isn't it?" Percy said. "He told ye reyt to ya face that if ye passed ya exam ye still wouldn't get promoted to inspector unless ya wife stopped workin' as a barmaid?"

"That's what ah find so hard to believe," Dolly said.

"There were nae two ways aboot it," Bright added.

"Aye, an' even if ah give up me job there's nae guarantee they'd gi'm the promotion anyway," Pat said. "Ah knah what's goin' on, ah knah what they think of is. They think ah'm common. It's me they want rid of, not him. But that's the police force fo' ye. They expect ye to run ya whole bloody life accordin' to the way they want an' then they might not gi' ye the promotion anyway. Well, they can think what they want, ah'm not livin' me life to suit them…thar a bunch o' bloody snobs, that's ahll they are."

"Ye know, wi like bein' ya friends," Percy said. "But if ye wanted to change your mind, we'd understand."

"Ah won't be changin' me mind," Pat said. "Friends are more important than anythin' else to me."

Bright saw his moment. "Aye weel, ah'll propose a toast then." He raised his glass. "To hell wi' the Chief Constable."

And the four of them laughed and touched glasses and chorused: "To hell wi' the Chief Constable."

* * *

Shep drove up the gravel driveway to Spring Bank Farm and parked the A40 outside the main house, a grey, three storey Georgian built by the owner of a long demolished iron foundry. He'd timed his visit so that Phyllis Ritchie wouldn't be home and he could speak to her husband alone. Six months had passed since Robbie McBride had tried to kill Bernard Ritchie. Big Mac had been charged with attempted murder and held at the county gaol at Morpeth ever since. Ritchie hadn't fully recovered from his injuries and likely never would. While Bright's efforts at the scene had restored Ritchie's breathing doctors had had to open up his skull to relieve bleeding in the brain. The full extent of the neurological damage was still not known but those who'd seen him spoke of a man damaged permanently.

The home help, a brisk middle aged woman with a duster in hand, let Shep in and showed him to Ritchie's study. It was afternoon but Ritchie spent most of his days in pajamas and dressing gown. He'd been confined to home since leaving the hospital a couple of months earlier, his movements restricted to downstairs where a bed had been set up in his study. He shuffled rather than walked and his gait was unsteady enough that he needed a walking stick. When he spoke there was a slushy sound to his speech, which could have been the result of the partial denture he wore to replace the teeth he'd lost in the assault, or an indication of brain damage. Certainly, he paused often in his speech and struggled to remember things. When Shep saw him in an armchair beside the bed he was struck by how shrunken Ritchie was and how much older he looked. His complexion was sallow, his eyes dull, his shaven skull a livid patchwork of scars. Shep hadn't seen Ritchie since visiting him in hospital shortly before his discharge and if anything he looked worse. In the past Ritchie would have been attentive to the point of ingratiating in welcoming Shep but now he didn't even try to get up.

Without waiting to be asked Shep sat in a leather cushioned chair across from Ritchie.

"How ye feelin' the day, Bernard?" He spoke loudly and clearly, the way he'd speak to someone who was a bit slow.

Ritchie seemed to have trouble meeting Shep's gaze. "A bit better today, actually," he said with a wan smile. "Contrary to how I may appear."

"Good," Shep said. He wanted to dispose of his business quickly. "We have to make a decision about proceeding to trial. Ah'm of the opinion you're not goin' to be well enough to give evidence on the stand and, quite frankly, ah don't think it's a good idea for ye to testify at all. But we can't keep remandin' McBride indefinitely. He's pleaded not guilty an' he wants his day in court. He wants to tell his side of the story an' ah don't think that's something we can allow. What ah'm proposin' to do is to reduce the charge from attempted murder to GBH in exchange for a guilty plea. That'll keep the evidence to a minimum, it'll take no more than a few minutes and he'll go to jail. Mebbe not for as long as he would if convicted of attempted murder but long enough to make the point."

Ritchie pursed his lips in an effort to frame the words that came with such difficulty now.

"I'm sorry, Jack, what is GBH?" It was a question he would never have had to ask before.

"Grievous Bodily Harm," Shep said. "It's just a step down from attempted murder but it gives the judge a lot more leeway in sentencing - he can impose anything from two to twenty years. The incentive for McBride is he'll serve a much reduced sentence from what he would otherwise expect. The incentive for you, for all of us, is that we keep a lid on the whole sorry business."

Ritchie seemed to ponder Shep's words for a long time. Finally he said: "I suppose."

"Ye suppose?" Shep said shortly. "Let me set ye straight on somethin', Bernard." His accent broadened, reflecting his anger. "Ah'm not doin' this oota o' the kindness o' me heart to spare ye any public embarrassment, ah'm doin' this for Phyllis. It's her good name ah want to protect, not yours. The last thing ah want is ye goin' to court an' stuffin' everythin' up."

Ritchie looked down at his lap and said nothing more.

"Ahlright then." Shep got up to go but paused with his hand on the door handle. "An' just so ye know, Bernard, what ye did to Robbie McBride's lad was bloody disgustin'. Speakin' fo' mesel ah hae nae sympathy fo' ye at ahll. If it had been one of my bairns ah'd hae done the same thing - only ye'd nivah hae got oota the hospital. An' ah want ye to be in no doubt, if ye sae much as lay a finger on another bairn fo' the rest o' ya life ah'll finish what McBride started."

*   *   *

The day after his meeting with the Chief Constable Bright leaned inside Shep's office and asked: "When ye were made inspector were ye telt one o' the conditions o' gettin' promoted was that your wife couldn't work?"

Shep looked up from the morning paper. "No. Nobody said anythin' like that to me. Is that what ya meetin' wi' the Chief was aboot?"

Bright said: "He telt is if ah wanted to be promoted to inspector Pat couldn't continue to work as a barmaid. Ah just wondered if there was owt more to it than that."

Shep put the paper down. "Ye cannit say ye weren't warned, Jimmy. Ah telt ye a long time ago the way things work in the police force. Everybody has to know tha place an' that includes your missus."

"Aye, an' that meyt be ahll var weel fo' some folk," Bright responded. "But me an' the missus happen to think it's not the Chief Constable's place to tell ah hoo to live ah life. Ah'll not waste me time tekkin' the inspector's exam, ah'm content the way things are. Bob Heslop can stick his promotion up his arse."

Shep smiled. He'd been right about Bright from the start.

Bright turned to go but Shep said: "Come in an' shut the door. Ah hae a bit of business ah want ye to do fo' is."

Reluctantly, Bright closed the door and sat down. Shep leaned back in his chair.

"Ah want ye to tahk to Robbie McBride fo' is. Ah want ye to tell him if he behaves himself an' agrees to a guilty plea we'll reduce the charge from attempted murder to GBH. That way he'll get nae mair than two, three year an' with good behaviour he'll be out in 18 months."

"Ye can promise him that?" Bright said. Shep could reduce the charge against McBride but after that the most he could do was send a recommendation for clemency to the Crown Prosecutor who would pass it on to the Assize Court judge but there was nothing to bind the judge to any agreement made between the police and McBride.

"Ah can put in a word where it'll do the most good," Shep said.

Bright had wondered if Shep would try to keep Big Mac from testifying about Bernard Ritchie interfering with his son. A judge might well consider it a serious enough provocation to warrant a lenient sentence - and when the truth came out the police would be compelled to bring charges against Ritchie. From where Bright stood he could see little incentive for Mac to bargain. And, from what Nellie McBride had told him, he doubted Mac could be persuaded to change his mind. Nellie took the bus up to Morpeth twice a week to see her husband and she'd told Bright across the back fence that Mac had no regrets about what he'd done and was looking forward to the case going to trial so he could tell the world about Ritchie in open court.

"Ah doobt Robbie McBride would be willin' to bargain on somethin' like this," Bright said. "This is his kids, his family. Ye can imagine what it's done te them. From what Nellie's telt is he's detormined to bring it oot in court. He wants iverybody to knah what Ritchie did an' he wants to see charges brought."

"Aye an' he'd probably like to win the Treble Chance an' all," Shep said. "If he's goin' to stick to his not guilty plea on attempted murder he's not going to be tried in open court like he thinks, with reporters there to hear what he has to say. It'll be heard *in camera* because the evidence involves sexual abuse of a minor. An' if he wants that brought up his son will be interviewed first by the prosecution and the defence and whatever child welfare experts and trick cyclists either side wants involved - an' that's not just goin' to be unpleasant for all concerned it's goin' to drag things oot a lot longer. Either way, it's not goin' to get him what he wants. Bernard Ritchie isn't going to admit to anythin' an' McBride's lad is too young to take the stand. An' ye know as well as me, provocation is no excuse for attempted murder. Just think about that for a minute. It's attempted murder we're tahkin' aboot heeyah, Jimmy, not a smack in the gob. He'll be convicted an' he could get twenty years. Wi' teym off fo' good behaviour he might get oot in fifteen. Does he really want to take that chance? If he cares aboot his family sae much ask him how much good that's goin' to do them."

"An' what aboot Ritchie?" Bright asked, "He's got nae part in this?"

Shep's eyes shaded, he lowered his voice and leaned forward.

"Ah'm goin' to tell you somethin' now an' ah want your word of honor it won't go beyond these four walls?"

Bright hesitated then nodded.his assent.

Shep continued: "Phyllis Ritchie came t'is personally an' asked is to dee whativah ah can to protect her in this - an' that's what ah'm goin' to do. She knows about Bernard. She has no illusions where he's concerned, but she never dreamed he'd ever be a threat to kids." Shep rapped his knuckles on the desk to emphasise his point. "Think aboot it fo' a minute, there's nothin' to be gained from prosecutin' Bernard Ritchie. Ahll that will happen from bringin' it oot in the open is that Phyllis Ritchie will hae to resign from the bench. She's the one who'll pay the price, not Bernard. Even if he was to be prosecuted an' convicted he's not goin' to go to gaol. It's a first offence, he's a sick old man, he'll get a suspended sentence an' probation, that's ahll. An' we'll lose a bloody good chief magistrate an' that's not somethin' wi can afford." Shep leaned back and added: Ah'll be the first to admit it's not as clean and tidy as we'd ahll like but wi hae to maintain appearances, Jimmy. Wi hae to maintain appearances."

"Aye an' what aboot the damage done by keepin' up appearances?" Bright responded. "Ye knah yasel the way these things work. This won't be the only time Ritchie has interfered wi' a bairn. It was goin' on for years with Keith McBride. Tha's likely umpteen others oot there wee'd come forward if…"

"It's the only one we know aboot," Shep cut him off.

Bright looked disgusted. "An' we wonder why folk hae nae respect for the law."

"Ah don't care if no bugga has any respect for the law as long as they do what tha told," Shep said sharply. "An' anybody wee doesn't like it can kiss my big fat hairy arse."

Bright assumed that meant him too.

"So will ye do it or not?" Shep pressed.

"Ah'd sooner ye fund somebody else," Bright said. "Ah live right next door to them. It meks things var' awkward."

"That's why it's better comin' from ye. They know ye, they trust ye." Shep paused as something else came to mind. "An' if stayin' at West Lea is goin' to be a problem fo' ye after this mebbe it's time we moved ye closer to the station. Ted said just the other day we've got a transfer comin' up."

Bright thought about it. There were three police houses closer to the police station, each of them nicer than the house at West Lea. Something good could come out of this for him after all.

"Ahlreet," he said, "but ah cannit move till the end o' the year, ah've already put me leeks in."

Two days later Bright drove to Morpeth to see Big Mac at the county gaol. Damp and draughty even at the height of summer the gaol held up to 120 prisoners in Dickensian dreariness. Bright sat down with Big Mac at a heavy metal table in an interview room painted green and cream with no guard to watch over them. Mac had acquired a prison pallor and dark shadows under his eyes suggested he wasn't sleeping well. Bright offered him a tab and the two of them talked about leeks for a while.

But then Mac shrugged and added: "It'll be a while afore ah see another leek show."

"Actually, Mac, that's the main reason ah'm here," Bright said. "Ah've got a message fo' ye from D.I. Shepherd that ye might want to gi' some thought."

Mac smiled a humourless smile. "Ah wondered if tha'd be somethin' like this. Got ye deein' tha dorty work noo hae they, Jimmy?"

Bright looked stung.

"Ahll ah can tell ye is it comes from D.I. Shepherd an' it's a genuine offer."

"So it's Shepherd wee's deein' the Ritchies' biddin' is it?"

"Shep doesn't care aboot what ye did to Bernard Ritchie," Bright added. "But ya right aboot Phyllis Ritchie. He does care aboot hor an' he doesn't want ah to suffer because o' what ah husband did."

"Oh aye, that meyt be a little embarassin' fo' them wouldn't it?" Mac said. "An' what aboot mah little lad? Wee's ganna explain to him why his dad is in gaol while the bloke wee interfered wi'm this past three year is gettin' away scot free?"

"Not exactly scot free, Mac. Ya lucky ya not sittin' in heeyah on a morder charge, then there'd be nae chance of a bargain."

The tip of Mac's cigarette flared as he took a pull.

"Ah had ivery intention o' killin' him when ah went there," he said. "An' ah woulda killed him if ye hadn't pulled is off him."

"Ah knah ye would, an' ye'd be gannin' away fo' life," Bright said. "An' hoo would that help Nellie an' the kids?"

Mac looked ambivalent. "Ye don't think at a time like that though, de ye Jimmy? Ya goin' on pure emotion. Ye want to kill the bugga wee hort ya bairn an' that's ahll there is tee it."

"Shep says he'll reduce the charge to GBH if ye'll plead guilty," Bright added. "He'll put in a word fo' ye wi' the croon prosecutor an' that should carry some weight wi' the judge. He says he can just aboot guarantee ye'll only get two or three years. If ye keep ya nose clean ye'll be oot in 18 months."

"Just aboot guarantee, eh?" Mac said. "An' ah'm supposed to say nowt aboot what drove is tee it? Aboot what Ritchie did?"

"That's the offer on the table, Mac."

"An' if'n ah'm not interested?"

"If ye stick to ya guns an' plead not guilty to the attempted morder charge ye won't be tried in open court, Mac. Ye'll be tried in a closed court. Whativah ye say won't matter because naebody will ivah knah, it'll be suppressed. There's nae reporters allowed in a closed court, there'll be naebody there from the papers or the television. No information aboot the case is allowed oot an' even if ye went to the papers yasel an' telt them ahll that happened they couldn't print it because they'd be in contempt o' court."

"Aye but ah can still speak me piece to the judge."

"Wouldn't dee ye any good, Mac. Ah'll hae to gi' evidence against ye. Me an' Alec Newell, both. Ritchie's secretary, Agnes. The patients wee were in the waitin' room when ye borst in. A top barrister might mek a little bit o' difference but ah divvent think ye've got that kind o' money de ye? Ye'll still be fund guilty of attempted morder, an' even if the judge sympathises wi' why ye did it he's bound by the sentencin' rules to gi' ye the minimum, an' the minimum fo' attempted morder is 20 year. An' if he doesn't hae any sympathy fo' ye he could put ye away for 30 year."

"So ah plead guilty to GBH an' nowt aboot what Ritchie did to mah lad will come oot – even when iverybody in Bedlin'ton knahs it's true?"

Bright paused. "Aye, that's aboot the extent of it."

"An' that's supposed to be justice is it?"

Bright hesitated. "Ah don't think anybody could call it justice, Mac. It's just…life. It's the way things work oot sometimes."

"Sometimes?" Mac snorted. "Ah'll the time, more like. Iverythin' is pushed under the carpet so the nobs can gan on livin' tha lives like nowt ivah happened even when iverybody knahs what a bunch o' shites they are."

"Nowt new aboot that," Bright said.

"An' the rest o' us wee knah the truth can just gan an' tek a runnin' jump, is that it? An' you're happy to gan alang wi' that?"

Bright looked pained. "No, ah'm not happy, Mac, but ah've larned to be realistic aboot things. A situation like this, ye hae te tek the lang view. It's not a matter o' justice or gettin' back at somebody that did ye wrong. Ye look at what does the least harm to ye an' yours so ye can gan on wi' ya life. Because ah'll admit, tha are people in positions of power wee knah hoo to work the system against folk like ye - an' me an' ahll believe it or not. So, in the end wi' divvent hae much of a choice at ahll. If ye torn this offer doon, Mac, ye'll be sentenced in a closed court an' ye'll get at least 20 years fo' nearly killin' a man wee'll be painted as a leadin' member o' the community. An' ye an Nellie and anybody else can complain as lang and as loud as ye like an' it'll ahll fall on deaf ears. Ya two lads will grow up wi'oot ye. Ye'll be an aad man by the time ye get oot an' that doesn't help anybody. As far as ah can see, Mac, if ye say no to this bargain tha's nowt ye can dee to keep that from happenin' because if tha was ah'd tell ye. But from where ah'm sittin' ah think the best ye can dee fo' yasel an' fo' ya wife an' bairns is te tek the bargain that's bein' offered ye."

Mac twisted in his chair and stared angrily at the prison walls that would be his horizon for the next 20 years if he didn't take the offer Bright had described. His eyes welled up, tears trailed down his cheeks and spotted his prison shirt.

"Ah divvent sleep var' weel in heeyah," he said, his voice thick and phlegmy. "Prison is noisy. Ah suppose ah should hae expected that but ah didn't. Ah nivah expected to be put in prison so ah nivah give it any thought. But it's noisy ahll the time, even through the night. Blokes shoutin' an' screamin' an' carryin' on. Ah'm in here wi' robbers an' thieves, ahll manner o' bloody wasters. Ah knah ah don't belong in here, but ah made up me mind; ah'd dee it if ah could mek things right by me little lad. An' it's not just because ah think Ritchie should be seen fo' what he is, it's because ah want me son to knah that what was done to him was wrang. Not just hearin' it from us, from his mam and dad, but from the rest o' the world. From the police an' the courts, from the grown-ups wee are supposed to knah right from wrong. So he understands…it wasn't him wee was to blame." Mac wiped his face with his cuff and turned back to Bright. "Ye knah hoo wi' fund oot?"

Bright shook his head.

"Nellie was cleanin' oot the lads' toy cupboard an' she picked up Keith's money box an' she thought it felt a bit heavy, like, fo' what shoulda been in it. So she oppined it up an' it was full o' haff croons. Two pund, seven an' six in haff croons. She asked Keith where he got it ahll an' he said it come from Dr. Ritchie. He said Ritchie gave him haff a croon ivery time they played tha secret game. That's what Ritchie called it, tha secret game. Wi trusted him. He was the family doctor…fo' bloody years. Wi thowt he was tekkin' good care o' Keith, treatin' him fo' low iron. Wi were glad he was tekkin' such an interest. An' ahll the time…" His voice trailed off. Then he looked Bright in the eye. "Ye knah hoo many times two pund, seven shillin' an' sixpence in haff croons works oot at, Jimmy? It's nineteen times. Nineteen times owa three year."

*   *   *

The Sunday after the August Bank Holiday weekend was warm and sunny and Pat and Jimmy decided to take a run out to the Lake District for the day. The drive to Carlisle was a pleasant couple of hours and soon afterwards they reached Keswick where they got out and took a stroll by Derwent Water before seeking out the familiar comforts of a pub. They were in no hurry to get home so they took a roundabout way back, taking the B652 through Haltwhistle.

They encountered little traffic until a few miles short of Morpeth they came on a line of cars at a dead stop. The road was a narrow two lanes that ran past open fields and Bright thought there must be an accident up ahead. He got out and looked over the cars in front and saw a group of thirty to forty men gathered at the side of the road as if at a fair. There was an open gate to a field where a dozen or so cars and vans were parked on the grass. Many of the men had whippets on leashes and that was all Bright needed.

He ducked down and told Pat: "Ah knah what's gannin' on, ah'll back in be a minute."

He walked up to where a couple of men stood in the road blocking traffic. Beyond them was a straight stretch of road and in the distance another, smaller group of men who'd stopped traffic coming the other way. The distance between the two groups was a couple of hundred yards.

As he came up past the car at the front of the queue Bright saw half a dozen men kneeling in the road, each of them holding a whippet ready for release. One of the two men keeping the traffic back gestured to Bright to stay where he was. A man at the side of the road, the starter, called "ready" and everybody fell quiet. The starter shouted "go" and to the urging of the crowd the dogs dashed off down the road to the waiting arms of their owners.

Bright knew some of the men but not all. They would have come from all over Northumberland at the prospect of making a bit of money off their dogs. He wasn't surprised to see Michael Leary there with his eldest lad, Brendan. The Learys were regulars at every illegal dog meet in the northeast.

Annoyed, Bright went up to the man who'd waved him back and thrust his warrant card into the man's face.

"Ye knah what this is?" Without waiting for an answer he added: "Ye lads can pack in what ya deein' right noo, stop holdin' up traffic an' had yasels away yem, the whole lot o' ye."

The man grinned uncertainly but made no effort to move and instead looked to the crowd at the side of the road. But Bright had already been seen and a voice called out: "Jimmy! What are ye deein' ahll the way oot heeyah? Are ye lost o' summick'?"

A man with thinning sandy hair and a red brick face detached himself from the crowd and Bright recognised John Jacks from West Lea. Jacks was a long time whippet breeder and a member of the membership committee that approved Bright's membership at Netherton Club. He took Bright by the elbow and steered him to one side while his mates waved at the cars to go.

"Wa just aboot done here," Jacks said. "We've only got another couple o' runs an' we'll be on wa way."

Bright looked around, no longer so certain of his ground. He saw Mick Leary watching.

"Ye know ya breakin' the law," Bright told Jacks.

"Aye but wa not deein' anybody any real harm are wi, Jimmy?" Jacks responded glibly.

Bright was trapped and knew it. "Aye, ahlreet then, just finish up as soon as ye can."

"Ah yar a good lad, Jimmy," Jacks said and gave him a pat on the shoulder. "Sorry if we held ye up, like."

Bright looked for sarcasm in Jack's face but saw none. He walked back past the line of moving cars, got into the Consul and started forward.

"What are they deein'?" Pat asked. Then she saw the whippets. "Tha nivah stoppin' traffic just so they can race tha dogs are they?"

"That's exactly what tha deein'," Bright said.

"Hoo can they do that?" she asked. "They're not allowed to dee that, surely?"

"No, tha not."

"So what did ye tell them?"

"Ah telt them te get a move on."

She watched the knot of men at the side of the road slide past and saw Jacks give them a cheery wave.

"Mind, thar a cheeky bunch of buggas aren't they?" Pat said. Bright gripped the steering wheel hard, stared through the windshield and said nothing.

*   *   *

Big Mac was scheduled for sentencing the last day of the autumn Assizes. The corridors of Moot Hall were almost empty. Only two courtrooms were in session, courtrooms 3 and 4, both occupied with arcane legal matters that pertained to low profile cases. Mac's case was last on the docket for courtroom 4. Because it was a Friday and nothing of importance remained none of the newspaper reporters had come back from lunch. The public benches were empty except for Shep and Bright on one side of the aisle and Nellie McBride and her sister, Noreen, on the other. The others were the clerk of the court, an assistant Crown Prosecutor, the bailiff and an usher. The judge, Mr. Justice Waldron, was a small, balding man with a fussy manner.

Shortly before four-o-clock the clerk of the court called Mac's case. When

Mac came up from the holding cells into the dock escorted by a prison guard he was wearing his best suit with a white shirt and a red tie. He'd had a haircut but his complexion was grey and he'd lost weight. He looked around the courtroom, saw Nellie and her sister and gave them a quick smile of encouragement. The clerk of the court leaned up to the judge's bench and said something that was inaudible to the rest of the court. Waldron listened without reaction, searched out some papers and took several minutes to read them. The courtroom was so quiet that when Nellie's sister cleared her throat it echoed.

"So, a guilty plea has already been entered in this case?" Judge Waldron inquired at last and the clerk confirmed that it had. The judge turned his attention to the assistant crown prosecutor.

"Is there anything further to add to the evidence before me?"

The assistant prosecutor stood up and said: "No, m'lord, no further evidence."

Mr. Justice Waldron muttered to himself and went back to his reading. It was an excruciatingly long time before he seemed satisfied.

"Mr. McBride?"

"Will the prisoner please rise," the clerk of the court said.

The guard behind Big Mac nudged him and Mac got to his feet.

"Is there anything you wish to say to the court before I pass sentence?" Waldron asked.

Mac glanced at Bright. "Ah, not really your honour."

Waldron knitted his fingers together and peered at Mac through his glasses. "This was an extraordinarily violent crime. An unprovoked and vicious assault that inflicted injuries of a horrendous nature on the victim. The victim is an elderly man who was unable to defend himself and the injuries he sustained were so severe that he must now contemplate a lifetime of incapacitation. Not only will he be unable to return to the life he enjoyed prior to the commission of this crime, it is a crime that also deprives the community of a long established and respected medical practitioner. The reaction of any civilised society to such a crime can only be one of abhorrence. It is, therefore, of the utmost importance that the court impose a sentence that reflects the disapproval of the community for the severity of the crime. I have taken into consideration the facts that the defendant has no prior criminal record, that he is a former member of His Majesty's Armed Forces, that he was honourably discharged from the army and that he has admitted his guilt in this matter. One can only speculate on what dark forces impelled him to commit this crime but no combination of circumstances, however dire, can be considered the remotest justification for an act of such willful barbarism. Mr. McBride, it is the sentence of this court that you be imprisoned for a term of twelve years."

Mac swayed in the dock.

"No...no!" Nellie shouted.

"This isn't right," Mac said, bewildered, "It's supposed te be 18 months, that's what ah was telt, 18 months."

But nobody was listening and Mac grew more agitated.

"This isn't right." He pointed to Bright and said: "He made a promise... he made a promise te me..."

"That's quite enough," Judge Waldron interrupted and rapped his gavel. "Bailiff, take him down."

"This is what ah get for cooperatin'" Mac cried despairingly. "This is what ah get..." The guard in the dock hustled Mac down to the cells, his protests ringing up the iron steps till the trapdoor closed over him.

Nellie McBride fled the courtroom, sobbing, with her sister trying to comfort her.

Shep remained expressionless. "Ye can never predict what a judge is goin' to do," he said, matter of fact.

Bright stared at him, his raw, slabbed face, his blank, unreadable eyes.

The clerk of the court closed the session and Judge Waldron left the bench.

"Just give is a minute," Shep said and Bright waited while Shep went down to the well of the court and spoke to the assistant prosecutor. Bright couldn't make out what was said, just that the prosecutor nodded in response to something Shep said then gave an indifferent shrug.

Shep came back to Bright. "He says they got my recommendation for leniency alright. They passed it on to the clerk of the court and they have to assume the judge saw it. That's ahll ah could do, Jimmy, that's ahll anybody could do. It looks like the judge decided to go his own way on this one."

When Bright stepped out into the corridor Nellie McBride went for his eyes.

"Bastard...bastard...bastard..." she screamed, her voice hoarse and hysterical.

Bright seized her wrists and held them tight till Shep and the usher were able to pull her away.

In a voice hardened by the years the usher barked at Nellie and her sister: "The two o' ye betta get out o' here right now if ye know what's good fo' ye."

Noreen put her arm around her sister and steered Nellie down the corridor to the exit, her anguished sobs trailing after her. The usher followed them for a short distance then turned back.

"Bloody rubbish, folk like that," he said.

Bright and Shep each lit up a tab to give Nellie and her sister time to get clear of the courthouse.

"He cannit even appeal," Bright said.

"Don't waste your sympathy on the likes o' them," Shep said. "Folk like that are always gettin' themselves in strife. They go from one mess to another an' they can never fathom why. They cannit help themselves an' there's nowt ye nor nobody else can do to help them an' ye might as well accept it."

1962

John Glenn becomes the first American to orbit the earth; Marilyn Monroe dies of a drug overdose; the Cuban missile crisis brings the world to the brink of nuclear war. A stellar year for TV debuts includes That Was The Week That Was with David Frost; Steptoe and Son with Alfred Brambell and Harry H. Corbet; Z Cars with Jeremy Kemp and Brian Blessed. Top films are Lawrence Of Arabia starring Peter O'Toole; To Kill A Mocking Bird starring Gregory Peck; The Longest Day starring John Wayne, Robert Mitchum ,Henry Fonda, Richard Burton, Richard Todd and more; Dr. No starring Sean Connery. Top record hits are The Young Ones by Cliff Richard; Telstar by The Tornados. The Beatles make their first chart appearance with Love Me Do.

Severance

With their thuggish contemporaries gone the lads of Fifth Remove were
free to enjoy their final year of school unmolested. Angie had left school the previous
spring and gone to work in a bank and Nick only saw her on weekends now. Which
suited him because she was ready to get married and have children and all he
could think about was getting away. There was a new mood in the country, a new
confidence. Music, film and fashion crackled with new energy. On TV *That Was
The Week That Was* pilloried the old order and helped fuel a national giddiness at
the realisation that nothing was sacred anymore. There was a new film called Dr.
No with a handsome young actor called Sean Connery whose masculine swagger
set the template for a new kind of British male. There was a thrilling new group
from Liverpool called The Beatles who looked and sounded like nothing anybody
had ever seen before and sparked riots wherever they played. There was a sense of
momentum building towards something as transformative as it was unstoppable.

While the prospect of escape from Bedlington dangled tantalisingly
in front of him Nick had no idea how he would make that escape. He thought
of joining the Royal Marines but the minimum enlistment of nine years was
daunting and going down the pit or joining the police force were out of the
question. His only real talent was writing but he could see no way of making a
living from it - until it occurred to him that a job on a newspaper might be the
way out. So he wrote to The Evening Chronicle in Newcastle and asked about
a job as a reporter. A week later the news editor wrote back that not only was
he too young, he would need a university degree before he could be considered.
University had never seemed a realistic option to Nick. He would need at least
six 'O' levels to get into Bedlington Grammar where he would have to study for
two more years and earn two or three 'A' levels before he would be eligible for
university and it would be another four years after that before he got a degree. To
Nick that was too much time away from the real world. He was thinking seriously
of just taking off and seeing where life might take him when another letter from
the news editor at The Chronicle arrived advising him that the paper hired one
editorial office boy a year and if all went well that young man would go on to join
the reporting staff. The letter also said that because there was only one opening a
year competition was fierce and attracted applicants from the best schools in the
northeast. Nick fastened onto it like a dog onto a meaty bone. He was required to
write a thousand word essay entitled: 'Why I Think Journalism Is An Attractive
Career.' In a lather of inspiration he wrote it in an afternoon and typed the final
version on a borrowed typewriter to show he knew how to type, even it it was

with two fingers. A week or so later another letter arrived telling him he'd made the shortlist and should come in for an interview.

The afternoon of the interview he reported to the staff entrance at the Chronicle building, a soot stained bunker between the Groat Market and Pilgrim Street. He waited in the dimly lit lobby with its worn staircase and clanking iron lift till the outgoing office boy came down to get him. Nick followed him upstairs along a dingy passageway and turned a corner into a blast of light and a room like a rubbish tip. A tip populated by scavengers who picked among the peaks and troughs while sheets of copy paper fluttered around them like seagulls. Reporters, sub-editors and editors toiled together in an unremitting din of clacking typewriters, ringing telephones, the hiss and thump of pneumatic tubes and voices raised in urgency. A round-the-clock drama that started in the late 1800's and hadn't taken a day off since.

Nick was shown to a chair outside a row of offices where he waited until called to face his inquisitors; a panel of editors from The Evening Chronicle, The Journal and The Sunday Sun. With them was Charlie Close, the Chronicle news editor whose name Nick recognised from the letters he'd been getting. There was a single chair in front of a large wooden desk and on the other side four serious looking men in dark suits. Nick was more excited than nervous and after this one glimpse of the world that awaited him he believed absolutely that this was where he was meant to be. The men in suits took turns asking him about his favourite and least favourite subjects at school, what sports he played, what hobbies he had, what books he read, what films he saw and what he watched on television. They asked him about current affairs. They asked him the name of the new Chancellor of the Exchequer. They asked him what the Common Market was. They also asked him the name of his favourite television programme and when he said *That Was The Week That Was* he sensed a positive undercurrent. Their last question was: What would he do if he didn't get the job? Without hesitation he said he would keep coming back till they couldn't turn him down. As it came out of his mouth he knew he'd gone too far. He sounded too pushy, too full of himself. But the words hung in the air like laundry on a line, adolescent hubris for all the world to see. Afterwards, he fretted all the way up to the Haymarket. There was something about the silence that followed those few brash words, the indifferent manner with which he'd been dismissed. By the time he got off the bus in Bedlington he was crushed. His only chance and he'd thrown it away by being too clever.

The letter from the Chronicle came in a couple of days. It was too soon. They couldn't have finished all the interviews. He opened it apprehensively and read that the job was his. He had a sensation of rushing upward, his consciousness soaring giddily inside his skull like the nose cone of a rocket racing toward the retreating ceiling. His life was about to change. Forever. Perhaps those final few words that came out of his mouth were what sealed it for him after all. What else was a newspaper reporter supposed to do but keep coming back till he got what he wanted?

*   *   *

When Bright went into the station on Monday morning he found a note waiting for him on the duty desk from Gail at the Crown Prosecutor's office in Newcastle. He was relieved to see it was Evan Thompson who'd taken the message and all it said was to call Gail back. She was a secretary Bright had spoken with the previous week to ask if there was a copy on file of a recommendation from D.I. Shepherd for sentencing leniency in the case of Robbie McBride.

Bright had tried to let it go, tried to let it slide the way he had with so many things before to keep the peace. It wasn't as if him knowing would do anything to help Big Mac. And it wouldn't make him feel any better to learn that Shep had sent in a recommendation and the judge had ignored it. But instead of fading into the recesses of memory it had nagged at him. Not that he felt especially guilty for what had happened to Mac or the part he'd played in it. What he wanted to know was if Shep had lied to him.

Bright swiveled the chair so he had his back to Shep, who was in his office with the door open, and dialed the number for the Crown Prosecutor's office.

When Gail came on she told Bright: "Ah've looked everywhere it would be an' ah cannit find it anywhere. As far as ah can tell no such recommendation came through this office." She sounded like she was in her early twenties.

"Could it have gone directly to the judge?" he asked.

"Not without it bein' seen as an attempt to influence the judge," she said. "We're the proper channel for sentencin' recommendations, anything that's supposed to go in front of a judge along those lines has to come through here first."

"Thank ye, pet," Bright said. "Ah appreciate you're lookin' for is."

"Ah'm sorry ah couldn't be more helpful," she added.

"Ye told is what ah needed to know," Bright said. He put the phone down and leaned back, deep in thought.

*   *   *

Nick started at The Chronicle the first week of September and stepped from one world into another. His pay was four pounds, seventeen shillings and sixpence a week and he took home a little over three and a half quid. His mam took two pound a week for room and board and he paid without objection because it wouldn't be for long. He had a job in the toon. And not just any job, a job that had thrust him into the exciting orbit of a big city newspaper. He'd gone from envying the confident, smartly dressed types he'd seen on the streets of Newcastle when he was a kid to becoming one of them. The great public buildings, theatres, cinemas, department stores and restaurants were the backdrop to his new life and the great issues of the day were his conversation. He loved the feeling of being on the inside. He loved the way newspapermen talked so knowingly about big name politicians, business leaders, sports stars and celebrities. How they knew all their vices and frailties; who drank too much, who strayed and who didn't, who was on the way up and who was on the way down. There was a sense of not only being close to history but of coming to grips with it, holding it up to the light and turning it inside out. What impressed him the most was the power reporters had and how they could use that power to shape events.

Nick was guided through his first week by the former office boy, Joe, who was now moving up to the reporting staff. Daily responsibilities included opening the mail, typing out the weather forecast and the shipping movements on the Tyne, running copy, answering phones, taking messages and getting lunch from the canteen for the senior editors. His boss was the news editor, Charlie Close, a massive white haired man who loomed around the office like a frigate under full sail. Charlie's secretary, Denise, a curvaceous brunette of about twenty, apparently was unaware of the effect her tight skirts and sweaters had on the men around her. When she and Nick opened the mail together, hip to hip in the seductive warmth of the secretarial nook, he couldn't watch her nimble, scarlet tipped fingers at work without thinking of them around his cock.

Among the duties not mentioned in Nick's job description was fetching reporters from the pub. He'd grown up around people whose main form of recreation was drinking, but the Chronicle was his first introduction to people who, if left alone, would drink all the time. One morning Charlie beckoned him around 10.30 and told him he had to bring three reporters back from the pub.

"Try The Long Bar first," Charlie said. "If they're not there try The Beehive, the Grapes, the Black Boy, The Vic And Comet and The Bridge."

The Long Bar ran the width of a city block and had the musty atmosphere of a railway tunnel. With no natural light the only illumination came from plastic yellow shells on the walls that kept the bar in a perpetual twilight. Coming out of the morning glare it took Nick a minute or two for his eyes to adjust. He walked down the tunnel, a row of badly used tables and chairs on one side, the bar on the other divided by partitions of curved wood and beveled glass to give the illusion of privacy. The drinkers were all men and many of them drank alone. Some were on their way to or from Central Station, some had just got off work from Swan Hunter or Vickers and some had the fugitive look of office workers who'd slipped away from their desks for an early top up. At the far end of the bar a couple of boisterous young squaddies filled up on beer before boarding the train back to Catterick. But there was nothing merry about it. Not the way you'd see people enjoying themselves at night. It had the ritualistic feel of an essential function, a medicinal need that had to be serviced. The air was sour and soupy, like the bottom of a lake inhabited by sickly, etiolated creatures that grubbed around in the murk and snapped at anything that came close.

Nick found the reporters behind a partition a third of the way down: John Parsons, Bob Carr and Mick Young

"Ah shit," Parsons said.

"Mr. Close says you're all needed back at the office right away," Nick said.

"Fuck off, there's a good lad," Carr said.

"Tell Charlie you couldn't find us," Young added and the three of them returned to their drinks.

Nick had no idea what to do next. He thought the mere mention of Charlie's name would be enough to send them scurrying back to the office but apparently not. He returned alone and perplexed. He didn't want to lie but he didn't think getting three reporters into trouble would win him many friends in the newsroom either. In the end he told Charlie he couldn't find them.

"Aye," Charlie nodded. "They told ye to say that didn't they."

Nick was lost for words.

"I know, they shouldn't put you in the middle like this," Charlie said. "Go back and tell them I want them here now, and don't take no for an answer."

Nick heard the echo of the words that got him the job; the boast that he would never give up, that he would keep coming back till he got what he wanted. Now he was being put to the test. He went back to The Long Bar. He found the three reporters still talking about work and still equally reluctant to do any.

"Mr. Close knows ya here an' he says ye have to come back right now - or else."

They appeared not to hear him except for Young who glanced over his shoulder and said: "We told you, we're not here."

Nick was stumped. How was he supposed to get three grown men out of the pub and back to work when the threat of the news editor's ire wasn't enough? He trudged up the long slanted corridor to the editorial department wondering what Charlie would think of him now. But, instead of going in to face Charlie, he went into the photographer's department to talk to Sid, the darkroom assistant and the first lad Nick knew with a Beatles haircut.

"Say what ye like," Parsons was saying, one hand cupped around his pint, "it's not about information anymore is it? It's about entertainment, if it's not entertaining enough nobody's going to read it."

"It used to mean something to work for a big daily newspaper," Carr grumbled. "Not anymore."

"Not when you're writing for mental midgets," Young muttered.

There was movement on the other side of the partition, a furtive scuffling then a blinding flash.

"You sneaky little sod," Parsons shouted. He reached around the partition to grab Nick's arm but Nick was already running for the door. The three reporters went after him, eyes aswirl with neon snowflakes. Nick had a good start but the camera was heavy and they gained on him up Grainger St. From her desk on the second floor Denise looked out the window and saw Nick running down the back lane laughing, the three reporters close behind.

"He's got them, Mr. Close," she called over to Charlie.

Charlie nodded without looking up. "Good lad."

Nick darted across the lobby, up the stairs and along the corridor, pausing only to duck into the photography department to give Sid the camera. He ran the last few steps to the editorial department, slowing to a walk at the last minute. Across the corridor the three reporters spilled into the photography department and confronted Sid. Only John Parsons had the breath to speak.

"You hand over that fucking film."

Sid looked blankly back at him. "Camera's not loaded," he said.

*   *   *

Nick thought of university as an oasis of higher learning where admirably focused young people pursued intellectual growth with a monkish zeal and was surprised to learn from Julian Gill that it was mostly about drinking and fucking. Julian had the delicate good looks of a poet and the soul of a libertine. From Scarborough he'd gone to Durham University where he earned a history degree, which he said was: "All about fucking old people and old people fucking."

He shared a bungalow in Jesmond with Phil Hart who was from Manchester and claimed to have cheated his way to an economics degree at Manchester University. Phil asserted that it was his goal to work for The Financial Times and make a bundle manipulating the stock market. The two of them were the lights that burned brightest in a string of dimmer bulbs who made up the dozen or so graduate reporters at the Chronicle. They played pranks on each other, stuck mock memorandums up on the notice board and wrote bogus news stories that satirised the sensationalist tone of modern newspapers. They were indulged because of a long tradition of tolerance for bad behaviour in journalism, which held that the worst behaved reporters were often the best.

The two of them never went straight home from work. Instead they did the rounds of the pubs and clubs and used their press passes to get backstage at concerts where they'd invite visiting pop stars to post-concert parties at Jesmond with promises of free flowing drink and women. A seemingly unlimited cast of amiable and attractive women passed through the bungalow providing cooking, cleaning, laundry and sexual services. Nick was impressed at the way Julian and Phil treated women. They got away with murder and he wanted to be just like them. Seeing in him an eager pupil they were happy to teach him all they knew. More and more he missed the last bus home and stayed over at the bungalow where the curtains were always closed and the party never ended. With every week that passed he felt more at home in the city, increasingly confident of his place among the only cosmopolitan crowd he'd ever known. His ties to Bedlington fell away like streamers from an ocean liner leaving the dock. He hadn't seen Angie in a couple of months and while they hadn't broken up formally it was clear they belonged to different worlds and faster and faster his was spinning away from hers. She was his first love and he was hers but now they were part of each other's past and it was time to leave the past behind. He was ready. Ready to go out and grab the world by its big wide hips and shag the living bejeesus out of it.

Whenever the orbits of his old life and his new life crossed it served only to emphasise the growing distance between them. Dave had left school at 15 and got a job at a garage ten minutes from home. Spelk, who'd got four 'O' levels, was working for the civil service at Longbenton. Nick invited them to a party at the bungalow in Jesmond once but they were painfully out of their depth. They couldn't keep up with the conversation, they didn't get the jokes and they had no idea when Phil or Julian was taking the piss. Seeing them there told Nick all he needed to know - they couldn't go where he was going. And it was Spelk who provided the parting memory that Nick would cherish forever.

They woke up late and hung over on Sunday morning and Julian and Phil did what they usually did the morning after a party, which was to go down the pub and start drinking again. They found a corner table and set about reviving themselves through the administration of more beer. All except Spelk whose skinny frame made it difficult for him to process as much beer as the others. He sat at the end of the table pale and withdrawn, like a pterodactyl folded in on itself, and sipped listlessly at his pint.

"You should have a Guinness," Julian said. "You need something to coat your stomach."

"Absolutely," Phil added. "Set you up in no time."

Spelk ordered a pint of Guinness but gagged on his first sip.

"Oh come on," Julian scolded him. "You can do better than that."

"Drink it as fast as you can," Phil urged. "You have to get it into you before it can do you any good."

Spelk struggled through the Guinness but when he was done his pallor had turned from pale to grey.

"You're not drinking fast enough," Julian said. "You have to coat your stomach and slow the withdrawal of the alcohol at the same time. You better have another one. You'll see, a few minutes from now and you'll be a new man."

"He needs something to soak up the stomach acid," Phil added. "He should have something to eat."

"They have scotch eggs," Julian suggested.

"Just the ticket," Phil said.

Spelk had another Guinness and forced himself to eat a scotch egg and then became very quiet. The others forgot about him till he lurched to his feet, grabbed the table with both hands and made an anguished "aaaahhhhhh" sound. His thin body convulsed into an 'S' shape and something from deep inside rippled upwards. Everybody reared back from the table, Spelk clamped a hand over his mouth, his eyes bulged and two jets of vomit spewed out his nose. A woman at the bar screamed and then there was silence.

"Sorry about that, ladies and gentlemen," Julian said. "Afraid Puff the Magic Dragon is a little under the weather today."

*　　*　　*

Nick's new life was not without its trials. As office boy he occupied the bottom rung on the editorial ladder and there were those who didn't hesitate to step on him. Christopher Betts was an English Language graduate from London University who sought to enhance his image as a man about town by wearing a straw boater everywhere he went. One day in the newsroom Betts took Nick aside and in the confidential manner of someone doing him a favour said: "You know, you really should do something about that accent of yours, you'll never get anywhere in life if you don't learn to speak properly."

Nick was dismayed. He thought he'd improved his accent substantially since joining the Chronicle. Geordies usually adapted their accent according to where they were and to whom they were speaking. To each other, in the home, in the pub or on the street they would speak dialect. To others, especially those in authority, they would moderate their accent and their vocabulary for ease of communication. It was a delicate balancing act because any working class Geordie who went too far might be accused of putting on airs. And, according to the protocols of inverted snobbery, there were Geordies who refused to adapt their accent to anybody anywhere because it would compromise their working class integrity. But journalism was an occupation that required communication with everybody and brought with it an enviable social mobility. And Nick felt no loyalty to the working class. He'd spoken properly at his job interview and had tried to polish his accent even more since then, knowing that to some Geordies he already sounded posh. Which made Betts' advice all the more galling. Not just because he was a snob but because he'd seen through Nick's artifice and found him wanting. Secure in the armour of his double breasted blazer, university tie and home counties accent Betts seemed to Nick a caricature of a British officer lecturing some native in a distant corner of the Empire on how to behave on his own soil. And he was pained at the thought that Betts might be right; that Nick had a long way to go before he would ever be taken for a gentleman, especially in his own backyard.

*   *   *

Bright poked his head into Shep's office soon after opening time. "Ye feel like gannin' owa the club?"

Shep looked up from some paperwork. "Ah wasn't but ah could - is it important?"

"Ah think so."

"Aye, ahlright then."

"Back room?"

"That important?" Shep said.

Rain pelted Bright's face as he walked over to the Top Club, one hand in his coat pocket curled protectively around a large brown envelope. He stopped at the front bar, ordered a couple of pints of Fed and told Col Beatty he and Shep weren't to be disturbed. Then he went to the cheerless back room, sat at the table nearest the door and lit a tab. Shep arrived a few minutes later, unbuttoned his coat and sat down.

"Ah cannit be long," he said, "Ah've got a dinner at the masons the night." He downed half his pint in a single swallow and lit up a Capstan. "What is it that's so important then?"

Bright opened the envelope, took out a couple of sheets of paper stapled together and slid them across the table. "Ah want ye to read this," he said.

Shep put on his glasses and looked over the papers, double spaced carbon copies of a sworn statement. As he read his face grew grave, his massive body tensed and a couple of times his eyes flicked up at Bright. When he was finished he leaned back, one huge hand resting on the papers.

"What's this supposed to be?"

"It's a sworn statement from Tommy Locke," Bright said.

"Ah can see that," Shep added. "Where did ye get it?"

"Ah arranged it," Bright said.

"Ye arranged it?" Shep repeated. "What do ye mean, ye arranged it?"

"Ah arranged fo' Tommy to mek that statement."

The statement was signed by Thomas Locke, witnessed and stamped by Donald Keene, a barrister Shep had never heard of.

"*Ye* arranged for Tommy Locke to mek a statement like this?"

"Ah'm sorry, Shep," Bright said. "But ye left is wi' nae choice."

Shep looked away. "Ah cannit believe this. Ah cannit believe ah'm hearin' this." He turned his gaze back on Bright. "Ye knah it's a load o' bloody lies don't ye. Top to bottom, there's not a word o' truth in it. The man's a villain. He's tryin' to fit me up an' you're goin' along with him?"

Bright shook his head. "Ah've known fo' years, Shep. Everybody knows, they've just been owa frightened to dee owt aboot it. It was me that went to Tommy an' asked him if he'd mek a sworn statement. It wasn't that hard. He's had enough o' ye, like ahll o' wi'."

Bright read Shep's face now as easily as he read the weather, saw the calculation in his bloodshot eyes.

"It's not worth the paper it's written on," Shep said and pushed the statement away from him.

Bright pushed it back. "It's your copy."

Shep stared hard at Bright but this time Bright was ready if Shep should lose his temper.

"So a barrister's seen that?"

"He's got the top copy…fo' safekeepin'." Bright said.

Shep shook his head. "Ahll ah need is a minute wi' Tommy an' he'll change his mind. He'll retract that statement and then ye'll hae nowt…nowt."

"He's not goin' to change his mind," Bright said.

"We'll see," Shep said. "Ah've known him a canny bit longer than ye have."

"Tommy's gone away on hol'day for a couple o' weeks," Bright said. "Ah telt him not to tell anybody where he was goin'."

Shep hesitated.

"What are ye hopin' to gain by this, Jimmy? What do ye think's goin' to come o' this? Ye think you're goin' to get shot of is? Is that what ye think? Because if ye do ah can tell ye you're makin' a serious mistake. This will go nowhere, ah know too many people."

Shep's accent had slipped, the Geordie in him was coming out.

"An' ye an' me…" he made a sideways slashing motion with his hand "…wa finished. Tha's nae way forward fo' ye from heeyah. Ye mark my words, ah'll hae ye oot o' Bedlin'ton afore the end o' the month. Ya wife'll hae to gi' up that job she likes sae much at The Feathers. See hoo the two o' ye like Wallsend or North Shields. See how lang ya marriage lasts there. From what ah've hord she probably won't even go wi' ye."

But Bright wouldn't be baited.

"Ah think ya forgettin' somethin' aren't ye?" he said. "If it wasn't fo' me it's ye wee wouldn't be here noo. Ah stuck me neck oot fo' ye when naebody else would. What was it ye said at the time - nearly 40 year on the force an' ye couldn't trust any bugga? They were ahll ready to gi' ye up back then. Ah was the only one wee stood by ye, the only friend ye had. Weel ya ahll oot o' friends noo, Shep. Folk have had enough o' ye tellin' them hoo to live tha lives."

Shep was taken aback by the force of Bright's words.

"Ye cannit leave folk alane te live tha lives in peace, can ye?" Bright continued. "Ye love bein' in charge. Ye love bein' the big man that knahs iverythin' aboot iverybody. An' ye've been deein' it fo' sae lang ye cannit help yasel' anymore."

"Ah'm a polis," Shep said indignantly. "Folk divvent knah what tha deein' haff the teym, some bugga has to tell them."

"Ye used me to put Robbie McBride away for twelve year," Bright said. "Ye decided that's what he deserved an' ye nivah gave it a second thought. Ye divvent gi' a shite aboot the grief it caused his family - or mine. Christ almighty, Shep, ah live next door to his wife, ah see ah ivery day."

"Is that what all this is about, that little gobshite?" Shep looked incredulous. "Ye were telt not to get owa close te ya neighbours. Ah knah because ah telt ye."

"Aye an' hoo the hell am ah supposed to dee that?" Bright retorted. "Ah live right in the middle o' them. Ye used is because ah was close to them."

"Robbie McBride is exactly where he should be an' ah thought ye would hae realised that bi noo."

"Aye an' ah thought ah could trust ye so it looks like both o' wi were wrang, doesn't it?" Bright said. "Folk have had enough, Shep. They want ye gone."

"Folk?" Shep said derisively. "What folk?"

"Tommy Locke fo' one. Me fo' another. An' tha's plenty more but tha owa frightened to tell ye te ya face."

"But you're not, eh?" Shep gestured dismissively at the statement on the table. "An' this is the way ye gan aboot it?"

"Ya twenty month past ya retirement, man," Bright said. "Ah looked in ya personnel file. Ye can retire any time ye like noo on full pension, nae questions asked. Tha's nae reason fo' ye to stay on exceptin' ye want tee - an' you're the only one wee wants ye tee."

"Ye really think ye can force is into retirement on the strength o' Tommy Locke's word? The man's a joke, nobody's goin' to take his word owa mine."

"Ye might be right aboot that," Bright said. "But tha's mair than Tommy's word against ye. That statement is just part o' it. Tha's a ledger ye knah nowt aboot an' ahll. Tommy doesn't just keep a record o' the bets he teks in an' the money he pays oot. He's kept a record o' ivery payment he's made to ye owa the past seventeen year. Amoonts, dates, iverythin'. Ye've done var' weel fo' yasel' oot o' Bedlin'ton owa the years, haven't ye, Shep? Nearly seventy thoosand pund bi mah reckonin'. Ahll the croon prosecutor needs is a copy o' ya bank records an' ah divvent think he'll hae any trouble gettin' a court order once he has the ledger an' Tommy's sworn statement. An' when he gets ahaad o' ya records ah'm guessin' he'll find an entry that'll be a close match fo' ivery amoont an' date Tommy sent ye money. Ah don't think ya word's goin' to hold up very weel against that de ye? Ah don't think anybody's goin' to believe ye won it ahll on the horses."

Shep was about to say something but couldn't stifle his fury.

"So...this is the worm turnin' is it?"

In those few words Bright knew just how much he'd come to dislike Shep.

"Ah divvent get any pleasure oot o' this, if that's what ye think'," he said. "But ye don't leave is wi' any choice. Ye lied t'is. Ah cannit trust ye anymore."

"Gi's a year," Shep said. "Gi's a year an' ah'll step doon, nae problem." Bright shook his head.

"Six month then," Shep tried. "Six month so ah can get me affairs in order."

"Ah promised Tommy ye'd be gone bi the time he got back from hol'day," Bright answered. "Ye can hae a week te get ya affairs in order. If ye haven't tendered ya resignation by the twenty second Mr. Keene is under instructions from me to forward the statement an' the ledger to the croon prosecutor's office."

"A week…a week?" Shep said disbelievingly. "An' this Mr. Keene, this barrister pal o' yours weeivah he is, he's happy to go along wi' you blackmailin' a senior police officer is he?"

"Actually, Shep, he thinks ah'm lettin' ye off light," Bright said. "He doesn't think ye should be given the opportunity to resign."

Shep sagged in his chair and looked around the empty walls. Bright watched him struggle to take in all that had happened in the last few minutes. When he spoke again it was with a mixture of contempt and resignation.

"Mind, ah picked the right bloke when ah picked ye didn't ah?"

*   *   *

Soon after the pubs closed the bus station at the Haymarket swarmed with drinkers trying to get home. The steel railed enclosures reminded Nick of cattle yards except these cattle sang, shouted, pushed, fought and spewed. As he passed the motorbike shop he noticed a cluster of dark shapes in the alleyway alongside and heard voices raised in confrontation. He would have kept walking if his eye hadn't been caught by something odd, a white disc bobbing on the shadows. Chris Betts' straw boater. Nick went over to take a closer look. He could make out four figures, two holding Betts against the wall and another standing apart.

"Take your hands off me…give that back to me…" Nick heard the cultivated tone so far from home in a Newcastle alleyway.

"Fuckin' puff," one of his assailants said. "Think ya good de ye, ye fuckin' puff?"

Then the other: "Hoo aboot ah shit in ya hat an' put that on ya poncy fuckin' heed."

The figure watching laughed and Nick recognised the laugh. Rocky Banks. The pair menacing Betts were Billy Finch and Blackie White. They'd been drinking and must have been waiting for the same bus as Nick when they'd seen Betts on his way home.

"Only a fuckin' puff'd wear a hat like this," Blackie said.

"I'm not a poof if that's what you're saying," Betts responded.

"I am not a poof," Blackie mimicked in a high, sissy voice. "I am not a poof."

Nick stood beside Banks.

"How, lad."

Rocky turned, peered at him in the darkness and recognised him. "How," he said and turned back to watch Billy and Blackie with their victim. The times might be changing but Rocky, Billy and Blackie weren't.

"Hoo ye been, like?" Nick asked.

Rocky shrugged. "Ahlreet."

"Ye workin'?"

"Day labourin'."

"Wee's that?" Billy said out of the shadows.

"It's Nick Bright," Rocky answered.

Billy grunted and turned his attention back to Betts. "De ye fancy 'is, like? De ye wanna gi's a gobble?"

"Aye, gan on," Blackie said. "Gi'm a gobble ye fuckin' puff."

"He's not a puff," Nick said.

Rocky didn't bother to turn his head. "Hoo de ye knah, like?"

"He warks at the Chronicle, same as me," Nick said, his accent pure Bedlington.

"Nick…is that you?" Betts called urgently. "Do something for god's sake, go and get a policeman."

Nick and Billy grinned.

"Ah am deein' somethin'," Nick said.

"What's he deein' showin' off in a stupid fuckin' hat like this if'n he's not a puff?" Billy asked.

"He doesn't knah any better," Nick said.

Rocky sniffed, vaguely amused. The other two paused and Betts' fate hung in the balance.

"He must be fuckin' stupid, gannin' around the toon in a stupid fuckin' hat like this," Billy said and swatted Betts across the face with the straw boater.

"A fuckin' fairy hat," Blackie said.

Billy and Blackie stepped back and Billy spun the straw boater off down the alley.

"Oh for heaven's sake," Betts protested.

"He's a posh cunt, but," Rocky said.

"Aye," Nick agreed. "He's a posh cunt."

The spell was broken. The moment for violence was past. Nick and Rocky stepped out into the drizzle of light that illuminated the bus shelters and Rocky offered Nick a tab.

"Me brother died," Rocky said.

"Died?" Nick said. Rocky's older brother, Johnny, had worked at the Doctor Pit.

"Aye, he got hissel' killed in an accident," Rocky said. "He went for a piss up a side tunnel an' pissed on a 'lectric cable."

Nick shrugged and tried to hide the satisfaction that piece of news gave him.

"It was his ahn stupid fuckin' fault," Rocky grinned.

The 3A to Bedlington pulled up to the bus stop and Nick and Rocky turned towards it.

"Bus is heeyah'," Rocky called over his shoulder. Billy and Blackie sauntered after them leaving Betts in the alley to forage for his hat.

The bus ride home felt like an eternity and Nick knew now he had to cut his ties with Bedlington. The next day he mentioned to Julian and Phil how desperate he was to get away from home and they said he could have the spare room at the bungalow till he found a place of his own. It was a 17-year old boy's wet dream. Not only would he be in Newcastle all the time now he would be living at the best party house in Newcastle.

It was an easy move, everything he needed he could carry in two suitcases. When he looked around his bedroom at West Lea for the last time, the bed stained with spent dreams, the built-in cupboard with the sliding doors and its pile of discarded toys reminded him of a stage set whose adolescent dramas had played to an audience of one. The view of the back fields, the arc of red brick houses, the line of trees that marked the edge of the old cemetery marked the confines of his old life and no longer meant anything to him.

He tried to write a note to his mam and dad but stuck on the word 'Dear.' He saw so little of them it would be days before they realised he'd moved out. It was better if he called them, it would let them know he was serious. He tried his dad first but when he called the police station from the Chronicle he was told his dad was away at court all day. He called The Feathers next and his mother picked up the phone.

"Ah just wanted to tell ye ah've moved oot," he said.

There was a pause at the other end.

"Eee,ah divvent believe it," she said. "Is this ahll the notice ya ganna gi' wi?"

"It happened really quick," he said. "Just this week."

"Where ye goin'?"

"Ah've moved in wi' a couple o' lads from work."

"What did ye tek wi' ye?"

"Ah took me claes."

"That's ahll?"

"Ah don't need anythin' else."

"Hae ye telt ya dad?"

"Ah cannit get hold of him."

"Ye couldn't hae tried very hard," she said. "An' this is your idea of enough notice is it, a phone call?"

"Ah would hae said somethin' sooner but ah nivah see ye."

"Ah cannit believe ya movin' oot wi' not even a proper fare-thee-well te me an' ya dad."

"Ah just telt ye, ah got the chance to move in wi' two lads from the paper. Ah'm there most o' the time noo anyway."

"An' hoo de ye think this meks us look? As soon as ye get a job ye cannit wait te leave home."

She was worried about appearances. He almost laughed.

"Aye, weel, ye winnit hae is aroond te spoil ya fun anymore, will ye?" he said and hung up.

That Friday his father came to the Chronicle in uniform. Nick went down to the lobby warily. He thought his dad would have something to say about the way he'd spoken to his mother but he didn't, he was surprisingly matter-of-fact about it all.

"Ah just want to knah - are ye sure this is what ye want?" his dad asked.

Nick shrugged. "Aye."

"Ye knah, ye could stay home for another couple o' year an' save a bit money. Tha's plenty o' lads dee that."

"Ah got the chance to move in wi' these lads from work," Nick replied. "They've got a great place up at Jesmond. It only takes is ten minutes to get in."

"Ya mam thinks it's ahll a bit sudden, like." His father paused. "But, she doesn't knah hoo young lads are, hoo keen wi are to get away from home when wa ready."

Aye, Nick thought. Us lads together.

"Weel," his father added with an air of finality, "noo ya workin' ye can mek up ya ahn mind. When ah was your age ah'd been workin' fo' three year an' then ah went into the Royal Navy. So, as long as ya sure?"

"Aye, ah'm sure," Nick said.

"Don't forget to keep in touch." He went to ruffle Nick's hair but Nick ducked away. His father smiled awkwardly. "Gi's a call from time to time then, bonny lad, just to let wi know hoo ya gettin' on." And he put his helmet on and left.

That afternoon, after the final edition had been put to bed, Charlie beckoned Nick over to his desk. "I heard your father was in to see you today. Is everything alright?"

"Aye," Nick said.

"Is he unhappy about your current living situation?"

"No," Nick said.

"Well, he should be," Charlie said. "I heard you'd moved in with Julian Gill and Phil Hart and I don't think that's the right kind of livin' arrangement for a lad your age. You're a bit young for the antics they get up to over there. The two of them should know better than to ask you."

Nick was alarmed. "They're just tryin' to help is, Mr. Close. You're not goin' to give them wrong are ye?"

Charlie smiled. "No, I'm not. But I'm not letting you stay there. The paper has a responsibility to see you're properly looked after. I have a place in mind where I think you'll be better off."

Nick's head reeled. He wanted to live at the bungalow. He wanted to live with Julian and Phil. He wanted to get up to the same antics they did.

"I'd like…I'd rather stay where I am," he said desperately.

Charlie peered over his glasses, amused. . "Aye, I bet you would. But you're not the best person to judge are you, son? You'll be better off at the place I'm thinking of. You might not thank me now but you'll thank me in the years to come."

Nick was furious and there was nothing he could do about it. Just when he'd broken free of parents who took no interest in his life he was taken hostage by somebody who took too much interest. When he told Julian and Phil all they did was laugh.

Charlie put him with Mrs. Perry, a widow in Gosforth whose only son was serving with the RAF in Germany. Mrs. Perry was a friend of Charlie's and had taken in lodgers from the paper before. Short and plump with a rosy complexion she looked as if she belonged on the cover of a cookbook. Her house was filled with the smell of baking and the kitchen shelves were stocked with all manner of home made jams and pickles. When she wasn't cooking, baking, knitting or sewing Mrs. Perry was volunteering at the church or delivering Meals-On-Wheels. Her house was a two storey detached with a cement grey exterior that belied its cosy interior. Nick was given the bedroom in the attic, which had been Mrs. Perry's son's bedroom, and was reached by a sliding ladder attached to a trapdoor. The shelves were filled with books about aircraft and model airplanes built by her son. The double bed was smothered by a quilt of white cotton, a huge billowy mattress and pillows stuffed with goose down so that when he settled into them he felt as if he were nesting in his own little cloud. The first night it took him only a minute to fall asleep and when he got up the next day he felt better rested than he had in weeks. He was to remember the sleeps he had at Mrs. Perry's house as the best he ever had.

Room and board cost him thirty bob a week and Mrs. Perry gave him a key to the front door. On weekdays he had cornflakes for breakfast with toast, jam and tea. Saturdays were two boiled eggs with toast and Sundays bacon and eggs with mushrooms, tomato and fried bread. Despite his resentment at having to leave the bungalow he settled into his new digs quickly. After a few weeks he had to concede that perhaps Charlie did know something he didn't; that he *was* better off at Mrs. Perry's. It was a while before he could put his finger on just what it was that felt so right about it till he realised as he settled down to sleep one night that, for the first time in his life, he was in a house that was at peace with itself.

1963

John Profumo, Secretary Of State For War resigns in a scandal involving call girl Christine Keeler; thieves steal two and a half million pounds from a Royal Mail train; President Kennedy is assassinated in Dallas. Doctor Who debuts on the BBC with William Hartnell as the doctor. Box office hits are From Russia With Love starring Sean Connery; Alfred Hitchcock's The Birds and Tom Jones starring Albert Finney. Top record hits are How Do You Do It by Gerry And The Pacemakers, Sweets For My Sweet by The Searchers, Please Please Me, From Me To You, She Loves You and I Want To Hold Your Hand by The Beatles.

New Horizons

The last week in July Evan Thompson drove Pat and Jimmy to
Woolsington Airport to catch a charter flight to the Costa Del Sol. They left with
enough time to stop at a pub along the way for a couple of drinks and were in
high spirits when they were dropped off at the airport. The past year couldn't
have gone much better for Bright. Shep had gone into retirement and nobody
tried to talk him out of it. Ted Dunlop offered to organize a retirement dinner
at the Top Club but Shep said he wanted no part of it. Morpeth decided to
discontinue the detective inspector's position at Bedlington and Dickie Prichard
was promoted to detective sergeant. With Bright's encouragement Alec Newell
was given the detective constable's job, which was where he wanted to be. The
only officer at Bedlington superior to Bright now was Ted Dunlop and the two
of them shared the same approach to the job - anything for a quiet life. Nick had
left home and Bright had organized a move from West Lea to a better house on
Acorn Avenue. With Shep out of the way and Pat content at The Feathers life for
Bright was as perfect as it could get. Bright knew his place in the world and was
happy with it. And just when he thought life couldn't get any better he won the
top prize at the Netherton Club Leek Show, a ten day package holiday for two to
Torremolinos.

He and Pat checked in their luggage, collected their boarding passes and
joined the queue of holidaymakers straggling across the tarmac to the waiting
Dan-Air Comet. There was an excitement in the air, anticipation mixed with
apprehension because for most of the passengers, including Pat and Jimmy, it
would be their first time in an airplane. And they weren't the only ones to have
a few drinks before coming to the airport. Instant bonds were formed out of the
nervous chatter and by the time it was their turn to board they'd made friends
with the couple in front of them, Chick and Edie from Chester-le-Street. Chickie,
as he liked to be called, said he was a greengrocer because he'd always been "a bit
fruity."

The aircraft was smaller inside than they expected and smelled of warm
plastic. Pat and Jimmy got seats together with Chickie and Edie and Pat asked
a stewardess to bring them drinks as soon as they'd taken off "...so if the plane
crashes we'll ahll die happy."

Chickie and Edie laughed and the stewardess pretended she hadn't heard
it before.

When the plane was fully loaded the cabin crew closed the doors and
ran through the safety drill. They'd barely finished before a man in the back of

the aircraft called out: "What happens if ah shit mesel?" followed by raucous laughter.

There was a long wait before the engines started up and the same boisterous crowd in the rear began singing 'Why are we waiting.' They cheered when the plane started moving but settled into a queasy silence as it taxied out to the runway for take-off. The pilot wasted no time. As soon as the Comet was in position he throttled all four engines up, the plane shuddered and jolted forward prompting involuntary gasps from some of the passengers. Pat clutched Bright's hand as the plane picked up speed. It seemed to take forever to reach take-off speed and window seat passengers watched nervously as the tree line at the end of the runway rushed toward them. Then the Comet tilted sharply upward, the ground fell away and the shuddering stopped. Pat and Jimmy felt themselves pressed back into their seats and joined everybody else in an exhilarated "whoooo!"

A palpable relief swept through the cabin and excited passengers pressed their faces to the portholes to watch the houses and cars below shrink into a toy landscape. The engines settled into a soothing drone as the plane climbed into a pale blue sky and banked southeast toward the coast and faraway Spain. When the Comet reached cruising altitude the seatbelt and no smoking signs blinked off and two stewardesses rolled a fully laden drinks cart out of the galley. Pat and Jimmy and Chickie and Edie decided they'd toast the start of their holiday with Spanish champagne. Bright felt as if he'd ascended into heaven. Life stretched ahead of him like one long holiday. He bathed in the radiance of Pat's smile and raised his glass.

"Happy days." he said. And they all joined in: "Happy days."

*   *   *

A couple of days before Christmas Nick got a call from the commissionaire in the Chronicle lobby to tell him a Corporal Miller from the Royal Northumberland Fusiliers was there to see him. Nick went downstairs wondering what Eric wanted. They hadn't seen or spoken to each other in years and Nick had no interest in renewing their acquaintanceship. If he hadn't known it was him, Nick would have passed Eric in the street without recognising him. He was burlier than Nick remembered and his light brown hair was flecked by the sun. He had a confident bearing, his badges and buckles gleamed and his boots shone like beer bottles. Army life suited him. He held his black beret with its red and white hackle in his left hand and offered Nick the other. Nick took it, less than enthused.

"Surprised to see me heeyah, ah bet," Eric said.

"Aye," Nick acknowledged. "What do ye want?"

"Ah just wanted to catch up wi' ye," Eric answered with a small self-conscious smile. "Ah knah wi'v nivah been close or owt, even though wa related an' ahll, but tha's a few things ah wanted to tell ye. Things to dee wi' the family ah thought ye should knah, like."

"What things?"

If Eric wanted to make friends with him after all these years Nick thought he'd left it a bit late.

"Just some things ah think it's important fo' ye to knah," Eric said. "Things ah think ye would *want* to knah." He looked uncomfortable in the small lobby where they could easily be overheard. "Ah think it would be betta if wi could tahk somewhere else. Can ye get oot fo' a cup o' char o' summick, it'll not tek lang."

It was close to lunch time and while Nick wasn't inclined to spend a whole hour with Eric he sensed an earnestness behind the awkwardness. And he was curious. What did Eric want to tell him after all these years that was so important? Probably nothing. That was usually the case. People thought they had something important to say and it turned out to be nothing at all.

"Ah'll hae to clear it wi' me boss forst," Nick said, slipping back into Bedlington dialect. Minutes later he buttoned his overcoat against the cold as he and Eric walked up Pudding Chare to a coffee bar in the Bigg Market. The coffee bar was hot, smoky and crowded, condensation dribbled down the windows and Christmas music played tinnily in the background. Nick ordered a cappuccino, Eric ordered the same and paid for both of them. They found an empty table and pulled up a couple of blocky wooden chairs. Eric said he was stationed in Germany and was on a five day Christmas leave.

"It's free both ways if ye divvent mind sittin' in the back of a Herc' wi nae heatin'," he said.

Nick spooned the foam on his cappuccino.

"Ye've done alright fo' yasel' then," Eric said. "Gettin' on at the Chronicle an' ahll."

"Aye it's ahlreet."

"Job wi' a future, ah suppose. Tha's ahlways ganna be newspapers isn't tha?"

"Probably."

"Are ye…what do they cahll it…a cub reporter?"

"Junior reporter."

Nick loved his new life. He'd been promoted to the reporting staff three months earlier and he loved the freedom that came with it. He loved the challenge and the unpredictability. He loved coming into the office each morning and checking the daily assignment diary to see what he'd be doing for the day; Newcastle magistrates court, a coroner's inquest, an agricultural show, an interview with The Rolling Stones.

"Ye were ahlways good at English though weren't ye? Compositions, like?"

Nick shrugged. Eric took a pack of Rothman's from a tunic pocket and offered one to Nick. He lit their tabs with a shiny steel lighter embossed with the regimental badge of St. George slaying the dragon.

"Ye gannin yem fo' Christmas?" Eric asked.

"Depends what ye mean by yem."

"Bedlin'ton?"

"Nah, ah haven't been there in yonks. Tha's ahll kinds o' Christmas parties goin' on heeyah."

"Ye divvent see much o' your mam an' dad then?"

"They hae their life, ah hae mine."

"That's not hoo ya mutha sees it."

"Aye weel, she's not the most reliable source o' information is she?"

Eric seemed amused.

"Actually, that's the reason ah'm heeyah, what ah want to tell ye, like. Ah've been thinkin' aboot this fo a while an' ah think it's somethin' ye desorve to knah…an' it doesn't look like anybody else is ganna tell ye…"

Nick sipped the scalding capuccino. Outside Christmas shoppers hurried past, their breath steaming in the winter air.

"Ah hae nae idea hoo ya ganna tek this," Eric went on. "But ye knah hoo ahll these years ye've ahlways thowt wi were cousins? Weel, actually, wa not. Wa not cousins. Wa bruthas. Ye an' me are bruthas."

Nick looked blankly at Eric. He had no idea how to react. He'd cut off any feelings of affection for his family long ago.

Eric persevered. "Me mutha, Dot, isn't me real mutha. Your mutha is mah mutha…ye an' me hae the same mutha."

Nick knew as the words came out of Eric's mouth that he was telling the truth.

"My mutha is your mutha?"

"Aye."

"Wi divvent hae the same fatha though?"

"No, not the same fatha."

"So wa haff bruthas?"

Eric smiled. "Aye, haff bruthas."

Nick remained expressionless. He couldn't understand his mother being wanted by any man, let alone two.

"Ye divvent look very surprised," Eric said.

"Ah am…an' ah'm not," Nick answered. "Ah ahlways knew tha was somethin' gannin' on wi' the two o' them but ah nivah knew what it was. Ah just thought it was nowt te dee wi' me. Tha was a lot they did that was nowt te dee wi' me."

"They never telt ye then, even after ye left home?"

"No, they nivah telt is nowt."

All those years, Nick thought. All those years of keeping it from him. Of making him part of their lie. Of imposing its bitter consequences on him without him ever knowing why.

"So, hoo did ahll this come aboot then?"

Now that it was out Eric had relaxed and the rest followed easily.

"Ye knah hoo your - wor mutha was in London durin' the war an' wor Aunty Vi was there workin' fo' some rich family? The way it was telt te me, like, she looked up to Vi an' Vi had been in London a couple o' year so she knew ah way aroond, like. The two o' them would gan to the NAAFI in Piccadilly Circus to meet soldiers an' wor mutha would play the piano an' she an' Vi would haad sing-songs. Ye knah what the two o' them are like when they get together even noo. Neither one o' them's shy when they've got a few drinks in them."

Nick remembered his mam and his Aunty Vi through the pub window in Arnold, leading the singalong, how they thrived on the attention.

Eric added: "What they were after was te find themsels a yank an' get married an' gan owa to America when the war was owa. They were a pair o' good time girls is what they were. That's what Dot called them. They'd only gan oot wi' yanks cos the yanks had money an' wor lads didn't. The two o' them would get tabs an' nylons an' chocolates from the yanks fo', ye knah, showin' them a good time, like."

Nick had no trouble picturing his mother and his Aunty Vi at the NAAFI in London during the war, picking up American soldiers, taking them for all they could.

"Only it didn't work oot the way they thought it would," Eric continued. "The yanks warn't stupid, they knew what was gannin on. They were happy to have a good time but that's ahll it was. They had nae intention o' gettin' married.

Then wor mutha went an' got ahsel pregnant, an' weeivah the fatha was, he didn't want te knah. He wasn't ganna let hissel get trapped into marryin' some English tart an' hae to tek ah yem. If she thought hor bein' pregnant was a way o' gettin' the fatha to stand by ah she was mistaken. She was left on ah ahn. She had to gan back yem to Ashin'ton in disgrace an' face ah mutha an' fatha. Ah fatha telt ah she couldn't get rid of is, she had to have is. So they sent ah to some norsin' home up in Edinburgh where lasses went te hae illegitimate babbies an' that's where ah was born. When she came back it was decided ah would go to Dot an' she would bring is up because she was the only one o' the three daughters that was married an' respectable at the time."

Nick remembered how his grandather on his mother's side used to refer to his daughters as his 'three disgraces.' Now he knew why.

"So y'ar a bastard then," he said.

"Aye, ah'm a bastard," Eric smiled. "That's why ah nivah liked ye when wi were grahin' up. Ye had a proper fatha, ye had a proper family even if wor mutha was a tart. Ye ahlways had mair than me but ye nivah seemed te appreciate it. An' ye had a mutha an' fatha wee wanted ye."

"That's what ye think," Nick said.

"At least ye knah wee ya fatha is. Ah'll nivah knah."

"Did ye not ask ah wee ya fatha was?"

"O' course ah did," Eric answered. "Ah asked ah a few times but she wouldn't tahk aboot it. The last time was just afore ah went in the army. Ah thowt the least she could dee was tell is then. But ye knah what's she's like. If she doesn't like the way things are goin' she gans off ah heed. She meks a fuss warse than if she'd just answer the bloody question. It's hor way of not dealin' wi owt she doesn't want te face up te." He tapped his tab into a full ash tray. "The thing is ah divvent think she knahs wee me dad is. Ah think she got knocked up by some bloke one night when she was drunk an' either it was somebody she didn't knah or the next day she couldn't remember wee it was. That's why she doesn't want to tahk aboot it. She was ashamed an' ah reminded ah o' what she'd done."

"An' ye reminded me fatha o' what she'd done afore she met him," Nick said.

"Oh aye, he knew," Eric said. "He ahlways disapproved o' me. An' ye must hae noticed the way they carried on aboot the yanks. They were ahlways rubbishin' the yanks, the pair o' them. The yanks could nivah dee owt right. Noo ye knah why."

Nick remembered the hot summer day in the orchard when his dad and his Uncle Don went on about the yanks and his mother and his Aunty Vi had been so quiet.

"Hoo come ye nivah telt is?"

"Ah divvent rightly knah," Eric said. "Ye'd think ah would, wouldn't ye, just to get back at ye, if nowt else? But, ah think ah was a bit ashamed mesel'. Ah mean, it's not somethin' ye want to brag aboot is it; that ya mutha was a bit of a hooah an' ye divvent knah wee ya fatha is? It's just givin' folk somethin' te hoy back in ya face, especially in Bedlin'ton." He leaned back in his seat. "Ah thowt they woulda telt ye bi noo but Dot said they were nivah ganna tell ye. Ah just think that's wrang. Ah think ye hae a right to knah the truth."

Nick smiled a wry smile. He'd been right all along even though he didn't know why. He always felt like he was in the way because he *was* in the way. He knew his mam didn't love his dad and he'd always wondered why she'd married him. Now he knew. It was because she had nowhere else to go. She was spoiled goods. No other man would have her. And his dad was so besotted by her he didn't care. He didn't even care that she didn't love him. He would take her on any terms. Their marriage was built on need. On mutual desperation. And the only way to make it bearable was by anaesthetising themselves with drink. By having fun. They had fun as if their lives depended on it because their lives did depend on it. Nobody was ever going to spoil their fun.

"Ah think wi were both accidents," Nick said.

"Ye were supposed to be the one they wanted," Eric responded.

"Ah knah," Nick said. "But that's not hoo it worked oot is it?"

"Ye poor bugga," Eric said.

"Aye, ah'm weel shot o' them noo though," Nick said. "Ah can gan me ahn way noo."

Outside the coffee bar they shook hands and went their separate ways without making plans to keep in touch. On the walk back down the cobbled slope to the Chronicle Nick felt strangely elated. He knew the whole story now and was stronger for it. The only person in the world he had to worry about was himself. They might not have intended it but it was the greatest gift they could have given him. Life was funny like that. You had to laugh.

THE END

Made in the USA
Middletown, DE
06 February 2021

33175845R00166